KLEOP

BLACK SEA

BITHYNIA-PONTUS

ARMENIA MINOR

PARTHIA

● ANCYRA

CAPPADOCIA

● PERGAMUM

ASIA

PAMPHYLIA

● EPHESUS

CILICIA

ATHENS

LYCIA

● ANTIOCH

RHODES

PHOENICIA

NEAN SEA

● JERUSALEM

ALEXANDRIA

ARABIA

NABATAEANS

EGYPT

RED SEA

PHARAOH

PHARAOH

volume II of kleopatra

karen essex

WARNER BOOKS

An AOL Time Warner Company

Warner Books, Inc., 1271 Avenue of the Americas, New York, NY 10020

Visit our Web site at www.twbookmark.com.

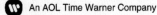 An AOL Time Warner Company

Printed in the United States of America

First Printing: August 2002

10 9 8 7 6 5 4 3 2 1

Library of Congress Cataloging-in-Publication Data

Essex, Karen.
    Pharaoh / Karen Essex.
        p. cm.
    "Volume II of Kleopatra."
    ISBN 0-446-53025-5
    1. Cleopatra, Queen of Egypt, d. 30 B.C.—Fiction. 2. Rome—History—Civil War, 43-31 B.C.—Fiction. 3. Egypt—History—332-30 B.C.—Fiction. 4. Mothers and sons—Fiction. 5. Queens—Fiction. I. Title.

PS3555.S682 P48 2002
813'.54—dc21

2002016802

Book design and text composition by L&G McRee

Pharaoh is for my daughter, Olivia Fox,
who for most of her life has had to share her mother
with the queen of Egypt

Kleopatra's Genealogy

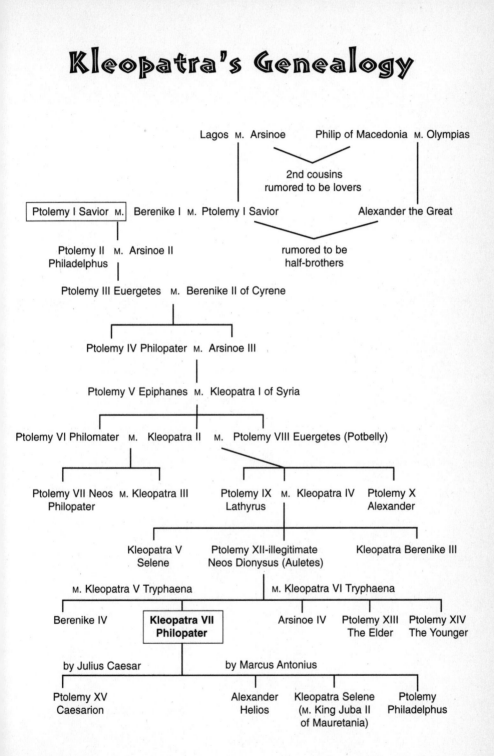

Part I

Alexandria: the 20th year of Kleopatra's reign

The queen stares at the phalanx of whores as if she is about to execute a normal rather than deplorable duty of state. Silent, tense, confused, they await her inspection and her command.

Charmion, the weary sergeant, the old warhorse long attached to an unpredictable commander in chief, has herded them to Kleopatra's chambers in utter silence. A great feat of intimidation, the silencing of a gaggle of whores. But that is the way with Charmion, who executes every duty with a diligence unanimated by emotion of any kind. She retains an implacable expression even while carrying out the bizarre wishes of the sovereign to whom she has sworn her life. An aristocratic Greek born in Alexandria, Charmion is not tall, but casts the illusion of towering height. Her bearing shames the carriage of a queen, even of the queen she serves. Though she is fifty-one, her sallow skin is smooth. Three wrinkles, delicate as insects' legs, trace from the corners of her brown-yellow eyes. Her mouth is full, a burnt color, like a river at sundown. Two tributaries, both southbound, run from her lip-locked smile, tiny signals of age, a result of the anxiety she suffers over the queen's behavior.

Unlike the queen, Charmion dislikes all men. Wordlessly, she has endured Kleopatra's relations with Antony with lugubrious countenance, as if she has suffered all these years from an intense constipation. Antony, charmer of maidens, actresses, farm girls, and queens, never elicits a smile from the woman. In her youth, the queen heard, Charmion had bedded with other women, though she could never confirm the rumors. Of Caesar, and of the queen's relations with him, however, she had approved, though her sanction was expressed only by absence of criticism.

Charmion has dressed the prostitutes herself, forcing Iras, the temperamental eunuch, Royal Hairdresser to the queen, to weave tiny jewels and trinkets of gold into their locks. For a prim woman, she possesses a talent for seductive costume. Knowing the Imperator's inclinations, she has chosen many large-breasted girls. On the most obscenely endowed, she has encased their sumptuous glands in loosely woven gold mesh so that the nipples, rouged to an incarnadine red, appear trapped in an elegant prison, eager for release. "Antony shall enjoy that," thinks the queen.

The courtesans regard their monarch, wondering what kind of queen, what kind of woman, sends prostitutes to her husband, much less approves their comeliness before she allows them to go to him. The queen, nervous, reading their thoughts, attempts to cover her trepidation with characteristic chilling authority. She rises to scrutinize her troops who are wrapped not with the armor of war, but with the luxurious weaponry of seduction. Reddened lips, slightly parted. Little invitations. Nipples: crimson, erect, acute, like hibiscus buds against stark white skin. Bare, nubile shoulders soft as dunes. Teasing one, an auburn tendril; grazing another, a crystal earring, sharp as a dagger, threatening to stab the perfect flesh. Luminous, kohl-rimmed eyes; vacant eyes, eyes without questions. Eyes that do not accuse, do not interrogate. Eyes that know how to lie. A naked belly and then another, larger, stronger, with a garnet chunk—or is that a ruby?—tucked in the navel. And of course, the prize—the female motherlode, coy, apparent, beneath transparent gauze. Some shaven, some not. Good work, Charmion, she thinks. Like all men, her husband craves variety.

A detail: long fingers, slender toes, adorned with rings, jewels. Excellent. Ah, but not this one. "She must leave," the queen says sharply, not to the half-breed beauty before her with fat, choppy hands, but to Charmion, who waves the girl out of the room. Antony, connoisseur of the female form, dislikes "peasant digits."

"Have we more?" she demands of her lady-in-waiting, knowing how thoroughly prepared she is for any situation, any disaster.

"Yes, Your Royal Grace. There are twelve alternates in the antechamber."

"Bring me two thin girls. Boyish. Young, please. Two waif-faced pretties without inhibition."

With a nod, Charmion leaves the room, returning with twin girls of thirteen, draped in the simple robes of a Greek boy, with one small breast peeking from the fold. The androgynous creatures curtsy low, remaining on the ground until the queen passes them, rising only at the snap of Charmion's fingers. Compliant in nature, schooled in ritual. That should please her husband. A fine mix.

"Yes, I believe we are complete now. Twelve in all.

"Ladies," she says in her most imperious voice. They stand at attention, but only Sidonia, the voluptuous red-headed madam of the courtesans, meets her gaze. "Marcus Antonius, my husband, my lord, proconsul of Rome, commander of the armies of the eastern empire, sits alone, inconsolable, gazing over the sea. He is despondent.

"I do not explain myself to the highest ministers in my government, much less to court prostitutes. But you, ladies, are the foot soldiers in my campaign. No longer are you mere vessels of pleasure, actresses in the erotic arts, receptacles of spilt semen. Today you are elevated. Sacred is your cause, urgent your mission. At stake is the Fate of Egypt, and your Fate and my Fate. At stake is no less than the world."

Now the ranks stare at her in disbelief, for what queen makes an army of whores? Puts the Fate of her kingdom in the hands of a dispatch of painted strumpets?

"You must revive my husband. It is as simple as that."

One of the girls, the one with the tough stomach and bejeweled navel, struggles to stifle a giggle, but Sidonia sees the stern raised eyebrow of Charmion arched in warning. She slaps the girl, who crumples to the ground in tears. Sidonia bows apologetically to the queen, kicking the girl with a sandaled foot, reducing her cries to a choked dog-whimper.

The queen is amused but remains nonplussed—a countenance at which she excels, thanks to her apprenticeship with the late Julius Caesar. "Tonight, ladies, you serve one of the greatest men in history. His courage is legend. His conquests span the world. His loyalty, his heroism, unparalleled. But he sulks alone in his mansion by the sea. The mighty lion cringes and licks his wounds. He must rally. He must become a man again. And we know, ladies, don't we, what makes a man a man?"

Every whore smiles. For all their differences—the queen of Egypt and courtesan slaves—they share the same intuitive knowledge. What every woman knows. What every woman uses.

"I am aware that there is gossip. And I am aware of those who spread it. They will be dealt with. As for you, you are to let all those who visit your chambers know that your queen sailed home into the harbor of Alexandria flying the flags of victory after the war in Greek waters. You are to say that the Imperator, my husband, is your most virile and demanding client, that you have heard with your own ears and seen with your own eyes his plans for victory against Octavian, the fiend who will terrorize our world if his ambitions are allowed to go unchecked. As you know, I do not allow soldiers to have their way with court prostitutes, politically convenient as it would be at times. The Roman army, should it descend upon our city, will not follow these rules. I encourage each of you to meditate on the Roman reputation for cruelty and degradation to conquered women and then imagine your Fates, ladies, in the event that the Imperator does not overcome his depressed condition and refuses to defend you against the Romans.

"Therefore, you shall succeed splendidly in rehabilitating the manhood of my husband and you shall spread with conviction to every man, minister, artisan, and soldier alike who enters your bed that the great Antony fights a war the way he makes love—with vigor, with passion. That his prowess in the sport of war is excelled only by his prowess in the sport of love. Let the word spread to all corners of the city, and let it be heard by sailors who will take the tales to other ports. I know you have the power to convince. I requested not only the most beautiful of you for this mission, but the most intelligent. The most shrewd.

"As you are cunning, I shall make you a bargain. If you do your job to perfection, you shall be given your freedom after Octavian is defeated. If you fail and my husband remains in his tower sulking like a baby, you shall be put into the fields to harvest the crops, or sent to the Nubian mines. Let me be plain: If you betray the throne, if you are heard uttering one word about the Imperator's melancholia, if rumors of his ill-humor are traced back to you, if you do not follow my orders to the letter, you shall die, or wish you had."

The smiles fade. To Charmion: "They may go."

Alexandria: the 3rd year of Kleopatra's reign

Kleopatra looked out the window at the scene that had greeted her all the mornings of her days before her flight into exile. There was little in the Royal Harbor to suggest Julius Caesar's occupation of Alexandria. The pleasure vessels of Egypt's Royal Family rocked lazily at the dock. The morning fog had lifted, revealing a sky already white with heat above vivid blue waters, and she was grateful that she was no longer breathing the deadening summer air of the Sinai.

Could it have been just yesterday that she was in the middle of that great blue sea, stowing away on a pirate's vessel to sneak back into her own country? She had dressed herself as well as she could without her servants, knowing that the last leg of her journey would be a rigorous one, and that she could not be recognized when she arrived in the harbor of Alexandria. She had let Dorinda, the wife of Apollodorus the pirate, help with her toilette, fixing and bejeweling the locks that had been neglected while she was in exile. She would have done it herself, but her hands shook with anxiety; she had fought with her advisers, rejecting their claims that it was too dangerous to reenter Egypt, and now she was faced with the task of using stealth to slip past both her brother's army and the Roman army to meet with Caesar.

Dorinda produced a silken scarf of spectacular colors and tied it about the queen's waist, making an impressive show of her young strong figure. Kleopatra looked in the mirror and wondered if, in the woman's hands, she looked like a queen or a prostitute in training. But that was a look that men liked as well as the royal demeanor. Perhaps Apollodorus might try to pass her off as a prostitute being taken to the mighty Caesar. Whatever got her into his quarters and whatever kept her there under his goodwill would do.

The queen allowed the woman to kiss her hand, giving her a pair of heavy copper earrings and a bar of silver for her personal purse before Apollodorus helped her lower herself to the small boat that awaited them just outside Egyptian waters. Dorinda put on the earrings and shook them wildly, jiggling her extravagant body as she waved good-bye.

Now it was just Kleopatra and Apollodorus in the small vessel. She wondered what might happen if they faced adverse winds. Would she have to row like a slave to get them to shore? No matter. She would do whatever was necessary and dream that it was an adventure, like when she and her girlhood companion Mohama fantasized their important partic-ipation in political efforts. She did not know at the time that such dan-gerous intrigues would someday be the reality of her waking, adult life. How she would love to have the company of that beautiful brown Amazon-like woman now. But Mohama, along with the rest of Kleopatra's childish fantasies, was dead, all victims of the political reali-ties set in motion by Rome and its determination to dominate the world.

Apollodorus completed his duties at the sail and settled down next to her.

"What do you suppose moves this man Caesar?" she asked. Apollodorus was a pirate, an outlaw, a thief, yet Kleopatra had come to value him as a sharp interpreter of human nature. But the pirate allowed that he could not figure the man, so paradoxical were the reports of his character. Talk of his cruelty and his clemency were mixed. In the war against the Roman senators, Caesar had spared almost everyone. He had captured Pompey's officers in Gaul and let them go. Some he had seized as many as four times during the war, and each time freed them again, telling them to say to Pompey that he wanted peace.

"If you submit to Caesar, he spares you. If you defy Caesar, he kills you," said the pirate. "Perhaps that is the lesson Your Majesty should take into the meeting. The towns in Greece that opened their gates to him have been rewarded. But the poor inhabitants of Avaricum—they are with the gods now—were turned over to his men for a drunken massacre. Merciful, cruel, I cannot judge. A complex man, but I am sure, a great man."

Suddenly it was dusk, and the pirate drew her attention to the harbor. In the fading sunlight, she saw the familiar Pharos Lighthouse, the landmark of her youth, and one of the great hallmarks of her family's reign over Egypt. The tower was bathed in diffuse red light that lingered as the sun sank behind her into the depths of the Mediterranean. The eternal flame in its top floor burned vigilantly. The imposing structure that had served as a marker of safe harbor for three centuries was the genius of her ancestor, Ptolemy Philadelphus, and his sister-wife Arsinoe II, and now it welcomed her home. This was not the first time she had approached her country from the vantage point of exile. But it was the first time she had returned to find a flotilla of warships in a V formation pointing dangerously toward her city.

"These are not Egyptian vessels," she said, noting their flags. "Some are Rhodian, some from Syria, some from Cilicia."

"All territories from which Caesar might have called for reinforcements," said Apollodorus.

"Warships in the harbor? What can this mean? That Alexandria is already at full-scale war with Caesar?" asked Kleopatra.

"So it appears. And now we must get you through Caesar's navy and the army of your brother's general, Achillas, before you can have a conference with Caesar. I do not know if my contacts at the docks can help us in these circumstances. As Your Majesty is well aware, in wartime, all policies change to meet the dire times. I'm afraid that our simple scheme of disguising you as my wife may not serve us in these hazardous conditions."

"I agree," she said. Her heart began the now-familiar hammering in her chest, its punch taking over her body and consuming her mental strength, pounding away at her brain. No, this cannot happen, she said to herself. I cannot submit to fear.

Only I and the gods may dictate my Fate. Not a heart, not an organ. I control my heart, my heart does not control me, she repeated over and over until the thud in her ears gave way to the benevolent slurp of the placid waters, calming her nerves as they slapped haphazardly against the boat. She put her head down and prayed.

Lady Isis, the Lady of Compassion, the Lady to whom I owe my fortune and my Fate. Protect me, sustain me, guide me as I make this daring move so that I may continue to honor you and continue to serve the country of my mothers and fathers.

When she looked up from her prayer, she saw that they had drifted closer to the shore. Trapped now between the Rhodian and the Syrian flotillas, she realized that she must take some kind of cover. How could she have so foolishly thought that she could just slip into the city where she was known above all women? She must do something quickly to get herself out of sight.

She shared these thoughts with Apollodorus.

"It is not too late to turn around, Your Majesty—" he offered.

"No!" she interrupted him. "This is my country. My brother sits in the palace as if he were the sole ruler of Egypt. Caesar, no doubt, is in receipt of my letter, and he awaits my arrival. I will not be shut out by these maritime monsters." She raised her hands as if to encompass all the vessels in the sea. "The gods will not have it, and I will not have it."

Apollodorus said nothing. Kleopatra made another silent plea to the goddess. She stared into her lap waiting for inspiration to descend upon her. She was for a moment lost in the intricate pattern of the Persian carpet that the men had thrown aboard the boat at the last minute for the queen to sit on. An anonymous artisan had spent years of his life stitching the rows and rows of symmetrical crosses into the silk. Suddenly, she pulled her head up straight and focused on the rug, mentally measuring its dimensions. Its fine silk threads would not irritate the downy skin of a young woman, should she choose to lie upon it. Or to roll herself inside of it.

The sun cast its final offering of light. Her companion's square rock of a body sat helplessly waiting for the decision of the queen as his boat drifted precariously close to the shore.

"Help me," she said as she threw the rug on the floor of the boat and positioned herself at one end.

Apollodorus stood up and stared down at the queen, who lay with her hands over her chest like a mummy.

"But Your Majesty will suffocate," he protested, stretching his palms out to her as if he hoped they would exercise upon her a modicum of reason. "We must leave this place."

The sun had set, and the boxlike form that hovered above her was only a silhouette against a darkening sky.

"Help me quickly, and do not waste our time with questions," she said. "Julius Caesar is waiting."

When the squatty Sicilian entered Caesar's chamber to announce that he had a gift from the rightful queen of Egypt to lay at Great Caesar's feet, the dictator's soldiers drew swords. But Caesar simply laughed and said he was anxious to see what the exiled girl might smuggle through her brother's guards.

"This is a mistake, sir," said the captain of his guard. "These people are ready to take advantage of your good nature."

"Then they, too, shall learn, shan't they?" he replied.

The pirate lay the carpet before Caesar, using his own knife to clip the ties that bound it. As he slowly and carefully unrolled it, Caesar could see that it was a fine example of the craftsmanship that was only to be found in the eastern countries, the kind he had so envied when he was last at Pompey's house in Rome. Suddenly, as if she were part of the geometrical pattern itself, a girl rolled out from its folds, sat up cross-legged, and looked at him. Her small face was overly painted, with too much jewelry in her thick brown hair, and a meretricious scarf tied about her tiny waist, showing off her comely body. The young queen must be a woman of great humor to have sent Caesar a pirate's little wench. She was not precisely lovely, he thought, but handsome. She had full lips, or so he assumed under the paint. Her eyes were green and slanted upward, and they challenged him now to speak to her, as if it was Caesar who should have to introduce himself to this little tart. But it was the pirate who spoke first.

"Hail Queen Kleopatra, daughter of Isis, Lady of the Two Lands of Egypt."

Caesar stood—a habit, though he remained unconvinced that the girl was not a decoy. She stood, too, but quickly motioned for him to sit. Surely only a queen would have the guts to do that. He took his chair again, and she addressed him in Latin, not giving him the opportunity to interrogate her, but telling him the story of how her brother and his courtiers had placed her under house arrest and forced her to flee Alexandria and go into exile; how her brother's regents were representative of the anti-Roman faction in Egypt; how she had always carried out her late father's policy of friendship with Rome; and how, most importantly, once restored, she intended to repay the large loan that her father had taken from the Roman moneylender, Rabirius, which she must have guessed was the real reason that Caesar had followed Pompey to Alexandria.

Before Caesar might reply to her speech, the queen said, "Shall we converse in Greek, General? It is a more precise language for negotiation, don't you agree?"

"As you wish," Caesar replied. From there, the conversation was held in her native tongue and not his—not that it mattered. He spoke Greek as if he had been born in Athens. He admired her ploy of simultaneously demonstrating her command of his native tongue while diminishing it in comparison to the more sophisticated Greek language. There was no pride like that of the Greeks, and this girl was obviously no exception.

But she had great charm and intelligence, so Caesar pledged her restoration, in accordance with her father's will and the nation's tradition. He would have done so anyway, but now he could do it with pleasure. Not only would it please the young queen, it would also irritate Pothinus, the dreadful eunuch whom Caesar despised. For Kleopatra's part, she pledged a great portion of her treasury that he might take with him back to Rome to satisfy Rabirius. A relief, he assured her, to have that clacking old duck paid and off his back. Kleopatra laughed, remembering the sight of Rabirius's great waddling ass as he was chased out of Alexandria.

"I do hope you are enjoying our city," Kleopatra said. "Are we occupying you as satisfactorily as you occupy us?"

Caesar felt he had no choice but to laugh. He told the girl about a lecture he had recently attended at the Mouseion, the center for scholarly learning that he'd heard about all his years. She had studied there herself, she said, and in her exile what she most had longed for was not her feathery bed nor the kitchen staff of one hundred who prepared for her the finest meals on earth, but the books at the Great Library, and the visits of scholars, poets, and scientists who engaged her mind.

Now secure that she was once again at home and in charge, she relaxed in her seat and called for wine, stretching her thin, shapely arm over the back of the couch and stretching her small sandaled feet in his direction. Caesar was startled at the way she so easily issued commands in his presence, but it was her palace, after all. Before he knew it, however, they were discussing the philosophy of domination, and he was drunk and praising Posidonius while she disputed every point.

"Posidonius has demonstrated that Rome, by embracing all the peoples of the world, secures all humanity into a commonwealth under the gods," Caesar explained. "Through submission, harmony is realized."

A tiny laugh, almost a giggle, escaped Kleopatra's lips despite herself. "Does Rome *embrace*, General? Is 'suffocation' not a more appropriate word?" she asked, her eyes wide and twinkling. He did not know if she was agitating him for the purpose of argument or to arouse him sexually. But with her enchanting voice that sounded almost like a musical instrument, and the way she moved her body with sensuous fluidity, she was succeeding more at the latter.

"Suffocation, perhaps, but only in the service of the common good."

"Whose good?"

"In Gaul, where I spent many years, tribes of men of the same bloodlines who speak the same language, who share common heritage, have fought to destroy one another since time out of mind. I soon realized that while my army was at war with the tribes, there was all the while a secret war in progress, one in which the tribes fought incessantly against one another. The same is true in Illyricum and in Dacia. What you might perceive as an effort at domination is really a means to force peace. Only by thralldom have they bought freedom from the tyranny of eternal tribal factions. But the first step is always the submission of the collective will to a man of resolute vision. Do you take my meaning?"

"I see," she said agreeably, and he wondered if she was storing up her thoughts to deliver an unexpected blow. "You do not aim to suffocate, but rather to unite."

"You are too young to have known Posidonius, my dear, but you would certainly have benefited by his acquaintance. He was most well-traveled, having studied the arts and sciences over most of the known world."

"Odd, we did not see him *here*, where the greatest philosophers in the world are known to gather," she answered, much to Caesar's annoyance. "And in any event, this unity of peoples you describe, General, is only pertinent to those whom you believe you must improve. How might it apply to we civilized Greeks, who require no improvement? How is it that we thrive under domination from a culture whose arts and philosophies are so thoroughly derived from our own?"

It was too much, really, but she said it so charmingly, knowing as surely she must that she held no real power over him. He could afford to be generous. She was so young, one and twenty, she had said, younger than his Julia would have been had she lived. "Surely the gods were drunk on the day they made an imperious Greek girl the queen of a filthy-rich nation. Surely I must be intoxicated to ensure the power of such a girl."

"The Crown thanks you."

"As you know, my child, as we have witnessed here in your own land, there must be a master. It's as simple as that. In accordance with the laws of the gods and the laws of nature. Otherwise, it's a muddle. 'The strong do as they will while the weak suffer what they must.' If I may quote a Greek to a Greek."

By this time, they were entirely alone. She had long ago dismissed the pirate, and Caesar his men. They sat facing each other on two white linen couches with a table of refreshments between them. The queen regarded Caesar for some time, and he allowed it, enjoying the flush of color across her high cheekbones and the way flashes of inspiration seemed to leap from her eyes. "Is it not possible for the two civilized peoples, Greek and Roman, to rule side by side; one race of men of military might in cooperation with another whose strength lies in the world of the intellect, the world of Art, Knowledge, and Beauty?"

"Possible, but not probable. If given the opportunity, men of means will always seek power and fortune."

"And women of means as well," she said.

"Yes, I have not seen that women lack ambition," he replied. "And if a woman has sufficient means, then perhaps many things are possible."

"I'm relieved you think so." She sat back, satisfied, her small hands folded in her lap, a quiet smile on her face as if she shared some lovely humor with herself alone. Caesar was sure that they had not finished with this line of discussion. But he wanted, at that moment, to seize her mind in his hands as if she were another territory to be conquered in the name of Rome and of unity. Yet she was not a woman to be merely taken. Here was a woman, he thought, who if giving herself of her own volition, would give the world.

"But we have parried enough, Your Majesty," Caesar said, rising. "You've vexed an old man quite enough for one day. Now come to bed. You are under my protection."

But she did not rise with him. "General, just when I thought your command of Greek was beyond reproach, I find that you make a linguistic mistake."

"Caesar does not make linguistic mistakes," he replied. What now? More argument with this fetching creature? Was she determined to try his patience?

"You said, *come* to bed, when surely you meant *go* to bed." Again, she looked at him as if she was either laughing at him or trying to seduce him. How could he, a man of fifty-two who had had hundreds of lovers, not rapidly discern which?

"No, dear girl. You know what I meant. I always make myself perfectly clear."

⌒ ⌁ 𓄿 𓅃 𓊖 ⌐ ◉ ◯ ⌐

The chubby boy king burst into his sister's chamber. Though it was early morning, he was dressed in formal robes and wearing his crown. Kleopatra barely had a moment to pull the cover over her naked breasts. Caesar sat up quickly, the dagger under his pillow already in his hand.

"What are you doing here?" the young king screamed, his bulbous lips quaking. "How did you get here?"

Caesar's soldiers followed the boy into the room; trailing them, Arsinoe, her panther eyes darting from Kleopatra to her lover. How old must the girl be now? Sixteen? She was the image of her treasonous, dead mother, Thea, only with marble green eyes instead of Thea's conniving brown ones. Arsinoe smirked but said nothing. She took her brother by the arm.

"Are you some kind of fiend or apparition? The entire city is on guard against you. How did you get into the palace, you ghost?"

Kleopatra did not answer but waited for Caesar to speak. Though he had just restored her to her own throne, he was dictator of Rome, and she at his mercy. At least for the moment.

"My good King Ptolemy," Caesar began, tossing the dagger aside, "I promised to repair relations between you and your sister, and I have done so."

Caesar's men, ready to seize the boy, looked to their commander, but he waved them away.

"But I don't want to reconcile with her," the boy answered, pointing to Kleopatra, who tried to retain as much dignity as a naked young woman in a roomful of strangers might. "She's a monster! Has she poisoned you against us? Has she?"

"Come now, there is no need for this kind of upset," Caesar said. "Let us set a meeting for later in the day—perhaps some reasonable hour after breakfast—and I shall enlighten you and your regents as to the terms."

Caesar's calm voice settling over the room evaporated the anger Ptolemy had released into the air. But the boy king did not relent. "What do you think you're doing?" he stammered at Kleopatra.

"Is this how you welcome your sister back to Alexandria?" Kleopatra asked, trying to imitate Caesar's mellow tone. "I have not seen you for the better part of two years, my brother. How you've grown." Though he was no taller, as far as Kleopatra could discern, he had expanded horizontally, reminding her of the girth her late father had acquired in his last years.

Caesar leaned toward the boy. "You know the terms of your father's will. You and Kleopatra are to rule jointly. It isn't for you to question. You shouldn't have run her out of the country in the first place."

"Run her out? She sneaked away like a common thief and raised an army against me!" he sputtered.

Laughable, Kleopatra thought. She would not put one ounce of her energy into bolstering such a fool before the Roman general, before the Alexandrian people, or even before the gods themselves.

"That's all over now, and I insist that you make up. It's all been decided. No need to create another dispute when harmony is so easily attained." Caesar smiled at Arsinoe. "Is that not what the philosophers tell us, young lady? You have your brother's ear. You must counsel him to be reasonable. You do not wish him to get himself hurt."

"No, General. I do not." Arsinoe folded her arms, making a bridge under her voluptuous breasts and chilling Kleopatra with her glazed stare. It seemed to her that Arsinoe had been assessing the situation and had come to some dark private conclusion. "Shall we go, Brother?"

The boy grimaced at Kleopatra, but let himself be guided away by his sister; more regal than he would ever be, she held his elbow and led him out of the room as if he were blind.

Kleopatra let out a sigh and fell back on her pillow, grateful to have awakened in her own bed, no matter what the circumstances, after two years of exile. She had not slept, really slept, in months, and even last night, she and Caesar were awake almost until dawn negotiating and making love. Fortunately, her energy for both of those activities was of the torrential sort. She had had years of practice for the former, both in her father's government and in exile where resources were limited. The latter, she was accustomed to with a man half Caesar's age, so that the passions of this older man, so distant, so polite, hardly troubled her at all. She thought of Archimedes—cousin, lover, comrade—still in exile, of his eyes as deep and dark as Nile silt, of his strong square shoulders, of the way he lost himself in a private frenzy after he had done with pleasing her, of the way his cries while making love seemed like prayers to some taunting goddess, and she ached with her betrayal. But what choice did she have? For here was Julius Caesar, undisputed Master of the World, who had made it safe for her to be in this room once more, where the sounds and smells of the sea rolled into her window. How many times had she wondered if she would ever set foot upon Egyptian soil again, much less sleep in her own goosedown bed? She had made a cold-blooded choice, but she had made the correct one. *In matters of state, let your blood run cold.* Her most trusted adviser, Hephaestion, whom she had left back in the Sinai with Archimedes, had drilled those words into her head for so many years now that she chanted them to herself day and night. She must have no regrets.

Caesar looked older this morning. The wine they had drunk last night in their orgy of conversation had blurred the lines around his mouth and eyes and the brown spots that covered his skin like tiny mushrooms. Archimedes would have been on top of her as soon as the last soldier had left the room, and she waited for what she assumed all men needed to do upon awakening, but Caesar merely yawned, stretching his arms in the direction of his toes, and groaning when he could not quite reach them. He seemed extraordinarily slim and fit underneath his aged skin, she had to admit. Not one ounce of fat marred his taut, lean physique. He had a narrow Roman nose and an elegant and knowing face, not handsome, fringed by his thinning brown hair. The frown lines at his mouth and the deep crevice under his lower lip formed a severe triangle. His ears were aristocratic and small, just as his fingers and toes were aristocratic and long. It was a well-proportioned face sitting upon a youthful neck that had yet to fall into jowl.

"What a fine, long neck you have," she said to him.

"Like Venus," he answered, nonchalant, and she smiled, remembering that Caesar claimed direct descent from that goddess. "We've all got it in the family.

"And you," he said, stroking her face. "The gods grace the faces of the young with morning dew. It won't be so when you're old like me."

Kleopatra accepted this with a smile while she assessed the new order of things. She was no longer in exile, waiting for the right moment to attack her brother's army. She was again the queen of Egypt. Caesar had overwhelmingly defeated Pompey and the Roman senate, thus making him the most powerful man in the world. And Caesar was now her benefactor and lover.

Yet she did not know whether her country was in fact occupied or not. Caesar acted like a guest who had made himself overly comfortable, rather than as a hostile commander who had entered the city with his standard raised, immediately engaging in a skirmish with the Alexandrian army. Kleopatra did not care what version Caesar put forth of the story. She believed he had entered her city with the intention of taking it. He had thought it would be easy; she was sure of this. He had just defeated Pompey and was confident of his invincibility. But he had underestimated the Alexandrian hatred for all things Roman, the old Greek and Egyptian pride that the city's citizens still carried in their very veins. They did not lay down their arms for the exalted Roman general. Far from it.

Now Caesar and his men were virtually barricaded inside the palace walls, so angered was the mob at his presence. Yet he did not act at all like a prisoner.

"General, I am unclear over certain issues. Are you at war with my brother or not?"

"Why no, of course not. I'm a friend to the Crown, as is all of Rome. I've told you: I came to Alexandria merely to chase down my former ally and old friend, Pompey, whom I had had the unfortunate task of defeating in Greece. I did not even wish to be at war with Pompey, but it seemed that no one could agree on whose policies would predominate in Rome. I came here to reconcile with Pompey, to bring him back to Rome and to his senses, and to make him see that the greedy senators who had incited him to go to war with me were acting in self-interest, rather than in the interests of either Pompey *or* myself.

"But your brother's eunuch, Pothinus, had already taken care of the issue for me. Upon my arrival, he presented me with Pompey's head." Caesar turned away as if to hide his sadness from Kleopatra.

"I may be at war with Pothinus," he said, as if working out the scenario for himself. "I may be at war with your brother's army but not your brother. We shall see what unfolds in the coming days."

How could a man be so casual about war? she wondered. Perhaps it was from a lifetime of waging it. And yet he seemed equally calm and dispassionate about everything, even those things that usually provoked the extreme emotions—debate, negotiation, money, sex.

They were interrupted by a knock. One of Caesar's men entered, not the least bit embarrassed to disturb the morning intimacy between their commander and the queen of Egypt. How often did they come upon such a scene? she wondered.

"Sir, so sorry to disturb you, but the boy king is speaking to an assembly of malcontents at the palace gates. He's torn off his crown and thrown it into the crowd. He is shouting all sorts of insults about the queen. He's getting them all whipped up out there. Shall we remove him?"

"No, no," Caesar said wearily. "Give us a moment. I'll fetch him myself and bring him in."

"We can handle it, sir," said the soldier.

"Yes, but I've got a way with him," said Caesar. "Besides, I shall make a little speech to the mob. I'll tell them their queen is back, and that Caesar shall ensure peace in their kingdom."

"Have the wine sellers discount their wares to the crowd," Kleopatra suggested, remembering her father's old ploy for placating his people.

"Excellent," Caesar replied.

"As you wish," the soldier said. Bowing courteously to Kleopatra but not meeting her eye, he left.

"My brother has always been a nuisance," Kleopatra said, leaning on her elbow.

"I imagine he has," Caesar replied. "Not to worry. He shall be made to understand."

"General?"

"You may call me Caesar, my darling young queen, and I shall call you Kleopatra."

"Caesar. Do be careful."

"Never worry over me," he said, waving his long fingers in the air, fanning away her concerns. "It isn't necessary. No one shall be hurt. At least not yet."

How cunning and stupidity could so seamlessly coexist in the same body, Kleopatra did not know. For here was her old adversary, the eunuch Pothinus, white lead rubbed into his wrinkled skin to make him appear both young and fair. His technique had failed on both fronts, and now his small dark eyes peered out from the perimeter of the thick circle of kohl and at the young queen, who did not shrink from his venomous gaze. Here was the man who had driven her from her own palace and into the treacherous heat of Middle Egypt and the Sinai, the man who had her brothers and sister in his thrall. He had been clever enough to drive Kleopatra away, but foolish, too. He did not understand that in cutting her off from the security she'd known all her life he had enabled her to find the depth of her determination and her strength. She had departed from him an adventurous and clever girl, and returned a woman of unstoppable resolve.

And now the fool thought that he might defy not only Egypt's queen but Julius Caesar as well.

"The king does not wish to be a prisoner in his own kingdom," Pothinus said to Caesar. "It is unnecessary and unseemly."

The boy king sat sullen in his chair next to Arsinoe, letting his regent speak for him. Arsinoe, too, exercised tight control, showing no emotion over the proceedings. Days earlier, Caesar and his men had gently removed the boy from the crowd he'd gathered in front of the palace. Ptolemy had been midway through a temper tantrum, throwing his crown to his subjects, denouncing Kleopatra as the traitor who would sell the nation out to the Romans and Caesar as the dictator who would murder the king and make Kleopatra sole ruler of Egypt. Caesar had instructed his soldiers not to harm the boy; he knew that Ptolemy had no mind of his own, that his emotions were easily whipped up by Pothinus.

"My dear fellow, who knows who is a prisoner of whom in these strange circumstances. To some minds, Caesar is prisoner of the Alexandrians."

Kleopatra had become accustomed to Caesar's manner of referring to himself in the third person, but it never failed to startle her ear.

"Because if Caesar steps into the streets, he is attacked by this mob that you cannot seem to control. And Caesar does not wish to make war on your mob."

"I am quite certain that if Great Caesar wished to leave Alexandria, the mob would cooperate," the eunuch said. Kleopatra wondered how long Caesar would tolerate this fool.

"Ah, but Caesar does not wish to leave Alexandria just yet," the dictator replied in a most pleasant tone. "Not only is his business here incomplete, but Caesar is prisoner of the northern winds which do not make sailing favorable. So you see, Caesar is a prisoner here on your shores. But *you*, my friend, are also a prisoner, though you may not choose to acknowledge it. However, if you set foot outside the palace gates, my soldiers will enlighten you. And the queen is also prisoner, is she not? We are all happy captives, and I suggest we make the most of it."

"By returning to Egypt, the queen defied a royal edict. She must suffer the consequences."

"The queen is the government itself, whereas you are an appointee. Do not forget that." Caesar maintained his agreeable demeanor, and Kleopatra noticed that the more sanguine he sounded, the more menacing he became. "Here is the will of Rome: Queen Kleopatra and her brother King Ptolemy the Elder shall rule in concert. I am their protector and adviser. As a show of my good faith, I hereby return the island of Cyprus to Egyptian rule. The princess Arsinoe and the prince

Ptolemy the Younger shall be its governors. As soon as the winds are favorable, they shall depart for those territories with a Regency Council selected by me."

Kleopatra and Caesar had plotted this the night before. She knew she would never be safe as long as Arsinoe was in Egypt. Dynastic tradition forbade two women to be in power at the same time, and so the only way to deal with one's sisters was murder or exile. Kleopatra explained to Caesar that Arsinoe must go if ever there was to be peace. She told him how their sister, Arsinoe's mentor Berenike, had raised an army against her own father, for which she was eventually executed. Arsinoe had spent her girlhood in Berenike's shadow. Did they have to wait until the girl took the inevitable action? It was not in Arsinoe's character to sit placidly by while Kleopatra and Ptolemy the Elder ruled the kingdom.

"If I were dead, Arsinoe would marry our brother and be queen. She would be unsensible if she did not try to have me killed. Besides," Kleopatra told him, "Arsinoe and Ptolemy have been sleeping together since they were children."

"Interesting," he replied. "We cannot have you dead, now can we?" Then Caesar had said that just as he had once banished the senator Cato to Cyprus to get rid of him, so he would now do the same with Arsinoe and the younger brother, who was presently a child of eleven, but who would soon become the same kind of nuisance as the present king.

"And we shall do it under the guise of goodness," Caesar had said. "A gesture of friendship and goodwill between Rome's new dictator and the Egyptian monarchy."

"May it be the first of many," Kleopatra had replied, and then she had walked straight across the room to Caesar, straddled him in his chair, and had him make love to her in that position.

Pothinus must have imagined what had gone on between Caesar and Kleopatra behind closed doors, and yet he refused to accept the verdict that their relationship cast upon his own Fate. Kleopatra's father had taught her to recognize whom the gods favored and align herself thusly—not out of self-interest, but in recognition of the supremacy of the Divine. The gods were with Caesar. That much was clear. And Caesar was now with Kleopatra. The final step to this equation, to any thinking person, particularly one who had studied logic and mathematics, must be clear. But Pothinus and Kleopatra's siblings chose to ignore this fact, for they made no move to cooperate.

"You mustn't send Arsinoe away!" said Ptolemy. "She is my sister and cherished chancellor, though she holds no formal office."

For the first time, Kleopatra realized that it was not necessarily the bonds of either family or sex that held Ptolemy to Arsinoe. He was afraid, and rightfully so, that without her, he would be even less of an obstruction to Pothinus's exercising complete control over Egypt and her resources. Arsinoe, on the other hand, probably comprehended this completely and had been using it to compensate for her unfortunate placement in the family's hierarchy.

"Dearest Brother," Arsinoe said, "if my duty to country lies at Cyprus, then go I must. We shall not let it separate us in spirit." Ptolemy moved to correct her, but she silenced him by taking his hand. "Now is not the time to discuss the issue. It is a private matter between us, and we need not consume the general's time with our familial arrangements."

How shrewd was this girl, Kleopatra thought. Berenike would have challenged Caesar directly, no matter what price she had to pay. Thank the gods that Caesar had agreed to remove Arsinoe from Kleopatra's kingdom. And thank the gods that Berenike and not Arsinoe had been the firstborn daughter. The eunuch Meleager who had attached himself to Berenike had been a genius conniver. He was dead now, slain by his own hand when his machinations failed. But Kleopatra shuddered at the thought of Arsinoe and Meleager combining their efforts to take over the throne. What a powerful team they would have made. As it was, Arsinoe's present regent was less adroit at disguising his intentions than was his charge.

"Great Caesar, I fear that your efforts to reconcile the family have had the opposite effect," said Pothinus, his voice full of false concern. "I fear you do not understand the intense blood bonds that flow through the veins of this family. See how you threaten the welfare of the king? As his regent, I simply must protest."

"Caesar has taken your protestations into consideration. But the fact remains. The princess and the younger prince set sail as soon as the winds are favorable. Now to the matter of the army."

"Which army is that?" the eunuch asked, and Kleopatra wondered if Caesar would simply take this idiot by the throat and rid them of him without further delay. But Caesar was patient, exercising, she supposed, the mercy upon which he so prided himself.

"The army that is encamped at Pelusium, commanded by General Achillas; the army that you were prepared to turn against the queen. I sent a message to Achillas, a message composed with the cooperation of the king, demanding that the army be disbanded. Achillas's answer was to murder the messengers. You will now send to Achillas and tell him that if he does not disband his troops outside the city walls, I shall summon every Roman legion from our eastern territories and turn them against him. Is that clear?"

"Amply, Great Caesar." Pothinus spoke with an expression of consternation on his face, as if he were suffering from acute dysentery.

"And the king and the princess Arsinoe and yourself shall not leave the palace until it is confirmed that the army is no longer."

"I see," said the eunuch.

"We are outnumbered here, but that will not be true for long. And may I remind you that the forces of Pompey the Great had us outnumbered five to one at Pharsalos. So do not become excessively confident in your greater numbers. I am not toying with you. Rome will be obeyed at any cost to you."

Pothinus nodded. Throughout the discourse, Arsinoe had kept her fingers tightly clenched around her brother's wrist, squeezing, Kleopatra suspected, whenever the boy moved to speak. What was she plotting? And how would she execute her plans? One thing was certain: no Ptolemaic woman would sit idly and let her Fate be dictated by a man, foreign or familial.

⌐🐪𝌆╮⌐◇◡

Julius Caesar's vanity saved their lives.

Though he had not much hair, his visits to the barber were frequent and regular, and he preferred a good Greek barber to all others, or so he claimed. He liked the way the man took time to heat and moisturize the face before removing the stubble with a razor, and he also liked how the barber let the thickest part of his hair grow longer than the rest, using the volume to cover his ever-receding hairline. He confessed all this to Kleopatra, who declared that Rome would never reach the

Greek standards of Beauty because what they treasured in life was not beautiful.

"I don't know why I suffer your insults," Caesar told her. "You are just a grandiose girl."

"Perhaps because you know I am right," she said.

They were snuggled in bed, falling into a deep, postcoital sleep, when the fighting broke out. Kleopatra heard the clash of swords and the rumble of men's battle cries coming through the window, startling her from the beginning of a hazy dream. Before she could articulate a thought, Caesar was up and dressed and telling her to neither worry nor leave the room. She thought of General Achillas at the head of the army, the preening, swarthy commander who had once tried to entrap her into a sexual liaison with him in exchange for protection against her brother and his regents. How she would like to see Caesar bring this man to his knees in defeat.

Luckily, when Caesar had been to the barber a few days earlier, the man had whispered in his ear as he leaned over the bowl of steaming water: "General, I shall pretend to clip the hairs from your inner ears so that I may whisper to you. There are things you must know." And Caesar, intrigued, gave his permission, though he was privately mortified that anyone might think he had unsightly ear hairs that required removal. The barber informed him that Pothinus and another eunuch, an army commander named Ganymedes, had sent to Achillas demanding that he march his army of almost twenty thousand men into Alexandria in secret and launch a surprise attack on Caesar and his small legion of two thousand. It was only a matter of days before the palace would be under attack. "And he plans to have you murdered, sir. Just as he murdered the Roman general Pompey."

"Why are you telling me this?" Caesar asked.

"I am a very old man, sir, and I have seen many fat and worthless Ptolemies and their eunuch advisers come and go. This lot is no different. When you throw these creatures out, I believe you will be most kind to those who helped you."

"You have correctly assessed the situation on all fronts," Caesar said. While the new information necessitated immediate action, he did not act so impetuously as to leave the barber's company without a fresh haircut and shave. Groomed, he revealed to Kleopatra what he had learned and what action he had taken. He had immediately dispatched a messenger to his allies in Asia Minor for reinforcements, with a special offer to Antipater, Prime Minister to Hyrcanus of Judaea, giving the Jews a last chance to redeem themselves for aligning with Pompey in the recent civil war by sending troops. Caesar knew his men could hold out against the superior numbers for a few weeks but not forever. He explained to Kleopatra that lesser numbers often worked to one's advantage because it inevitably made one's opponents lax. And then he sighed. "Poor Pompey." He also reinforced the barricades around the palace quarter, denying anyone admittance or leave. "We are going to be besieged," he said to Kleopatra. "At the right time, I shall engage Achillas in combat. But in the meanwhile, we are not going anywhere."

"That is as I wish, General. I want to get to know you in the extreme."

"By the way, you didn't need to say good-bye to Pothinus, did you?"

"Where is he going?"

"To Hades, I suppose."

"Oh?"

"It is the Roman custom to avoid inauspicious language. An old superstition, but customary nonetheless. Let us just say that he *did* live, but it is no longer true to say so."

Now Kleopatra went to her bedroom window, stood next to Caesar, and watched the Egyptian fleet sail into the harbor, effectively blockading Caesar's smaller navy and cutting him off from supplies and reinforcements by sea.

"Make use of your young eyes and count the vessels," he said. "I believe they are seventy-two in number, more than twice what we've got." Kleopatra confirmed his count and asked his strategy. "Oh, it's all been done before," he said. "When I've lulled them into thinking victory is certain, I shall entice them into combat. The Egyptians are excellent sailors, but not known for fighting man-to-man. We'll lure them close to our boats and then we'll board their vessels. They will be easily defeated on those terms, I assure you."

"You're awfully confident," she said. She could not yet hear the sounds of confrontation, but she remembered how frightened she had been as a child when the mob rioted against her father outside the palace walls.

"Fortune makes confidence unnecessary, my dear."

She was not sure when the moment of clarity had arrived. She had not plotted it, exactly. But when she realized that she was securing the Fate of herself and her nation, she was pleased.

Caesar was not Archimedes, her childhood friend, Kinsman, and subject. She could hardly dictate to Julius Caesar where he placed his semen. With Archimedes, she could tell him that she would not produce a royal bastard, and he could agree with her that it was the wrong thing for both herself and for Egypt. He was a bastard himself and he knew the precarious Fate of such children. She could tell Archimedes that he might penetrate her as much as he wished, but he might not deposit his seed inside her body. And Archimedes had been content with the arrangement and had disciplined himself to arrive at the moment just before climax and then quickly withdraw. All men know how to do this, he had told her, but few wish to bother. Few are making love to queens, she retorted. And he agreed.

If fifty-two-year-old Julius Caesar did not know how babies were made, then it was not Kleopatra's job to tell him. He had had only one daughter, Julia, whom Kleopatra had met while visiting the home of Pompey with her father. Caesar had married Julia off to Pompey to secure the two men's alliance. But Julia had died trying to give Pompey a son. Kleopatra knew that Caesar had been in Gaul when his daughter had died and that he had regretted not being there at the hour of her passing. Kleopatra told Caesar that she and Julia had become dear friends when she and her father were exiled in Rome, that the older girl had been somewhat of a mentor to the twelve-year-old Kleopatra. In truth, Kleopatra had thought Julia a silly goose and had avoided her company. But it heartened Caesar to listen to an eyewitness to Julia's happiness with the elder Pompey, who was even older than Caesar, and this was not fable. Julia and Pompey were rarely out of one another's arms, as nearly as Kleopatra could tell.

She had not yet brought up the subject of another heir. She had never been pregnant, and she did not know the signs. She would send for Charmion as soon as possible; though Charmion had never been pregnant either, she would know precisely what to anticipate and how to tell if one were with child. At present, there was no one in whom

Kleopatra might confide. Though her bleeding was only a few days late, her body had begun to stir—not in ways she had heard women speak of, but as if an odd energy had manifested itself and come to mingle with her.

One morning after Caesar left her bedroom, she had the vision. She was accustomed to rising early, meeting with her advisers and her War Council, sending correspondence to foreign leaders to raise an army, and negotiating with governments and independent merchants and importers to keep her retinue and soldiers fed. These days, there was little she might do but lie in bed like a courtesan, imprisoned as she was in her own palace, while in the streets Roman and Alexandrian soldiers engaged in heavy fighting. She would like to have joined them; she had ridden with her troops in the Sinai, leading them to their encampment, making speeches to rally them to her cause. It seemed unnatural that a woman of her temperament should be cut off from the action of battle, from the events that were to determine her own Fate, and yet when Caesar demanded that she stay away from the fighting, she acquiesced—not because she wanted to obey him, but because she suspected that she held within her body the key to their future. Not the future of Egypt or the future of Rome or the future of Kleopatra or Julius Caesar, but the future of the world. And only before this phenomenal goal would she lay down her desire to participate in the war.

She had begun to think of the seed within her as a son, and she hoped she was correct. How much more difficult it would be if she bore Caesar a daughter. Even the Egyptians, who had been governed by women of will, would never accept the daughter of a Roman intruder as their queen. To Rome, the child would be a mere bastard born to a foreign mistress. The girl would not even be a Roman citizen. But a son—Rome might be coerced to change its customs and its laws for a son of Julius Caesar, even if that son was born out of wedlock and even if Caesar was already married to that woman Calpurnia about whom he never talked, whom he had married for political expediency. Divorce was not only recognized but easily attained in Rome. Why, Romans seemed to marry only for political alliance anyway. What was a Roman woman with a few connections in that city compared to the queen of Egypt, the descendant of Alexander the Conqueror, who not only commanded the treasury of her ancestors, but whose country was

the door to the countries of the east, the territories Rome had been trying to subdue once and for all for over a century?

The boy would be the unity of east and west, of Caesar and Kleopatra,
of the three hundred dynastic years of the Ptolemaic empire and the
sweeping landscape of the Roman conquests. In his small and fragile
body would run the bloodlines of Venus on his father's side, and of
Dionysus and Isis on his mother's. Of Alexander the Great and his mother, Olympias, who wore snakes in her hair and put terror in the hearts of
men. Of King Philip of Macedonia, one of the great warriors of the
Greek world. Of Ptolemy the Savior, first Macedonian pharaoh of
Egypt, and Julius Caesar, conqueror of Gaul, Britannia, and Spain, and
dictator of Rome. These would be just a few of the boy's ancestors. Their
legacies would collect in his small body, nurture him into manhood, and
then reveal themselves in his ability to rule the world in peace and harmony. The boy would put an end to Greek and Roman rivalry, for in him,
the very highest and best of those cultures would make itself manifest.
He would be the first of a new race of men, a hero, a new kind of Titan.
The people ruled by his father and those ruled by his mother would unite
in a joint government that would go beyond the limits of either republic
or monarchy. It would complete the vision of Alexander, who did not live
to see his dreams come to fruition. The locus of the new ruler's power
would be Egypt, the land whose fertile soil fed half the world, whose civ-
ilization had achieved greatness thousands of years before either Rome or
Greece was born.

Kleopatra remembered the dream she had had long ago. She was
walking in the forest when she came upon Alexander, who was hunting
the lion with his legendary Kinsmen, including the founder of
Kleopatra's dynasty, Ptolemy, the great king's companion, general, and
historian. Ptolemy shot Kleopatra with an arrow that, instead of killing
her, turned her into an eagle—the symbol of the Ptolemaic dynasty.
The palace crones had interpreted the dream to mean that Kleopatra
would one day rise to become queen. But that was merely one level of
its meaning. Now she understood the complete message. Alexander had
chosen her, his spiritual daughter, to carry out his vision. He had subdued the bellicose Greeks into one nation. Then he had ridden across
Asia Minor, Egypt, Persia, and into that strange and impenetrable land
called India. Wherever he went, he was welcomed. What other man or

god in history was hailed by the very people he conquered? It was because Alexander did not bring hardship upon his conquered people, but rather alleviated it. He brought a vision of harmony and unity, even if he used military might to do so. Did he not love all the peoples and religions of the world? Did he once impose his Greek gods on any nation or tribe of men? But, depressed over the death of his beloved Hephaestion, he had let himself get weak with fever and drink and died on the road to Babylon. Now—some two hundred fifty years later—Kleopatra would carry out his ambitions. As soon as she was able to leave the palace, she would visit his tomb and tell him what she planned to do.

She had watched her father grow old and feeble in his efforts to negotiate with Rome, to appease Rome's appetites for Egypt's money and resources. She had vowed before the goddess that she would not repeat the pattern that put him in his tomb. And now she had the solution. She need not appease Rome. She would give birth to a new kind of Roman. And if she and Caesar could have one child, why could they not have many, one to preside over every nation of the world? She was young and in optimum health, and he, old as he was and engaged in military actions the day long, still came back to the palace every night and made love to her.

Kleopatra put her hand over her belly. It was no larger than it had been a month ago, but now she felt a new energy stirring inside. Her hand tingled as she stroked the smooth skin. The muscles were so firm that she worried that her womb would be too tough to house a tender baby. Would they give way when the child started to grow inside her? She would rub creams and ointments into her skin and coax the muscles to stretch as much as they could to make room for the child, the new emperor.

Kleopatra lay back down on her bed, reconciled to spending the day indoors. It seemed to her that protecting herself from falling off her horse in the heat of a battle, or from the knife of one of her brother's assassins, was the very least she could do while the future of the world nestled quietly inside her womb.

Arsinoe lacked Berenike's height, which was a problem. Berenike had been as tall as most men, if not taller, and she had not had these infernal large breasts that were good for keeping the attentions of men but got in the way of shooting. Still, when Arsinoe pulled back the bow, its string cutting through the leather glove and into her fingers, she saw the target as if it were the only object in the world. In that moment she was not a human at all but an isosceles triangle of bow, arrow, and princess, with the arrow in a straight line to infinity—only infinity was cut short by the black target before her. She released, falling forward slightly, easily hitting her mark. It would have been easier if she did not have to hold her bow six inches from her chest, diminishing the strength with which she fired. But she had slapped her right breast many a time to the point of bruising, and she did not want to suffer the injury again. It was not form that mattered in the end, but the completion of one's intention.

Ganymedes handed her another arrow. He was slim for a eunuch, probably because he had trained in the military from early boyhood and kept up a strict regimen of swordsmanship and exercise at the gymnasium. He was young still, perhaps thirty, and he wore his hair long and curly like the Greek boys of earlier times whose lovers immortalized them in statuary. He had no facial hair save eyebrows, and was fair enough to be called effeminate. To assume that his character followed suit would have been an unfortunate mistake.

Arsinoe thought him rather beautiful, far more attractive than her pudgy brother. Every night that horrible creature, the image of their late father, came to her room, and she rolled up her nightshirt and let him suck her nipples and rub against her until he spilled his filthy seed all over her thighs. Then he would fall asleep and she would clean her legs and pray to the gods to kill him, until, mumbling prayers to the underworld, she drifted off into fitful dreams. But he was king, and if he were to die a sudden and mysterious death, the little one would probably be no better. Arsinoe prayed that Ptolemy the Younger would stay long in the nursery, that she would not have to let more than one brother at a time suckle her breasts and feel between her thighs. There was no ridding herself of either of them, at least not yet. Berenike would have slain the elder one in his sleep or castrated him, dealing with the consequences later, but Berenike had been executed because of such impulsive moves. At least now Pothinus was dead, and if Arsinoe decided that she could no longer bear her brother's nocturnal visits or his silly outbursts in which he pretended to rule the nation, the absence of the eunuch would make it easier to get rid of the boy king. As it was, the boy's outrage over the execution kept him ranting without cessation, and though he was slightly less interested in making Arsinoe play with his penis, he still relied on her day and night to be the audience to his tirades.

Kleopatra was her biggest problem. But by bedding down with the old Roman general, something she had probably dreamed about since girlhood, her older sister was sabotaging herself and committing political suicide, thus creating one less impediment to Arsinoe's rule. The mob would undoubtedly drag Kleopatra out of the palace and slay her in the streets. She had been a Roman-lover like their father since she was a small child. When she was away with the now-dead king in Rome, bribing those monsters to put them back on the throne, Arsinoe and Berenike would make puppets out of their images, shooting them with arrows until it looked like the Parthian army had come through and emptied their whole pouches into the effigies. Then the two princesses would fall on the grass and laugh until they were sick to their stomachs. Berenike would wait until Arsinoe had no breath left in her body. Then she would cover her with kisses and touch her in all the secret and wonderful places that their idiot brother seemed incapable of finding. Arsinoe would lie in reverie until Berenike got bored and went to her grown-up women. She missed Berenike terribly, though she would like to do those same things now with a man. Not someone disgusting like her brother or the eunuch or the elderly Caesar, but one of the young soldiers who stood guard over the royals, one who had a lean, strong body and handsome eyes. She saw no chance of this at present. She was closely watched day and night. Even in the future, when she would finally escape to head her army, she would still be expected to remain chaste until she chose a husband. It would have to be that way to preserve the monarchy, unless she, too, chose to sell herself out to another creepy Roman with lupine teeth. She had spurned the advances of the snake, General Achillas, though he was handsome almost beyond compare. When he approached her and suggested an alliance based on sex in exchange for his protection, she felt the spirit of Berenike rise up inside her and she slapped him across the face. "I shall leave you to your brother's charms, then," he replied, and she knew that if she did not act first, he would eventually make her pay for what she had done. So she made a plan.

She would choose the next king—not one of her brothers, not a conniving military man like Achillas who sought only power, but some beautiful Greek prince like Seleucus, the handsome Graeco-Syrian whom Berenike had chosen and who had died in battle against the Romans. Together, and in memory of Berenike and all that she stood for, he and Arsinoe would break this ridiculous custom of brother-and-sister marriages that kept the entire world laughing at them and their bizarre ways. Kleopatra only *thought* she was exercising her will and having it her own way. She was merely a Roman's whore, and if that's not how she saw herself, then she was not being realistic. Arsinoe would be different.

Arsinoe placed the proffered arrow into her bow and pulled back with all her might until her arm quivered. The eunuch came behind her and placed his arms over hers as if helping with her form. He took the weight of the stance from her, and she felt herself relax, only to tense again from having a beautiful man, even if he was a castrated one, embracing her from behind. He whispered, "The uniform of one of the Roman pipe-boys will be in the trunk in your chamber. At the hour of midnight, put it on and be prepared to leave." Arsinoe's bow arm started to shake again. "You will not be alone," he said. She felt him pull her arm back until it hurt.

"Release," he ordered, and the two of them let go at the same moment and hit their mark.

Kleopatra watched the spider's tiny jaws devour the leg of some long-dead insect. She could not discern what the thing had been, so crumpled and distorted were its small remains. She had never observed a spider's activities from this angle at this proximity, and she found herself mesmerized by the creature's persistent, rhythmic chewing. She was grateful for her acute eyesight. The spider was perched upon his elongated legs, negotiating his bulbous body this way and that so that his repast need not be disturbed when the dead thing shifted. He would not know impatience, Kleopatra thought, admiring the way he kept coming at his prey one way and another without any acknowledgment of discouragement or fatigue.

Caesar's long legs were stretched out in front of him, feet crossed at the ankles. Ptolemy the Elder sat opposite him, twisting a fold of his linen robe with both his hands. Kleopatra completed the triangle, sitting adjacent to the two men, continuing to watch the spider gobble his victim on the corner of her brother's chair while he sat unaware of the arachnid's valiant efforts inches from his arm.

The war—for now they were clearly at war, but with and against whom was still slightly unclear—had gone on for weeks, with Caesar waiting patiently for reinforcements to arrive. He was certain that he would not be disappointed, despite some messages from Rome's eastern client kingdoms that few Roman troops could be spared because the Parthians would not let up in their attacks on Syria. Their best hope for reinforcements lay with Antipater of Judaea. "Pompey had such trouble with those Jewish warriors," Caesar had said earlier that morning. "They *resisted* him and frustrated him terribly. He repaid them by forcing them to side with him and against me in this recent war. I believe they will not let me down this time. After all, they do need to make amends."

"I wonder if they are a different race from the Jews with whom we have lived in peace here in Alexandria for so many hundreds of years," she had asked, amazed at her arch tone. "They are almost thirty percent of our population. Perhaps we know better how to *embrace*. And to think we have done so without the wisdom of your Posidonius."

Caesar did not argue with her; he never did. She could not bait him into a good Greek-style dialogue. He treated her as if she were a precocious child whose sarcasm amused him in his dotage. That's one way of diminishing my power over him, she thought. She knew that despite the fact that he did not exhibit the typical male ferocity in bed, he took great pleasure in coming to her every night for lovemaking, which was followed by a long conversation until they fell asleep, naked, she on her back, he curled about her, his breath on her forehead like a soft wind.

They were able to spend lengthy amounts of time together because

General Achillas had kept with his strategy of enforcing the siege on the palace quarter, attacking Caesar's troops if they attempted to venture beyond the barricades. It was only a matter of time before he ordered an attack on the palace itself. The only thing preventing this, Caesar concluded, was the fact that the king was held hostage.

It was a little awkward, however, the king's forces fighting against Caesar while Caesar both befriended and imprisoned him. But Caesar did not allow him to think he was a hostage. He would take long walks with the boy through the palace gardens, asking him for his opinions, and telling him that only together might they resolve this dreadful crisis. When Ptolemy was so bold as to inquire over Caesar's relations with his sister, Caesar simply looked at him and asked, *Are you not a man?* He declared to the boy that he was protector of all the children of the dead King Ptolemy Auletes, and not until harmony reigned among the heirs themselves and the heirs and their subjects would he, Caesar, get a good night's sleep. He was awfully sorry that he had had to execute Pothinus, but the eunuch was damaging the situation by claiming that Caesar was no friend to Egypt, that he intended to make Kleopatra its sole ruler, and worse, that he intended to annex Egypt to Rome's empire and institute a policy of extracting exorbitant taxes from its population. Ptolemy had reluctantly accepted Caesar's action, and had almost stopped trying his sister's patience by complaining about it.

Caesar, too, had made it plain to Kleopatra that she must reconcile with her brother. She did not know if he really meant for this to happen, or if he had a larger plan that he would eventually reveal to her. She did apprehend that her bedroom relations with Caesar did not figure into his political policies. She had once thought otherwise, but now she was forced to sit in this room with her tedious brother and pretend anticipation of the day when the two of them might rule as king and queen, brother and sister, husband and wife. The dictator of Rome had his own agenda, independent of hers. She did not believe he would make concessions to her unless her ambitions were in accordance with his own. She could not figure if he was engaging in a bit of political dissembling by pretending friendship with the king, or if he merely intended to dally with Kleopatra until the war was over and he could safely return to his larger business of conquering the world in the name of Rome. Would he really leave her alone in Egypt with her brother? Didn't he know that as soon as his ships left the harbor, Ptolemy would have her assassinated and make Arsinoe his queen? And if Caesar knew that reality but was ignoring it, would he think differently when he discovered Kleopatra's secret?

Aulus Hirtius interrupted their silence. A slender man with a soft voice and a love of literature and fine foods, Hirtius was one of Caesar's men whose company Kleopatra enjoyed. She had apologized many times to him for her inability to provide those things he loved in any abundance while the war was in progress, and had promised him that as soon as victory was achieved, they would celebrate with fine feasts and a long tour of the Great Library. She had had the cooks prepare meals as best they could while the siege was on, and the Romans seemed suitably impressed, but the banquets were inferior to the delicacies they might experience when supplies were once again flowing abundantly into the palace.

Hirtius bowed formally to the royals, handing Caesar a letter. "A dispatch from our man behind enemy lines, sir. Sealed for safety and authenticity."

Caesar held out his hand for the knife Hirtius knew to give him, and cut the seal. He unrolled the letter, read it quickly, and then scanned it again. The expression on his face did not change. When finally he looked at Kleopatra, she detected only one eyebrow raised slightly above the other, the singular way she knew that Caesar registered surprise.

"Do prepare yourself for a shock," he said to the boy king, who immediately clenched even harder the wad of fabric he'd been wringing, as if he were a washerwoman doing laundry.

Kleopatra waited, and Caesar did, too, apparently giving the boy a moment to collect himself.

"It appears that last evening Princess Arsinoe escaped the palace barricade dressed as a Roman page. She went straight to Achillas."

The boy king jumped to his feet, his robe a net of wrinkles where he had been clutching it. It looked for an instant to Kleopatra as if the spider's web on his chair had leapt upon his stomach, and despite the news they had just received, she almost grinned at his childish, slovenly appearance. Caesar merely looked at him, waiting for an explanation.

"I had no idea," Ptolemy protested. "I swear. I *swear!* She told me nothing."

"This is a serious blow to the peace between us," Caesar said calmly. "I trusted you to keep your family members under control."

"But I didn't know," he said. "She tricked me, too." He looked very hurt, his mouth turned down into a deep frown, his plump cheeks quavering just as his father's used to do when he got upset.

"Surely you must know that this does not reflect well upon the trust I've so carefully built between us." If Kleopatra had to judge, she would have said that Caesar was seriously grieved by the news. His demeanor was convincing; nonetheless, she did not believe that he was either surprised or upset. "There is more."

"What more could she do to me?" asked the wretched boy.

"Oh, so much more. I'm afraid your lack of control in the situation has led to an entire chain of unfortunate events."

"It's Pothinus, cursing us from his tomb," Ptolemy cried. "You should have left him be."

"What is the rest of the news, General?" Kleopatra asked, cutting short her brother's histrionics.

"She's had General Achillas murdered. She's made some eunuch named Ganymedes commander of the Egyptian armed forces."

"She has no right to do that!" the king exclaimed. "She is not king!"

Kleopatra stifled her own response. Caesar answered quickly, "No, she is not. But she's managed to get a substantial number of the tribes of the city to declare her queen."

Kleopatra sat still. She had always known this day would arrive, though she had never suspected it would come so quickly. The Alexandrian populace regarded her brother as an ineffectual child, the puppet of whatever courtier had his ear, and herself as a Roman collaborator. They had despised her father for his propitiating policies with Rome, never understanding that the days of the illustrious Ptolemaic empire were over and that Rome was the immutable beast that would either trample over them or allow them to remain unscathed—the latter only if they made themselves of good use. Kleopatra and her father were resigned to this reality, whereas her brothers, her sister, and the Alexandrian mob preferred to live inside the fantasy that if they defied Rome, if they gathered their forces and put up some resistance, the Romans would just leave them in peace. That had not been the case with the rest of the world, of course, and Kleopatra always knew that Rome would never, under any circumstances, withdraw its interest in this nation that was not only the world's largest producer of grain, but was also the singular gateway from the west to the coveted lands of the east. She did not intend to play the suppliant to Rome either, but she had a more ingenious plan than engaging in some inglorious war she would inevitably lose. Her battle would be fought on higher ground.

But now Arsinoe had joined the ranks of deluded Ptolemies determined to restore the great glory of the past. Good, Kleopatra wanted to say. When the Roman reinforcements arrived, they would just kill her.

Ptolemy looked beseechingly at Caesar. "What am I going to do?"

"My good young man, you must take control of the situation. The queen has no sway with her sister." Caesar looked apologetically at Kleopatra. "So you must go to her and this Ganymedes and negotiate."

"But what if she has turned against me?"

"Do you think she's capable of that?"

The king exhaled, shaking his head. "No. She's deceived me, but I do not believe she's turned against me. Ganymedes has influenced her, that is all. Or perhaps she means to gather her forces and break me out of here."

Caesar gave him a grave look. "Is that what you and she have been planning?"

"No, no, I have already told you. I had no idea what she was up to."

"But did you ever say to her that you *wished* someone would rise up against Caesar and break you out of your besieged palace? Did you incite her unwittingly? Did you imply to the poor girl that it was her responsibility to free you from me? I heard you say she was your 'most cherished chancellor.' I will be very displeased if all the while you and I have been discussing peace, you have secretly plotted with your sister against me."

The boy turned to Kleopatra. "It's her, isn't it? You and I were in perfect agreement until she sneaked back into the palace. She's the one who turned you against *me*. She's probably the one who made Arsinoe do this, too."

"I have no truck with my sister." Kleopatra's voice was ice cold. Why couldn't the idiot see that he had been betrayed?

"You'd better watch your back," Ptolemy said to Caesar. "She's going to murder you in your sleep!"

"You are out of control, King Ptolemy," Caesar said evenly. "You have been deceived by one sister and now you suspect the other. Is Kleopatra outside the barricade heading up an army? No, she is sitting right here, working with us toward our common goal. You are negating all my hard work at peace between yourself and the queen. Really, you must calm yourself."

Kleopatra almost opened her mouth to ask her brother to realize that Arsinoe had private ambitions. But she felt that anything she said would interfere with *Caesar's* private ambitions. She was not privy to them—or rather she no longer believed he had shared with her all of his thoughts—so she decided to sit quietly and allow Caesar to orchestrate his plan, whatever it might be. Hirtius stood immobile next to his commander, his countenance entirely calm. She would imitate his implacability, letting Caesar conduct the scenario. It was difficult for her to remain passive, but she intuitively felt it was the wisest course of action. She did not want to disturb Caesar's plans. She had no choice but to trust him.

"Your Majesty," Caesar began, for the first time using the formal salutation to address the boy. "You must go to your army and to your sister. You must gain control of this unfortunate turn of events. I have no wish to harm the young princess. She's a formidable girl, I know, and headstrong. If she calls off her madness, she won't be hurt. She will be free to go to Cyprus with her younger brother and there reign in peace. You must tell her that. Caesar's mercy is known far and wide. She may rely upon my word."

"But what if she refuses to listen to me?" Now the boy was very nervous. The color had drained from his face and he stood frozen in front of the Roman dictator. His belly moved in jerky little spasms as he breathed. Kleopatra thought he might vomit at Caesar's feet.

Caesar stood, putting a long arm around the boy king's shoulder. "You must pull yourself together," he said. "I—that is to say, Rome—and your country and Queen Kleopatra are depending upon your strength and your diplomacy."

"You mean, I am to leave the palace and go to her."

"Yes, of course. I cannot do it myself. I'd be assassinated. Kleopatra cannot go. Who else but you, sire? It is certainly a job for the king."

The combination of flattery and onus was not lost on Kleopatra, but she saw that her brother remained ignorant of Caesar's ploys. If he intends to play these kinds of games with me, Kleopatra thought, he will have to be less transparent. Perhaps Caesar stepped up the level of his manipulative techniques as his opponents grew in formidability. She certainly hoped so. At any rate, he needn't have expended any more of his shrewdness on Ptolemy, who was now softly crying as Caesar gave Hirtius orders to prepare for the king's release to the Alexandrian army.

"Think of me as a father," Caesar said. "I know your dear King Ptolemy Auletes died when you were still very young. You were not able to benefit from his counsel, but remember always that you shall have mine."

With those words and an extra admonition not to disappoint, Caesar bid the young king good-bye. Ptolemy looked at Kleopatra, waiting for her farewell. "May the gods be with you," she said, thinking that he would surely need their help when he finally realized the true nature of his beloved Arsinoe.

"That's right," said Caesar, giving the boy one final pat on the back. "See how easily peace might reign between you?"

When Ptolemy was gone, Caesar sat back in his chair. Kleopatra waited for him to explain his true mind to her, but he said nothing, looking at her as if she were a new acquaintance to whom he had decided to be polite but distant.

Kleopatra finally spoke, taking a risk. "That was quite a performance, General."

"Can you not delineate theater from diplomacy, my dear?" Caesar asked. "I suppose you are correct; it is so like a play. No matter the quality of the performance, the ending is always the same."

"You have no experience with the women of my family if you think Arsinoe is going to negotiate with our brother."

"I have ample experience with women of all nationalities, my dear. You must trust me to know their minds."

"I don't mean to scoff, General, but my sister will never surrender her power or her new title or her will to my brother."

Caesar sighed. "Don't be tedious, Kleopatra. When I wish you to know my mind, I shall enlighten you. Until then, please be a darling and come sit on my lap."

"I am not your pet," she said. It would not do to be just another person who did Caesar's bidding. She had learned from Hammonius, her informant in Rome, that the dictator had seduced the wives of many of his fellow senators—Gabinius, Crassus, Sulpicius, Brutus, Pompey—and also that she was not the first queen to lay down sexual favors for him. He had bedded the queen of Mauretania, not to mention the king of Bithynia—everyone, reported Hammonius, but his sour-faced, barren Roman wife.

"What is troubling you?" Caesar posed this question as if he was inquiring about the weather in Spain at this time of year. Kleopatra felt her fury rise. Privately, he had acted as if they were partners, equals, queen and dictator acting in concert toward a common goal. She had grown so confident of her power over him, yet now she wondered if he would even take into consideration the fact that she carried their child. Perhaps he would laugh the conception off as another folly of war and return to Rome without giving their son a thought. Her father had had dozens and dozens of unacknowledged bastard brats roaming the palace halls. But he also had five legitimate heirs. She must think carefully before she revealed her news. She must wait until she was certain that Caesar shared the vision. Until then, she would let him make love to her, but she would hold her heart outside the arrangement. For that was a woman's downfall.

"I am worried over my brother's safety." Two could play his game.

Caesar allowed himself the smallest grin. "Then let my old and war-weary arms smother your youthful anxieties."

She went to him. He took her into his lap as he might have once done his daughter. She laid her head against his chest and listened very carefully for a heartbeat. Relieved when she found it, she let herself rest in its cadence.

�⌁𓀀𓏤𓏭𓊍𓂋𓊖◇𓂋

Caesar stood on the muddy banks of the Nile in wet soil the color of eggplant. He had forbidden Kleopatra to be with him at this horrible ordeal—not because he thought she would not be able to bear it, but because he did not want her to be linked with the death of the boy king in the minds of the people. After all, she was the one who had to stay and govern them.

When would they learn? Caesar asked himself. How many faces of the dead would he have to see before it was all over, and how many of those faces would be familiar to him? He would never be the one to capitulate, much as he would sometimes like to lay down his sword and go to sleep for a good long while, a sleep that would not be interrupted by a call to battle or an emissary bursting into his dreams in the middle of the night with stolen news of the enemy, or by the snaking dysentery that seemed an inevitable part of every campaign. He was tired of it all. Not physically tired. Physically, he was always the same. He had not been a vigorous young man, so he did not waste his later years mourning the absence of youth's lost strength. Caesar had found his true physical reserves in middle age, and they remained fresh and intact now into his sixth decade of life. Just the other day he had found himself jumping ship to avoid a sword through his gut and swimming two hundred yards to another of his ships, all while wearing his heavy armor. Not only that, but he had leapt into the water so carelessly that he forgot that the latest dispatches from Rome were still unread in his breast pocket.

That would teach him to react out of fear, rather than to call upon Mother Venus, who had protected him all his days from any serious injury. She would have stopped the Egyptian swordsman, because she was not yet ready to take Caesar. He knew. He had always known, and that was why he feared neither death nor injury. That was the secret he would never reveal. Whenever the dropping sickness overtook him, he saw her face, and she talked to him, telling him what to do. The last time had been in Pompey's abandoned tent at Pharsalos. Caesar had felt the spell coming on, and he had asked his men to give him a few moments alone in his adversary's quarters. The men did not question him; they never did. He had gone inside, struggling to reach Pompey's folding chair before he blacked out. As soon as he was in the darkness she was there, her eyes as blue and limpid as the waters of a clear lake, and she was telling him to pursue Pompey into Egypt.

Caesar was confident that she would inform him when his time was up, when the gods of the underworld demanded their inevitable meeting with him. Until then, he had no reason to fret. That is why he chastised himself for jumping overboard like a frightened boy, like a virgin in battle, when he might just have whispered her name. As it was, he had had to swim the long way to the other vessel with only one hand to tread the water, the other carrying the letters high above his head. Worse, he had left his purple cloak behind as a souvenir for the enemy. It pained him to think of his garment in the hands of some strutting Egyptian. Very unpleasant. The swim had been neither convenient nor pleasurable, but it did not fatigue him. Yet his men had made such a ruckus when they realized what he had done, saying that Caesar was like the gods, for neither did they age. He had aged all right, but the men were correct about one thing: The body of Caesar did not really tire.

The mind was another story. He was tired of the sameness of human experience. He noticed that when he ate, he was tired of food, tired of *chewing* it, for that was the very definition of monotony. Food was simply food; the experience was the same with each of the day's meals. Why did intelligent men set such store in consuming a well-prepared meal as if it were their first or their last, when they had many times thus feasted and would do so again and again? He was weary of the sameness and regularity of the necessary human functions—eating, sleeping, digestion and elimination, bathing, warring—and even more so of the uniformity of human nature. The greed, the lies, the petty fears, the lusts, and particularly the transparency of those things in almost every human being he encountered. He wondered if all people experienced this fatigue with life, or if it was a characteristic particular to himself. He would like to take the discussion up with Cicero, if he could once again win the old coot back to his side. That, he realized, was one of the very things of which he was so tired—the winning back of Cicero. Oh, he had done it all before, hadn't he? What might await him now? Would the next decades be so tediously like the last?

How many nations must he subdue before the message was clear?

How might he spread the word of his desires to all the peoples of the earth so that he would not have to keep up the monotonous task of invading and annihilating? Perhaps he should commission an oral poet, one such as the legendary blind man, Homer, to spin tales of his conquests. Then he would send legions of poets forth to all corners of the earth to recount the stories of Great Caesar's victories over his enemies, to tell tales of the horrors wreaked upon those who defied him. He would give traveling bards a special stipend to take the tales into lands he wished to conquer, inspiring terror in the people, who would then beg their leaders to lay down their arms and negotiate. It would certainly be more economical than sending legions everywhere. What a good idea, he thought, congratulating himself. He would pass it before Kleopatra this very evening, for she did know so much about poetry, and even more about ways to shape public opinion in one's favor.

He was not tired of *her*, neither of her supple body nor of her less flexible but infinitely interesting mind. It would be difficult to leave her. He had not experienced the emotion of regret in decades. Would he carry it far from the Alexandrian shore? He did not know, and this alone pleased him—the fact that his future emotions regarding the young queen were not a foregone conclusion. She was the only surprising thing he had left. Something to which he might look forward. The only other adventure he might anticipate was death. Perhaps that would be interesting. Perhaps death was a reward rather than a curse. He would have to die to know, wouldn't he?

His soldiers wanted to go home, but he realized that for them and for him, home was a theoretical place. They had been away for so long and on so many campaigns that campfire tales in the open air of a strange land were more familiar, more like home, than Rome. For what was Rome now but an idea they fought for? His idea, Pompey's idea, Cicero's idea, the senate's idea. All different, but in the end the same. A place where power might be changed into money, and the reverse. Did it matter so who was in control as long as mouths were fed and pockets lined?

Caesar took a deep sigh, letting his shoulders relax, relieving the weight of his breastplate. He looked down at the murky water. The boy king looked just like another drowned body; neither his lineage nor his title could protect him from the soggy Fate. What an equalizer was death. Already fat, the water had bloated him further, his bulging eyes taken to caricature. So unseemly for a royal to be dredged out of the river this way, scooped into a net like the day's fresh catch, his glittering armor catching the slanting rays of the sun as they hit the river. The king had perished along with some of his followers who had optimistically tried to escape in a river vessel too small for their numbers. Where they intended to sail Caesar did not know. Where did they think they might escape him? Escape Rome? He might have let the bodies remain at the river's silted bottom, but he wearied of the rumors spread by the superstitious Alexandrians that whoever drowned in the river would inevitably rise again. No need for that to happen. And no need for anyone to wish it to be so once Caesar left Egypt. He wanted Kleopatra to have as little difficulty as possible once he was gone.

Was he dreaming that she had begun to behave exactly like his sweet Cornelia when she began to suspect that she was with child? The secretive smiles, the complete obedience, the tender and unconscious stroking of the belly when she thought no one was watching. The way she covered herself protectively with her arms. The downcast eyes. A perpetual look for docile Cornelia, but he never dreamed he would see the same demeanor in Kleopatra. Each day when he returned to the palace, she was waiting for him in the bedchamber. Yesterday, she had actually fallen at his feet, hugging his pelvis so close to her face that he did not know whether she was ready to perform sexual favors or pray.

"The gods have spared you," she had cried, and then she had looked up at him with tiny tears in the corner of her virid eyes. So unlike her. The menacing intellect she had once used to gain equality with him was now hidden, and in its place was the lush, enveloping softness of womanhood. He had no doubt the more caustic elements of her personality would again emerge once she was on terra firma as queen and no longer required his services to ensure her authority. But it was nice, this radical change that allowed him to enjoy her without challenge or effort.

Caesar stood over Ptolemy's body. "Strip the armor and display it in the marketplace," he said to Hirtius, who gave the command to the men.

"And the king's body, sir?"

"A respectable tomb, but without spectacle. Do I make myself clear?"

"Always, Caesar."

Caesar took one last look into the dead boy's eyes and turned away. An heir. What would he make of that? It would cause as many problems as it would solve, bring as much sorrow as joy, he was sure, for that was the nature of life. But it would be interesting. Perhaps there were a few surprises left after all.

⌒🦆𓏏𓏏𓈖𓏤🔲⌐🔊⌒⏌

Kleopatra watched the war from her own balcony like a spectator at a theatrical production. It was as if she had already read the text of the play, what with Caesar unfolding his plans to her at night, and then the next day enacting them to the letter. During those times, she learned that Caesar was right; Fortune was on his side. It seemed true that if Caesar wished something, it inevitably happened. It was as if he were dictating to the gods and not the opposite. Kleopatra thought that Alexander probably had possessed the same gift—that is, until the end, when the gods decided to reclaim their mastery over the mortal man. At some point, they would exact that toll from Caesar, but until then, it was clear that they kissed him with blessings. It was impossible to learn the personal secrets of Alexander—how he had gained influence over both the divine and mortal worlds—but here was Julius Caesar, in Kleopatra's own bed, where she might observe his ways and learn how he managed to wield power over the gods themselves.

Ganymedes had had the palace entirely surrounded by land and by sea. His ships outnumbered Caesar's navy, and to worsen the siege, he had pumped salt water into the wells used by the Roman army. But Caesar did not get discouraged; in fact, to Kleopatra he seemed nonplussed, mildly inconvenienced. He was certain that the Jewish forces would not let him down—they could not afford to disappoint him again—and so he told Kleopatra that they would make the best of things in the interim. She knew that the Roman army was only days from dying of thirst, and had told him so.

"No matter," he had replied. "There's always a way if men are willing to work. My men are bored anyway. They despise being on this end of a siege. They find it rather embarrassing. They'll relish the task." She did not know what he had in mind, until he urged her to look out her window. There, she watched Caesar's men dig deep tunnels, working day and night, to reach the drinkable wells near the shore. When she congratulated him on the discovery of the wells, he replied, "Roman ingenuity." He added, "A race of men who do not mind work," as a slight against the Greeks, who were thought to have grown indolent in the centuries since the great days of Pericles.

Finally, the Roman senate sent Caesar a small flotilla from Asia Minor. They had taken so long with naval reinforcements that Kleopatra had begun to wonder if they wished Caesar victorious in Egypt, or if they had a covert agenda. She asked him about the matter, and he replied that undoubtedly his enemies in Rome wished him vanquished. "But the wishes of my enemies are of no consequence to the Fate of Caesar," he said.

He promised Kleopatra that the next day would prove eventful, and he did not disappoint. In a night-long meeting with his admiral from Rhodes, to which he allowed Kleopatra attendance, she listened to them devise their plan. They would sail right up to the Egyptian ships, engage them in battle, and quickly set them afire.

"After we defeat the fleet, we shall take Pharos Island," he said.

"All on the same day?" she asked.

"Why waste time?"

The next day, it happened exactly as Caesar had said, giving more credence to Kleopatra's theory about his relationship with the gods. He burned most of the Egyptian fleet, including a merchant vessel carrying a large shipment of books to the Great Library. "A mistake," he said to her by way of apology. And she did not fault him, for he loved literature as much as she and would never have done such a barbarous thing intentionally.

She felt a barrage of emotions as she watched ship by ship be overtaken and burned, great flames soaring into the blue Mediterranean sky as if competing with the fire atop the towering lighthouse. These were her ships, her men, her navy. Only circumstance had made them her enemy. Once reinstated, these same men would have to pledge loyalty to her. What did they care whether they served one Ptolemy or another? These were the same men who would have faced her mercenary army at Pelusium, had Pompey not been defeated by Caesar and fled to Egypt for quarter. Today they were her enemy; tomorrow they would have to be her defense. It was an insecure position, and she did not know if after the war she should bring her own army into the city for extra protection, or whether that would only increase hostility. She had a recent letter from Hephaestion saying that many of her mercenaries had deserted because they received better offers from the Roman generals to go to Syria and fight the Parthians. He could keep the rest paid and fed for another month, but no longer. What were her orders?

She had no orders to give. Inertia simply did not suit her, and yet it would not be intelligent to take action independent of Caesar. Would the rest of her life be like this? Was she just another useless Ptolemy hanging on to her throne by playing the suppliant to Rome?

The child, she realized, was the only means by which she might escape the Fate of her ancestors. It was the solution she had prayed for all those years ago at the feet of Artemis of Ephesus, when she—fourteen years old and a lover of small animals—had slit the throat of the lamb with her own hands and watched its blood run like a red river into the sacrificial bowl. She had sworn before the goddess to be different from her degraded ancestors, and now Artemis, virgin goddess of the hunt, the very one who had rendered a man blind for simply looking at her naked body, had not begrudged Kleopatra the pleasures of sex but had gifted her with pregnancy. *The gods are good to those who serve them.* She heard the voice of her father in her head and felt a chill run through her body—the sign that his spirit was still with her.

She had told Caesar nothing of her suspicions, which were now confirmed by the fact that two months had come and gone without her shedding so much as a drop of blood. One night, in the elation over the destruction of the Egyptian navy and the reclaiming of Pharos Island, she and Caesar had made love in a great burst of fury, faster and with more heat than they had done before, though that was the very day that Caesar had swum a long distance in his full armor. Yet he seemed younger and less fatigued than ever. She hoped that vigorous sex did not harm the unborn, but there was no one she might ask without arousing suspicions. One word from her on the subject and there would be a chain of gossip from one end of the besieged palace to another, as if the details of her love affair were not enough fodder to keep that machinery in constant operation day and night. She knew that most of her subjects did not understand her reasoning in the affair, but she held the faith that someday soon, she would stand before them and explain to them what she had done on their behalf and for their futures.

After their lovemaking, Caesar had lain on his back, eyes closed, recovering from what was surely the last task in his long and demanding day. Kleopatra had snuggled to his side, wrapping an arm around his chest so that his underarm hairs tickled her chin. Another remarkable thing about Caesar—he had no disagreeable body odor. He used only the most delicately scented oil, one that would not have disguised the masculine effluvium. Though he had exerted himself in pleasure, and though she had a nose like a tiger, Kleopatra could detect only the faint aroma of myrrh on his body. Was this yet another of the ways that the gods had blessed him?

"In a few days I shall leave you."

He did not open his eyes to deliver this news. Kleopatra was afraid to sit up. She refrained from tightening her grip around his chest.

"Oh?" She wondered if she sounded authentically curious, or if the shock and desperation she felt infiltrated her tone.

"I've received word that Mithridates of Pergamum is marching toward us from the east with the Jewish legion. They say Antipater is escorting the high priest of Judaea himself. I must go to meet them."

"I see," she said. "Will you be coming back?"

He opened his eyes and looked at her. "Darling," he said. And then he chuckled.

"Perhaps I am becoming too much trouble," Kleopatra said. "Perhaps it would be easier to leave me to face my sister's army on my own." She despised the anxiety that had crept into her normally confident tone. I sound like some pathetic courtesan, she thought. Is this what pregnancy did to women? If so, she would never do it again.

"I'm leaving a small garrison here to protect you. I'll be back in a matter of days if all goes well."

"What is your plan?"

"You'll have to trust me, my darling," he said, kissing her forehead.

"If Arsinoe has me killed, will you call an end to the war and support her as queen?" she asked, feeling bile rising into her throat.

He did not respond, but exuded exasperation without uttering a word or a sigh.

"It would certainly be an easier solution than maintaining a war machine," she said.

Was this the time to tell him about his son?

"Kleopatra, you are so dramatic these days. What is wrong with you? I believe you are proving Aristotle's claim that a woman is irrational and incapable of reason."

"Men are rendered irrational in the presence of women and falsely conclude that it is the female who is irrational," she retorted quickly. She had not spoken to Caesar this way in months, and she wondered if he had grown lax in his treatment of her. Did he mean to treat the queen of Egypt as an ordinary mistress?

"Nonetheless, you are not yourself. What is the matter?"

"I believe it has to do with my condition. They say it causes a woman's humors to descend and her emotions to rise."

"Are you ill, my child?" he asked, and she wondered if he contrived the worried look on his face. "Should I be concerned?"

"Not unless one considers carrying the child of Julius Caesar a cause for alarm."

"I do not consider it so," he said evenly, no change in his calm expression. She waited, but he said no more.

"Have you nothing further to say on the matter? Are you not even surprised? Do we mean nothing to you?"

"I have known for some time, Kleopatra. You can keep nothing from me."

"Why is that? Are you all-knowing like the gods?" She wanted to antagonize him. If he did not commit to one emotion or another she would go mad.

"I have lived two and one-half times longer than you, dear girl. There is nothing I haven't seen. I have thought your thoughts. And if I have not, I have observed others thinking them. But no matter. You need not surprise me to please me."

"Are you pleased?" She held her breath, trying not to look at him in anticipation. Unable to resist, she shot him as cold a glance as she could summon, but inside, her stomach churned. She hoped her anxiety was not harming their child.

"What man would not be pleased?" he asked. He sat up a little, turned on his side, and held out his long arms, waiting for her to sink into his chest. When he wrapped his arms around her, she felt him shudder.

"You are unhappy."

"I am thinking of Julia," he said. He looked away, but she could see that his eyes were watery. "If she and her son had lived—my grandson—Pompey would not have come to such a humiliating end."

"Then let *our* son be that force for unity," she said, and she hoped that she did not sound as if she were pleading.

He said nothing, but continued to hold her to his chest.

"Think on the meaning of it, my love," she said. "Think of what he might represent to the world."

"I have considered all that," he replied with none of the rapture that reflected her own thoughts. "But it will not be so easy as you think. You do not know the obstacles that await you in my country. They won't take it well."

"Opinion can be changed."

"Ah, but not so laws."

"Laws are made by mortals. You have passed enough interesting legislation to know that," she said.

"I must go to sleep now," he whispered in her ear.

"Shall I have an artist sketch your likeness so that I may someday show it to our son?" She allowed a bit of coyness to invade her question.

"You must learn to eradicate doubt, Kleopatra, or you shall not make a good mother to our boy."

"May I still not know your plan?"

"Now more than ever, it is crucial that you do not. But mark the words of Caesar. By this time next week, we shall be rid of at least a few of our most pressing problems."

He drifted off to sleep, leaving her vulnerable, ignorant of what he would do next, and praying to the gods that she had not been a naive girl all along, believing the tender words of an inveterate diplomat and seducer.

She did not sleep that night, or the next, or the next. She lay awake stroking her stomach and praying to the goddess. After Caesar had gone, she roused the priest in the middle of the night, and had him make a small sacrifice. Alarmed at her urgency and groggy with sleep, the priest had his attendants light the torches in the temple and bring in a small goat. Its entrails were the image of good health, he assured her, and so Her Majesty's intentions were honored by the goddess.

Kleopatra tried to be consoled by this analysis, but she had never felt so alone. Her supporters and Charmion were trapped behind enemy lines. She was entirely dependent upon Caesar's goodwill and authority, and besides his cryptic word and his good but implacable humor, she had no solid assurance that she might rely on him. His men might as easily murder her in her bed as protect her if her sister's soldiers burst through the barricades and into the palace. Why should they stop an assault on her? Some would consider it a service to Rome to slay

Caesar's foreign mistress—especially if it were known that she was carrying his child. If Caesar had already guessed, others may have, too.

She passed the rest of the night with her hands on her stomach talking to the boy, calling him young Caesar, telling him her plans for his future, who his mother was, who his father was, his ancestors. She recounted tales of Alexander, from his boyhood through his conquests of kingdoms and nations. From the library she sent for a copy of the story of Alexander hunting the lion and read it to her unborn child.

"Alexander's father, too, was a great warrior, but never forget that Alexander surpassed him in achievements. So might you, difficult as it may be for your tiny self to apprehend. And Alexander's mother struck fear in the hearts of men, as apparently your own mother has done to her own brothers and those who advise them. And I shall do so even more and with greater ferocity when you are a grown man and rule at my side." Kleopatra smiled at the thought of inspiring fear in men. Roman soldiers thought they held dominion over everything, including the sowing of fear in the hearts of others. "They may have to share their domain with us," she said, hoping her son already had a sense of humor, of irony, that would put him in good stead with his father. "And do not forget, Alexander's detractors said the same awful things about him that they say of your father, that he was mad for power and that he ruled Fortune. Those were the jealous Greeks, the Spartans and Athenians who had to abdicate their power to the greater man. Those on the decline always criticize those on the rise." She promised to take him to Alexander's tomb and get his blessing as soon as he was old enough to be taken out of the palace. She hoped his little spirit was ready to take on the weight of his earthly mission. *If the philosopher is correct, and all knowledge is but remembering what the soul already knows, then you must come into this life with full memory of all that has gone before you.*

She calmed herself this way, communicating with her son so easily that she was certain his soul was present with her in the room, until finally, her aloneness and her fears were lifted. She thought that she might be a fine mother, one with the power to inspire greatness in her offspring, for what else might be the purpose of a queen who out of necessity would pass along her throne? She patted her stomach until she believed she had calmed the child as well as herself, and then she drifted off to sleep as the vaporous light of dawn floated lazily into the room.

Days later, Caesar burst into their chamber with the news that her brother was drowned, Ganymedes dead, and her sister in chains. Caesar had outfoxed Ganymedes, of course. He had made a great show of sailing out of the city with his legions to join Mithridates. He did meet up with the reinforcements, but in the middle of the night, when the Egyptian army was deep in slumber, they sneaked back through the western gate, taking them by surprise and easily vanquishing them.

Caesar smiled more broadly than ever before. Kleopatra's first thought was not *thank the gods*, but rather, *now I shall owe Caesar everything*.

Unless the gift of a son was equal in his mind to the gift of a throne.

Arsinoe looked at her brother's death mask and felt nothing. The artist had improved his features, making him appear a bit thinner and more secure than he had ever looked in his short lifetime; nonetheless, there was nothing to miss in that round and vapid face. Never again would she have to see the ridiculous expressions he made as he reached for his pathetic moment of ecstasy. The awful contortions of an already disgusting face. The moaning and groaning as he struggled with something inside himself, or so it seemed, struggled against his own horrible pleasure. And then the inevitable mess at the end. She would never have to do that again, which was the thought she had held firmly in her mind as she and Ganymedes had forced her brother and his men into the boat that would take them on the long trip down the Nile; that was, if they made it, what with human cargo twice the weight the vessel could support. Either way they would have perished—by the hands of the Egyptians who would be furious at the king who had capitulated to the Romans, or by nature herself as she dragged them to the river bottom.

There was nothing here to mourn, and yet the Roman soldiers kept looking at Arsinoe as if she was supposed to have a certain kind of reaction. She had cried her tears over the serene death mask of Ganymedes, who had been executed by the Romans for political expediency. Arsinoe had begged for his life to the Roman commander, but was told that the eunuch had too many militaristic ambitions to be spared. She knew that he was being killed merely because he had almost outsmarted Julius

Caesar, and undoubtedly the crafty old Roman could not tolerate the existence of one who had almost bettered him in battle. If it had not been for the late arrival of the Jewish forces—bullied into joining their conqueror's cause—Arsinoe would at this moment be queen of Egypt and Ganymedes her Prime Minister. And Kleopatra's head would be on the executioner's block, and it would be Julius Caesar's filthy Roman armor and not her brother's displayed in the marketplace, though she would have undone her brother anyway.

Arsinoe remembered the first time Ptolemy came to her chamber. It was right after the death of their father, when the eunuch Pothinus— dead now as well—had insisted the marriage between Ptolemy and Kleopatra take place. Kleopatra had agreed to the ceremony, but afterward she refused to let Ptolemy into her bed. The boy, red with humiliation and anger, came rushing into Arsinoe's room, calling her his true wife and queen and promising that he would see Kleopatra if not dead, then in exile. And he had made good on that promise.

Arsinoe had had no choice but to comply with his salacious wishes. She had no one to look after her interests but the unsavory boy who removed his clothes and slipped under the blanket beside her. And so she succumbed, playing the role of lover with all the passion of an actress, for she remembered what sweet love had felt like and she could enact it for this fool who actually believed she enjoyed touching his putrid flesh. She could not tell him that compared to the body of the fair and taut Berenike, it looked to her like uncooked, milk-fed veal.

She turned away from the sarcophagus and met the faces of her captors, Roman soldiers who eyed her leeringly, staring at her body. She was not afraid, and returned their gaze with an imperious and defiant stare like the one Berenike had given at her trial. She had heard that Caesar had given strict orders to the men not to harm her in any way. Surely he had disobeyed the wishes of his mistress in that regard, for she knew that Kleopatra wanted nothing more than to see her dead. Then and only then would that whore of the Romans be safe.

Well, let the Roman-lover try to have her executed. Arsinoe would face her death bravely and with dignity, just as Berenike had done when their own father demanded her death. And she would leave behind her a trail of animosity against Kleopatra and the Romans that would destroy them all, for she knew that many of the tribes of Alexandria were disappointed that Kleopatra had prevailed.

She dared not hope for life. Alive, she was of no earthly use to her sister. She could be nothing but a threat, because there was still the younger brother who was already twelve years old, and Kleopatra would soon have to face the reality of his existence and of her own position. And at any point in his life, under the influence of an ambitious courtier or of his own volition, Ptolemy the Younger could decide that Kleopatra was not his ally, and he could have her murdered in her sleep and replaced with the seemingly compliant Arsinoe. After all, the two of them had grown up together in the nursery, and after his mother and Berenike were dead, who had mothered him but herself? To him, Kleopatra was a half sister, an inconvenience, a threat, or all of these things, whereas Arsinoe was a full and true sister, an affectionate sibling, the closest thing to a mother the boy would ever know.

She knew the reason she was presently kept alive, and it had nothing to do with Kleopatra. She had heard it from those within the palace who attended her and who secretly still supported her. Julius Caesar had told Kleopatra that he would not execute a girl. Not that he cared who lived or died, but he did not wish to mar his reputation for mercy. And that was that. Apparently, Kleopatra had shut up for once and did not argue with Caesar to do her bidding. Arsinoe doubted that Kleopatra was trying to follow her lover's example for mercy. Julius Caesar could afford to be merciful; a Ptolemaic queen fighting for the throne could not. Kleopatra probably had an alternative plan for Arsinoe's demise and was not yet ready to reveal it to Caesar. If Arsinoe's sources were correct, Kleopatra must have revealed quite a bit of news to Caesar in recent weeks. Unless Kleopatra had suddenly taken to doing her own laundry, there was only one reason for a woman to go two months in the palace without sending bloody linens into the baskets for cleaning.

Arsinoe's women could not help but to notice this discrepancy. And Arsinoe had laughed and replied that she had always suspected Kleopatra was not a real woman. Perhaps she did not bleed like one.

With a Roman sentinel flanking her on either side, Arsinoe stepped out of the mausoleum and into the light. The winter air had dried out the city, and the sky was as gray as the metal of a sword. It was as if the whole of Alexandria had taken on the color of war. The young princess looked down the long colonnade that lined the Street of the Soma. The vines that snaked up its columns had shriveled up for the season, leaving those tall, elegant Greek flutes wrapped in dead brown leaves. She did not know if she would ever see her city again. She was to be taken prisoner in the palace, and then sent to Rome to be marched in Julius Caesar's victory parade. His prize. How she wished she might find a way to take her life before that humiliating moment. But something kept Arsinoe from pursuing that line of thought. Surely she could have a servant sneak in a vial of poison or a dagger. How complicated could that be? On the other hand, she might gain something from this long voyage to the city of her enemy. She had spent her life pretending to be one thing or another—a compliant lover, a nurturing sister, an ally. Only with Berenike had she passed those rare and early moments of authenticity in her short life. She would now rely on her ability to dissemble. She would allow herself to be paraded in front of the Roman vermin, because that was the price to pay for access to the Roman mind. Once given that access, Arsinoe would fill eager ears with stories of her sister, of how Kleopatra's ambitions were only seemingly in line with those of Rome. She would tell long tales of how Kleopatra had deceived her father, her brothers, and her sister, only to serve her own ambitions to be queen. It was all Arsinoe might manage in the way of revenge. She knew that Kleopatra would continue to call for her demise, and she could not blame her. If the gods had been good to Arsinoe and if she had been in Kleopatra's place, she would do exactly the same.

Dear Your Majesty,

It has come to my attention that you no longer require *any* of my services. Therefore, forgive me if I do not return to my position as your adviser and to the Order of the Brotherhood of the First Kinsmen. As you recall, I am a partner in a very lucrative import business with our friend Hammonius, and I am needed in Rome. I shall go where I am needed. It was a pleasure and an honor to serve you. If I was not assured that you were receiving equally good service in my stead, I would return to you immediately. But it does appear that you are well taken care of in all regards.

I am leaving all further matters of the army to the discretion and administration of Hephaestion, a man equally loyal to you and, given his physical condition, perhaps more suited to be part of your new regime.

I shall always honor the memory of your father and the kindness he bestowed upon me. If Your Majesty finds in the future that she needs me, I shall return to her immediately and without question. Until then—

Your Cousin and Kinsman,

Archimedes

She could not say that the sight of his penmanship and the hurt and bitterness that bled from the words did not go straight to her heart and wound her. She had disappointed him and injured his pride, and he had deserved much better from her. He had been loyal, he had been willing to lay down his life for her, and he had loved her. For those sacrifices he willingly made, he received in return the news that she had become the lover of Rome's dictator.

Why is it that a man might have had such a liaison and thrown it off as either necessity or dalliance? Why is it that a man, particularly a king, might have arranged to keep them both? Caesar—indifferent, implacable Caesar—might have tolerated an alternative lover in her bed, but Archimedes, with his Greek passion and temperament and masculine pride, would never play the lover to another man's mistress, especially if she were carrying his child. She was glad Archimedes was going straight away to Rome. She could not bear to look upon his face, his keen, moist eyes that undressed her even before he laid his hands on her body, his beautiful long neck, his brown locks that tickled her face when he was on top of her. Sometimes she could hear his laugh inside her head, or remember the way he bit her neck with hot teeth, and she would thrill to her core, blushing, covering her face with her hands lest she have to explain this sudden color to anyone, especially Caesar.

She missed him. But she did not have the luxury of wallowing in that sorrow. Caesar had planted inside her belly the course for a different kind of future.

At least she was spared the ritual of mourning for a husband. She had had the foresight to rush a divorce through the Egyptian court as soon as her brother left the palace. She argued that she could not stay married to someone with whom she was at war. That fact, combined with a word of encouragement from the Roman dictator, and the divorce was quickly granted. She did not have to go to his tomb and beat her breasts or enact any such nonsense over the brother-husband for whom she felt not one iota of affection or even respect.

With Ptolemy the Elder interred and Arsinoe in prison, Kleopatra went to her last sibling, Ptolemy the Younger, and explained to him the situation. He was the youngest of a fairly large family and had the characteristics of one who was positioned as such. He had been indulged in some ways and kept ignorant in others. Too young to have a keen sense or memory of the coups of his mother and eldest sister, he had been allowed to play the role of prince in the nursery. He had grown accustomed to Arsinoe and the older brother calling him "King of the Seleucids," for they, with Pothinus's ample encouragement, had promised him they would conquer the lost empire of Seleucus for him and allow him to rule over it. Kleopatra told him that the Romans had long since conquered the lands once ruled by Alexander's companion, and that they were fighting the Parthians now to keep their domain. The boy seemed surprised.

"That doesn't mean that I shan't have it in the future," he said. "Pothinus always said that Rome would destroy itself, either with or without help from us."

"Whether that is true or not, only the gods know," she replied, trying to be patient with this pudgy boy, this ugly reminder of her stepmother, Thea. "In the meanwhile, the papers are being drawn up for our marriage. Caesar wishes us to follow the traditions of our ancestors and the terms of our father's will."

"I am to be king, then?" he asked.

"Yes."

"Then I shall have a Regency Council? Like Pothinus and Achillas and Theodotus were to my brother?"

"Julius Caesar and I are your Regency Council," she said.

"But he is your lover!" the boy said. "If you are to be my wife, then how is it proper that your lover be my regent?"

"Dear Brother, listen to me. Despite the foolishness you have heard all your life from your brother and sister and their silly eunuchs, you must adjust to the present situation, to the order of things as it exists, not as you wish it to exist in your fantasies. Now, if you simply follow the wise counsel of Caesar and myself, you shall not fall victim to the same Fate as your elders."

"And if I do not?"

How tedious was this conversation. The boy did not know how fortunate he was to be alive at this moment, to be free, and not to be chained to Arsinoe, waiting to be paraded through Caesar's triumphal arch and into Rome. She had suggested it, but Caesar declined to follow her advice. To rule Egypt legally, she required a male consort. Neither Rome nor Egypt was prepared for that man to be Julius Caesar, at least not yet. Since the time when Ptolemy I had married his son to his daughter in imitation of the pharaohs, the pattern had been the same. To change it so quickly, on the tail of a civil war, would not be wise. "One thing at a time, darling," Caesar had said. "You mustn't be impatient. It's the surest road to failure."

Kleopatra accepted the judgment of Caesar, but she was already tired of explaining things to this preposterous boy. Did he really think she would allow him to reign with her once her son was born?

Perhaps she would banish Ptolemy the Younger to a faraway island, letting him rule it in name while someone loyal to herself kept an eye on him. Hephaestion would find such a place, and this boy was probably deluded enough to be kept contented in such a situation. Once the people of Egypt saw the son of Caesar and Kleopatra and realized the honor and power the boy brought to their nation, they would quickly forget about this last male Ptolemy. It would be Kleopatra's union with Rome that would restore the empire of her ancestors. Why could the members of her family, not to mention the majority of the Egyptian people, not realize that fact? For it was stamped all over the earth by the boots of Roman soldiers.

"If you do not follow my counsel, then you shall have to face the consequences. But why make trouble for yourself? We shall both take on the title of Philadelphus, Brother and Sister Loving, to let the people know that we shall not be at odds, that you will not conspire with others against me as your brother did."

"But you are not my lover!" he insisted. "You are the lover of Julius Caesar and everyone knows it."

"Yes, that is true, and that fact will also serve us." If this worm thought he would exercise the rights of his ancestors and find his way into her bed, particularly while she was carrying the child of Caesar, he was more deluded than he appeared. More than anything, she hoped that she did not pass on any of the characteristics of the male line of her family to her son. It would not do to keep breeding the likes of these boys.

"I want to see Arsinoe."

"That is not permissible. Arsinoe is Caesar's prisoner." What tripe Arsinoe would put in the child's head—rise up against the Romans for the glory of Berenike! Oh, Kleopatra could just hear the incendiary speech Arsinoe would give the boy, her last stand in Egypt before she was taken away forever.

"Then I shall never see her again?"

Was she having sexual relations with the little one too? How deep was their bond? Kleopatra wondered. Even if Kleopatra was able to eliminate Arsinoe's influence, how long until another conniving eunuch got hold of the boy and reminded him of his destiny as the last son of Thea? The last hope for Egypt to be ruled by the untainted blood of a Macedonian king? The only barrier between an independent Egyptian nation and one dominated by Rome? He was not so very young, not too young to have his head filled with treasonous nonsense.

She looked at his round, red face and his corpulent body, far too opulent in size for one so young. A ripe piece of fruit waiting to be plucked by the purveyors of political intrigue. She wondered how long she would have to tolerate him as a factor in her life. Suddenly, she felt very tired. This creature was draining the very life from her body.

"As I said, only the gods can know the future."

Alexandria: the 20th year of Kleopatra's reign

*T*he rustle of silks against thighs, the jingle of jewels. The sounds Antony shall hear as the women are led to him. *Would that it were me,* she thinks. *Would that I were the object of sexual delight able to ignite that bold leader of men.* But the man who shared her bed these many years, who used to make such sport of petting her, pleasing her, who never failed to move her to rapture, wants her no more.

Antony sits drunk in the mansion he built by the sea—Timon's Retreat, he calls it, after the Athenian who was betrayed by his friends and settled into a life of misanthropy. He spends his days staring out at the sea and at the lighthouse built three hundred years ago by Kleopatra's ancestor, Ptolemy I Soter, the father of the House of Lagid, the general to Alexander the Great. The tower has stood as a beacon to ships at sea, guiding them into the city, ships bearing the cargo and the culture that have made Alexandria the center of the world. Now its flame burns for an inebriated recluse. A sacrilege against the memory of her deified ancestors. *This cannot be. She will not let it be.*

No one can humor Antony, much less inspire him, not her (especially not her), not even his sons. Not little Philip, not Antyllus, the great strapping mirror of himself. Philip in his innocent observation did not help matters. "Father, your face looks as wrinkled as your old clothes." A tragically accurate simile. Nonetheless, she halts the procession of the prostitutes. She will go to him one last time, a precursor to an army of whores. Her last attempt.

Antony is haggard; he bears the look of a beaten man. He has spent the day staring down at the peasants who make their way by pillaging ships that wreck upon the shore. "That's the life," he says to Kleopatra, not even taking his gaze from the window. "That's how I wish to live henceforth. A scavenger feasting on plunder. An outlaw beholden to no one." He turns around. For a moment, his eyes shine bright from within his red, bloated face. She sees a glimpse of Antony of better days, before he had the countenance of an insane child.

She intends to seduce him. She wishes to rekindle his desire for her, for surely that was an impetus for some of his actions in the past. Sex always cheered him. It used to invigorate him so; Antony, who always made great art of pleasing a woman. Her attempts to reason with him have failed, so she resorts to the role of seductress—ironically, the role in which Octavian and her enemies in Rome have cast her. She has dressed fetchingly, though it has taken a great deal of her energy. Adorning herself, even allowing the slaves to adorn her, is now laborious. She cares so little for the cosmetic tricks on which she once prided herself. Nonetheless, she believes she has created the illusion of beauty. But for all the Roman claims that she has him entirely enchanted, Antony barely acknowledges her presence, much less the pains taken to appear pleasing to him. He is in the grip of Dionysus, but is a joyless Bacchant. The medicine for misery fuels his agony.

She takes Antony's leathery hand and leads him to the pillows. She nuzzles her shoulder under his, trying to let the warmth and strength of his body please her. She tolerates the sour aroma, recalling the times they made love after battle when his odor must have been even stronger. But the smell of victory, no matter how acrid, is erotic; the smell of defeat is not. She tries to concentrate on those moments when passion and power and glory met and she experienced utter annihilation under his enormous body. The wine and the war cannot have dissipated that devastating masculinity entirely. Beyond the drunkenness and the despair, she knows that he is still Antony.

How many times have they sat quietly like this, putting all problems and grievances aside, blocking out the world and its demands, reveling in the simple fact that in his hand hers was like a child's, a doll's? "Your Royal Grace is but my small toy," he would say to her. "You rule a kingdom, but I shall have you under my power." He would sweep her into his arms and carry her to wherever it was— the bed, the bath, the floor, the table, the balcony, the garden—that he felt like making love. Antony never ceased to enjoy the audacity of having a queen, and an imperious one, serve his pleasure.

She strokes his hand in the old way, praying that her slow fingertips grazing his tough-hide skin will remind him of those days. She turns the great paw and caress-

es the soft center of his palm. She brings it to her lips and gently bites the flesh with her front teeth, nibbling, licking, in the way that he used to love so.

He ignores her. She puts his hand on her breast and squeezes it so that it engulfs the flesh over her heartbeat. He stares straight ahead, silent but for a wheeze that has of late invaded his breathing. His hand is a large dead thing limp against her chest.

Impatient, irritated at this slovenly, lethargic creature who calls himself Antony, she drops his hand and stands up.

"Antony," she addresses him, not liking the admonition in her voice, but unable to suppress it. "We must talk. We must make plans. Our allies in Italy are homeless. Octavian has confiscated their property to give to his soldiers in payment for their services. In payment for betraying you. Our friends in Italy have lost the lands of their fathers. I am told by my men that the Antonians are still loyal, that they wish to support you. But you must give them something to support. We must give a sign that we are strong, that we are ready to fight again."

He says nothing, but rises to sit on the ledge of the window, looking through bloodshot eyes out to sea as if he anticipates some mystical revelation to come from those waters. She wants to shout, "What are you looking for out there? Look at me." But she continues: "Can you not see that we still might win? We lost a battle, not a war. And even that point may be contested."

He leans his head against the sill and closes his eyes. "I leave all further matters of strategy up to you, my dear. You excel in these things, I believe. You and your network of impeccable spies."

He throws his empty glass out the window and turns toward her. His red eyes blaze like a furnace. "Would you let me be one of your merchant spies, darling?" he hisses. "The gods know I'm fat enough, eh?" He strokes the girth of his stomach in self-disgust. The gesture chills her.

"Bribing officials in foreign lands for you, my darling, while I'm selling spices to the markets, silver to the minters, perfumes to the whores. Yes, especially that. I'm an old whoremaster from way back when, aren't I? Just ask anyone. Just ask Octavian. My love, give me leave to grow a beard, don a Greek robe, and join the fleet of fat informers on your very handsome payroll. The gods know I need the money." He glares at her with what she could only interpret as hatred. Then he tosses his head back and laughs, the acrid smell of stale wine on his breath filling the room, making her nauseous. The sickening catch in her stomach as much in anguish over the dissolution of her husband as from an intake of foul air—the poison in his heart escaping through his mouth like a noxious gas.

Unwilling to admit defeat, for never will she face that possibility, she tries again.

"Octavian has put up his own estate for auction to demonstrate his need for money, while his henchmen spread the word that any who bid on it will face certain execution." She speaks slowly, calmly, and waits for his reaction. Octavian's duplicity always roused his anger, for whatever lies are told of Antony now, no one can say he is not a loyal and straightforward man. Instead, he displays his ironic smile, which used to anticipate some clever joke but these days casts a shudder in her soul.

"Have you nothing to say, my darling Imperator?" she asks sweetly, trying to recover her womanliness, trying to let him know that to her, he is still the warrior, the victor she fell in love with so many years ago. Without meeting her eyes, he returns his gaze to the infernal sea. "Fulvia and I lived long and well in a confiscated house. It belonged to Pompey, but the poor fellow lost his head right here in Egypt and no longer had the need of it."

He laughs the shrill, consuming laugh of a madman. He hops off the ledge and into the room. That small exertion gives her a second's hope that he has come around. But he looks at her and laughs again. She knows she has lost him. Pounding his massive fist on the small table, he cries, "More wine, you bastards. More wine."

The patter of the slaves' bare feet running up the stairs. The sound of Antony's fist again hitting the wood like meat on a butcher's slab. The boy, dark, slight, craven, entering the room of the lunatic giant. The wine bottle teetering on the tray. Antony, grabbing it in a greedy, fierce swipe. The boy losing his balance, falling into the immense shadow of the besotted old Titan pouring the liquid down his throat. The queen, alone, unattended, meeting the eyes of the boy who shrinks back in fear, sliding away from her on his backside, out of the elongated shadow of the fallen demigod with the bottle stuck to his lips like a horn singing the call to battle.

Divine Lady, Lord Dionysus, Pallas Athena, goddess of war, how is this a proper Fate for a warrior? She leaves his quarters at once.

Alexandria:
the 4th year of
Kleopatra's reign

Caesar watched her eyes light up and then dart away from his. He knew by now what excited her, and he could tell that the mention of his Master of the Horse had aroused the interest of the queen. Was there a woman on earth who did not respond that way to Antony? They responded to Caesar, too, but that was because they knew his power. If the two men were side by side disguised in beggar's clothing, Antony would still be able to seduce any woman, from washerwoman to queen. Kleopatra's face at this moment was evidence of that. And why not? Antony was a physical specimen sent by the gods to remind mortal men of what they might strive to achieve. His native beauty was startling, a masculine ideal in the way of old Greek statuary, but without the taming effete qualities. Antony was the male animal in its pure and glorious form. There were those who said Antony shared himself with men as well as women, but Caesar doubted that Antony had carried on with men past the first time he shaved his beard. Who knew? Drunk, one fine young bottom was as lovely as another, its owner's sex be damned. Why the Romans were rabid on the subject of sexual relations between men, Caesar did not know, because virtually every Roman he knew had used his slave boys when women were scarce, or, in many cases, for the kind of vigorous sex men needed without the tedious challenge of seduction that women demanded. Why could the Romans not be as sophisticated as the Greeks?

Caesar remembered watching Antony in Greece in battle atop his horse, the sun on his bare bloodstained arms delineating his huge muscles as he swung his sword, his highly arched nostrils drawn back with each thrust, with each slaying. More beautiful than a bull. It was cold, and smoke billowed from Antony's nostrils as he murdered his way through enemy ranks like Herakles himself facing his adversaries. What must he have looked like to a man who had to face his wrath? It was as if time had stopped for that moment. Caesar had never experienced anything like it—as if the gods had decided to slow the rapid linear stream of events to show him the true beauty of the human form. Antony was perhaps the only man Caesar had known who made the act of killing a beautiful performance. Of course Caesar would never say this to him, or to anyone, for that matter. Some thoughts—most of one's private thoughts, in fact—must remain one's own observations. It would not do to let others into his mind, except for *her*, because she was so very exciting to talk with. Really, only Cicero was as interesting, and what was a debate with an ugly old man compared to that same experience with a stunning young woman? Cicero always smelled of one poultice or another. His health was not good, his sleeping patterns even worse, so that he was always in a bad mood. Kleopatra smelled like the inside of a flower, and she generally slept like a child and awoke energized, with that eager look on her face, as if her dreams had been wonderful and she was challenging the waking day to gift her with something of equal delight.

He must write a love poem about her. Another of his secrets, for what respectable Roman general wrote love poetry? Again, so less sophisticated than the Greeks, whose masculinity did not diminish with sensitivity and love of beauty. Truth be known, Caesar was a bit defensive about his love poetry. Oh, he read a poem to this friend or that one, or to the odd lover, usually one who did not have such great command of Latin. He had written an entire series to Venus, of course, and now he would compose one to this girl who so reminded him of his ancestress. Not that Kleopatra had the beauty of Venus. Were she not the queen of Egypt, with royal carriage and dazzling clothing and jewels, she might not be thought beautiful at all. The nose was far too beaklike to have been carried off by a mere woman. But somehow the face of a queen tolerated it quite well, and it added to her authority. Had she been a conventional beauty, her power might have been diminished. Somehow, what would be considered flaws on the face of an ordinary woman only enhanced the genius that radiated from every expression Kleopatra offered. If he had had such a daughter, he might have tried to change Roman law and make her a senator.

"Why have you stopped speaking, General?" She looked at him warily.

"I must write a poem about you," he said. "You are poetry itself, it seems to me."

"You are saying that because you are tired of our negotiations and you merely wish to win each point. But I am not softened by your flattery." She gave him her coy smile. He thought she looked relieved to be off the subject of Antony.

"Are you not happy that I have no ill feelings over your girlish lust for Antony?"

Now her eyes turned a colder shade of green and she dropped her smile. "I did not say that I experienced girlish lust. I said that as a young girl, I was intimidated by his handsomeness, almost to the point of embarrassment. I am certain that as a woman and a queen I should be less under his spell."

"Oh, I doubt that."

He sensed she was holding back some bit of information about Antony. But what could it be? She was only fourteen the last time she saw him. Surely she had not indulged in an affair at that tender age? No, despite her passion, he suspected she had led a fairly chaste life. Knowing Antony, he would have less preferred a virginal princess than the brothels of exotic Egyptian whores.

They sat in the Royal Reception Room, built by her father and dedicated to the god Dionysus, where she and her father had entertained countless foreign visitors. It was here, she said, that her father had often regaled his guests with performances on the flute. A true artist, she said, and Caesar wondered which was closer to the truth: the stories that he had heard about the daft king, or Kleopatra's version of her father as a wise eccentric. Perhaps both were true, for what man was merely one man? Through the course of any given day, Caesar himself might be many men—warrior, commander, dictator, politician, lover, poet, scholar. And the Roman mind could be so unkind to men who were considered odd. Perhaps he himself might have enjoyed the king and his music, for Caesar transcended conventional Roman thinking.

"In any case, Marcus Antonius is my *Magister Equitum*."

"Master of the Horse? Is that a cavalry position?"

"No, dear girl, it is the second in command to the dictator. He is presently the ruling official in Rome."

"Shall we continue with our negotiations, General? Or would you like to hear more stories of my past, when my father's music filled this hall and I was just a child? Or perhaps you would like to hear more of the heroics of your Master of the Horse, how he marched his men across barren desert to reinstate my father to the throne."

Caesar sighed, looking up at the vaulted ceiling upon which was painted a scene of the god reclining in a forest surrounded by satyrs and nymphs. He knew Kleopatra had opened the Royal Reception Room so that he might feel the splendor and wealth of her throne. Yes, it was fantastic, certainly more opulent and beautiful than any structure in Rome. The marble columns, giant mosaics of scenes from the god's life, the golden throne, the eagle of Ptolemy that crouched above her head staring him in the face as if to defy him to harm this great woman, this descendant of the House of Alexander—all these things were stunning to the more austere Roman eye. But if she thought that Julius Caesar would be intimidated by a visual feast of wealth and power, then she underestimated him. But he admired her for using her resources.

"I assure you, I have heard all the stories of Antony's adventures, for he is the preferred storyteller at every event, and he does not disappoint his audience. Had he not been born a great orator and warrior, he surely would have made his fortune as an actor. And why, dear Kleopatra, would I wish to listen to you taunt me with your affection for my favorite lieutenant?"

"You are grieving me with this topic of Marcus Antonius, a man I have met only once in my life and briefly at that. Would you care to return to our business?"

They had been spending days together in the Great Library, where she had scholars pull off the tall shelves the scrolls Caesar most wanted to see. Yesterday he had read a conversation with Socrates, written in Xenophon's own hand. Nights were spent feasting, celebrating their victory. They had slept very little, and Caesar knew that despite the fact that he felt as well as always, he looked drawn. This morning in the mirror the barber had shaved away his stubble, revealing deep creases that ran down the sides of his cheeks. Kleopatra, on the other hand, had color in her complexion. Perhaps it was youth, perhaps cosmetics. In any case, she made him feel alive, more so than he had in years, more so than battle, more so than victory itself.

"Yes, I would. Tell me, in what denomination will you provide the money to pay Rabirius? I do not wish to lose any of it in the foreign exchanges, which can be so costly."

"Will gold do, General? I seem to recall a Roman affinity for that particular metal."

She took not one moment longer than he to adjust to the business at hand. She was formidable, he thought. How she would throw those old crones in the Roman senate into fits of madness with her cool negotiating skills. He wished he might bring her into those chambers to teach those old fools a lesson.

"Gold will suffice."

"It is an extraordinary amount. Extortion, some might say."

"A small price to pay for your seat on that lovely golden throne."

"Very well. My father accepted the bloodsucker's terms and I shall honor them. Now, about our son's legitimacy."

"Kleopatra, how are you certain that the child is a son?"

"The astrologers have told me so. And so has my own intuition, which is usually more accurate than all the predictions of the soothsayers."

"Without further arguing that point, the child will not be considered legitimate in Rome because, as you well know, I have a wife."

"Yes, but is divorce not readily procured in Rome?"

"My dear, it would be an outrage for me to divorce my Roman wife in order to legitimize a foreign-born son."

"Has the outrage of others ever stopped you before?"

He had to remember that she would never back down unless he exercised authority over her, and that would ruin everything. Besides, he could not resist the notion of a son. Why had none of the women he had married or bedded with given him a boy? Perhaps the constant rigors of military life and the inevitable diseases that followed one along the campaign trail had made him sterile for years at a time. He had heard from his men that after bad bouts of malaria, they were unable to give their wives children for two, sometimes three years. How often had he contracted that little misery? He had not been in the marsh for some time. Perhaps that, and his victory over Pompey, had made him more potent than ever.

He wanted a son. Pompey had had two. Fine strapping men, whom Caesar would eventually have to reckon with. Even Rabirius, a man who pin-curled his hair, had produced a son. Cato, Bibulus, Gabinius, all had sons. True, many a great man had produced a male issue who, perhaps to spite the father, took up the role of rake and failure. Cicero's young son Marcus, whom the orator had recently sent to the philosophers in Greece for instruction and correction, promised to that vein. And that sort would never have done for Caesar. Perhaps it was just as well that he had been spared that Fate. For what boy would wish to meet the challenge of comparison to Julius Caesar? There were those who charged that Brutus was really his son, and Servilia herself was not above suggesting that it was true, particularly when she wanted something from him. At times, the somber, moralizing Brutus had acted the part of the son to Caesar, but that was usually when he, like his mother, sought favor. Caesar had looked into Brutus's face since the boy's birth for signs of inherited traits from the Julian clan, but he saw none. Or nothing conclusive, at any rate. Why had the gods denied Caesar, their favorite? Perhaps they were saving this as a late-life reward, a son of the House of Alexander, an heir brought forth from the loins of this marvelous girl. How could Caesar not honor a gift from the gods?

"Before we address the issue of our son, should we not clear the smaller details of our negotiations. For example, I am wondering who will pay the troops, the three legions I shall leave behind when I return to Rome."

"Are you protecting me, or are you protecting Rome's interests from me?"

"Clearly, your interests are Rome's interests. I didn't go through all this trouble to see you queen again so to have your lovely neck slit in the middle of the night."

"I might have offered to pay them, but with the enormous extraction of gold from the treasury, I am afraid that will be impossible."

"Then I shall have to take them with me."

"Then I shall have to recall my army from the Sinai and bring them into the city."

Was she threatening him?

"I do not consent to that. What if you have as much control over your army as your brother had over his? No, I'm afraid that won't do. Egyptian armies seem to have minds of their own."

"And what are you afraid that army will do?"

"Besides rise up against you at the urging of the first eunuch who gives them a speech? I have told you: I intend to march back through here within the year on my way to Parthia. Those savages will continue to menace us until I go there myself. At that time, the gates must be open and the way clear. I have fought one war here. I will not fight another."

"Then it is clearly in *your* interest to keep your legions here, regardless of my desires. I suggest you find a way to pay them and to feed them. And also to discipline them. I won't have another band of rapists and thieves on my hands the likes of which Antony and Gabinius left here."

"Those were mercenaries. These are the soldiers of Caesar. Do not think they would disobey me, even in my absence."

She looked at him like a child might who has wearied of playing a game. "Why do you not annex Egypt to the Roman empire? Surely it is not merely for the love of your mistress. Is it because of what Cato told my father? That there is not a Roman honest enough to serve as its governor?"

How lovely it would be to tell her that he left her country independent for her sake. How magnanimous he would appear.

"Otherwise, General, I cannot figure it."

But she would never believe it. "Anyone sent here would not only line their pockets with your treasury, but would also use the location to gain control of all territories to the east. Such a man would have to be feared, and then subdued."

She leaned forward so that she was perfectly in line with the eagle, her face almost as feral as that of the beast. Caesar felt as if both of them were getting ready to lurch at him. "Then *be* that man. Do you not think it is a wise plan? Be my king, line your pockets with my treasury, and together we will subdue the eastern territories. No one could touch us."

He had thought of that, of course, dreamt of it, played with the idea of it over and over in his mind as he lay beside Kleopatra at night. It was an excellent notion. Unconventional, of course, never having been done. And completely out of line with Rome's idea of government. That would not stop him, however. But how much easier it would be to execute if he first subdued the Parthians, conquered those long-haired horsemen of the bow who had troubled Rome for so many generations. Rome would never accept a king, and Caesar would never accept being a king in Rome. But Rome was not Egypt. In Parthia, Judaea, Egypt, Media, all the territories he intended to have as his own, a monarchy would be necessary.

"And we will pass our kingdom to our son."

"It's not impossible."

She smiled sweetly at him. "Of course it's not impossible. Whatever is our combined wills cannot fail."

He thought she would come to him and sit on his lap as he liked her to do. She was looking a little fatter these days, just around the middle. Pregnancy softened the taut lines of her body, rounding her in very pleasing ways. Instead of approaching him, she said, "So you will pay them?"

"Pay whom?"

"Your legions. Is that not the issue at hand?"

"Yes, yes, I shall pay them if you will feed them," he replied, shaking off his dreamy affection. It was the first time a human being had disarmed him in so many years. "Your granaries are full these days. It's the least you can do."

"Agreed."

"And when Caesar returns in one year with his legions, the granaries will be open to us, I trust?"

"Agreed. But at a price. Only the gods know how many ravenous men it will take to defeat Parthia."

"A very low price. Less than the exporters pay."

"Yes. Egypt's cost. I just don't want to lose money. Also, I want Cyprus. Just because Arsinoe will not be here to govern it does not mean it shouldn't be returned to the empire of my ancestors. You and Clodius conspired to steal it from my uncle just so that you might get Cato out of your hair. You caused my uncle's death. I wish compensation for that, and for the lost revenue the island used to bring us."

"Now, Kleopatra, I won't be paying any retroactive revenues."

"But you will send the Roman governor home?"

"Yes, yes." What did he care? When his plan was made manifest, it would all be his anyway. His, hers, the boy's. The elements were moving together in Caesar's mind like pieces of a puzzle. A few were yet missing, but the picture had begun to take shape.

"Now the matter of the boy. The matter of the kingdom. The matter of our Fates. Yours, mine, his. What is your hesitancy?"

"You want everything too quickly, Kleopatra. It is a disease of youth. I spent ten years subduing the tribes of Gaul. Oh, I would have preferred to have done the job in less time. But it took ten years."

"I cannot wait ten years to know the Fate of my son. And at your age, you may not have ten years to decide it."

"As long as we are being blunt, let me say that you will have the wrath of Rome against you if you push the issue. Calm yourself and trust me. Surely you see that Egyptian sentiment toward Rome is not exactly high. You do not wish to turn your people against your son."

"No, I do not. But this brings me to my final request. I agree to put off the matter of our son's legitimacy in Rome for one year. But there is something you must do for me."

He knew that she knew what he was thinking—that there was precious little that Caesar must do for anyone. But he wished to indulge her as he would a spoiled child, as he would have done Julia and her son if only they had survived. Why should he not take this opportunity to pamper her and the unborn son? He had worked hard. There were those who said he only did as he wished for his own gratification and reward. That may have been true. And yet he asked so little of others outside the loyalty and labor of his soldiers. Why should he not grant the request of this delightful creature, particularly if it may help along the status of his heir? He knew that whatever Kleopatra asked of him henceforth was not for herself but for the seed of the man that grew inside her, for that was what happened to extraordinary women once they were with child. Never again did they think as the singular creatures they once were. Inevitably a large portion of their own ambitions were poured into their sons. Kleopatra would be no exception.

She interrupted him with the melody of her voice. "Oh just say yes to me, my darling. I wish to give you an experience you shall never forget."

Caesar tossed a chunk of meat into the crocodile's gaping snout and the animal snapped down on it with such fervor that the dictator laughed. Kleopatra watched the years seem to melt from his face as he smiled. The afternoon sun fell over the temple, turning its sandstone pillars a soft gold and changing Caesar's craggy skin into a youth's complexion. The High Priest himself had blessed the meat from the sacrifice to Sobek, the crocodile-god, and watched, too, as Caesar fed the six leathery beasts in the sacred pond.

"I do believe they are divine," Caesar said to Kleopatra. "Look at that fellow in the middle, the one who fights his mates for the food. He must be fourteen feet long. I should appoint him my captain."

Kleopatra translated this to the priest, who replied that the animal was indeed regarded as special. "Just as Great Caesar inspires fear in the hearts of his fellow men, so does his favorite crocodile subjugate the others of his species."

Kleopatra saw the dictator try to suppress his ironic smile as he accepted the solicitous offering.

He seemed younger, lighter than he had been in the city. He was no longer at war, of course, but Kleopatra thought the change was greater than a relaxation from that anxiety. He was neither so cynical nor so all-knowing. He seemed genuinely delighted with the Egyptian countryside, with the exotic beauty of the terrain, with what must seem to him their arcane customs, and especially with the evidence of corruption. He had laughed out loud when Kleopatra explained to him the purpose of the hidden tunnels in the temple. In earlier times, the priests would speak through the walls to the worshippers, pretending to be the voice of the god. They would order specific and lavish offerings of food, which they would consume that evening for dinner.

"I'm pleased that my country entrances one who has seen so much of the world," Kleopatra told him.

"That is true," he answered. "But I have never seen anything like Egypt."

The way Kleopatra saw it—the reason she had undertaken the trip—was that the message had to be sent, and sent directly, not by third parties. The people of Egypt must be shown the alliance with the great man, and they must be given an inkling of what that alliance might mean to them and to their country. She would not send proclamations or pamphlets or make new coins. She would go to them as she had done in the past and present herself and her intentions. Twice before this method had proved successful. She would not start in Alexandria, where animosity toward both her and Caesar was high. She would begin with the rest of the country and then use the vast amount of goodwill she collected to influence the proud Graeco-Egyptians in the city. Soon, she was certain, she would have their support as well. Like the current of the Nile that flowed from south to north, so the goodwill she amassed in southern Egypt would float upward. She was sure she would not fail.

The barge was three hundred feet long and was followed by a flotilla of ships carrying Caesar's legions. Though they had won the war, and though Kleopatra had the widespread support of the native people in the lands beyond the Greek city of Alexandria, they had no idea whether to anticipate trouble. Besides, Kleopatra did not think it a bad idea to demonstrate the might of Rome united with the sumptuous wealth and charisma of the queen. She insisted that half the ships fly the Roman flag and the other half the Egyptian, solidifying the alliance. When they came to a settlement or a city, Caesar and Kleopatra would stand on the front deck, surrounded by statues of Aphrodite and Apollo, in full view of the spectators. Sometimes they displayed themselves from the upper deck, which housed an arbored garden and a huge alabaster statue of Aphrodite with the infant Eros and another of Isis suckling Horus. And in the event that the populace still did not understand Kleopatra's condition, they were left with the image of baby Horus sitting on a lotus blossom right above the vessel's rudder as the barge floated away.

In a small ceremony at the ancient city of Thebes, Caesar removed the laurel wreath he wore at all ceremonies and replaced it with a garland of flowers in the tradition of the Ptolemaic kings. To the Egyptians, it signaled precisely what Kleopatra said it would—that Caesar demonstrated respect for the customs of their country and would be delighted to be the male consort of their queen, resplendent in the seventh month of her pregnancy.

In the mornings, the rulers took their meals privately in their chamber, sheltered from the heat. Languorously they ate dates, mangoes, bananas, and drank chilled goat's milk, reciting poetry to one another, and, when the mood took hold, lazily rolled together and made love. In the evenings they supped in the dining room with their guests—Caesar's highest-ranking men, Greek and Egyptian dignitaries from the cities they visited, and clever Alexandrians Kleopatra had invited along for Caesar's amusement. Of these, he preferred the conversation of Sosigenes the astronomer. Long after the queen took to bed, Caesar would stay up with the bearded scientist staring into the night sky. In the mornings, he would awaken full of their conversation about the placement of the stars, the length of days, weeks, months, and the calendar year. Sosigenes was working on a more precise yearly calendar, one that did not have to be adjusted to accommodate the days left over at the year's end, and Caesar had decided to put more funding to the cause.

"Imagine the convenience of a calendar that actually matched the days of the year," he said, his left elbow propped on the cool white sheets of their bed as Kleopatra fed him a slice of papaya with her fingers. She thought of his own daughter, Julia, and how she used to feed Pompey this way, and how odious it had seemed to the adolescent Kleopatra before womanly passions had taken hold of her. She regretted her harsh judgment of Caesar's daughter, who had probably been as much in love with the much older Pompey as Kleopatra was with Caesar.

Caesar took in the terrain along the Nile, never tiring of its diversity. Rows of new crops freshly planted revealed the rich black soil on one side of the river; on the other side, so much sand. Flat huts of sun-baked clay and straw interrupted the monotony of green. Sugarcane crops and other willowy foliage covered the banks, along with tall bamboo shoots and communities of palm trees short and tall. On the fertile land, a small flock grazed lazily, ignoring the late afternoon sun. Midday, a strong arid wind whipped up the heat, slapping it against the skin like punishment, but Caesar didn't mind. "So preferable to the cold," he said. "Once you've spent a winter buried in the Alpine snow foraging for food, it's hard to complain over heat."

From Luxor they had sailed to Edfu, known as the killing place, where Horus—falcon-god, hawk-god, son of Osiris the god of gods—slew Seth to avenge the murder of his father. There, he cut his wicked uncle into sixteen small pieces. "Merciless," was Caesar's comment.

They had stopped at the temple of Horus at Edfu, where Kleopatra was particularly friendly with the priests, and where she insisted on purchasing a huge vat of the famous and delicate jasmine perfume made by the temple workers as a gift for Caesar's wife. Caesar liked the black granite statue of Horus, with one eye the sun and the other the moon. "God always sleeps with one eye open," said a priest, and Caesar replied that he understood why; that he, too, had developed the same habit out of necessity. At the end of their visit, the High Priest stood on the temple platform where he traditionally made his predictions. Silver robes shimmering in the setting sun, he announced that the child born to the Roman general and the queen of Egypt would be a great man, a man who united the old and the sacred—Egypt—with the new and the mighty—Rome. And then he reminded his audience that sacred might was greater than military might—"In the event that I am ignorant of that fact," Caesar whispered to the queen. The priest ended with a prayer to the god for peace among nations "so that the boots of foreign soldiers do not mar the crops gifted to the people of Egypt by the Divinity," and Caesar almost laughed out loud.

As they sailed south from Edfu, the green on the eastern bank of the Nile gave way to desert. The heat thickened and mountains dug into the desert floor like an animal's claws. Kleopatra wanted to come this far into southern Egypt to show Caesar the outer reaches of her country. She herself had never ventured so far into her kingdom, close to the Nubian lands of dark-skinned people who played soft-sounding musical instruments that used to so please her father. She wanted to show Caesar the double temple at Kom Ombo built by her ancestors for Horus the Elder and Sobek, the crocodile-god. Her father had been in awe of the temple, and had further decorated it, building a great gate opening into the courtyard.

The temple's columns shot from the courtyard like ancient stone trees, as tall and solemn as any in Egypt, but capped with fluted Corinthian elegance. Kleopatra asked to see the tributes to her father inside, the ones of which he was most proud. They entered the great hall with dual passageways into the temples. Mighty vultures painted in bright colors took flight across the ceiling. On one wall, King Ptolemy Auletes was seen bringing offerings to Sobek, who had the body of a tall man and the head of a crocodile; on the other wall,

Horus performed purification rites over the king. Most magnificent was the wall painting of the king with a host of Egyptian deities: Sobek; Sekhmet, the lioness-goddess; Horus; Isis; and Thoth, the ibis-headed god of wisdom and writing.

"A good likeness of your father?" Caesar asked.

"Perhaps when he was a young man, and slightly less heavy than in his old age," she said wryly. "I do not believe he could have been more than forty years older and one hundred pounds heavier than this when the painting was made."

"And what is the difference between the elder Horus and the younger?" Caesar asked.

"The elder is the falcon, the healer god. Worshippers suffering from disease and ailments make the pilgrimage to this temple. The younger Horus is the son of Isis and Osiris. They are the same god. Perhaps one needs a Greek or Egyptian mind to understand the complexity." These days, the two of them laughed together at her slights on the Roman mind.

"I shall let that pass," he said, "in honor of your father and the beauty that he created here. One feels haunted by the spirits of two great civilizations."

"This is what my father did to rebuild the support of his people," she said. "My father always said that the gods are good to those who honor them, and that the people honor those who honor their gods. He was right. And this is what I shall do in Alexandria as soon as I return. When you come back to me, you shall marvel at the things I've built in your honor."

"How clever you are for just a slip of a young girl," he said.

"I allow your patronization only because you are the greatest man on earth," she whispered to him, standing on her tiptoes and brushing his cheek with her lips. Then she blushed, wondering if she should have shown such affection to a foreign man in the chilly and solemn atmosphere of the temple.

"If Your Majesty bathes in donkey's milk, she will never age or lose her beauty." The wife of the priest at the precinct of Aswan looked grave and sincere.

"Is that your own secret for eternal beauty?" the queen asked, looking for wrinkles in the grandmother's skin and finding none. The dark
eyebrows were stern crescents over eyes like midnight sky, and the
woman's lips were still crimson and plump like those of someone half
her age.

"Oh yes, Mother Egypt. I shall procure you a large vessel of it to take
back to your palace in the north, for I am sure the donkeys there are not
fed on as rich a grain as we give them here."

Mother Egypt. She had never been called such a thing, and yet she
liked the sound of it. A title that indelibly linked her with the country
and its land and people. She would like to be mother to Egypt, to feed
and nurture and care for it along with its truest benefactor, the Nile.

"I would be most grateful to you," Kleopatra said, and then dismissed her company. She invited the important ladies of every community they visited to spend one hour with her in the afternoons, taking
light refreshments in the shaded garden atop the boat away from the
sun. But she was weary of small talk now and returned to her cabin
where Caesar was alone, stalking the room like a trapped cat with no
sense of mission or destination.

Caesar was pressing to return to Alexandria; in fact, he just that
morning insisted upon sailing back swiftly. He had received disturbing
dispatches about the state of things in Rome. Harsh weather on the seas
had cut off all correspondence for several months, but now a pile of old
letters filled with disastrous news had been heaped into his lap, rushed
from Alexandria by a swift vessel that had easily caught up with their
leisurely cruise. Last night he had paced their chamber instead of engaging in his usual long conversation with Sosigenes under the stars. Today
he was in considerably foul humor. A cloud of cynicism had descended
upon him once more, and he no longer took pleasure in either Kleopatra
or any of the delights she provided for him on their tour. His food went
untouched except for a little wine that he drank to settle his nerves. The
lines on his face had reappeared and he looked thin and tense.

"I dare not hope it is leaving me that is causing this sudden consternation." She could take the awful transformation no longer. He kept his
dispatches close to the breast and did not share the contents with her.
She wondered if they contained messages from or about his wife,
Calpurnia, the daughter of his friend Piso. Perhaps Piso himself had

heard of the affair between Caesar and the queen and had written to chastise him.

"I have lingered too long in your company, madam, and my enemies have taken advantage of it."

"It is merely ten days since the last battle was fought," she protested.

How dare the world intrude upon their pleasures? And especially at this time, when Kleopatra had never felt so alive. She did not understand why women sequestered themselves during pregnancy, acting as if they had been taken by a mysterious illness. She felt as if the child inside her was giving her energy; as if she were now more than herself, the combined force of the two beings in one body. She felt vigorous and strong and invincible. And if the women in her service cautioned her about overexertion, she attributed it to a failing of theirs, not to the condition itself. Perhaps she was not a mere woman after all. She had so longed for a female confidante during this time, one who faced pregnancy with the same fearlessness that she felt inside. She missed Mohama. Surely the desert girl would have been just like her, if not more vigorous, had she lived to bear a child. They would have been like two Amazons together, carrying warrior children into a world that awaited their majesty.

But apparently pregnancy did not so affect the sire. Caesar looked glumly at her.

"I've spent the last twelve years expanding the borders of Rome beyond the wildest dreams of its most ambitious men, putting money into their pockets, slaves into their households, beautiful foreign women into their beds, and yet it is never enough."

"What is it, my darling? Won't you confide in me? Just this once? I can't stand to see you so upset. I've put my life and my future and my heart into your hands, and it frightens me to see you this way. I worry that you are out of love with me, that Egypt has finally bored you, that I am out of trickery to keep you here, and that is why you are going."

She did not like to hear herself make these vulnerable declarations, but she had grown so close to him in the last weeks. They had called a halt to their rivalry and had slid gracefully into the idylls of love. She would have to work hard to suppress the tender feeling that she'd grown so accustomed to showing him to dissemble for him again.

"If you must know, King Pharnaces, the monstrous son of Mithridates of Pontus, has taken it upon himself to seize a good amount of Anatolia. I am the commander of the legions in closest vicinity and so I must go." Caesar added, muttering to himself, "He shall never be sorrier than when he meets me."

"It is merely duty that sours you so?"

"The sons of Pompey have regrouped in Africa and are planning a rebellion against me. From Anatolia, I must make haste to Africa before they can sail to Italy. I did not count on them being such a menace. Why won't they simply accept reality?"

"I see."

"Perhaps I can send negotiators. But I doubt it."

The boyish look of a few days past was long gone. His voice, even his eyes, were impatient. "In Rome, my supporters as well as my enemies are so deeply in debt that they are murdering one another in the streets. No one can tell if Antony is trying to put the rebellion down or encourage it. Apparently he has claimed Pompey's estate with no intention of paying for it. Or so Cicero says, the old troublemaker. Who knows who is telling the truth. I must soon return to Rome before there is no Rome to return to. I am sorry. I do not wish to leave you. I have— enjoyed myself."

It seemed so hard for him to say those few words. Not because the expression of emotion was difficult, but because he seemed astonished that he had been swept into the joys of their passions. And yet she knew, not by his words, but by his attentions over the past weeks, that he regretted taking leave of her, of her country.

"All the gods are with you, General, and now, even the old gods of Egypt, especially the crocodile whom you so lavishly fed."

He gave her a faint smile and held out his arms.

She moved into his chest, turning her face to the side so that she might hear the slow steady drum of his heart. "We will never lose one another. I am sure of that. The gods won't allow it. Nor will I."

He backed away from her, taking her chin into his hand. How did a military man keep his hands so soft? The hand that had brought death to so many now firmly cradled her face. "The surety of youth is so different in tenor than the surety of age. I cannot explain it, quite. One is based on calculation from experience, the other on will and hope."

"And who is to say which is stronger and more accurate?"

"No, I believe you, Kleopatra. I believe we are inextricably bound."

Alexandria:
the 5th year of
Kleopatra's reign

To: Kleopatra VII, Queen of Egypt
From: Gaius Julius Caesar, Dictator of Rome
(Dispatched from the city of Athens)
My dear Kleopatra,

How delightful to hear from you so soon after my departure. Your letter caught up with me in Antioch. Your messengers are devoted and determined men. You have pleased Caesar greatly with the commencement of construction of the monument in my name and my honor. I shall look forward to being greeted by its majesty when I next sail into the Great Harbor.

First, some business between us. I have rewarded Antipater for his support in the war against your brother's army by sanctioning his government in Judaea and by exonerating that territory from its yearly taxes. I would like you to demonstrate some gratitude as well by lessening the taxes on your own Jewish population for a period of one year. This was the suggestion of Antipater, and I trust you shall see fit to implement it. You must follow the example of Caesar and reward those who demonstrate loyalty, particularly at a cost to themselves.

The nuisance King Pharnaces has been put down. In brief: I came, I saw, I conquered. He contributed to the expediency of my victory by directing his charioteers and foot soldiers to attack my legions uphill. Such arrogance. We demonstrated no mercy, for he had slaughtered the Roman soldiers he had defeated, and some, he castrated to indicate his scorn. For those who merit it, however, Caesar retains the quality of mercy. I have made visits to more than one of Pompey's allies in Syria and neighboring territories and I have pardoned them for little more than modest sums of money pledged to show their loyalty. By their own volition the people of these territories heaped upon me the wreaths of gold customarily offered the victor. From Marcus Brutus, who is to me as a rebellious son who necessarily takes opposition against his father, I demanded nothing, though he caused me grief by his allegiance to those who made themselves my enemies. He requested I give audience to Gaius Cassius who gleefully had aligned with Pompey, and whom I neither like nor trust, but whom I pardoned at the urging of Brutus.

And now I make haste for Rome via Athens to assess conditions in the capital. My detractors have accused me of staying too long in your country. I reclaimed Anatolia in four hours, so it is inconceivable to them why it took eight months to make peace in Egypt. After all that I have done for my country, I am begrudged one week of rest after eight months of siege and battle.

I trust you are well and that you will keep me apprised of your condition.

Yours, C. Julius Caesar

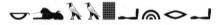

To: Gaius Julius Caesar, Dictator of Rome
From: Kleopatra VII, Queen of Egypt
My dear General,

Please be advised that I have implemented the favor you requested to the Jewish citizens of Alexandria, for which they have expressed much gratitude, and for which the rest of the city remains resentful. I trust the bitterness will not endure. The Alexandrian Jews are grateful at a distance that you have allowed the rebuilding of the walls of Jerusalem and have excluded their temples from the ordinances against assembly, for they are a deeply religious people as you know and any intrusion upon the ritualistic worship of their terrible and singular god causes them great consternation. They stand alone as the one culture that has remained untouched by the customs of the native people and the Hellenes alike.

I am pleased to announce the birth of our son. He has his parents' determination and aggression, for he came into the world very quickly, so quickly that I have wondered if my womb was not a hospitable place. Perhaps he sensed the intensity with which I have missed his father, and he could not wait to escape the dreadful feelings of my longing. I know that men are rarely interested in the details of labor, but you are the rare kind of man. I gave birth in the Egyptian way, sitting in a special chair that the midwives say makes the baby come faster, under a great canopy decorated with lovely, fragrant garlands and holy amulets of all kinds. To keep my good cheer, Charmion brought in a statue of the dwarf-god, Bes, and whenever I felt pain, I looked at his big triangle ears and laughing eyes.

I have named your son Ptolemy XV Caesar so that he might carry the identity of both his parents, but the Greeks in Alexandria have already dubbed him Caesarion, or Little Caesar, which I suppose is appropriate enough. They seem to say it with more affection than disparagement, and I take this as a sign of growing acceptance for our union. He has his father's height, for the midwives said they have never seen a baby so long. His fingers and toes are thin and elegant. I believe he has inherited the lengthy neck of Venus that runs through your family. His skin is ruddy like many of his Macedonian ancestors, his hair is rather dark, and his eyes are the ubiquitous blue of infancy. I am told by his astrologer that they will change to the gray tones of Alexander's. And why should our son not carry Alexander's eyes into the future? He will surely bring to fruition the vision of his ancestor.

The astrologers foresee a pensive character, slightly withdrawn in nature, but an expansive thinker and an intellectual. His constitution is strong, and he will contract none of the childhood diseases. They foresee tumult in his sixteenth year, but peace thereafter in his life. I imagine him to grow up thoughtful, perhaps truly the first of Plato's Philosopher Kings. He will study with the scholars here at the Mouseion, as did his mother and all his ancestors before him. Then we shall send him to Greece to study military strategy. Much of this he shall learn, however, from reading his father's written accounts of battle.

I am enclosing herewith a coin that I have issued commemorating his birth. I believe the image of the queen as Isis—an image to which my subjects are accustomed—suckling the baby Horus, will hearten the people both Egyptian and Greek, and spread through the Two Lands of Egypt the joy that comes with the birth of a future king. The Greeks associate Isis and Horus with Aphrodite and Eros to the extent that there is no difference in their minds between the native deities and their own. But I hope the coin reminds you of our time together at the temple of Horus in a land that I believe you found enchanting.

Will you see Little Caesar within the year? Shall I bring him to you once the quarantine is lifted? We do quarantine royal children for a period of six months. Though his astrological chart says he is not susceptible to illness, no chances may be taken.

Remember my confession to you that as a girl I escaped to the marketplace where I hoped to hear tidbits from gossiping merchants about Mighty Julius Caesar and his Exploits in Rome? I did not dream at that time, or perhaps I did, that I would one day listen firsthand to the observations of Caesar himself, whispered into my ear late into the evening for my amusement. Please do not spare me any details of your travels or your travails. I do so long to have you here, letting your wisdom wash over whatever youthful inexperience remains after my years of tumultuous rule, and listening to your insights into political schemes and human nature. I also miss vexing you. Until I see you again, your words will be like the fingers that so affectionately brushed my face, so do not spare those words, dear General. I cling to each one.

In the meanwhile, I shall devote my every thought to the health and safety and nurturing of your son.

Yours, Kleopatra

⌐⟍⟋⟍ 𝕀 𝕀 ▦ 𝈜 ◉ ◇ ⌐

From: Gaius Julius Caesar in the city of Rome
To: Kleopatra VII, Queen of Egypt
(By private messenger)
My dear Kleopatra,

Caesar assures you that the news of the birth of his son is presently his singular source of gladness. Though he returned to Rome in triumph, recent events cloud his many victories.

There is murder in the streets of Rome—not among the enemies of Caesar but among his friends. Caesar charged Antony with gaining Cicero's favor, and he has done the opposite, forcing the old man to eleven months of exile in Brundisium. The two despise one another, and I have not been able to repair it. Cicero executed Antony's stepfather in the mess of the Catiline conspiracies of many years ago. I advised against it, but he did not heed my warnings, and Antony, an affectionate man of great familial loyalty, will never forgive him. Besides, the two are temperamentally opposite, fire and ice. Cicero, whom I have taken pains to cultivate despite his unfaithfulness to me and my causes, has never forgiven Antony a minor, manly indiscretion with a certain Volumnia Cytheris, an actress whose company Antony keeps. Years ago, when poor

Pompey was still alive and Cicero was vacillating between the two of us,
Antony passed his house in an open carriage with Volumnia, and Cicero, who
is rather prudish, treated the incident as if it were a crime against the Republic
itself. Kindling his outrage was the fact that Antony's mother, Julia, was also
present. Only a moral bankrupt would subject a pious Roman matron to such
an indignity, Cicero declared, though I assured him that I share Antony's
enjoyment of people of the theater, despite their dramatic temperaments. Cicero
himself has recently put away his wife, Terentia, and taken a teenage bride. It
is also rumored that he whispers words of love in secret to his secretary, a
learned Greek slave, Tiro. And yet he does not forgive the passions of others. Perhaps it is the urgency, ferocity, and youthful vigor of Antony's ardor
that he resents.

That is the background of their feud. I was forced to stop in Brundisium and
personally rub salve on Cicero's wounded vanity. Meanwhile, in my absence,
Antony conducted a personal war against young Dolabella for committing adultery with his wife, Antonia, whom he is now divorcing. I do not doubt the
charge, but the true reason for divorce is so that Antony might marry Fulvia,
the widow of our mutual late friend Clodius, with whom he has bedded for so
many years. Fulvia is an absorbing woman, with political ambitions more complicated than the many plaits and ribbons she weaves into her hair. The gods
only know how many husbands she's buried and will bury before she is called to
Hades. Her most recent husband, Curio, was killed in North Africa by
Pompey's son. But she will tame Antony for the better, and he demonstrates fine
judgment in calling such a taskmaster to the cause of his discipline. The first
order of her reign: Give up Volumnia Cytheris. He has sheepishly agreed.

Dolabella and Antony both owe in personal debt more than the sum of the
treasury of many a nation, due to their extravagant living and poor management.
While Caesar was away in the cause of his country, Dolabella proposed a new
debt law favorable to his situation and then barricaded the Forum to guarantee
its passage. Antony charged the barricades and destroyed the placards announcing the law. Hundreds died in the skirmish. I have chastened the both of them,
though I have dealt with Antony more severely. I have deposed him of his powers and named Marcus Lepidus co-consul for the year, and I have thrown his
dissolute friends out of the houses he stole for them and returned them to the
state, where they might be auctioned off to assist in paying Rome's legions. I shall
forgive Antony, for he is good-natured, the greatest warrior in Rome next to
Caesar himself, and highly influential, but only after dishonor has humbled him.

After settling these many problems, Caesar personally faced hostile Roman legions who had the audacity to march straight into the city demanding their settlements from the war. I confronted them in the Field of Mars, and demonstrated my disdain for their mutinous actions by addressing them as "citizens." I acted delighted to grant their discharge, whereupon they protested that they were not mere citizens but soldiers, Caesar's soldiers! And then begged to be kept in my service.

At this moment, my enemies are organizing against me in Africa. I had intended to meet and put an end to these insults to my honor, and yet conditions in the capital make it impossible to leave. My personal attention seems to be the key ingredient in the solution of all present problems.

It is the express wish of Caesar that this missive had been delivered in his person to receive the delight of your smiles and sympathies as you read of the tribulations of his public life. There is no other in whom he has ever wished to confide or to seek comfort for life's many difficulties. In the meanwhile and in his absence, he has written and dedicated a short verse to you:

Venus, your placid countenance is a seduction, an illusion.
From the waters of your canal flow Eros, who fills the ocean
of the heart, cresting like the cimmerian torrent of the Black
Sea.

Yours, C. Julius Caesar

To: Gaius Julius Caesar, Dictator of Rome
From: Kleopatra VII, Queen of Egypt
My darling Caesar,
I have read your letter a thousand times and then a thousand times more to our son so that he might know of his father's brilliance, his glory, his wit, and to know that his father is not merely general and statesman but poet—a complete man by the definition of the Greek philosophers. How I long to kidnap you and shelter you from your many worries. If you were here in Alexandria with me, I would see that all evidence of the honor you deserve was heaped upon you every day of your life. And at the same time, I would guard our private life together so that every day I might sit upon your lap and listen to your stories

of foreign lands and of battles fought and won and of the friendships and adversaries you face in your capital city. That you continue to unburden yourself to me is my joy. I think often of the happiness of our few days together after the war when you began to reveal to me the contents of your mind. Would that I could do more than receive your distant thoughts in letters. For it pains me to know that time and distance stand between us and I am not able to know what you are thinking at this very moment, nor to share with you my thoughts and ideas as they take form and then quickly transform into the next. We are made anew each moment, are we not? I have found, dear General, that that is your particular genius—the fact that you approach each of life's many hurdles with a fresh mind, always open to the inspiration of the gods as to how to solve a particular situation. Was it Venus herself who directed you to shame your soldiers by addressing them as citizens? It seems to me that you and I share in common that the gods whisper directly into our ears. Perhaps it is because we are sanctioned by the Divine as leaders of men. You are every day a new man, and that is why those who cling to the old ways fear you. I believe this is another of our common traits—the desire to part with traditions that are no longer relevant to present-day realities. The changes, of course, are not simply to serve ourselves, but to further all mankind.

I fret over your health, dear one. I worry that someday in the heat of battle or in the throes of debate on the senate floor, you shall be overtaken by your malady. Why am I not there to watch over you, to hold you to me while you make your strange voyage to some unseen place, and then to mop your brow with my own handkerchief while you take shallow breaths and return to the earthly realm? I treasure the moments I spent with your head in my lap, watching you come back to me from your journey to the unknown. Do you recall what you said? It seemed to me that you were still lost in the place between this world and that one when you looked at me with misty and distant eyes and said, "She is you and you are she." And then you closed your eyes again and your hands went limp at your sides, sliding off your chest, and you fell into a peaceful sleep as if you were just a small boy taking comfort in his mother's safe and tranquil presence.

I have seen the same look now on the small face of our son. He is strong, like both his parents. Though he is but three months old, he holds his head tall, looking intently at all who attend him as if he wished to impart to them the secrets of life that he has carried forth from his time with the gods. I have spoken to him at length about his position in life, so that he seems to have absorbed it into his very being. His countenance expresses the seriousness and the weight of his lineage and all that to which he is heir. His eyes are a dark blue, I cannot say that they are yet the gray of Alexander's, and they are shrouded by rather heavy and sensuous lids. His brow is well-defined for an infant. He has a philosopher's thinness despite his vehement enthusiasm at the breast. I nursed him myself for two months for that is the Egyptian way. The native midwives say that precious life-enhancing fluids are passed to the child from the mother's milk in the early months, and so like a peasant I held him at my breast before releasing him to a wet nurse. I find the Egyptian women's knowledge of spells and remedies far in advance of those of Greek women. For example, I have bathed in donkey's milk brought back from Aswan under the advice of the wife of the Egyptian priest, and already my skin has recovered its youthfulness after the birth. (I hope I am not boring the General with these tedious details. I feel certain that if he were here, I would share every thought in my head with him from the profound to the banal and he would indulge all of them as if I, too, were his child.)

I long to hear more of you, though the financial demands you placed upon me before you left keep me busy day and night with enterprises that will replenish my treasury. I have increased the laborers in the Cypriot copper mines so that our revenues from that territory you restored to us should double in the coming months. Duties on merchants have increased, much to their chagrin. I have toured the linen factories myself and with the craftsmen have invented new dyes that are sure to bring greater demand for our cloth from rich Roman ladies, and have granted new licenses for the export of jewelry and other adornments to a whole new generation of merchants. When you see a lovely Roman girl wearing Egyptian finery, do think of me. I was tempted to raise the price of beer, but was assured that public opinion would sway very far away from me if I did.

So you see, dear General, despite the burden you placed upon my people, I am still your devoted one. (I do hope the money has finally placated Rabirius and that he plagues you no more with his demands.) I live only for your happiness, for my son's future, and for our future together. Though we must tolerate this lapse in our togetherness, when next we meet I am certain that it shall be as if we had not spent a day apart.

Yours, Kleopatra

From: Hammonius in the city of Rome

To: Kleopatra VII, Queen of Egypt

My dear Majesty,

Your old friend and faithful servant reports to you on the conditions in the city of his exile. Yes, yes, I can see your smile spread as you read of my woe, and I do admit that I have grown as prosperous as a king while in the service of your father and your Royal Person here in this strange and ghastly land. But Your Majesty, please believe me when I say that no amount of gold can truly compensate for not having one's two big feet planted firmly on olive-drenched Greek soil.

Your Majesty, I believe I can explain the recent silence of Julius Caesar. One month ago he was pulled away from the problems in the city to face his enemies on African shores, where the sons and remaining allies of Pompey united with King Juba of Numidia to continue the Roman Civil War. The dissenters were mighty in numbers, for they had the many thousands of the king's archers and horsemen and another army that rode into battle on fearsome elephants. Once again, Caesar was outnumbered by his enemies. It is said that food and supplies were so depleted that he forced his soldiers to dismiss their slaves, and was reduced to feeding seaweed to his horses. And yet, as the gods would have it, Caesar was victorious. The soldiers say that he drilled the newer recruits in the arts of war himself, demonstrating the finer, more subtle artistry of swordplay, when to advance and retreat, and how to maneuver one efficient mortal blow. This personal instruction from so great a man made his young soldiers fiercely loyal to him. The African soldiers had no real loyalty to the Pompeians, who demanded much of them and promised little, and the fearsome reputation of Caesar was enough for whole legions and towns to come over to him at his request. Still, the sheer multitude of the enemy was awesome, and at the onset of the deciding battle, some of the less-experienced men tried to run away. It is said that Caesar stood back so that he might catch them in their retreat and personally point them in the direction of the battle. The deciding battle was fought at Thapsus, and then Caesar moved on to Utica, where his enemies easily surrendered to him, but for Cato, who died by his own sword.

And now, Caesar has made a glorious reentry into the city. The rabble was represented in record numbers in the streets of Rome for the forty-day Thanksgiving festival (twice longer than any victor has previously enjoyed) accorded to Caesar for his victories abroad. Caesar was given permission to celebrate Four Triumphs: over Gaul, Egypt, Pontus, and Africa. His victories over his fellow Romans go unmentioned, or at least uncelebrated. The senate was extremely indulgent of Caesar upon his return to Rome, voting him dictator for another ten years and inventing a new office for him, Overseer of Public Morality, through which he is vowed to restore discipline. His opinion will heretofore be delivered first at all senate meetings. He will not only nominate all magistrates, but himself will sit on the magistrates' bench. And he will give the opening signal at all public games, which will undoubtedly thrill his throng of common admirers.

I witnessed each spectacle staged for the Triumphs, and I attended a banquet for the public where I sat at one of twenty-two thousand dining couches and feasted until my rebellious spleen sent me running to the public latrines. There was no end to the food served. I believe that millions, not thousands, of tender sea eels, quails, pigs, geese, goats, lambs, hares, cows, chickens, and ducks were eaten by the population at large, while the more fortunate of us with high political connections were also treated to peacock (eaten to encourage immortality), oysters, and even tender morsels of songbird, once said to be a favorite of Darius the Persian. You will also be pleased to know that rare spices imported from Egyptian merchants at great expense peppered each dish. And then Caesar made a great store of giving two thousand denariis to each legionary, claiming it was more than twice what they would have received from Pompey, and that he aimed to be "rich *with* the Roman people, not their robber."

The parades called to mind the Grand Procession of your ancestors, revived by your father when you were but a girl of nine. But the Romans added the ingredient of cruelty, missing from our more festive and holy Greek and Egyptian celebrations, for people and animals lost their lives brutally. One such was a huge blond creature whom Caesar had defeated in Gaul. He was strangled for the crime of defending his tribe against the Romans. Your own sister Arsinoe was marched in chains along with a four-year-old African prince, who amused the crowd with his playfulness. He obviously thought the festival had been staged in his honor, so generous was he in waving to the throng. But soldiers who complained that the cost of the celebration was eating into their settlements were beheaded! Gladiators murdered their opponents in blood-drenched reenactments of the battles won by the Romans. And I, an old man who has seen so much inhumanity, turned my head away from the slaughter of hundreds of lions and giraffes done only for the pleasure of cruelty. This awful display lacked any of the noble intentions of manly sport and took all honor and dignity from hunter and animal alike.

Caesar himself was escorted in his parade by seventy-two high officials, whose slaves carried vats of burning perfume to neutralize the fetid odor of a large mob on a hot day. He had a boy with him, Gaius Octavian, his grandnephew, grandson of his sister Julia. The boy is thin and pale and looks perhaps to be about eighteen years old. I inquired of him, thinking he had performed valiantly in Caesar's service, though his appearance betrays not a trace of military ability or potential. I was told that he had not participated in any war, and those with whom I spoke were also puzzled as to the place of honor he was given in the Triumph, when the great Marcus Antonius, who committed impossible feats of heroism in the wars, was given no special honors at all.

The parade itself was spectacular. Artisans had worked day and night to paint gigantic scenes of Caesar's victories that were carried by slaves. The people cheered wildly at the paintings that made Rome's enemies into cowards. A final note: Many plays were staged during the celebrations, but without the finesse of craft so beautifully displayed in Greek theater. And also, Your Majesty, I wish you to hear of this from myself, your servant who loves you. Caesar's soldiers invented rather nasty songs about the General, but also about Your Royal Person, and sang them as they marched. The General was called every kind of profligate lover, every man's wife and every woman's husband, who conquered first the king of Egypt, and then for measure, surmounted the queen. Caesar showed much perturbation at this crudeness, and directly challenged the notion that he was once plaything to the king of Bithynia. How strange these Romans are in their thinking. I discerned that the true insult was the idea that he had once played the passive partner. I suppose that is the result of a mentality in which domination and conquering exceed all other human Virtue. Thank the gods we are not Romans!

These are the recent doings of Julius Caesar, reported to you herewith on this heated day in the month of August in the violent and chaotic city of Rome, from which, praise the gods, I shall gain some respite next week at the suburban villa of a wealthy and sonless (and therefore unwatched!) widow who enjoys the company of a well-read and affable fat Greek man.

Your Majesty, I shall remain in your service so long as you wish; otherwise, I would retire to Crete, where I would hire two Greek women to cook for me and five more to furnish me with love.

Your faithful servant and Kinsman,

Hammonius

To: Ptolemy XIV, King of Egypt
From: Arsinoe IV, Queen of Egypt
(delivered by secret messenger)

My dear brother,

This will be brief. I am imprisoned in the stinking city of Rome and under surveillance at all times. Fortunately, some Roman matrons, appalled that a Royal Female was paraded like a common criminal in Caesar's parade, have taken pity on me and send me small gifts of food and grooming articles through their servants. One of these servants is a Macedonian freedwoman who hates the Romans with all her heart. She is smuggling this letter to you through her own brother, a servant to the merchant who supplies wax to our palace candlemakers. Please treat him well. He delivers this at great risk to his life, and he is the only person who might deliver to me your response.

Dear brother, I realize you are but thirteen years old, but you are the only barrier to the great nation our ancestors conquered falling irreparably into the dirty hands of Rome. You must begin to school yourself in the ways of war, for the only way to combat might is with greater might. Say that you wish to study military strategy and go to Greece at once. Kleopatra will be relieved to be rid of you, for you are the only threat to her plan to sell Egypt to the Romans and rule it as their prostitute queen. She is a deluded fool who does not know that she and Julius Caesar are as despised here as they are in Alexandria, and, I am sure, the rest of the world. I have done what I can to fill the ears of influential Roman women with tales of her ambitions and her evil. They hate her already for her alliance with a Roman man married to a Roman woman. They do not speak good Greek, but it is passable enough to convey important ideas, and I believe I was effective in bringing our hated usurper sister one step closer to ruin.

Thanks to the goodwill of these few women, I am being sent to the city of Ephesus, where I will be given sanctuary at the temple of Artemis, whom the Romans call Diana. I shall still be a Roman captive, but from there I shall surely be able to be in contact with you should you go to Athens. Fear nothing. Simply act. We must keep ourselves nimble and alive for the moment when Kleopatra destroys herself. The Fate of Egypt depends on it. Do not worry. We still have many supporters and we shall prevail.

Lovingly yours,

Arsinoe, your rightful Sister and Wife

⌐◢⬛🐖𓏏𓏏🏛⌐◉◯⌐

From: Julius Caesar, Dictator of Rome

To: Kleopatra VII, Queen of Egypt

My dear Kleopatra,

Forgive my silence. I was called away from Rome to fight my enemies in Africa. Again, I was the victor. Upon my return, I face as many enemies as triumphs. As our old friend Clodius used to say, it never ends, darling. Your letters were a comfort to this graying general in his many trials.

Conditions such as they are, I have put off the campaign to subdue the Parthians for another year, and yet I do not wish to wait another year to see you or Little Caesar. I wish the two of you to make haste for Rome. I have proposed a new piece of legislation to some of my most ardent and influential supporters that would allow me to take an additional wife in order to produce an heir. My supporters believe that with the proper timing, the bill has every chance to pass into law.

Please send word of the approximate day of your arrival. You shall stay in my own home outside the turmoil of the city. It is a lovely villa on Janiculum Hill, which affords the very finest view of the city, though it has not the vastness of the quarters to which you are accustomed. I believe it will comfortably house up to ten members of your travel party and no more than twenty-five of your servants. I shall visit you there whenever time permits. I shall also provide you with an amusing Roman entourage for your entertainment. There are those who fear your arrival and those who are dying to meet you. Many feel both sentiments. For myself, I do not care what others think. I miss the presence of the one who understands me.

I would also like you to include my friend Sosigenes in your travel party. The Roman calendar is completely out of kilter with the solar year to the point of chaos. Only the priests know what day it is and have to announce it to the populace, and I believe that on most days, they, too, are guessing. I intend to lengthen this year in order to set it all straight, but I require Sosigenes' mind and his calculations to do it properly.

Until we meet again, I remain,

Yours, C. Julius Caesar

To: Gaius Julius Caesar, Dictator of Rome
From: Kleopatra VII, Queen of Egypt
My darling,

I am on my way to you immediately and plan to arrive at the port of Ostia in mid-September. I will happily bypass the more convenient port at Brundisium and sail all the way around the boot of Italy to reach you sooner. Still, there is one small matter that troubles me. Would you please lift the ban on the worship of the god and goddess dearest to me? I do not think I should enter a city that forbids the adoration of Isis, as that is the goddess with whom my own people identify me and to whom I pray daily. My late father, whom I loved above all until I met you and gave birth to our son, was called Neos Dionysus. He was not only the god's most avid worshipper, he was the god himself here on earth, or so the Egyptian people believe with all their hearts. And so my darling, you see my dilemma. I trust you will repair these religious matters immediately, and that such issues are within your jurisdiction as Pontifex Maximus.

Yours always,
Kleopatra

To: Hephaestion, Prime Minister of Egypt
From: Kleopatra VII, Queen of Egypt
Dear Prime Minister,

You must complete all our business in the Sinai and return immediately to Alexandria to resume your post in my cabinet. I must leave the city in two weeks for Rome, where Julius Caesar has requested my presence. I shall take my son with me, of course, but I am leaving my brother the king here in Alexandria. You are to act as his Regent in my absence, and you are to keep him under the strictest watch. I intercepted a letter he wrote to his treasonous sister who is presently in Ephesus, where the Romans exiled her. I suppose it would have been unpopular to strangle such a young girl, though if they understood her feral hatred of themselves, they might have risked the good opinion of their citizens and done away with her. I am going to Rome to solidify relations with Caesar and his government, and to seek legitimacy from the Roman senate for my son.

Caesar has indicated that this is not an impossible task. You are the only adviser in whom I might trust without condition now that Archimedes is out of my service. As we are allies of Julius Caesar and under the protection of his legions, there is no longer reason to maintain a mercenary army. Please leave the details of disbanding the troops to one of your staff and return to me immediately.

I will not postpone the date of my departure. As the Romans say, *carpe diem.* And yet it is not just the day that must be seized now but history itself. I shall not arrive a moment too late.

Your Sovereign Queen, Kleopatra VII Philopater

Alexandria:
the 20th year of
Kleopatra's reign

S*he stares into the mirror in her chamber. Iras the eunuch removes the gold twine holding her curls. It unravels in his hands—a sad reminder of her failure to entice Antony. Iras holds the shredded glittering mess to the light to evaluate its condition. With a pursed look of distaste, he discards it. A diviner spreads the cards upon her table, reading aloud his forecast of gloom. She does not look at him but continues to regard herself as he echoes the words of the miserable astrologer she sent abroad with Antony, that fool who told him that Octavian was born under a more favorable stellar configuration than he. The knowledge surely unmanned him more than the position of the stars at the time of his birth. I should have had the diviner drowned for causing Antony private misery, for infecting a great man with the poison of self-doubt, she thinks. Iras raises an eyebrow. The queen dismisses the enchanter.*

Iras, grave as a goat, brushes her hair in silence. He looks worried, more worried even than Charmion, to whom the queen reveals every desperate thought, and whom the queen does not trouble herself to comfort. But Iras is tender and sentimental, as are many of his castrated brethren. Unlike many of his kind, he is devoid of bitterness. He was, he has confessed to the queen, a lover of men before his manhood was removed; he was never certain that the gods had intended him to be a male in the first place. He believes his mother cursed him in the womb, changing his sex midway through his fetal development.

"I didn't mind, Your Royal Grace. They were entirely superfluous," he said of

his missing genitals. "I don't miss them at all." He is Antony's age, fifty-four, though he looks older. Unusual for a Syrian, his skin is lined with an intriguing network of creases. The pasty white lead makeup he uses to make fair his ruddy complexion calls much attention to this convoluted map on his face—a map leading nowhere. Like the queen, he kohls his dark eyes, tints his lashes with inks, and uses the juice of mulberry on his cheeks and eyelids. He does not ochre the palms of his hands and feet as women do, but applies the same for the queen every morning, gingerly working the powder into her skin as if he has never performed the act before. He looks neither male nor female, but has the androgynous features one acquires in later years, and is given to a eunuch's paunchiness. Sometimes the queen leans her head to rest on his belly as he crochets impossibly small shiny objects and delicate amulets of protection into her hair with the nimble concentration of Arachne weaving her dazzling tapestries. These days, she often tells him that he is the man in her life, which makes him giggle and blush. Exceptional for a eunuch who has access to the powerful, his ambition is confined to shaping and costuming the Royal Hair.

Iras pinches and unpinches his lips and arches his brows spasmodically, exhaling in annoying little spurts. The queen knows he waits for her reassurance that what the diviner said is by no means Divine Law. He adores Antony, laughs too loudly at his jokes, flirts with him, and believes him to be a great man.

"No matter, Iras," she says to him. "Do not tattle on me to the priests, but I place no emphasis on the words of the soothsayers. Yesterday when I went to the temple to preside over the sacrifice, the priest made a great store out of a few maggots swimming in the animal's organs. But I asked myself, what is the significance of a cankered sheep's liver, in comparison with one's own intuition? You must do as I do. Follow not these charlatans, but the inclinations of your mind and the stirrings of your heart. We must endure the rituals, but ignore the prognoses."

"Blasphemy, Mother Egypt!"

"Nonsense. I have not lost any of my fervor for the gods, but I've wearied of those who speak for them on earth."

Iras holds her hair in his hands. "You are my life, Your Royal Grace."

"And you, Iras, are a lovely part of mine."

Edified, the eunuch slips into his own internal reveries, dreamily pin-curling her hair for sleep. The queen stares into the mirror, assessing her condition. Despite all the troubles, despite the business at Actium, she is still a young woman. Her eyes are alert, large, almost green, she likes to think, and are green with the proper cosmetic assistance. They are not innocent. She seduces with her eyes—their appeal, her knowingness. What is behind those eyes? men wonder. What accumulated wisdom, what richness lies behind those spice green eyes? And they must—if they are curious, if they respond to challenge, as all great men do—find out. That is her charm and she knows it. She is a mountain of mystery that must be scaled for the secrets within—secrets men wish to possess but do not—to be revealed. It is said that she is ravishing, though she knows she is not. She knows that power and mystique are often mistaken for beauty. She depends on the ancient chemistries of the alluring Egyptian women and on the talents of the eunuch Iras to enhance her natural charms. This evening she wears no cosmetics. Bathed, oiled by the body servants, clothed in a nightgown, the face into which she stares is her own, unpainted, unadorned. She is still young-looking, though she is nine and thirty. Contrary to the warnings of the Greek doctors, the active and demanding life she has led has preserved her vigor and youth, and not robbed her of it. She has borne four children, yet she is as taut as a girl of fourteen. I am like the women of ancient Sparta, she thinks, strong horsewomen, wrestlers, fighters—warrior women who swoon to the smells of war, not the scent of perfume. Such am I and such were my sisters and all my ancestresses. The women of Macedonia, the women of Sparta—the ancient women who rode with, fought with, ruled with, and often ruled, their men. The unconquerable women.

The poets say that wars are fought for the love of such women. But the Trojan War began as began the war with Octavian—not over a woman, but over money. Spartan money. Helen's money. For who could have taken a Spartan queen if she did not wish to be taken? The preening Paris? And who could have defeated the man who could have taken a Spartan queen against her will? No, it was a war fought over money and turf, like the war with Octavian, like all wars.

Always she believed it beneficial to remain dispassionate about one's enemies. The philosophers, the suffering of her father, and the counsel of Caesar taught her thus. But she does not possess the mental discipline to squelch her fury against the conniving intriguer, who has busied himself serving her to the Roman people as the villain in his dramatic play. He reinvented her: Monster. Seductress. Prostitute. Viper. Enemy of Rome. The most maddening of these was prostitute, as if the queen descended from Alexander the Conqueror was, or could be, for sale. He called her "The Oriental," though he knew her blood was pure Macedonian Greek. Cunning though he is, he fears me, she thinks. He paints me as Rome's enemy for an excuse to come here and steal my money. And so it has always been and ever shall be. Money. My money. The treasure of the Ptolemies. The sweet honey that has drawn the flies of Rome to our borders for centuries. Would that I could res-

urrect Caesar from Hades to make him account for naming Octavian his heir. If I had been then the woman I am today, it never would have happened.

It is almost daybreak. Iras has fallen asleep on her bed, snoring softly, his painted lashes fluttering as he dreams. As much as she craves sleep, she must wait for the report from Sidonia, the madam of the whores. Surely Antony cannot last much longer. He is no longer young in that way. Or is he, but not for her? The sun forbore to rise. A tightness in her chest chokes the air that reaches for her lungs but never seems to arrive. If I cannot breathe I cannot sleep, she thinks. These days, rest is a rare and precious commodity.

Rome:
In the 6th year of
Kleopatra's reign

They arrived quietly according to Caesar's wishes, as quietly as a queen, a young prince, and a retinue of forty might slip into gossip-dominated Rome. He housed them at the tranquil villa in the south-eastern portion of Janiculum Hill, where the ever-curious Kleopatra might look out upon the city without causing the tongues of its inhabitants to wag with her regal presence. Not only did he not wish to incur needless gossip about his mistress. He did not trust his fellow Romans to welcome a son of Caesar born into a monarchy—a son who would be king of a rich and powerful nation—with anything else but the sharp point of a dagger. He hoped Kleopatra would content herself with the lovely view of the olive groves, spiked here and there with cypress trees, and the rolling hills of lavish wildflowers blooming past their usual time. It was the autumn season after all, the most beautiful time to be in Rome, when the light was so lovely it seemed to come to the city filtered through the eyes of a gentle goddess. Even she—the queen of the queen of all cities—who presided over the magnificent Alexandria could hardly complain.

After all, they were together. That was what she wished, for all her letters insinuated that she would like to bring her son to the city of his father. He knew that he would encounter problems; wicked rumors would spread about the nature of her visit, about the age difference between them, about the plans he was making that included a foreign queen in his grandiose design. But it was all worth it to see her face again, to hear the music of her voice even when she discussed serious matters, and to see that the paternity of his son was not in question, for he carried many of Caesar's features upon his little face and body.

There was more of the father than the mother in the boy, which was how it ought to be with sons. Kleopatra had been correct; Little Caesar had a very long neck for a one-year-old child, and he carried his imperial head proudly upon it. His eyes were blue—like the first Ptolemy and almost like Alexander, or so Kleopatra thought, not realizing that both Caesar's maternal grandmother and Venus herself carried that same shade of twilight sky in their eyes. It also appeared that he would have his father's high brow and fairer skin, though Caesar had been so long in the sun that he no longer knew the true shade of his coloring. The look of intelligence and the already apparent pride, the boy could have inherited from either or both parents. But how thrilling it was to look upon a face so like one's own, to recognize one's character, one's traits, in the early stages of a new life. In those first moments when he held the boy with the ever-disapproving Charmion looking on as if he, Caesar, had not the strength or the intelligence to hold twenty pounds of boy, the futility he had so recently been battling melted in the child's keen stare into his father's eyes.

He was a splendid boy, so serious and so beautiful, not at all like a child, but as if he was already acutely aware of his position. Kleopatra had selected his attendants on the basis of their intelligence and loyalty. All were under the merciless supervision of Charmion, who scoured them for the slightest hint of boredom or lack of patience or even poor use of grammar that might infect the child's ear for language. Kleopatra was certain the boy would inherit her gift for languages, though Caesar believed that such an extraordinary facility was given directly by the gods and not passed through blood and semen like color of eye and curl of hair. He hoped that Kleopatra would not be disappointed in the ways in which the boy did not live up to her expectations, for he had seen many an ambitious mother damage her son. Sometimes, however, as with Servilia and Brutus, and with his own mother, high expectations yielded high results. No matter. He would exert his own influence over this little creature. He would show him the ways of war as only Caesar

could, for the ways of the intellect Kleopatra would assign to the scholars at the Mouseion.

As requested, she had brought at least one of those studious men with
her to Rome—Sosigenes—his long beard cutting a path before him as he
greeted Caesar. Her retinue was as extraordinary as everything else about
her. Charmion, who watched over the queen and the prince as if she were
a feral cat mother and they her tender kittens, was in command of everyone. She dared to give Caesar threatening looks, as if to let him know that
should he disappoint her mistress, she was not above castrating him in the
middle of the night. She let it be said around the house that her life was
nothing to her, that she lived entirely in the service of the queen, for
whom she would happily commit any atrocity. Caesar wondered if he had
ever met so imperious a personage as Kleopatra's head lady-in-waiting,
and he realized that he had not. Along with Charmion and a host of
women, Kleopatra had brought her favorite astrologer; a rather boister-
ous philosopher fellow whom she said would entertain her guests with
clever discourse; and a terribly overpainted eunuch, the Royal
Hairdresser, without whose talents, she said, she would never again
appear in public. Caesar shuddered to think what the Romans would
make of such a creature. Better to keep him hidden. Kleopatra proudly
introduced two Greek engineers with pinched faces and wrinkled brows
whose ideas she thought Caesar would find enlightening. Among the servants were the queen's scribes, her special messengers, the cosmeticians
with whom she collaborated on the creation of her powders and perfumes, body servants who had undergone a special anointing ceremony to
be able to touch the Royal Person, dressmakers, and a fat old man whose
sole responsibility was purchasing interesting foreign stones and gems on
the queen's behalf. She had brought her own laundresses, for she did not
want her clothing touched by the Roman fullers, who used decayed urine
to remove stains. Two Greek doctors of medicine were also on board
because, as Charmion said, it was impossible for Roman medicine to
affect a Greek body. Oh yes, and there was a terribly arrogant Greek chef
who had already insulted his kitchen help with "suggestions for the
queen's diet." It seemed to Caesar that they were an officious bunch, jolly
to parade their Greek superiority over their military betters. Following
the human travelers were trunks and trunks of clothing and personal
effects for both Kleopatra and the child, and even more containers of

gifts she intended to present to "her new Roman friends." Knowing she was to receive Cicero, she had brought rare and beautiful manuscripts from the Great Library, as well as a case full of books to donate to the library Caesar was building in the city.

Everyone, even Caesar's wife—especially Caesar's wife—was dying to meet her. He knew that Calpurnia would suffer at the sight of Kleopatra's youth and imperial demeanor, and particularly on beholding the boy, who had the qualities of the Julians all over his long baby face. Yet her curiosity was winning the battle against her pride. She was undoubtedly spurred on by Servilia, who was pushing with all the subtlety of a battering ram for a banquet at the Janiculum house. Everyone wanted to meet the queen and form their own opinion about her. Caesar wondered if some of the men did not want to see if they might steal her away, so great was the chatter about her presence and her charms. Luckily, he was still not receiving Antony, who would certainly elicit an uncomfortable level of interest from one so passionate as his queen. That would be unseemly and problematic. But it seemed a waste of her beauty, her intriguing intelligence, and her lovely and exotic gifts not to grant his friends and associates this opportunity. Besides, he intended for her and the boy to become permanent fixtures in his life, if not in the city of Rome. The Romans might as well get used to her. They were only human; surely they, too, would fall in love and see the wisdom of Caesar in incorporating this sumptuous and exquisite being into his world. She was, in blunt terms, an asset—to Caesar, to the nation he governed, and to the empire at large. He would have to take the risk that their judgment, their vision, and, if not those two things, then their greed, would supersede their fears.

Kleopatra had not stood under the sun's heavenly warmth in a month. It shone in the distance, she could see, and yet heavy clouds shrouded Janiculum Hill, waiting to shower her alone while all the rest of Rome might be happy under the pure blue shelter. She stood on Caesar's terrace overlooking the Tiber River and the jumbled mess of a city that spread like a rash on the opposite bank, the city that was so near and yet so distant. It was a cramped, horrible, and noisy place compared to the luxurious sprawl of Alexandria, and she did not mind that

Caesar had housed her where she could see it without having to spend her days and nights a victim of its incessant noise. The river was the color of peas, of moss, a pale stream—dirty, she was told, by those who had swum its currents. It was a malarial pool into which small Roman boys were thrown to learn how to swim and to acquaint them at a tender age how to stoically survive both fear and filth.

The red tents that housed last night's festivities fell to the ground like dying cardinals. Slaves rolled them quickly into long tubes, anxious to finish the cleaning before the inevitable afternoon rains fell upon the cloth. The Romans were so cruel to those who served them. How many lashes would be exacted for a few drops of water on cheap wet wool? There was no song among these tall, fair-skinned laborers who she assumed were Caesar's captives from Gaul. They spoke a language that did not number among the ten that were in Kleopatra's repertoire. But as she listened to them, her ear began to pick out the words for "yes" and "no," for "hurry up," and for "bring this to me." Their dialogue was peppered with Caesar, Caesar, Caesar. She listened carefully, trying to discern their word for "queen" so that she would know if they were talking about her.

A tiny drop of water hit the bridge of her nose. Was the sky ever truly clear in Rome? Did the gods ever unequivocally give Helios his claim over this strange town? It seemed that even through the brightest sun the sky perpetually waited to open up and flood the city with its tears. Kleopatra looked up at the dark pearly clouds hanging over her head, knowing she would not long be able to stay outdoors today. She did not like this anticipation, this marking of time in precious open air, waiting for a wet blanket of rain to send her running inside. She was forever waiting in this place. Waiting for Caesar, waiting for the right time to act on their plans, waiting for word from home, waiting for a visit from Hammonius, her eyes and ears in town. Ever since she had met Julius Caesar, she had spent less time in action and more in anticipation. She feared that alliance with him was transforming her into an ordinary woman, one who waited for the decisions of her male master to know her own Fate. The idea made her furious, and whenever it arose, she calmed herself with the knowledge that Caesar's masculine allies also waited upon his judgment, but without the additional benefits of proximity that she was afforded as his companion, his lover, and mother of his only son.

Kleopatra had discovered that Julius Caesar had many plans that did not include her, though she could see that she had inspired them. His stay in Alexandria and tour of Egypt left him determined to rebuild his capital in grander proportions, befitting an empire. His building projects spanned the city, with crews working into the darkness to tear down old, cramped houses, decayed temples, and filthy shops to make way for sleeker and more modern buildings. He appointed his supporter Varro to begin building a public library modeled after the Great Library of Alexandria. When his discharged soldiers flooded the city's already overburdened housing, he got the idea to form new colonies all over Italy, giving the veterans land grants if they knew how to farm, or setting them up with shops if they were of the merchant class. Thus far, he had settled eighty thousand soldiers, and often sat awake at night wondering what he would do with the remaining thirty-five legions still armed and under his command when—gods willing!—he would no longer require their services. He ordered that one-third of the slave labor on all public works projects be replaced by free workers, and then he took those workers off the state dole, which put him in such good stead again with his conservative colleagues that Cicero ran around telling people that Caesar was "practically a Republican again." And while he was busy overseeing all of these things, Kleopatra, who had administered the enormous bureaucracy of the Two Lands of Egypt with vigor and determination since her eighteenth birthday, waited for him to come to her and tell her of his progress.

Rome itself was a city of waiting, and this past year it had waited even longer than usual for the year to end. For Caesar, under the advice of Sosigenes, had extended the year to four hundred forty-five days, so that the new year would begin according to the correct solar timing. Caesar's new calendar was named after himself, the Julian Calendar, and the seventh month would henceforth also bear his name. The year would now be three hundred sixty-five and one-quarter days. The compromise Sosigenes and Caesar had reached about how to accommodate that awkwardness was to add one additional day every four years.

"Is that the best you can do?" Kleopatra had asked them.

"It is far better than having the months fall every year in a different season," Sosigenes answered defensively.

"Or having the priests dictate which day of the week it is," Caesar snapped.

And so they officially instituted the new calendar, making Rome's already anxious population spend an additional ninety days in a year that had been one of their most unhappy. But the people of Rome were accustomed to waiting for their annual disasters—civil war, bloodshed in the streets, proscriptions from the winners, heads of the latest accused of treason hanging in the Forum, and finally, the floods. "At least in the new year, the floods will arrive in the proper season," Caesar remarked.

Every year the Tiber rose over its banks and into the streets, forcing the city's denizens to move their furnishings one story up, were they lucky enough to occupy two floors of a house. If not, they were ankle deep in infested waters, wading in their soggy housing until the deluge drained away. The wealthy, of course, owned homes on higher ground and were not affected. How different from the munificent, life-giving annual inundation of the Nile, welcomed, prayed for, washing the crops and blessing the people with food and prosperity. How apt, Kleopatra thought. In Rome, even the river brings dread.

The Romans made statues of beautiful gods to represent the river—mighty male and female figures in repose—and it was a miracle that the gods did not rebel against them for it. What god consented to represent such pollution? Why was the Tiber so unclear? Was it the sewage that was briskly swept from under the Roman houses and into its waters? Or perhaps it was all the bodies of criminals and unsavory characters who had been flung into its torrents in the four hundred years of the city's existence.

Cicero had stated as much last night. "The only proper treatment for one who has broken the law is to tie him up, put him into a sack with a wild and hungry beast, and throw the screaming and remorseless bundle into the Tiber," he had said in his sonorous voice that invited no disputation. He had attended the banquet with his seventeen-year-old bride, Publilia, having divorced his lifelong mate, Terentia, and married the teenager, who came with an enormous dowry that helped diminish his debts. Now, it was explained to Kleopatra, his beloved daughter, Tullia, had just died, leaving him bereft. The bereavement irked Publilia, who thought Cicero gloomy enough before Tullia's death. Cicero was working frantically to raise money from other sources so that he could send the girl back to her family.

"Is that really done?" Kleopatra asked about Cicero's preferred method of execution, not bothering to hide her horror. In Alexandria, quick-acting poison or beheading were the only means of execution; not painless, perhaps, but expeditious.

"Of course," he said condescendingly, as if talking to a naive child. "The law is sacrosanct. No one may break it without repercussion. How are criminals punished in Egypt?"

"We do not throw them into the river that gives the land its life," she replied. "Execution is a duty in Egypt, but never a joy." What would the dignified, religious Egyptians think of this bestial practice? They resented their Greek monarchs as it was, the very people who had rescued them from the bitter tyranny of the Persians and brought order and prosperity to the country. They resisted Kleopatra's relations with Rome, not apprehending that only by alliance could she save them from domination by these cruel men. What was the spiritual state of a country in which the man most revered for his political and philosophical views advocated such expressions of cruelty? Would that every embittered Egyptian ear could have been at last night's dinner.

Caesar's banquet to introduce Kleopatra into Roman society had come off as a success, or so the queen believed. She hoped that she had been able to observe this odd cast of characters who inhabited Caesar's life without allowing them any indication of her opinion of them. It was a strange assembly of family, allies, lovers, and enemies. Caesar's confidence was so great that he invited those who had taken up arms against him to his dinner table and treated them with deference. Perhaps fifty guests attended, and Kleopatra wondered if any other than herself and those in her retinue who counted themselves Caesar's admirers could be called Caesar's unqualified friends. Many of the guests had fought with Pompey against the dictator and had been the recipients of his famous clemency—notably Brutus and Cassius. Cicero had not fought at all, but had gone over to Pompey just the same. Not content to merely forgive, Caesar rewarded with extravagant posts those who had warred against him. Brutus had been appointed governor of Cisalpine Gaul. Cassius was given a prestigious post in the provinces, which did not satisfy him, and so he was in Rome pursuing yet more favor. And Cicero was given the commission to head the building of Caesar's new Forum.

It would have been difficult for Caesar to distance himself from these men entirely, since they were wrapped like snakes around his politics, his life, and his history, the ties so twisted that the lines between friend, brother, and enemy were ineluctably blurred. Brutus, rumored to be Caesar's son by Servilia, had recently married Porcia, daughter of Cato, Caesar's mortal enemy, who had spent the last decade of his life chiming away like a bell in a windstorm against Caesar's tyranny. Cassius was married to Servilia's daughter Junia Tertia, Brutus's half sister. Servilia, though present with her husband, Silanus, showed no sign of resigning her post as primary female confidante in Caesar's life, which irked Kleopatra. Servilia also lorded over Caesar's wife, Calpurnia, a somber, ugly woman who wore plain clothing and no jewelry while Servilia was draped in golden plunder from Gaul that she proudly told everyone was a gift from Caesar. It was no surprise to Kleopatra that Calpurnia had borne Caesar no children. She had a face and demeanor that would frighten semen away, while Servilia, at fifty, had a sensuality that slipped past the lines in her face and the excess flesh that had settled around the curves of an undoubtedly once comely body.

Kleopatra wore a frozen half-smile on her face like the moon at midmonth. She was determined to be gracious, and yet it was difficult with Servilia prattling on and on about the history of her gold necklace in front of herself and Caesar's wife. "It was the prize possession of Vercingetorix's wife," she said, stroking the glimmering square that hung just above her breasts. Its big red garnets stared out like a demon's eyes. *You look older when you gloat,* Kleopatra wanted to say, for Servilia's smile made crinkles around her eyes and fat mountains out of her already heavy lids. Calpurnia said nothing, but smiled with crooked weakness. Her face lacked symmetry, and Kleopatra wondered if it was because she had not the vigor to raise both sides of her mouth. She seemed sluggish, passive, a woman worn down by gossip, loneliness, and duty, the last comprising the two most prominent syllables in a Roman woman's vocabulary. It had been explained to Kleopatra that Calpurnia was the daughter of Piso, one of Caesar's wealthier supporters. She had been given to Caesar in marriage to solidify the friendship and so that Caesar might have full use of her dowry for his military ambitions. While Caesar traipsed about the world, Calpurnia skulked about their small townhouse in Rome, reading books, spinning cloth like a good Roman matron, and waiting for him to return. When he returned, he spent so little time with her that he might as well have been away. Thus did

Hammonius gather this gossip by spending as much time as possible in the beds of rich Roman women. Kleopatra felt some sympathy for Calpurnia, imagining what her life must be, how lonely, and without the comforts of children. But Hammonius assured her that a Roman woman's first love was duty to family, and if Calpurnia obliged her father by being a patient and silent wife to the great Julius Caesar, then she was gratified.

"How easy for you to say, Hammonius, when the world itself is your home, when you have freedom, money, and love in your life, and no one save the queen of Egypt to report to," Kleopatra had admonished the big bear of a man in her service. Why did men think women were so unlike themselves?

Servilia was still on the subject of her necklace. "The Gauls may be savages, but they certainly know how to work a piece of gold. Never have I seen such fine hammering." She traced her middle finger around the square's perimeter as she dared to eye the queen, who regarded her back. "Calpurnia does not care to wear gold," Servilia said. "But Your Majesty obviously has a great appreciation for a fine piece of jewelry, if I may say so. You must encourage Caesar to show you his collection from the tribes of Gallia Belgica. The earrings alone are a phenomenon. You must ask Caesar to make a gift to you. They would be so lovely on Your Majesty's delicate lobes."

"I wonder how they would compare to the treasures of the ancient Egyptian pharaohs which are in the Royal Vaults," Kleopatra said dismissively. To whom did this conniver think she spoke? And yet Servilia was hardly content with female intrigues. The tentacles of her influence had no boundaries. In the middle of a discussion with an old woman about the splendid olives sold on Velabrum Street in the Aventine Hill, she interrupted a discussion between Caesar and Brutus, the latter pleading a case for Cassius, who reclined on a couch at the opposite side of the room with a snarl on his face. "I don't know why you keep passing over him for key appointments," she said, poking her head between the two men and raising a brow toward Cassius. "He is married to my Tertia now and he is family, Julius. Where is that famous forgiveness of yours, my dear? He has apologized. What more does he have to do to prove himself?"

He might wipe the arrogant look off his face and be civil, Kleopatra thought,

but she said nothing, astonished at Servilia's insolence. Kleopatra's opinion of Roman women had not changed in the ten years since she had
last visited the city. Either they were overly bound to duty and knew no
life outside the small domestic circle in which they reared their children
and bolstered their men for the rigors of public life, or they were dom-
ineering and determined usurpers of power. She wondered on which
side of the fence she would have fallen if she had been born an ordinary Roman girl, and she feared she knew.

Servilia was whispering to Caesar, "You so favor Marcus Lepidus,
and I understand it is because he is rich, darling. I don't fault you. He's
my son-in-law, too. But you are positively hurting Cassius's feelings and
turning him away from you again." She turned to Brutus. "Isn't that
right, dear?"

Brutus tilted his head to the right and back again in agreement with
his mother. "I have said my piece on his behalf, Mother, but Caesar is
Caesar and not to be commanded."

"Perhaps not by you, dear," she answered, looking directly at
Kleopatra. "But a woman has her ways."

⌐⟋🐂𓏏𓏏𒀭⌐◎◇⌐

"For our Royal Guest of Honor, whose great ancestor founded her
magnificent city after a dream vision from the blind poet he so loved."
Hermogenes the singer bowed to the queen, his springy curls toppling
forward. He thrust his head and hair back dramatically and began his
song. Kleopatra relaxed to the lovely lilt of his tenor voice singing
Hecuba's sorrowful lament as she awoke after the fall of Troy, wondering if the ignorant women of Rome even knew that he had referred to
Alexander, who was guided by Homer in a dream to the pastoral seaside
fishing village where he set down the perimeters of what was now
Alexandria. The singer's sweet notes were accompanied only by the delicate strings of a lyre, the instrument Kleopatra's mother, who died
when Kleopatra was so young that she could only conjure her music in
fantasy, was said to have plucked ever so gently. Thank the gods for good
Greek music that stopped the venomous chatter of these Roman
mouths, the words whose poison competed for space with their food
and wine. Did they not know that her command of their language was

as good as their own? That she understood every subtle insinuation made about herself and Caesar? The songs were a glorious respite, even though the Romans ate noisily through the performance, paying no heed to the singer's grace and nuance. But the queen smiled broadly at him, motioning one of her servants to send him a message that she would receive him at a later date and gift him with a special treat from Egypt.

Iras had knotted Kleopatra's hair too tightly, and she longed to let it down to make her headache go away. There would be no escape, however, until late into the evening, after everyone was sloppily drunk enough to have their servants cart them away. After two blissful songs, Hermogenes was dismissed by the long arm of Cicero, which looked to Kleopatra like an old lizard, his five insistent fingers forming a craggy snout. Cicero reached into the deep folds of his tunic and pulled out a document. He was going to read his own work to the guests. She had suffered this indulgent Roman custom as a girl of twelve, but back then she had been allowed to fall lazily asleep against her father's grand belly. Now, as queen and guest of honor, she would have no such privilege. Cicero had a long, pointy face and a nose to match. At perhaps sixty years of age, he was thin, and like many intellectuals, lacked any indication of physical vitality—that is, until he spoke.

He began: "My friends, Your Majesty, Great Caesar, honored guests, I would like to read from a philosophical dialogue I started to compose at my beloved home in Tuscany. In my bereavement at the death of my daughter, only philosophy has given me comfort."

Eyes immediately turned to Publilia, who reclined on Cicero's couch in his absence, twirling a lock of her hair. If she caught the slight to herself, she gave no indication.

He continued: "And so I have set upon the task of exalting the worth of that great discipline in daily life, and the further task of proving that the wise man is always happy. I dedicate this work to my dear friend and protégé, Marcus Brutus, who is a kindred soul in the pursuit of a virtuous life."

He unrolled his paper and read, holding it as far from his eyes as his long arms could reach. "Would obscurity or unpopularity prevent the wise man from being happy? No, I say. We must ask ourselves whether the popular affection and glory we so long to win are not more burden than pleasure. It is imperative to understand that popular glory is not worth coveting, and that true dignity is in knowing that the true glory is in not having any glory!

"As the musician does not adjust his melody for the taste of the multitude, then why should the wise man follow the pleasure of the crowd? Surely it is the height of foolishness to attach importance to the opinion of the masses when one looks down upon them as uneducated workers. The truly wise thing is to despise all our banal ambitions, all honors bestowed upon us by the crowd. The trouble is that we never do manage to do so until it is too late, until we have good reason to regret that we had not looked down upon them before! For one avoids troubles if one refuses to have anything to do with the common herd."

Kleopatra watched Caesar during the reading. How pointed did Cicero have to be before Caesar interrupted him? Why should he tolerate—smile through—this criticism of his populist leanings in his own home? At his triumph, Caesar had given three hundred twenty thousand citizens one hundred denarii, ten pecks of corn, and six pints of oil each—acts of extraordinary generosity for which the people loved him. Hammonius had described the looks of gratitude on their faces as Caesar made his speech about sharing the glory and the riches of the empire with ordinary citizens. How dare this man criticize his actions?

Kleopatra scanned the faces of the guests, who were smiling placidly while they ate Caesar's food and drank his wine and accepted gifts from his mistress and ally. Brutus listened intently to Cicero, as if he had never heard such wisdom uttered from human lips; Servilia struggled with a partially cooked egg; Cassius—if Kleopatra was correct—listened not at all but eyed Brutus's pretty wife, Porcia; and the rest continued with their dinners. Not one objection was raised, not even by the host himself. He just grinned ironically at Cicero as if the orator were reciting a dialogue on the treatment of farm animals.

Cicero had now leapt to the subject of the miseries of exile, another implicit criticism of Caesar, who he blamed for keeping him eleven months at Brundisium after the war in Greece.

"Besides, one can hardly give credence to the opinion of a community which drives good and wise men away," he was saying as Kleopatra sat on her hands to control herself. Her stomach churned at Cicero's attack and Caesar's lackadaisical attitude. Did no one understand? Or did all understand, and were taking pleasure in this insult to the man who had shown himself to be their better? Kleopatra suspected the latter. Were they testing at this close range the mercy and forgiveness of Caesar? Were she in command, she would call in Caesar's guard who sat eating directly outside the tent and have each guest systematically slain.

"The next section of the dialogue is a discussion of how even the blind should be happy," Cicero said, unrolling yet one more page.

Kleopatra thought that that would be the perfect moment to tie his hands, shut his mouth, and put his eyes out. The Romans may like spectacle, but they could not compete with authentic Greek theatricality. She was angry, true, but also deeply worried. Caesar had no qualms about sweeping across continents, conquering tribes and lands, but he did not move to put these insolent Romans in their place in his own home. She would interrogate him afterward on his motivation, or lack of it. She hoped he would send Calpurnia back to town and spend the night at the villa; in fact, she would insist upon it. Mercifully, none of the diners would sleep at the villa, since it was fully occupied by Kleopatra's party.

Kleopatra could not breathe. She felt suffocated, as if the heavy red billows of the tent above were pregnant with some kind of fire water that would soon be dropped on her. If one sat long enough in an enclosed space with Romans, the collective smell of the urine-based stain remover used on everyone's clothing eventually took its toll on one's senses. Though they seemed immune to it, and though they covered it with expensive oils and perfumes, Kleopatra's sensitive nose easily detected it. She knew she would have to pay a price for her exit in the middle of Cicero's reading, but she could sit no longer. She raised a finger in the direction of Charmion, who stood immediately. "I need air," she said to no one in particular.

Outside, the dusk had taken on a spectral glow. The clouds' flaming centers burned through the deep blue of the twilight sky. It looked to Kleopatra as if something was being born, some new star in a far-off sky cracking through the vapors and entering the universe.

"You are ill?" Charmion put her hand on Kleopatra's forehead to check for fever as she had done since the queen was a small child.

"Please undo my hair, Charmion. It is like a band of torture around my brain."

"I am going to flog that chattering eunuch," Charmion replied, removing the pins that held Kleopatra's thick brown hair in its tight bun at the nape of her neck. She had kept her coiffures simple in Rome, though the wealthier local women seemed to favor as many hair ornaments as an Egyptian prostitute. Kleopatra thought they might be disappointed at her sleek elegance, as if they expected her to wear ceremonial robes every day. She closed her eyes and let her head rest against Charmion's belly while Charmion rubbed her temples.

"Pardon me!"

Porcia had left the banquet and stood embarrassed before the queen. "I did not see your lady exit with you," she said. "You looked ill, Your Majesty, and I thought you might need assistance."

The young woman was probably Kleopatra's age, with light mushroom brown eyes and olive skin. Her eyebrows were dark and dramatic, like the wings of a hawk. Kleopatra looked for signs of her father, Cato, in her face, but Cato had been an old and weathered man when Kleopatra met him twelve years ago. Porcia was a beauty, but with a furrowed, serious brow that eliminated any appearance of coyness about her looks. Kleopatra had heard that she was scholarly like her husband, Brutus.

"That is very kind of you, madam," Kleopatra answered. "Please sit with me for a minute. I am glad we will have this moment to speak, just the two of us. I wish to express my sorrow over the death of your father. When my own father was at the worst of his troubles, the senator made an extremely generous offer to help him. My father was gratified to have been treated so well by such a highly respected Roman of his rank."

"It is very gracious of you to remember him, Your Majesty. Would you believe that you were also spoken of in the house of Cato?"

"How so?" Kleopatra could only imagine what Cato had to say about her liaison with Caesar.

"When my father returned from his duties in Cyprus, he told all his children of the small princess from Egypt who spoke many languages and acted as her father's diplomat, though she was still a child. He used you to shame us over our lessons!"

"And were you inspired to try harder?"

"No, Your Majesty, we were inclined to give up altogether in the face of your many accomplishments. My father was a man of impossible idealism and virtue. I don't believe I ever pleased him."

"Surely your marriage pleased him?"

Porcia said nothing. She looked at her feet, at Kleopatra's feet, and then met the queen's eyes. "I know that my father was instrumental in the death of your uncle, the king of Cyprus."

"The king took his life of his own volition," Kleopatra said. "There is no need to apologize."

"But my father's presence in his country drove him to the act. Or that is what I have been told. I am certain this caused great grief to his brother, your father."

"Yes, it was the catalyst for a rebellion in our city. Our subjects were furious that my father could not help his brother. But what could he do? Still, I remind you that the senator did offer us his assistance. We hold no grudge against him or against his memory." Kleopatra remembered the humiliating circumstances under which her father had met with Cato. The old man, though forthright and seeming to want to help, had forced the king to come to his private quarters—humiliating enough—and then received him while he sat on his toilet, plagued with dysentery. How close the king's men had come to slaying him on the spot and putting him out of his misery. And what misery they would have saved Caesar if they had done just that. But here was this sincere creature apologizing for her dead father's notoriously inflexible ways.

"That is gracious and kind, and the gods will bless you for your generosity," Porcia said. "It unburdens me to know that there is no animosity against my father's soul from you or from the late king."

"But this is the way it must be," Kleopatra said. "There are those who would blame our host—my friend and ally and benefactor—for the death of your father. And you seem not to hold him in dishonor."

"Your Majesty, if Caesar were a less generous and merciful man, I would be a widow and my children fatherless. My father was not a man to kowtow to anyone or anything, neither a regime nor a man. He knew that in committing suicide, he would deny Caesar the pleasure of giving mercy. He took his life for his own reasons and according to his own plans. I revered him in life and will honor his memory. But what can I say of Caesar? Despite their philosophical differences, he is like a father to my husband."

"And your husband? He is genuinely reconciled with his spiritual father?" And if so, why is he so thick with Cicero, and why does he listen to Cicero's insults against Caesar with a whimsical smile on his face instead of taking up a sword as a real son would do?

"He has never lost his boyhood affection for Caesar. I have counseled him to concentrate on their common interests and history, and not their differences."

"How like a philosopher you are, yourself, madam," Kleopatra said. "Would that you had spoken tonight instead of the orator."

"No, that is far too illustrious a compliment. I have simply learned to adjust to the price of politics and war, Your Majesty," Porcia answered. "It is a woman's burden to suffer the machinations and destructions of men."

Yes, Kleopatra thought. For a woman not born a queen, for women who hold no power of their own, that is precisely their Fate.

Kleopatra peeked out the small square window of her chamber, watching as Caesar gave Calpurnia a chaste kiss before letting the footman put her into her buggy. The two treated one another formally, more like nephew and matron aunt than husband and wife. Kleopatra supposed the lack of collective time spent together made them little more than strangers, or perhaps polite but distant business partners. She did not enjoy thinking of the impediments to her own happiness with Caesar. His wife. Her brother-husband, the craven thirteen-year-old under watch in Alexandria. Roman law. They were obstacles, to be sure. But obstacles could be removed.

The last of the carriages took off into the night, the bright torches of a bodyguard on horse lighting their way, making a tunnel of flames through the thick darkness. Kleopatra felt momentary relief, and then remembered that her evening was hardly over. She met Caesar in the corridor, a tiny candle burning in her hand.

"Let us gaze upon our Little Caesar," she said. She realized that she could not rest at night until she saw that her son was safely asleep, especially in this house where so many of Caesar's enemies had just dined. Though no one mentioned the child—out of deference to Calpurnia, she supposed—everyone knew that his mother had brought him to Rome, and that he carried Caesar's name with Caesar's consent. Surely they did not think she had named him Caesar out of mere respect for a political alliance. But she and Caesar had decided that they would make no formal announcement about their son, at least until he could obtain a quick and blameless divorce. "How about adultery?" Kleopatra had once asked him. "That seems to be a popular factor in Roman divorce." "I already used that one once," he had replied, referring to his second wife, who had been caught in flagrante delicto with his friend Clodius. "Besides, no one would believe it of Calpurnia."

One of Caesar's personal guards stood outside the door to the child's chamber, his face scarred to disfigurement on the left side. The sword at his side made a sharp crescent shadow on the wall like a new moon. He waited for Caesar to address him, and then a smile broke across the right side of his face. "I let the prince hold my sword, General. I'm getting him ready for your training, sir."

"Be careful, Trebonius, that my son may soon be as skillful as a Gaulish marksman."

Trebonius stepped aside to allow them entry, and Kleopatra asked Caesar if he might not be allowed to at least sit down on his evening watch. "They are accustomed to marching thirty miles a day, my dear," Caesar whispered. "Standing the night long is a luxury."

Two Egyptian attendants slept on thick mats in the boy's room, breathing a synchronous tune. They did not awaken; the child must have worn them out. The prince lay in a small crib with slatted sides that Kleopatra did not like—it reminded her of a sarcophagus. But he was sleeping soundly, the moonlight on his gleaming baby skin, his breathing soft and hushed.

"Look how serious he is even in sleep," Caesar said.

It was true; the boy looked as though he carried on a philosophical dialogue with himself or some unseen dream partner. His delicate little eyebrows were tensed together, and his pupils rolled about beneath the lids.

"He is making a rebuttal to Cicero," Kleopatra whispered.

Caesar did not reply, but gently wiped his long index finger on his son's forehead to smooth his wrinkled brow. "There, there, my prince. You have no such worries. Your father will take care of you."

"First his father must take care of himself," Kleopatra hissed. She kissed her baby's moist, warm cheek, breathed in his scent, and motioned to Caesar to leave the room with her.

She walked ahead of him to their bedroom, waving away her body servants. "Good night, ladies," she heard him say, as he paused at the door to give his cloak to the valet, and entered the room after her. His bodyguards' swords clanked with finality as the men settled into their posts. The guard, he said, was for her. Caesar used no guard despite the pleadings of herself and of his supporters. "The love of the Roman people is my guard," he always said.

"You are tense, Kleopatra. Would you like to have a bath?"

"I am not tense, General. I am concerned."

"Did you not enjoy yourself?"

"I did not enjoy sitting idly while the enemies of my partner and ally attacked him in his own home while he did nothing more than feed them more food and wine."

"Do you mean Cicero's reading?" He brushed her concerns aside with his hand. "He means to admonish me for my popularity with those he deems unsavory. He is like one's tired old father, darling. To be respected and ignored."

"You often talk of his influence. Does he suddenly have none?" she asked. She took the last pin from the hair Charmion had loosely rewound, letting her mane fall around her shoulders. She would have liked to stop this conversation and soothe the tension in her head with long strokes of the hairbrush, but she continued. "And what of Brutus? He is thick with Cicero. He took up arms against you along with that Cassius. What a snarling, arrogant fellow he is. Why do you entertain your enemies, General? Why do you allow them such proximity?"

"Brutus is an intellectual, and, like Cicero, his animosity is born out of devotion to a system of government, the beloved and dying Republic, not out of malice toward myself. Cassius I tolerate because Brutus and Servilia have begged me to do so, and they are not technically family but have been close to me for many years."

Kleopatra removed the emerald brooch that held the folds of her chiton, releasing her cleavage and letting the fabric flow. She stopped undressing and turned to Caesar. "Is Brutus your son?"

"No, no, he's the essence of his father and his grandfather and all the virtue-loving, solemn Republican Brutuses since time immemorial. Can't you see that there is nothing of me in him while our son wears my imprint on his face?"

"Please, my darling, this is no time to be angry or impatient with me. I am not your enemy. I am the one who loves you. But I do believe that I was singular in that emotion at today's banquet."

"You do not think my wife loves me?" She could not tell if he was taunting her with mention of his wife or if he expected an answer.

"Your wife is an enigmatic woman. I do not presume to know her feelings. But the rest, I believe, I can assure you. They do not love you. Why is it that you delivered death to my enemies, yet treat your own as if they were your precious pets or errant children?"

"Because you are young and vulnerable and you require protection. I am old. I have lived long enough for life and for nature. I require nothing because already I have all."

You do not yet have the things we have planned together, she wanted to scream, but screaming at Julius Caesar did not seem an appropriate measure. Was he trying to tell her that those things were her dreams and not his? Was she just another person to be placated by him?

"And Servilia? Do you have her down as another traitor?"

"She is Brutus's mother. A mother chooses a son over a lover." She was aware that Caesar would quickly apply this formula to herself, but she was not going to take it back.

"Is that a universal law? Is that what I might expect from you?"

"Is it what you would expect from your own mother?"

"Yes," he said. "Of course."

"Then I will not apologize for what is simply a woman's instinct. If we were not so, then men may not survive."

"Why are you so grumpy, darling?" he asked. "Was Cicero nasty to you? He can be so. I have seen it. His health is not good and it causes him to criticize people."

"No, no, he courts me. He wants the rare manuscripts I have brought from the Library. He also talks about us behind our backs. Hammonius has heard this from many sources."

"Ah, but that is just how he is. He is very critical of all women, except his daughter, Tullia, who never uttered a word that would offend him her entire life. That is what he thinks makes a great woman. He is not naturally predisposed to one of your status or temper."

"He has limited experience with queens," she said.

"And I believe he means to keep it that way."

"I despise him. He rants about living the pure and simple life, renouncing riches, and refusing public honor, and yet he owns houses all over Italy and is making a fortune off his commission to build your new Forum."

"Is he?"

"You know he is."

"And how do you know he is? Did he tell you so?"

"I have told you, General, that I pay good money to have eyes and ears throughout the city even though you will not allow me on its streets."

"I am protecting you and the boy from both physical danger and rumor, which can be even more deleterious. And I must insist you stop worrying so over Cicero."

"What about the rest? Do you not fear that they will rise up against you once more? All they require is a leader."

"What can they do to me, Kleopatra? I have survived three hundred battles. Did you know that? Can your young imagination even fathom three hundred battles? Why should I fear anything at all?"

Not even losing me, she wanted to say. "Not even death?"

"I have said one hundred times in your presence that it is far better to simply die than to waste one's time fearing death. Do you think I am merely being glib?"

She sensed that he was losing patience with her. "Can you not manifest just a little fear? If not for yourself, then for me and for your son? What will happen to us if you are not alive to protect us?"

"That is why we must concentrate on our futures, darling, our plans. Not on petty disloyalty and grim death. I have no doubt that you are entirely correct in thinking that our guests tonight who once fought with Pompey against me would not be very sorry to see me fall. But they will come around. They have to, you see. I am going to give them no choice."

"I see." She tried to take comfort from his resounding confidence. "I am glad to hear you say it. Because the only way that Rome will ever have peace, and the only way that you and I will be able to see our ambitions come to fruition, is to use the means by which Alexander united the Greeks—and it was not by inviting them to dinner."

"I don't need you to give me a history lesson, Kleopatra. The senators are a thousand times worse in their bickering and their hostility than the warring tribes of Gaul, and they will be dealt with similarly if necessary."

"Do they not wish for peace?"

Caesar had removed his tunic and was now reclined, his eyes closed, his deep breaths melting the lines on his face. She wondered if there would be lovemaking tonight. "Kleopatra, would you please finish the removal of that great mass of white linen and come to bed?"

"Shall I put on a nightgown?"

He opened his eyes and looked at her with a strong glint of desire. Perhaps he did not have everything after all. "I said I have lived long enough. I did not say I was dead."

She was weary of the bitter stew of fascination, suspicion, and disdain with which she was treated by the Romans. They did not approve of her, of course. Their rigid laws—the obsolete laws Caesar had vowed to change—practically forbade it. Her union with Caesar was thus far illegal. A Roman citizen could take no foreign wife, recognize no foreign issue born to him, or leave property of any kind to a child who was foreign born. But if you were Julius Caesar, there might be ways around all of these things, and the Romans knew it. Caesar had been able to enact a sheaf of legislation in his political career, either by legitimately winning his detractors to his opinion, or, when that was not possible, by various means of coercion. The Romans knew that he had a good chance of making his union with Kleopatra every bit as legal as his three marriages to Roman women. They fearfully anticipated that day, so they could not, on the surface, treat her with anything short of respect. And yet that courtesy was less than skin deep as far as she was concerned. Even Caesar's unqualified admirers seemed to her to be hedging their bets on him, which she detected in the slight irony with which they addressed her as "Your Majesty" or him as "Great Caesar." Only Caesar's two secretaries, Oppius and Balbus, who carried out his will, seemed purely loyal. But they were not strong men like Antony, for example, whom Caesar had banished from his favor. Kleopatra felt that both she and Caesar were admired and feared, but not liked. She was so tired of dissembling. She felt as if her garments were holding her together the day long, and when she removed them at night, her flesh seemed to spread around her as if she had just escaped, body and spirit, from prison.

When at last she saw the bear-round face of Hammonius, a face from her childhood, belonging to a loyal man who had loved and served her father as he loved and served her, she leapt into his arms and covered his cheeks with kisses, astounding the staff that attended her. Oh, it was good to feel like a child again, a child with a father who would protect her from all harm. Not that Hammonius had that power, but her arms around his affable Greek bulk brought that lovely feeling back to her for the first time in many years.

"Hammonius, you have been so long in Rome that you now dress like a Roman!"

He was draped in a fine white wool cloak with bright red trimming. Threads of gold ran through the fabric, adding shimmer to his solid girth. It was reminiscent of the toga, a garment that could only be worn by Roman citizens.

"And why not? I find the *umbro* so very convenient for walking in their miserable and unpredictable weather!" He raised the folds of the garment over his head, demonstrating the instant cover from rain. "Besides, in Rome, one never knows when the shit and filth of politics is going to be dumped on one's head!"

She grabbed him again, letting her cheek linger against his soft beard, which had now gone entirely gray, along with the thick mass on his head that was combed away from his forehead in rows of waves like a new crop of corn. But his skin was still fine and smooth, and despite his excessive weight, age had not diminished him. The light glowed as strongly as ever in his dark brown eyes. He was a testimony to good health by way of fully enjoying life. Hammonius loved food, wine, women, money, and all in excess—everything that the sickly Cicero said one must abhor in order to be wise and happy. But who was truly wise and happy? The scrawny insomniac who criticized everyone but his stoic Brutus, or this beaming mountain of a man who held her in his arms?

Hammonius released Kleopatra and picked up the prince, letting him rest on the horizon of his belly. "I believe I see a shadow of the late king in his face."

"How is that, Hammonius, when my father was fat, jovial, and dark, and the child is fair, slim, and serious?"

Hammonius sighed. "I suppose I would just be so happy to see the king's face again. It's a sad thing to grow old, Kleopatra, and watch those who have witnessed your life be taken by the god of death, who is omnipotent and remorseless. Someday soon I'll join Auletes, and he'll play his flute for me once more." A little tear escaped the old man's eye and he wiped it away with his big, woolly hand.

"You do not look like you are ready for the tomb. And you had better not die on me, because you are the closest thing to a father I will ever have again."

"Your father would be so proud of you. The poor man tried all his life to make alliances with important Romans, and they bled him dry. Now here you are in the home of Caesar. You shall exceed all your ancestors, Kleopatra."

Kleopatra sat close to Hammonius on the couch, absentmindedly smoothing her son's hair over his pointy head as she whispered in the Greek man's ear. "That is my aim, my friend. Because there is no compromise in this game. One must either rule side by side or be subdued entirely. That is the lesson I learned from so many years of watching them extort the money and the spirit of my father until he was drained of both gold and life. He might have lived many more years had he received better treatment from Rome."

Hammonius shook his head. "His troubles turned him into an old man at fifty! And look at me, sixty-two and still feeling like a boy of nineteen. And I mean that in every sense, my dear!" He kissed the prince's head with a great smack of his broad lips. "But what is wrong, Kleopatra? You look upset. Surely you are not offended by an old man's pride in his virility?"

"No, no, my friend. I am thinking that next year, Caesar will be the age of my father when he died. He won't listen to my warnings because he is so much older than I, and so believes that he has learned the lessons of power. But Hammonius, he believes he can win over his enemies by kindness and clemency."

"The merciful man is rarely victorious," Hammonius said. "One's enemies are like snakes; though one may learn to handle them, they are always poisonous."

"But he thinks himself invincible!"

"He is also wise, Kleopatra. You must have some faith in a man who has conquered half the world and has lived to enjoy it."

"Of course that is what he says, too. But I remain skeptical. And unfortunately, the future of my son and of our kingdom depends on his judgment."

Hammonius's carriage was spacious, with plush, cushioned linen seats, and heavy brocade curtains that could be opened for ventilation. Unlike so many vehicles, its canopy was pale so that the sun's heat did not settle in its weave. The carriage would be driven to the gates of Rome, where they would transfer themselves to litters that would carry them to see the new Julian Forum.

Julius Caesar, disgusted with the traffic that congested his city day and night, had made a law that forbade wheeled vehicles in Rome's narrow and swarming streets except for the purposes of trash collection and delivery of goods to the shops and markets. His new Forum, named after himself, was also built to relieve the overcrowding that suffocated Rome's streets and byways. He had sent word to her at the villa asking her to meet him there today at an appointed hour. He said he would send a party to fetch her, but she preferred to trust herself to her loyal Kinsman and friend. Hammonius usually kept himself busy in the city nosing into the public and private affairs of Rome so that he could send written reports to his queen. While he mingled with the city's wealthiest inhabitants, he made lucrative contracts for the goods that Kleopatra and her father before her allowed him to export from Egypt tax-free.

The carriage was so luxurious that its passengers could indulge in conversation without danger of chipping their teeth, even as they wound their way down Janiculum Hill, jostling along on the rural road paved with big stones like an elephant's toenails. Though the loud trotting of the bodyguards' horses invaded the carriage, the pair could still converse without yelling. Normally, if one was in a mood to socialize with one's fellow passengers, even a short carriage ride left one throaty.

Kleopatra had been avoiding the subject of Archimedes, Hammonius's protégé, business partner, confidant, and nephew, and she felt the tension of it in the air between them. She was certain that the particulars of her affair with him had been disclosed in detail to Hammonius, though it had occurred on the other side of the world while she had been in exile. Archimedes had indicated that he was going to seek refuge from her betrayal in Rome, and also in Hammonius, whose buoyant spirits would be a soothing emollient to his wounded pride and broken heart.

"And what of Archimedes," she said now, plunging ahead with her question before she could weigh the emotional cost of hearing news of him. She was prepared to hear Hammonius deliver an account from her former lover's point of view on how she hurt him—a man who would have easily given up his life for her and nearly did. "I am sure you know the circumstances under which he left my service."

Hammonius took her slender hands in his. "Kleopatra, what could you have done? You chose for your kingdom, and that is why you are a great queen. Again, I say that your father is now with the gods chanting your name, and celebrating the fact that he chose it for you so wisely. Glory to her father. Which Kleopatra in the family has ever lived up to her name so loyally and so brilliantly?"

"I am aware of the reasons for my actions, and I have no regrets. But I am asking you of my cousin. Is he well?"

"Well?" Hammonius dropped her hands and threw his beefy arms up to the gods in exasperation. "No, he is a whimpering, lovesick puppy. In his thirty years, no woman has ever turned him down, much less released him from her heart. He is wounded, of course, but he will recover. I got sick of his skulking around and sent him to Greece to lick his wounds. I told him to come back a man!"

"I hurt him very badly and without explanation. Please don't be hard on him."

"He believes that he is the true father of the prince."

Kleopatra's tender feelings hardened into fear. "He must be stopped from saying that."

"He only says it for my own ears. He knows better. And now that I have seen the long face and Roman nose of Caesar on the boy, I will tell him that his fantasy is just that."

"I love my cousin, but if I hear that he has publicly disputed Caesar's paternity, I shall take action against him. Tell him that."

"Kleopatra, you are a queen and are above all men. But don't forget that it is natural for a man to want progeny. Archimedes will never do anything that will cause you harm."

"Anything that jeopardizes the future of my son with his father causes me harm." Did he not realize how alternately delicate and complex were the ties with Caesar—the political alliance held together by her treasury, the geographical location of her country, and one tiny little boy, who could not yet even say his name? Her ambitions hung by the thread of feeling that Caesar was developing for the small facsimile of himself to whom she had given birth.

"Is there a chance that Caesar will claim the boy as his own?"

"He has already done so privately and to his immediate social connections. A public announcement will follow the enactment of pending legislation. Until then, it would be awkward. You understand, don't you?"

Hammonius pulled the chain to signal the driver to stop. "An old man's bladder is as demanding as a young man's prick!" he said by way of apology, and excused himself from the carriage to relieve his misery. They were still on the west bank of the river, south of Rome and her giant arched walls, but in sight of Tiber Island, whose triangular stone embankment wall pointed toward them like a river barge on a cruise. Hammonius finished his business in the outdoors and then invited the queen to stretch her legs before they continued into the city.

He pointed to the island. "The home of Aesclepius the healer," he said. The temple to the god of medicine had been built more than two hundred years earlier after a terrible plague swept through the city.

"'Tis both lovely and unseemly to have a sacred spot in the midst of this pestilent river," Kleopatra said. The river and the heavens had taken on the same preternatural pearlescent green. No sunshine came to bring normalcy back to the color of earth, water, and sky. Kleopatra felt as if she had sipped the mushroom broth at a Dionysian ritual, the strange brew that always turned natural things unnatural shades. The two sections of bridge that connected the island to both sides of the river spanned its waters like the graceful outstretched arms of a dancer.

"Do you know how the Romans say the island came into being?" he asked. "When the people expelled the last of the Tarquin kings, they threw his wheat crop into the river and it formed the island's mass."

"A pretty story of pride and independence, but undoubtedly apocryphal," she replied.

"The Romans have never taken kindly to men who wished for singular rule. It is not in their nature."

"What are you saying to me?"

Hammonius smiled at her. "I am telling you a story like I used to do when you were a little girl and were rapt to my silly tales."

"I think there is covert meaning, my friend. Do you think you cannot speak directly to me anymore because I am sleeping in the bed of Caesar? Come, Hammonius, you are my oldest friend and my most astute spy and adviser. You do not need to speak of myths and legends to make your point."

His face took on a look of gravity; his worried brow knitted his eyes into two giant teardrops. "Kleopatra, Your Majesty. Oh, sometimes I do not even know what to call you. One moment you are the little girl who used to sit on my lap, and the next, the most formidable woman in the world. The partner of Rome's dictator—may the gods themselves stand in your honor, Kleopatra."

"But there is more you wish to say. Come, come Hammonius. I know you as well as I knew my father. Neither of you has ever been difficult to read."

"When I came of age, I took the vow of the First Brotherhood of Kinsmen to protect you with my life. At nineteen, Archimedes took the same vow. Do you believe that either of us would happily thrust a sword into our bellies rather than break that vow?"

"I do believe it. Even Archimedes, whose pride and heart I have so wounded."

"It is our duty to protect and advise you, not merely to go along with your plans, or to comfort you."

Kleopatra did not think she could ever raise anger against this man, but why was he treating her as if she were a child, unaware of her position or of his? "Why would I wish for anything else? Do you think me not woman enough to know the truth of things? Do you think I need to be coddled like a painted princess?"

He looked at her very sternly, like her father used to do when he was about to forbid her to do something she wanted to do very badly. Her heart melted once more, because, like her father, Hammonius was of a jovial and harmonious nature, a man who had to force himself to be strict and stern.

"Archimedes has written from Greece. He visited Apollonia, where the commander who trained him in Athens now resides, teaching young Roman cadets military strategies. He had cause to meet Caesar's nephew, Gaius Octavian, the boy who rode in Caesar's triumphal parade."

Kleopatra's heart quickened. She had wanted to ask Caesar about this mysterious boy, but she did not wish to appear nosy. It disturbed him enough that she paid Hammonius big sacks of gold for information about his countrymen and their private doings that even he, Caesar, did not know. She sensed that her network of spies threatened the accord between them. But the boy Octavian had raised concerns in her mind. When she learned of the unearned honors Caesar had heaped upon him, she worried that he was Caesar's new beloved, though she had heard he was frail and wan and hardly out of childhood. But there would be no dictating to the dictator whom he might bring into his bed, and so she let go her curiosity about him.

She stood straight, moving away from the tree against which she leaned and grabbing Hammonius's sleeve. "Go on."

"Caesar sent the boy to Apollonia to study."

"Why would Caesar not participate in the schooling of his nephew? Is that not a worldwide custom, to educate our loved ones?"

"Apparently he has paid the families of two splendid Roman boys to attach their sons body and soul to Octavian's service. The boys are of great intelligence and skill, but not of patrician birth. Caesar gave their families great sacks of treasure from Gaul, which he said were the families' to keep as long as the two boys—one, an intellectual who shows great political promise, and the other, a military prodigy—are loyal to his nephew."

"Does that not demonstrate Caesar's mercy and goodness?" she asked. "Why should this generosity to a frail nephew rouse our suspicions?"

The moment she asked the question she had her answer. Why was Caesar heaping favor upon a distant relative that he should be reserving for his own son?

"Do you not think there is malice in Archimedes' wishing me to know this? He has ample reason to wish me to suffer."

"His vow supersedes even his heart, Kleopatra. He is angry with you, but still he works for your welfare. I believe this with all my might. But just in case an old man's judgment has become soft and sentimental, I had the information confirmed. Caesar's own family has reason to believe that he is preparing to adopt this boy, to groom him for power, and to make him his legal heir."

Kleopatra and Hammonius entered the Forum of Caesar through a small arch whose low height only emphasized the vastness of the square the dictator had leveled many city blocks to construct. Caesar had bought up dozens and dozens of homes and apartment buildings with the plunder from Gaul and demolished them, moving great mountains of dirt to fill the void and make the ground even. He had torn down the Curia, where the senate usually met, and rebuilt it elsewhere, a move his detractors had interpreted as a portent of things to come.

Kleopatra leaned on Hammonius's arm, still shaken by the news he had broken to her on the gloomy banks of the Tiber, indifferent to the grand temple to Mother Venus; to the basilica dedicated to Caesar's daughter, where court cases were heard; to the tall statues of the gods that formed a colonnade; to the luxurious gardens in the middle of the square. She was almost hostile to these things, as if it were arrogant or insolent of Caesar to try to impress the queen of Egypt—a nation of glorious monuments unfathomable to these Roman rustics—by building something of this scope. She was furious that her entire life was now hanging by a spider's thread that Caesar could clip at any time, sending her crashing down against the hard, unyielding dirt. Her least favorite emotion—humiliation—hung over her like a pall. She wondered if Hammonius was thinking that she was just a naive girl, the plaything of the aging dictator, and not his true partner at all. Was she in fact deluded to imagine that the vision of the world that she and Caesar constructed in conversations late into the night was real? Was he just engaging in fantasies with her so as not to spoil the sweet romance of their hours together? Was he playing her for a fool? And would she continue to play this game along with him when the future of Egypt and of her son were at stake?

If Caesar thought as much, he would be surprised to find out the truth. She had warned him: A woman chooses her son over her lover.

She did not know how she would master this Master of the World, but she would find a way. The gods were masters over all, and she had no qualms about appealing to them on her behalf. They had never disappointed her before, though she had sometimes been obliged to suffer difficult times before the deities revealed their true and higher purpose.

The temple of Mother Venus had eight exquisite Corinthian-style columns supporting its pediment, and striking statues of the goddess in her various incarnations on its roof—the enchanting Venus the Lover, the strident Venus the Victorious, the nurturing Venus the Mother. The building was small and delicate compared to Egypt's grand shrines to the deities, but Kleopatra sensed that with Caesar's visit to her country, mighty Egyptian proportions had crept into the Roman sense of architectural scale. Kleopatra remembered how small and cramped she had thought the Roman Forum when she saw it as a child. For those Romans who had not yet gotten the message, Caesar's Forum signaled that a new era of eastern extravagance would lace itself through the rigid harness of stringent Roman values, bringing a sense of affluence to all.

Kleopatra left Hammonius outside and entered the temple through its tall, narrow door, which allowed the building's only natural light. The stone walls were lined with torches illuminating vast collections of mounted jewelry and gems. Rays of emerald green, garnet and ruby red, and the ice white of diamonds and crystals danced through the temple's empty space like glittering spirits. Paintings from all over the world hung between the jewels, including one that Kleopatra recognized as a rendering of the pale moon-goddess Hekate soothing the troubled people of Byzantium during a siege, lighting the sky with her crescent and star. In the center of the room, a gold breastplate rimmed with silver trim and shot full of ivory inlays stood like mighty host. Undoubtedly, Caesar had taken it from some conquered king.

Caesar stood alone in the temple. "Is it to your liking?" he asked, looking as nervous as a drummer boy his first day at service.

"It's lovely," she said. She had expected every element of his plan to deceive her to appear on his face and in his demeanor. Instead, she looked into his eyes and for the first time saw expectancy, almost a hope. "But with this display of your war plunder, it seems more a temple to warlike Venus the Victorious than the Mother Goddess."

"How astute you are, my dear," he said. "When I rode into the camp of my enemies after the battle at Pharsalos and saw nothing but their cowardly retreating behinds, I promised the goddess that I would erect a temple to Venus the Victorious. I began to go through the collection of treasure from Gaul and Britannia, and I appropriated the best of it, as you can see. Our citizens so enjoy these displays of wealth confiscated from the conquered. But then something unexpected happened."

"And what is that?" she asked. She realized that she feared him, that she was protecting herself from falling into the net of his sway. He reached for her hand, which she reluctantly gave to him.

"May I show you something?"

He led her through this museum of his victories to the rear of the temple and into the sanctuary of the goddess. Sheltered under the vaulted ceiling was a gleaming gold statue of Mother Venus; her child, the baby Cupid, sat on her shoulder whispering into her ear, his round cheeks puffed, his lips pursed with secrets. She held another Roman child by the hand, who looked up at her for protection and guidance. The goddess had lively sapphire eyes, which looked forward into the future. Her body was draped in folds of gold that flowed behind her as if she were walking into a gentle breeze. To the right of the goddess was a statue of Caesar himself, tall and proud, wearing the laurel wreath of victory in honor of his many triumphs.

But this was not what Caesar had brought her into the temple to see. He said nothing, letting her attention fall upon his surprise. On the right side of the statue of Venus, at a distance close enough to be talked about but far enough to be considered respectful, was a full-length golden statue of Kleopatra, dressed as the goddess but wearing her own diadem, which was as bejeweled as the one Caesar had seen her with in Egypt. He had had the sculptor copy gem for gem the rich stones that she wore about her head. How had he remembered? Her face was as serene as that of Venus, and her body not so slim as it was but fuller, more womanly, the way she had looked when she was just a few months with child. Her eyes were not sapphires but bright polished emeralds, and her hair was swept back into a golden knot at her neck. In the ears, she noticed with a giggle, were the earrings that matched Servilia's enormous golden necklace. Snuggling her feet was an ever so delicate cobra, the symbol of pharaonic power, with a silver tail and opal eyes. Caesar pointed to it. "Lest they forget your true identity."

He waited for her to speak. "Do you approve?" he asked.

"I am speechless, General."

"There will be no question now of the position you hold. For these are the two women in my life: One gives me fearlessness in the face of death, the other gives me reason to stay alive."

She chastised herself for ever doubting him, for doubting her instincts about his commitment to her and to their future together. She did not know why he patronized his nephew, but this was a grand gesture—and a public one—of his recognition of her place in his heart and his life. Tears ran down her cheeks. Her arms were motionless at her sides, limp and heavy.

Caesar put his arm around her shoulder and with one hand turned her face toward his. "Have you nothing to say?"

"Its beauty is overwhelming, but it is even more beautiful to me because it came from you."

"I am not a king, Kleopatra. I cannot build a grand monument in your name, at least not in Rome. But I have done what I can to let this country know how I regard you."

"It is more than I would have asked of you, darling."

"And now when I tell you that I must leave Rome in a matter of days, you will think of this and you won't be upset." He had dropped his hands from her face and grasped her shoulders, forcing her to look for further meaning in his downcast eyes.

"Leave Rome?"

"I had hoped that my general Vatinius had forever cleansed the earth of the Pompeian menace, but it appears that his sons have gone back to Spain and joined forces with that scheming traitor Labienus."

"Must you go yourself? How can you leave Rome at a time when you are just setting up your government? It's dangerous, Caesar. You are not surrounded by those you can trust. That is what I believe, and I must tell you so."

"I trained Labienus myself, schooled him in every art of war so that now he is formidable enough to raise thirteen legions against me. I'm afraid that I'm the only one who can answer the challenge. There is no other commander to send."

"What of Antony?"

"I am not yet so convinced of either his redemption or his loyalty that I'm willing to put him at the head of my own army." He tightened his grip on her shoulders and spoke in a low voice, as if he thought the statue of Venus might be eavesdropping. "The loyalty of the army is the single factor that keeps the senate under my power. That is the situation they created when they sent me forth ten years ago to expand the empire. They got what they wanted from me, and they also got something they did not want—legions and legions of men loyal to Caesar and not to a senate or a country or a system of government. If I do not have the army, I do not have the dictatorship, and you and I, my dear, will certainly not have the unity of our nations the way we plan. Without the solid loyalty of the army, I am just another Roman senator who once did his duty abroad."

She let herself cry now, both in relief at the confirmation of his love for her and the misery that he was going back into battle. She had adopted his attitude of invincibility toward his safety, but the reality of war erased that confidence, and fear crept back into her heart. "Will you guarantee that you will be safe?" She sounded like a child asking the question. She realized it was foolish, that only the gods might guarantee anything, and they rarely did.

"I do guarantee it, Kleopatra."

"Oh, my darling, I want to believe you, but I would be foolish to do so."

"I give you not my word but hers," he said, casting a glance at the goddess's face. "She has promised that I will return."

"How so?" she asked skeptically.

"She is not ready for me yet, Kleopatra. She has told me so."

"She speaks to you directly?" Why not? Kleopatra had received so many signals from the gods that she did not doubt his assertion.

"You must never say anything about this. There is enough suspicion about me as it is." He slid his hands down her arms and clutched her wrists so tightly that her bracelets pressed into her skin.

She wriggled one arm away. "You can tell me anything. I believe you know that. If not, ask the goddess and she will confirm my loyalty."

"She comes to me. That is all. Is it so extraordinary? She is the mother of Aeneas, who founded our city. Aeneas married Creusa, and their first son was Iulus, the first of the Julian clan. Why should she not come to me?"

"Does she visit you in dreams?" Kleopatra had never told Caesar about the dream in which Alexander and Ptolemy the Savior appointed her the dynasty's next successor, but that was the first thing she thought about.

"Not dreams exactly. She comes during my spells. As soon as my eyes go black, her face appears and she counsels me. I have never told anyone this. But you, who understand so well the communion between gods and mortals, will understand."

"I do, my darling. It is just one more proof that the gods wish you to take your place among them."

He shrugged. "The people of Rome practically demand it. The Lupercalian priests are establishing a brotherhood in my honor. There are those who approve, and those who say it smacks of kingship, since the last Roman to be honored with a cult was Romulus."

"But it is natural for the people of Rome to want to honor the man who has brought them so much." Kleopatra did not understand why the Roman nobility so fiercely denied the ordinary citizen's need to connect the rulers with the gods. She thought the senators merely jealous that both the deities and the citizens of Rome had chosen Caesar and not one of themselves to rule over the empire.

"Yes, but that makes small-minded senators sleep even less well at night. They want their power without having to do anything to keep it. Whereas I have earned every honor and privilege."

"And that is why you shall prevail against them."

He kissed her softly. "You will not see me again until I return."

She was about to protest when she sensed a presence in the room. Caesar's secretary stood patiently. "Sir? The hour of the next meeting has arrived."

Caesar walked back with her to the entrance of the temple, where a committee of men awaited him, and Hammonius, her. He took her hand and bowed formally. "Your Majesty, it has been a pleasure discussing matters of state and religion with you."

"And with you, General," she said, giving him her finest regal smile, though the pain in her chest cut like a knife when she tried to take a breath. She said a silent prayer for Venus's infallibility. "Until we meet again."

She turned her eyes away from him before she gave in to more tears. That would not do before this assembly. She searched the crowd for Hammonius, who quickly took her arm, his fine Greek bodyguard falling in line behind them. He led her into the Forum, where she noticed nothing but a long stretch of umbrella pines, their strange inverted branches opening to the sky as if in fervent prayer.

Alexandria:
the 20th year of
Kleopatra's reign

*D*awn threatens. *The light creeps into the windows of her chamber, disturbing the perfect peace of darkness. Iras twitches his nose in his sleep as if the break of day disgruntles him even in his dreams. From the window facing the sea, over the treetops of the Royal Gardens, the queen sees the still-tranquil harbors and the causeway jutting out like a silvery finger, pointing the way to the Isle of the Pharos. On the island, the eternal flame of the tower lights the sea, its fire meeting the first rays of the sun in celebration of the day. Down the coast, Antony lies in the arms of a militia of whores.*

Charmion enters, the thin lines around her mouth drawn deeper from lack of sleep. A servant trails her with a cup of steaming infusion of Indian spices on a tray. Following the authority of Charmion's pointed finger, the girl places it on the window ledge next to the queen. Having delivered the beverage, she hops back as if she fears being bitten. She is a new girl, one the queen has either not seen or not noticed. Unusual. Charmion allows no strange servants into her private chamber.

"The girl was in the Imperator's retreat," Charmion says grimly. "I sent her."

The girl steals a glimpse of the queen's face but quickly lowers her big cow-eyes, wondering if Charmion will punish the insubordination. The queen holds the tea to her face, letting the steam rise to plump her skin and refresh her. The girl is small, perhaps fourteen, of mixed Greek descent. Her simple white chiton is open on the right side in the manner of the Laconian maidens. Through the gap, the queen sees her right leg shake ever so slightly.

"*Look at me, child,*" she says. The girl obeys, surprised at the friendliness in the queen's voice. The queen captures and holds her eyes, startled by the fineness of the child's features. Despite the mingling of foreign bloods her face is gifted with the outline of the Greek ideal. Kleopatra makes a mental note to speak to Charmion about her. Beautiful, guileless. She wonders if her son Caesarion has had her. More likely Antyllus. Like his father, he is given to seducing shy but willing creatures, while Caesarion, though king, requires being seduced.

"*What did you see, child?*"

"*I saw nothing, Your Royal Grace Mother Egypt,*" she replies, looking to Charmion.

"*I sent her to listen at the door. The servants are quite unreliable and do not speak the languages of the Imperator,*" Charmion wearily commands. "*The child is facile with many tongues. Her father is a learned Jew, but her mother an outcast. Tell Your Majesty what you heard.*"

The child's eyelashes flutter up and down like little insect wings. Tears well in the corner of her eyes. "*Singing, Your Royal Grace Mother Egypt,*" she answers with great hesitation.

"*Singing?*"

"*Yes, Your Grace. The Im-Imperator was teaching the ladies songs.*"

"*Songs?*"

"*Songs, Your Royal Grace. Songs like riddles. In the Latin tongue. B-b-bad songs. Coarse songs like soldiers sing. About coupling with beasts. Songs of that nature.*"

The queen exercises extreme discipline in refraining from laughter. Imitating the stern Charmion, she asks, "*At what hour was this? Surely they have finished singing their tunes by now.*"

"*Less than an hour ago,*" Charmion says. "*As the child was leaving, she heard the Imperator call out for more wine.*"

More wine, after drinking and fucking for twelve hours? The queen had hoped that her husband's melancholia would have been slightly more difficult to dissipate.

"*More wine, and a roast pig, Your Royal Grace.*" The girl is beginning to lose her shyness and looks directly at her queen. "*The Imperator demanded a roast pig with prune sauce, a pheasant fixed his special way—*"

"*Yes, yes, baked slowly and braised with grapes and wines. Go on.*"

"*And a goose with sweets, Mother Egypt. Yes, he said a goose with sweets. And, and, and—*" Suddenly the child falls to her knees as if stricken by Caesar's malady, hiding her face in her hands as if consumed by either disease or a paralyzing shame. Her back heaves up and down beneath the folds of the thin cotton dress.

"*Spit it out, child.*" *Charmion is losing patience.* "*Control yourself and tell the queen what the Imperator demanded.*"

The child raises her face to meet the queen. "*And three naked serving girls to carve,*" *she sputters quickly, lowering her eyes once more.* "*Your Royal Grace Mother Egypt,*" *she adds, gasping an intake of breath.*

Unable to restrain herself, the queen bursts into laughter. Charmion remains unyielding, suffering with resigned ennui Antony's antics. The child, however, collapses and weeps again on the floor at their feet, a supplicant awaiting punishment for carrying the news of the queen's husband's audacity.

"*What else did you hear?*" *the queen demands of her, signaling to Charmion to lift her up.* "*Do you know the sounds of lovemaking? Did you hear such things?*"

Charmion grabs a handful of the black ringlets and yanks them back, revealing the tear-stained face. "*Only singing, Your Royal Grace Mother Egypt. Only song. Forgive me. I believe I would know the sounds of lovemaking, but I heard none. Only the singing and the command for the foods and servants.*"

The queen looks at the lady-in-waiting in disapproval. Sighing, Charmion releases the girl's hair, takes her elbow, and raises her to her feet. She smoothes the loosened curls and almost tenderly straightens the child's garments, looking back at the queen as if to say, "*is this better?*"

"*You shall be rewarded for your excellent service. I need clever girls who speak languages and are loyal. You shall be called upon again. You may go.*"

The child looks to Charmion for confirmation of the order, as if Charmion is queen and Kleopatra the lady-in-waiting. Charmion nods her head at the door and the child walks quickly toward the exit.

At the thud of the heavy door closing behind her, Iras turns on his back and snores, but does not awaken. The hot, sweet concoction slides down the queen's throat, filling the emptiness inside, hurting as it makes its way into her stomach.

"*Does she know not to speak of this?*" *she asks. She likes the girl and wishes her no harm. She also recognizes that the child might continue to prove useful.*

"*She is fully briefed, Lady,*" *Charmion says monotonously, though with the solicitousness she never abandons. They sit in silence, the queen sipping tea, Charmion staring disdainfully at the sleeping form of Iras.*

Charmion says, "*The early shift heard the sounds of lovemaking.*"

"*Then we are successful,*" *the queen replies cheerily.* "*The first battle is won. Can victory be far off?*" *She cringes at the hollowness of her own voice.*

"*Do you wish to meet with Sidonia this morning after she is finished?*"

"I wish for nothing less," she snaps at the good woman who lives for her alone. "I see."

She thinks, *Once it was I who feasted with Antony into the morning hours. Once it was I to whom he made love between courses of pig and pheasant and goose and wine. Once it was I with whom he laughed and sang the prurient songs of war late into the night. And once, not so long ago, it was I who made Antony forget food entirely for days at a time, while he obliterated in me all thoughts of duty, family, and country. Once. But no more.*

Masking those anxieties she says, *"It is entirely possible, Charmion, that my plan has reversed itself on me, that Fate in her fickleness has delivered an unexpected outcome. This is what I get for meddling with the gods: Antony is sinking farther into the debauches of wine and women. Watch: He will find the pleasures so intoxicating, so reassuring to his failed manhood, that he'll never want to fight a war again. Why should he?"*

"Yes, Kleopatra, it is entirely possible." Charmion is terse; her lack of faith in Antony is well-known. *"You might do what we discussed,"* she adds with hope in her voice.

The queen knows that Charmion believes that she must negotiate with the enemy. The enemy of her husband. The rival of her own son. The monster Caesar hand-delivered to the world.

"I am not prepared to play the suppliant to the monster."

"The Lady of the Two Lands, Mother Egypt, the Queen descended of Many Kings, need never supplicate," Charmion retorts. *"She need only reveal her will. The kingdom of your fathers has prospered by alliance with Rome. And who is Rome now?"*

Kleopatra can hear Charmion answer her own question: *Not the man who sings and dances drunk in the mansion by the sea. Not the lascivious man-boy who amuses himself with naked serving girls while his enemy approaches from Greece. Not the man you chose. Not the man you chose this time.*

"It is not my will to align with the Typhon," Kleopatra growls. Charmion is the only person who might suggest such a plan to the queen and retain her head. Kleopatra does not suspect Charmion, but wonders if she is acting on her own intelligence or if she has been approached by others. She is sure that forsaking Antony is not a novel idea in the kingdom. *"I believe I make myself clear."*

Charmion asks no further questions, but returns to the business of administrating the queen's day. *"The War Minister requests a meeting prior to breakfast with the Cabinet."*

"The queen is currently indisposed with regard to the War Minister. I cannot listen again to his mad raving plans for escape through the east," she replies, grateful to be relieved of the discussion of the practical logic of betraying her husband. Sometimes the plan makes too much sense to her. "Does he expect the Royal Family and the Imperator to simply disappear into India? If he persists in attempting to sell me this plan I shall have him exiled.

"Cancel breakfast with the Cabinet. Send Sidonia to bed—to her own bed. And leave me alone."

"What work shall you do, Lady?"

The queen thinks, Charmion is hopeful yet that I shall write to the monster. She believes I am being secretive in my negotiations. From my chamber, she will exit the Inner Palace and go directly to the temple of Isis, where she shall offer a small sacrifice and pray to the goddess for me to desert my husband.

"We shall discuss it at the appropriate time."

"As you wish. Shall I remove the Royal Hairdresser?"

"I should think so. The queen requires a catnap."

Charmion opens the door to the antechamber. A tall Ethiopian slave enters, bowing to the queen. Turning to the bed, he picks up the sleeping eunuch, barely disturbing his slumber. Iras smiles with half-cloaked dreamy eyes at the queen, leaning his head against the hard, bare black chest. Curled up like a child in his father's arms, he is carried out of her chamber and into further revelry.

The queen's maidens enter, gathering up the rumpled bed linens like mice scurrying to collect a prize hunk of cheese. They replace the sheets with smooth, clean ones, remove her dressing gown, and place a fresh one over her head. She lies on her bed, big enough to sleep the War Cabinet, and a girl kneels on either side of her, massaging oil into each arm and hand. She is particular in the care of her hands. The shutters are sealed and the room dark once more. One small lamp is lit; through sleepy eyes, the queen watches Charmion in silhouette speak to the slave who carries the laundry in a basket on her head. The slave listens intently and curtsies obediently to the older Greek woman. The basket moves not. The queen's eyes grow heavy, and within moments, safe in the knowledge that the old sergeant carries her orders to the troops, she falls asleep.

She is still listening to the authoritative calm of Charmion's voice, to the soft patter of slaves' feet, to the whisper of the servant who extinguishes the candle with her breath, when the ghosts of the past arise and take hold of her dreams.

Rome & Alexandria: the 6th year of Kleopatra's reign

To: Kleopatra VII, Queen of Egypt in the city of Rome

From: Hephaestion, Prime Minister of Egypt in the city of Alexandria

To Her Majesty the Queen,

Recent events require your immediate return to Alexandria. Our sources have uncovered evidence of a worldwide conspiracy directed against yourself and the prince. I no longer trust the privacy of our correspondence, so I will reveal no further details until we are face-to-face. One of Hammonius's ships is leaving Ostia in two days. It is a luxury vessel, I am assured, and fit for you and the prince and whatever members of your party you wish to accompany you. Take no security risks. Employ all methods used from your time in exile when conditions were also uncertain. Above all, trust no one but your closest aides. Make certain that Charmion is always in attendance with the prince. It is my burden to have to alarm you, but it is also my duty. The urgent situation calls for your presence, as dynastic succession is at stake. Do not alert the Romans that there is trouble in Alexandria. Information was leaked to Caesar's legions here in the city, but I have personally seen to it that has been countermanded. I believe we are safe now in that regard. The excuse you must give for your hasty departure is the illness of your brother, the king. We believe he has been infected with the plague and the urgency of his condition requires your immediate return to Egypt.

Forgive my familiarity in expressing this sentiment, but I am looking forward to being in the Royal Presence once more. We have been through many trials together, and recent events suggest that our challenges are not yet over. Please do not delay your return.

Eternally your servant, Hephaestion

The last time she had entered her city's harbor she was wrapped stiff and suffocating into a musty carpet slung over the shoulder of a pirate, mentally practicing what she would say to the dictator of Rome to encourage him to support her over her now-dead brother. Whenever she became gloomy, thinking of the mountains that were yet to be climbed before she and her son and the kingdom of their mothers and fathers would be secure, she made it a point to think about how far she had come. Julius Caesar's only son was the prince of Egypt. A statue of her likeness was standing in a Roman temple, where the citizens would learn to associate her with the Mother Goddess, just as they did in her country. Egypt was still an independent nation. And these things she had accomplished on her own with the help of the gods.

The unobstructed sun warmed her face against the sharp bite of the ocean breeze. The sky was the pure azure blue she had not seen in so many months, spotted with benevolent clouds that sailed along with the ship, whirling tufts of snowy white dancing for her as her ship clipped into the Great Harbor. She put aside the apprehension raised by Hephaestion's cryptic letter and watched the sky-goddess's performance, the clouds her little round daughters bouncing merrily for the queen's pleasure. Why would Hephaestion have called the queen and prince back to a palace infested with plague? She did not question him but packed a few trunks, made hasty apologies to the Romans Caesar had charged with keeping her care and company in his absence, and departed with an alacrity that left them guessing. After all, too many members of her family had learned too late that an absent monarch soon became a deposed monarch. But word of her departure had spread about Rome even before she was gone. Cicero had sent a messenger to the dock with a long list of books he would like to borrow from the Alexandria Library upon her return.

The bright lining in the dark cloud of Hephaestion's letter was that she was able to send a curt note to Servilia canceling that woman's trip to the villa planned for the following week; duty demanded her immediate presence in her own capital. Whatever the crisis at home, she thought, she would at least be spared another encounter with that noxious woman. But Servilia did not respect Kleopatra's wishes. Instead, she sent word that the meeting must not be postponed. She would arrive the very next day.

Caesar was not two days out of Rome and Kleopatra was one day from departure when Servilia appeared at the villa. When that lady had announced her intentions to visit, Kleopatra had extended the invitation to her daughters as well, but Servilia arrived alone, allowing that the young Roman matrons were far too busy with their children and their household duties to make visits to the country. Kleopatra wondered if Servilia was insinuating that her regal lifestyle was too indulgent—a favorite criticism the Romans used against others who did not share their fanatical, though superficial, devotion to Stoicism.

"Whereas a mature woman like me has already reared my flock, and an active social life is my reward," Servilia said.

"You are alone?" Kleopatra asked. "I was under the assumption that Roman women must always be under the protection of one man or another."

"Or they under our protection, as the case may be." Servilia's oddly shaped eyes smiled along with her mouth. They were flat at the bottom and highly rounded on top, like the shape of the Alban Hills where Pompey had once lived.

Servilia said she had felt it her duty to tell Kleopatra the terrible things Caesar's enemies were saying behind his back: He is destroying the Republic. He wants to be a *god*. He wants to be a *king*. He wants to move the capital of Rome to *Alexandria*.

Kleopatra did not know if Servilia was jealous of her, trying to warn her, or simply seeking to destroy her union with Caesar for political purposes, working as her son's agent. In any event, she did not believe the woman was to be trusted.

"And what do his *friends* say of him, madam?" Kleopatra asked. "Would you have any way of knowing those details? For example, what does your son say about him?"

"Brutus and Caesar have ideological differences, that is all. From the time Brutus was a baby, his father filled his head with stories of how their ancestors rose up against Rome's tyrants. He was trying to instill

Republican ideals in him. He succeeded in the extreme, I'm afraid. I wish my son were not so literal. But I don't worry too much over it. There is a kindred feeling between Brutus and Caesar that is as deep as the familial, I can assure you."

"That must be a great comfort to Caesar," Kleopatra replied. What was Servilia's game?

"Your Majesty, the people of your country worship you as a goddess, is that not correct?"

"They believe that Pharaoh is their link to the gods, the gods' representative on earth. It is a tradition many thousands of years in practice."

"There are those who say you are whispering these thoughts into Caesar's ear! Thoughts that he should enjoy deification, too."

"I thought you knew Caesar well," Kleopatra answered.

"As well as anyone has ever known him, I assure you. Our friendship has survived every challenge," she said, drawing out each syllable of the word "every."

Until now, Kleopatra thought. "If that were true, you would know that first and foremost, Caesar is a Roman. His interests are Rome's highest interests, not his own. And secondly, he does not require a woman's whisper to put ideas in his head."

"We who know him well are aware of that fact. But I thought that Your Majesty would want to know what rumors were being put about. If we believe the philosophers, we must agree that knowledge is a form of power."

"Indeed. But who is instigating these rumors?"

"Many, I'm afraid. And your own sister had a hand in it."

"My sister? Since when does a political prisoner have the ear of the city's dignitaries?"

"Your sister had audience with a small group of Roman women who pride themselves in administering to prisoners. You know the kind of do-gooders I mean?" Servilia waved her hand to show her disapproval of such types. "Women who waste our natural female sympathies on the undeserving, when they should be at home minding the affairs of the family."

"Why would anyone listen to her? My sister is an enemy of Rome. She would not stop fighting her war just because she was defeated and in chains, I assure you."

"And she did not! She fueled the rumors of Caesar's outlandish ambitions with stories of how you and he plan to disband Rome's government and set up a joint kingdom somewhere in the east—Babylon, Alexandria, Antioch, Troy, take your pick."

Servilia waited for Kleopatra's reaction like a cat eyeing a cornered mouse.

"Did you say as much to Caesar?" Why was she taking the trouble to enlighten Kleopatra? What dark purpose hid behind that smooth, high brow? Why did she not take her information directly to the source?

"Yes, but you know how he is. He waved his long arm at me, leveling my fears into idle gossip that should be ignored."

"And my sister was believed?" Kleopatra asked incredulously, or projecting as much incredulity as she could muster. She wondered if Servilia knew how close she was to guessing the truth—the truth, but without the sinister undertones of vanquishing Rome's government to achieve their ambitions.

"Oh yes, because they wanted to believe her. Caesar has the great love of the masses, but some extremely powerful people fear him—and fear exactly the fruition of what the princess said."

"But surely you understand that these are the ravings of an hysterical and embittered girl?"

"Of course. But she was able to do some damage before she was removed from the city." Servilia clutched the arms of her chair as if she were about to stand, but she did not get up. Her square white fingernails turned purple with the pressure. "Your Majesty, may I break with all protocol and be utterly candid with you?"

"As you wish," Kleopatra said, stiffening, fearing the charge of this dauntless older woman.

"You may think that I wish to regain my—what shall we say?—former position in Caesar's life, but I can assure you that nothing is farther from the truth. I would have surmised the same thing when I was a young woman. But you cannot imagine the freedom that a woman gains at this stage of life without those sorts of concerns. What I am trying to tell you is that I have loved Caesar for more than thirty years, and my love for him is very far beyond wishing to be the object of his desire. We are old, old friends. He and I have always envisioned being very elderly together, unable to walk any longer without assistance; we would sit in our chairs and watch the young take over our duties while we had nothing to do but sip wine and smell pretty flowers. I do not mind that you are one of those vital young people who has already taken my place in the most enduring relationship of my life. You are welcome to that position. I am taking you into my confidence because I wish to grow old with Caesar in the manner in which I have described. If he is not care-ful—which he disdains to be—our pretty vision may not happen."

Kleopatra scoffed to herself at the notion of Servilia sharing Caesar's dotage. One woman would have that honor, and it would not be an old Roman crone but a formidable young queen.

"What are the objections of his enemies? You must help me. I do not quite understand the animosity against a man who has brought so much greatness to his country." Kleopatra waited for Servilia to answer. She was sure that Brutus was no friend—no son—of Caesar, and she won-dered if the mother was ready to confess that knowledge. For if some-thing was afoot in this woman's family, she surely had knowledge of it. Kleopatra doubted that a single olive could disappear from Servilia's kitchen without her having foreknowledge of the thievery.

"Your Majesty, it may be hard for a monarch to apprehend our ways, but the concentration of power in the person of Caesar is against our very constitution. That is my son's objection to the dictatorship. As for the rest of them, what has raised hackles is that Caesar is giving Rome away to those who are not Roman. He has been granting Roman citi-zenship to all free men of Italy, giving them the same rights and privi-leges as *true* Romans. He has appointed Gauls to the very senate, and he removed Roman officials of very noble blood from their positions in the provinces and replaced them with locals."

Crooks! Caesar had called the Romans he stripped of power and sent home. *Crooks, ingrates, inept thieves!* But the queen did not repeat this to Servilia, who was undoubtedly related to some of them.

"Lately, he has said in public that his goal is to give Roman rights to each and every free man in the empire! I must tell you that this idea—along with these strange Gallic creatures attending senate meetings in *breeches*—has completely infuriated his conservative critics, who believe we must keep Rome *pure*. Surely you see the wisdom in that?"

"The Gallic senators were his loyal allies in the war there, I believe," Kleopatra said. "Why should they not be rewarded? And if Gaul is now

Rome, then why should Gauls not be Romans? Romans do not have to become Gallic."

Servilia looked shocked, her eyebrows drawn into arching question marks. "And do you envision your own subjects someday being Roman citizens, too?"

Kleopatra did, in fact, look forward to the day when her own subjects would be given Roman citizenship. They would become Roman Graeco-Egyptians, combining the three most illustrious civilizations on earth. In her mind, it was a goal to strive for, not a change to be feared. For without change, there is no progress. But she did not think it wise to reveal too much to this woman, who undoubtedly soaked up information like a sponge.

"Madam, as your son was brought up on tales of vanquishing tyrants, so I sat on the lap of my father the king and listened to stories of our forefather, Alexander, and his visions of a world empire governed in harmony. Alexander embraced the people of the nations he conquered, and it seems that Caesar has decided to follow his example. Surely that cannot be an error?"

"Not in theory, Your Majesty. But this is Rome. You have not spent much time in the streets of our city. You have not heard the mob shout, 'Restore the Republic! Restore Rome to the Romans!' when Caesar passes by."

Caesar had told Kleopatra that the conservative senators paid mobs to chant these slogans in the streets. "They wish to walk backward in time, but it will never happen," Caesar had said. "Men throughout the world find the idea of equal citizenship intoxicating."

"And I hear that the mob also shouts 'Hail to the king!' when Caesar passes by. I suppose the slogan depends on who is meeting the day's payroll."

Servilia looked insulted. The question marks dropped, and her lips shrank from a broad, solicitous smile to two pursed prunes.

"Madam, the world is changing," Kleopatra pressed on. "Isn't it wise to change with it? It seems to me that even Caesar's enemies have benefited mightily by his progress. But it appears that his opponents wanted to reap the rewards of progress without paying the price of change."

Servilia stood. "I have said what I came to say. You are correct, Your Majesty. Many will ride the rapids of Caesar's sweeping changes. But there are those few—and I believe he knows who they are, those living ghosts of Cato—who cling to the old ways like barnacles. They have my son's ear, though Caesar still has his loyalty. My advice to you is this: If you wish things to go your way, you might encourage the dictator to stop pretending that the old ways no longer matter, and to toss the old dogs some fresh meat. Otherwise, I fear that their fangs will find a way into his thigh."

⌒⇀☜☡☡█⌐◉◇⌐

The colossal statues of her ancestors greeted Kleopatra at the Great Harbor. Try as Caesar might to rebuild Rome to meet Alexandria's proportions and majesty, there was still nothing in that sweaty and crowded place to rival this sight—Ptolemy Philadelphus and his wife Arsinoe II, taller even than Titans or gods, their aristocratic Macedonian features adapted slightly to make them more palatable to the conquered race, yet looming as impressively over humankind and nature as the greatest of the ancient pharaohs. Rome would have to climb a long way out of its provinciality to measure up to this, she thought.

The pristine white city of Alexandria sprawled languidly along the rocky shore and up the hills beyond the harbor. Caesar's monument, the Caesareum, looked as if it had been completed in her absence. Dwarfing the temple of Isis, it dominated the south shore, the twelve columns of its front and their stalwart black shadows facing the sea like a Greek phalanx. The day was clear, and the statue of Pan on the hilltop held a welcoming arm out to the queen. She could just make out the silhouettes of people in repose on the pine-cone shaped knoll, resting in the shade of satiny willow trees. She thought of Servilia's warning and realized that the truth of it was this: Alexandria, by its geographical situation, by its rich cultural history, by virtue of the grandeur of its proportions, its sheer beauty, and the ancient knowledge housed within its institutions, was a more appropriate capital of a world empire than Rome. That idea was bound to threaten the Roman senators, those aging men whose political power was seeping from them as quickly as blood from a slaughtered animal. Oh yes, and they bled a little more each day as Caesar pushed the boundaries of Rome's empire farther and farther into exotic lands where he would easily be hailed as king, just as they had once hailed Alexander. Though Caesar had never *said* he wished to be a king, it seemed to Kleopatra the unavoidable next step in his ascension.

The ship sat in the harbor until sunset waiting for safety clearance. Nut, the sky-goddess, softened the horizon, turning Zeus's dancing white clouds into slim, tawny fingers guiding the ship to shore. In the final moments of the daylight, when sky and city melted into a dusky blue dream, Kleopatra planted her feet on Egyptian soil. The ship's crew had disembarked and were kissing the ground and chanting the name of Ra, and she wished that she could join them.

She could not wait to eat food prepared in her own kitchens. The security protocol put into effect aboard the ship had taken her appetite away. Every plate of food for her and for the prince was tested by food tasters, and even then, Charmion suspiciously smelled everything before letting them put a morsel to their mouths. Sometimes Charmion made them wait to see if a toxic substance might have a delayed effect, and by the time Kleopatra tasted her meals, they were often cold. She and Caesarion slept in the same cabin, armed guards outside the door and attendants on pallets inside. The child's fitful sleep kept her awake much of the night, hunger gnawing away at her stomach. Two days into the voyage, she longed for privacy, for a fresh plate of food served directly to her, for a walk on the deck without two big sailors following her around. She longed to tell them that she followed the philosophy of Caesar, that she did not fear death and in fact preferred it to this anxiety over someone taking her life. But she did fear death, not on her own account, but because of the blue-eyed infant, who would survive neither the cesspool of Roman politics nor the snakepit of the Egyptian monarchy without his mother's protection.

And now, though no hostile militia, no rebellious mob, no disgruntled faction of citizens greeted her at the harbor, she wondered what trouble she had been called back to face. Hephaestion had kept her return quiet. No ceremonial party greeted her at the harbor, only the stately eunuch, members of his staff, and a wagon of attendants to help transport the Royal Goods back to the palace.

"Are you too tired to be briefed this evening?" Hephaestion asked as they settled into the carriage. She noticed that he had arranged for them to be entirely alone.

"Are you asking out of politeness, Hephaestion? I know you too well. You have already decided that we must waste no time in catching up. I'll wager that the order is already given to serve us dinner in my office so that we can talk."

"Your Majesty is ever wise. I would not trouble you if matters did not necessitate urgent action."

He had aged in her service. When her father had appointed him ten years ago, he was slim, his face unlined, his mouth still turned up buoyantly at its corners. The office was supposed to turn over to a new adviser annually, but the family's long history of being betrayed by its highest chancellor had persuaded Kleopatra's father to appoint the eunuch to the position for life. He was perhaps fifty now, close to Caesar's age, close to the age her father was when he died. Hephaestion seemed healthy still, despite the weight that had crept up his middle and into his neck and cheeks, puffing him up like a proud old rooster. He had not yet taken to the use of cosmetics like so many of his aging, castrated colleagues, save for a thin line of kohl around his fine brown eyes. His skin was much looser than when she had left him in their war camp outside the fort at Pelusium to sneak away with Apollodorus the pirate and meet Julius Caesar. Steely gray streaks swirled with his tight black curls. She wondered how many of the new visible lines chiseled into his smooth face could be attributed to his devotion to her.

She did not stop to make a small sacrifice at the temple of Isis to give thanks for her safe return, or, once at the palace, pay a visit to the state bedroom that she had missed so much in Rome, but went directly with Hephaestion to the room where the two of them had so often met to conduct government business. Hephaestion dismissed all scribes and attendants at the door and ushered her in. She sat in her usual chair with a cushion over the seat and golden arms like lions' paws stretched out in repose. Hephaestion took a small metal tool out of a black box on his desk, and with it loosened one of the stones in the wall. Carefully he pulled out the stone and placed it on the floor. He reached inside the empty space and produced a packet of letters.

"Is all this secrecy really necessary?" she asked. She was exhausted and lightheaded. Her body still felt the rhythm of the sea, and she pressed her feet firmly against the tile floor to try to accustom herself to land. She was hungry, too, and longed for a hot bath in her private quarters.

She could almost feel the warm water engulf her; her mind sank into a reverie imagining that pleasure. Hephaestion spread the letters on the desk in front of her, but instead of reading them, she closed her eyes. "Must I read these now?" Her eyes stung from too many days of the whipping sea winds and from too little sleep aboard the undulating vessel.

"I will tell you their contents. These missives are the correspondence between Princess Arsinoe, who calls herself queen of Egypt, and the king. They have been slipping by our censors thanks to the treachery of a servant to the Royal Candlemaker, whose sister was body servant to the princess in her captivity in Rome. A system of delivery was established even from Ephesus, where the princess is supposed to be under Roman watch. Clearly, she has found co-conspirators among her guard."

Kleopatra could only imagine the methods her beautiful sister employed to induce her captors to do her will, techniques perfected in the bedroom of her younger brother, whom she manipulated all his days. Would she never be rid of her sister's insidious sway?

"Princess Arsinoe has been sending envoys to the Roman army here in Alexandria to rise up against you, Your Majesty, and take the city back for her."

Kleopatra scoffed. "Does the fool think the men of Julius Caesar would so swiftly betray their commander?"

"Some of them are mercenaries gathered from Pompey's former eastern provinces, less interested in the glory of Rome than in gold. She made quite a few inroads with those men. She wrote passionate decrees promising money, land, citizenship, and marriage to Alexandrian wives for their cooperation. She was able to get the letters directly into the hands of their leaders."

Kleopatra shook her head. "Even in captivity, she still insists she is queen." She rubbed her ears as the masseuse had shown her to do to manifest vigor, letting her fingers work down her neck and into her rock-tight shoulders. "And so we are on the verge of another rebellion? Is that why you called me back here? What is going on, Hephaestion? Why did you have me say that my brother has contracted a plague? Why not just say he is a traitor?"

"It is not entirely untrue that he has manifested signs of the disease."

He had chosen his words carefully, but Hephaestion was a careful man. She did not like this state of semi-knowledge in which he seemed determined to keep her. He was not a conniver or intriguer like so many of his kind who had served the Ptolemaic dynasty, and never had he grabbed for power beyond the limits of his office. But he had a eunuch's unadulterated loyalty as well as the uncanny ability to mastermind. This was not the first time he was one step ahead of her, but she was sure that whatever puzzle he was putting together was for her well-being. He had proved himself a thousand times over, risking his own life to safely get her out of Alexandria when her brother's regime had made her a prisoner in the palace, and then serving her loyally in exile, even when her funds ran out.

"Why did you call me and my son back into a plague-ridden community?" She knew she sounded suspicious of him. "But wait, I saw no warning flags at the harbor and no hospital wagons in the streets. What in the name of the gods is going on?"

"There were signs of the plague a few months ago, but it has been safely contained by quarantine." Hephaestion fished through the letters, found the one he wanted, and put it in front of her to read. It was written by her brother, the present king, to a Roman lieutenant promising him one thousand talents and an estate near the Fayum if he could convince his troops to betray the orders of Julius Caesar and allow Arsinoe to enter the city. Kleopatra read: "'Arrangements have already been made with your comrades in Ephesus. The True Queen of Egypt needs only a word from you to return to her home.'"

"Here is another you will find of particular interest. After the candlemaker turned in his servant, we began to intercept the correspondence of the Roman soldiers. This is a letter from a Roman officer offering on behalf of a 'high-ranking Egyptian official one thousand talents for the assassin who is able to dispense with Kleopatra of Egypt and her son, residing in the city of Rome while she conspires for its destruction.'

"I have no way of gauging what their chances of success may have been had we not uncovered their plots."

"What ordinary man would not risk all for a chance at one thousand talents?" Kleopatra said. "That is more than sits in the treasury of most city governments. But which one is to blame here? Is my brother merely Arsinoe's puppet? Or does he have a mind of his own?"

"He is the age his older brother was when he raised an army against you."

Kleopatra picked up the letter again. It was chilling to read the call for one's own death. She put the letter down and sat back exhausted and numb, as if perhaps she were in fact dead and this bizarre meeting was a dream she was having about the living.

"Your Royal Grace, do you remember the advice I gave you so long ago after your father died and we had to take drastic measures to secure your position?"

"You said: In matters of state, let your blood run cold. I have never forgotten it."

"Have you found it wise advice?"

"More wise than I would like it to be."

Hephaestion knelt before Kleopatra, his face as still as a death mask. "I beg your forgiveness for what I have done in your absence."

"Prime Minister, please get up. I am far too tired for these kinds of dramatics. This is so very unlike you."

"Egypt cannot tolerate another war of Ptolemy against Ptolemy."

"My alliance with Rome was intended to prevent that possibility."

"But as we have now seen, nothing will stop Arsinoe from trying to usurp. And the king is her finest local instrument."

"But you say he is ill?"

"He is ill because I have caused it. The alchemist who makes youth potions for my mother confided to me that he had discovered a poison that could produce the same effects as the plague. I had been praying to the gods for a way to quietly dispose of the king, and then this! I took it as a sign. There was plague in the city and a warning had already been issued. I knew that no one would be suspected if the king took ill. And so I have had him fed the substance in his food. I can have it stopped if you wish, though I strongly advise against it."

"But what of my sister? She is the true instigator."

"At your command, I will arrange to deliver the same goods to the princess Arsinoe," he said. "She is not the only one with connections in Ephesus."

Royal Announcements issued on this fifth day of April in the Seven Hundred Thirty-fourth year from the First Olympiad, and in the Eighth year of the reign of Queen Kleopatra VII, Theas Philopater, Neos Isis, daughter of Amon-Ra, Pharaoh of the Two Lands of Egypt. Descended of King Ptolemy I and Queen Berenike I Soter the Savior Gods, Ptolemy II Philadelphus and Arsinoe II, Brother and Sister Gods and Ptolemy III and Berenike II the Benefactor Gods who conferred bountiful blessings upon the people, of Ptolemy IV Philopater and Arsinoe III, of Ptolemy V Epiphanes and Kleopatra I, Gods Manifest, of Ptolemy VI Philomater, Ptolemy VIII Euergetes and Kleopatra II, granddaughter of Ptolemy XI Soter, daughter of Ptolemy XII Theos Philopater Neos Dionysus Neos Osiris and Kleopatra V Tryphaena. Upon this land the Royal House of Lagid bestows many benefactions.

To the citizens of Alexandria and its Jewish residents:

Queen Kleopatra is returned from the city of Rome where she renewed the sacred title conferred upon her by the Roman Senate, Friend and Ally of the Roman People. Owing to the Queen's Majesty and Beneficence and Influence, the Roman people have regained the right to worship the goddess Isis and the god Dionysus. All Hail Queen Kleopatra, who has restored piety to the people of Rome.

Queen Kleopatra invites you to join her in honoring the memory of the late King Ptolemy XIV, who has been called to ascend to the gods, for games and theatrical performances in the Caesareum on the 20th day of April commencing at high noon and ending at sunset. All citizens and Jewish residents are encouraged to attend.

Honors will be paid to King Ptolemy XV Caesar, Philopater and Philomater, son and co-regent of Kleopatra VII of the Royal House of Lagid and Gaius Julius Caesar, Dictator of Rome, descended of the Julii Caesarians of Italy and the Greek hero Aeneas, Founder of the city of Rome and son of Aphrodite.

By invitation of the queen, the finest and most accomplished athletes, musicians, and tragedians from all over the world will perform and compete. Prizes will be awarded to the winners.

All Hail Queen Kleopatra who with the blessings of the gods makes all things possible!

The city of Narbo in Gaul: the 6th year of Kleopatra's reign

Caesar had trouble remembering if he had just won his three hundred fourth or three hundred fifth victory. His mind, so fine for detail, was growing ever more fuzzy. In Spain, though he had subdued Pompey's sons and their legions, he frequently forgot precisely against whom he was fighting. He just continued to fight, commanding his men without overreliance on the intellect. It was one's instincts that served one well in battle. But the battles—blood splattering the faces of his men; loose limbs dangling so pathetically from the bodies of the unfortunate; futile cries of pain, even more futile prayers to the gods yelped with one's last breath; gorgeous horses who had served so valiantly falling over their own legs and trampling the object of their loyalty—these scenarios were indistinguishable from any other battles he had ever fought.

There was one difference in Spain. *She* had come to him in the midst of battle and told him to relax his sword and follow her away from the ruckus. He felt the noise around him disappear as if he had gone completely deaf. He saw men's mouths agape in fury, in pain, but he heard nothing. Suddenly, the world had all the hush of an early morning snow in the Alpine mountains. He followed the unearthly presence through the silent tableau of battle and back toward camp. She looked so beautiful, her skin dewy, her cheeks pink, her blue eyes gleaming. Her body was draped in the thinnest weave of fabric, luminous in the late afternoon sun that rushed through newly sprouted leaves of thick-trunk trees, lighting her body through the dress. She was Spring itself, he thought, and as she looked back at him urging him to follow her form—the quintessential woman's body with its soft curves and high formidable breasts and long bare feet with sloping arches that he would like to tickle—he did not know if she was leading him away from battle because he had died or because she wished to seduce him. In the act of dismounting his hot, perspiring horse, he reached for her waist, and she evaporated like smoke as he tried to encircle her. The next thing he knew, he was in his tent, and a doctor with a face like a curious crab was squinting down at him, informing him that one of his men had found him fallen from his horse, unconscious.

Why had she not simply taken him at that moment? He would happily have left his body in the forest and disappeared in her arms.

He recovered, as he always did, remaining in Spain to clean up the inevitable mess of a provincial government changing hands. He settled all court cases, punished war criminals, forgave the remorseful, set up a new tax system, sifted through bribes to make all the proper appointments, collected the expected tribute, and now was on his way home.

He had done it again, pulled off yet another victory, and by now, so many senators had joined his cause—oh, out of fear, he realized, but still it was nice to see one's foes diminish in number. A large party of them had taken the trouble to meet him in the coastal city of Narbo to heap yet more honors upon him, as if waiting for him to reenter Rome would have been an insult. They named him Dictator for Life, giving him the power to appoint consuls, censors, tribunes. He was also supreme lord over the empire's finances and would henceforth appoint all its governors and highest provincial officers. It was declared that forevermore, Caesar would sit in a gilded chair whenever he received officials. What was next? he wondered. Were they—despite all the talk about preserving the old Republic—actually going to ask him to be king? Oh, that would kill Cicero, wouldn't it? And what posthumous suffering it would cause the soul of Cato, who would never rest for all eternity should Caesar wear a crown in the city.

But they did not mention naming him king, at least not yet. Caesar's guess was that this greeting party wished to secure their positions in his government—and secure their share of the loot from Spain—before the other senators and knights took their shares. He was not surprised to see Gaius Trebonius, whom he should have had executed for his execrable show as governor of Farther Gaul. Trebonius was not the only man who showed up to save his head. Indeed, as they stood in the sand, Caesar looked at the tops of many a suppliant head that had once conspired to do him wrong.

But here was Marcus Antonius, too, who had made the journey in a chariot, of all vehicles, and who leapt from it like an Olympic athlete and turned on every bit of his considerable charm when he saw Caesar's carriage. Antony looked so humble, his head lowered so that he smiled with his eyes. Then he walked toward Caesar, making a speech about Caesar's many accomplishments, his big arms swinging as he articulated each syllable as he was wont to do in his flashy Greek style of oratory. Everything about Antony was gleaming on this auspiciously sunny day—eyes, teeth, words, skin. Even the air about him seemed to sizzle with a barely visible shimmer of energy. Caesar was unsure if he was about to slip into another spell, and when the two men were just a few feet apart, he virtually fell into Antony's arms, which everyone took as a sign of reconciliation, particularly Antony, who hugged Caesar so tightly that he worried he would collapse his lungs.

"Praise the gods, Caesar, I am your son again," Antony whispered in his ear. And Caesar was comforted by that sentiment, because he knew that when he returned to Rome he would need all the filial affection from men of power that he could muster. There would be fewer friendly faces in Rome than here at Narbo, and Antony was the man to help meet those who groused over Caesar's extraordinary new powers. Antony was just the sort of son a dictator required, a son whose courage and golden words could turn the most cowardly soldiers into brave hearts ready to face the grimmest tasks.

"The senate has taken an oath to protect you, Caesar," Antony announced. "For all know that your health and wellness are the very anima of the empire. Even those who once called themselves your enemies are now sworn to give daily thanks to the gods for your very existence."

Caesar invited Antony to ride back with him in his carriage, which forced his nephew Octavian to ride in a second coach. He thought he saw the boy wince, but surely he understood that Antony's seniority entitled him to enter Rome side by side with the dictator. The sulking pride was the characteristic that worried him about his nephew—that

and his rather frail health, but that was no matter, because Caesar himself had proven that one might be thin and pale in youth and yet grow
into a man of power. Had he not bemoaned to his friends at the age of
thirty that he had done so very little with his life, whereas Alexander by
that age had conquered much of the world? The boy was merely a late
bloomer like himself. He attributed the sulking to his age, sixteen, when
a boy so desperately wished to be a man, and was either enthralled or
intimidated by those like Antony who embodied male strength. He
thought thrall a little healthier than the jealousy he saw flash across
Octavian's face. The boy had yet to fight a battle and yet Caesar had
heaped all sorts of honors upon him. Now Caesar was sending him
directly back to school in Apollonia where he might learn a thing or
two. In the meantime, what more did he want?

After so many years of being without an heir, suddenly he was rich in
sons. Antony, Brutus, Octavian. But they were sons with agendas and
ulterior motives. And yet the son of his blood, the little blue-eyed boy, he
could not recognize because of Rome's laws. Perhaps he would change all
that if he had the time. If the gods wished it. He was a little tired of pushing the gods to his favor. He felt that after all he had done, they should
grant him ease. He was ready for some personal reward. In Spain he had
thought he had been given some of that in the favors of Queen Eunoe,
the lusty wife of the Mauretanian king who had so helped him with his
Spanish operations. But she was like so many other lovers—eager to
betray her aging husband with another older man who was more powerful and whose patronage she sought. Caesar thought he could hear her
mental machinery churning away while he was on top of her. Human
beings were so entirely predictable. Only one had the ability to surprise
him still in ways that pleased. He hoped his messengers did not delay in
getting his letter to Kleopatra. He did not want to reenter Rome without
knowing that hers was one of the first faces he would see.

Rome:
the 7th year of
Kleopatra's reign

It seems like only yesterday that I was in Alexandria," Antony said, sweeping his toga behind him with his bare, beautiful arm and bowing. "And yet that cannot be so, for Time has worked its enchantment upon the young princess I met in there and has turned her into a most majestic example of the womanly sex."

She offered him her hand to kiss and he took it, lingering over it, and then looking straight into her eyes. "Your *Majesty*. It is a pleasure to address you as such, because in you alone does the literal meaning manifest."

Caesar smiled broadly at his friend's flirtation with his mistress as if at a precocious child, and Kleopatra thought he looked like a proud parent whose firstborn had just performed a new feat. She wondered if her lover would have been so gracious if he understood that the dignified countenance with which she answered Antony's coquetry concealed an alarming internal combustion.

The last time she had seen Marcus Antonius she had been a twittering girl whose knees shook every time he looked at her. She felt that he had known this, and had played with her girlish affection, staring directly at her with his deep, unabashed eyes, teasing her, and making her blush. She had looked forward to their reunion so that she might let him see how, as a woman, she had control over the way others affected her;

that she governed not only a nation and its people, but the entirety of herself, heart, body, and mind.

But years of living and warring had also enhanced Antony so that he, at thirty-seven years of age, was no less formidable an invasion to her composure than he had been ten years prior. He had the gift—even more highly developed than Caesar—of communicating with women on many levels all at once. Kleopatra felt that he was treating her as if she were girl, queen, mother, mistress to another man, and, of course, potential lover, in every glance sent her way, in every sentence. It seemed that even the things he said to Caesar also contained some hidden meaning for her. She could not reckon what it was, exactly, but she was aware at every moment, he was considering her; that despite the fact that the topic of discussion was war, the business of seduction whorled around every strategy. In ways, he was even more disturbing to one's calm than Caesar, who ruffled virtually everyone with his opaque irony. Antony caused a different sort of disruption—more visceral, easier to locate in the body.

Caesar and Antony treated one another with great solicitousness, like a married couple who had had a serious rift now put right and were careful not to upset their newfound rapport. Caesar had presented Antony to her as "my son," and she immediately felt a threat to her own son. Now that Caesar had been given the additional title Father of His Country, he called every breathing Roman male his son. How many sons did a man require? Caesar had taken the step of formally adopting the boy Octavian, he said, as a show of familial loyalty to his sister. An ancient Roman custom, he said. Simply a formality designed to bring one's family members into civic life. For how else was a youth to succeed? Caesar called Brutus—a man who had fought against him and who publicly honored the memory of Caesar's enemy, Cato—his son. Marcus Lepidus, Caesar's Master of the Horse, was also occasionally called son, which did not bother Kleopatra so much because, privately, Caesar had said to her that it was for Lepidus's money that he kept him so close. And now this great hulking warrior who had only recently ingratiated himself back into the dictator's life, and who did not appear to need the patronage of anyone, much less a father, was also given the term of endearment. What was the place of Little Caesar in this pond swarming with sons? How would a little boy, a minnow, survive in this pool of sharks?

Why were so many sons appearing just as she had become one step closer to securing her position? She had felt so hopeful as she sailed away from her paradise by the sea and back toward the hot chaos of Rome. With the death of the boy king, Little Caesar had been elevated to co-regent, unrivaled by any male in the dynasty. The child had been in a most positive mood ever since, as if he had understood that he had been given a great gift. As they sailed from Alexandria, he was laughing in the arms of his governess, sticking his tongue into the wind and for once acting like a baby.

"Now that he has the crown, he is not acting at all like a king," Kleopatra said to Charmion.

"I believe he is behaving exactly as many kings before him," Charmion said, and they both laughed, remembering not only the less dignified elements of family history, but the histrionics of her own father, who had loved playing the child.

Like the plague itself, the substance slipped to Kleopatra's brother had been quick poison. Within days he was dead, his body burned in a spectacular funeral pyre—for no embalmer would touch a body that had contracted plague, not even a king's body—and his ashes were placed in a golden sarcophagus along with a respectable amount of treasure, including the little red robes he liked to wear as a child when he pretended that he lorded over the eastern lands once conquered by his forefathers. The Royal Body and Treasure were placed in the Royal Catacombs near the temple of Isis by the sea. No one could understand how he had been so unlucky to contract the disease that had been lurking around the cheap inns and back alleys of the harbor but had not spread to the palace quarter, and it was put into the ether that like so many of his ancestors, the boy king had an exotic secret life that must have put him in touch with many questionable characters who might easily have contracted the disease elsewhere and brought it into his very chambers.

With the expedient demise of the king, Hephaestion wished to arrange to administer the same dose to Arsinoe, but Kleopatra would not allow it. Arsinoe was the prisoner of Caesar, and he alone must decide her Fate.

Caesar was now too preoccupied to take up matters of rivalry in Egypt. He was ready to take the bold, final step necessary to equal the achievements of Alexander, the conquest of the vast eastern territory of

Parthia that had confounded the Roman dominators for so many decades. And that, Kleopatra realized, was the true reason he had so completely accepted Antony back into his affairs. He appointed Antony governor of Macedonia, a key location in the operations against Parthia. She also knew an even deeper truth of the reconciliation. Antony was a commander to whom the Roman legions were fiercely loyal. It would not do to have Caesar away on the other side of the world fighting a war while a man like Antony remained in Rome and could call up so many troops to do his bidding. And that bidding might just be to unite with his rich friend Lepidus and a few of Caesar's most potent Roman enemies, and take the city for himself in the name of the Republic. In that event, Caesar and his legions would be banished from Rome unless they marched the thousands of miles back home and fought another civil war. Kleopatra knew that if she had the shrewdness to foresee this possibility, then Caesar did, too.

Antony had a naturalness to his demeanor, though, that made it difficult to suspect him of any participation in conspiracy. His smile, though lascivious, seemed to come from his heart, and not from some dark agenda of sexual or political conquest. If Antony intended to seduce her, he made it seem that it was merely because he wanted to, not because he had a larger purpose other than the dictum of his brawny male desire. And if he had any inclination that Caesar's affection toward him was based on suspicion and not love, he did not let on, nor did he behave toward Caesar as anything other than an admiring lieutenant and repentant son.

Kleopatra snapped to attention. This was no cat-and-mouse game for the affections of the queen. The stakes at hand were not a position between a young woman's loins but the position of her kingdom and its resources at her command to be utilized in their bid to conquer a powerful enemy.

Caesar opened the map slowly, as if he were spreading the folds of a maiden's nightgown, and Antony's rapacious eyes scanned the territories as they revealed themselves, as if they were the untouched mounds of the young girl's breasts. Caesar smoothed the parchment, his long fingers grazing the many lands he had already marched across and claimed for Rome. His hands so easily owned the world, she thought. He pinned the edges of the map with metal pegs. With his index finger, he pointed to Parthia.

He explained his plan. On the eighteenth of March, he would set out across northern territory, amassing along the way some sixteen legions and ten thousand cavalry. Following the River Euphrates south, he would launch the initial attack from that direction, sweeping through Carrhae and avenging the humiliating death of his former ally, Crassus. After his ignoble defeat, Crassus's head had been served up in a production of *The Bacchae* to satisfy the barbarous humor of the Parthian king. "The gods will curse us if we put off Crassus's revenge another year," Caesar said. "Some nights, I do believe I see his poor headless ghost." After vindicating Crassus, he would march north through Dacia, meeting up with Antony and his legions, and confront the barbarian chief Burebistas, who had been striking out against Roman settlements in Illyricum. It seemed that he found the consumption of wine intolerable and wicked and set about burning down Roman vineyards in the region.

"The man is a menace," Antony said. "I will have to control myself to wait for you to dispense with him, Caesar."

"Remember how much more we become when we are partnered, my son," Caesar said. "Together we are greater than a mere two." They smiled at one another like cats sharing a dead bird. Kleopatra did not know if she was suspicious of this mutual solicitousness because she feared for her son's position, or if the bond between the men indeed lacked a genuineness that they tried to disguise with calculated affection. It was nothing as sinister as the chill she felt when she was near Brutus, whose eyes turned into sad, small slits when he looked at Caesar, even if he was mouthing generous words. Perhaps it was the subtle rivalry between the two men for her attention that was causing the little flutters in her stomach. Something was amiss, but she could not define it.

"General, I thought you planned to come through Alexandria for supplies on the way east." Kleopatra thought she would broach this now rather than hold it in until they were alone. How long would it be before she saw him again if he did not come to Egypt? She had already made plans to ride with him as far as Judaea, visiting the Nabataeans to renegotiate the rental of their lands for date orchards.

"There is too much talk of moving the capital there, my dear. It would not do to fuel it by marching one hundred thousand soldiers past your door. I would like you to send the Egyptian contribution to the war—the grain, weapons, animals, and horses we discussed—straight on to Antioch, and Dolabella will see to the delivery."

So that was the plan. Kleopatra's contribution would be enormous, but her participation minimal—crucial to victory, but invisible to the world.

"The route through Alexandria is too long, Your Majesty," Antony offered. "Though it would certainly have its rewards."

"It wasn't too long for Alexander," she blurted, her tone wiping the smile from his face. She had offended him, but she did not at this moment care. The two men were grabbing the world for themselves while demanding that the queen work behind the scenes for their glory.

She worried that a wedge was coming between herself and Caesar, and she did not know its origins. She did not particularly think Antony was the cause. But her instincts were rarely wrong. In private conversation, Caesar always held close to the vision of empire they had created together—dictator of Rome and queen of Egypt united in the body of one small boy; Caesar presiding over the eastern Roman empire from Alexandria and over the west from Rome. Partnered with the queen but not her lord and master, until her son rose to be king of Egypt and eventually inherited his father's powers. He always said that once Parthia was conquered, there would be no stopping them. Kleopatra believed him, but also realized that his own plan provided him with an empire with or without her.

Caesar had called her all the way back to Rome—urgently, even—but since their reunion, he had been aloof. A change had occurred. He went about his duties as usual, including his duties in the bedroom, but with a detachment even greater than the distance he usually maintained between himself and all other humans. It was not as if he had lost interest in any of his endeavors, but he seemed to Kleopatra to float through the days like a shade revisiting the earthly plane, resuming the life he had led while living, but with only an illusion of the solid corporeal body of his human form. He had aged. Never one to eat enthusiastically, he had lost weight in Spain. His cheeks hung like empty saddlebags on his narrow face. Violet rings rimmed his eyes. Compared to Antony—skin flushed red, flesh pumped with muscle, radiant snow white circles making gleaming brown marbles of his eyes—Caesar looked yellow and ill.

She remembered where she had seen that awful color on a face before. It was her father in his last, desperate days.

"After settling things at Dacia, we'll march along the River Danube until the tribes of Germania are subdued. That should take us all the way into Gaul, in the event that Brutus requires assistance in keeping the peace there, and then southward home."

"It's an ambitious plan, Caesar," Antony said. "My only hesitation is that I won't be with you for its entirety."

"There is too much Roman empire and far too few able Roman men to run it," Caesar replied. "That is the biggest problem we face. I have stationed you where you are most needed. And if you will notice, it is not so far from me that I won't be able to call upon you if necessary." He turned to Kleopatra. "Or upon you, my dear." Caesar looked at his two protégés. "What beautiful bright stars you are. How marvelous the three of us are together. You realize the potential?"

Antony and Kleopatra did not look at Caesar but at each other. Something passed silently between them, something that could not be given a name, but was solid and real. Something that had everything and yet nothing at all to do with Caesar. It took place in less than a flash of a moment, but Kleopatra felt that whatever was planted in that fleeting instant was now an indelible part of her world. Antony knew it, too, she believed, because he was, for once, at a loss for words, holding his face in a stiff smile. Neither of them dared look at one another again, nor did they respond to Caesar's question. They waited for the dictator to elaborate, but he was lost in thought over his map.

"Potential, General?" Kleopatra finally said, breaking the silence in a halting tone.

Caesar took a piece of chalk and drew lines from Italy to northern Greece to Egypt and then back again to Rome. "And it doesn't have to stop there, does it?"

Antony dropped his smile and looked utterly serious. "No, it does not."

With his left hand, Caesar took the hand of Kleopatra; with his right, that of Antony. "The two of you will look glorious flanking me in my victory parade."

Kleopatra sat in a box seat in the Forum reserved for foreign dignitaries, squinting against the sky's white glare. She had left her son at the villa because Caesar worried over his safety. But she was not going to miss the drama today, not one that had been so carefully staged by the threesome they secretly and jokingly called the New Triumvirate—Caesar, Kleopatra, and Antony, the threefold partnership that would someday form a mammoth triangle of invincible power, its ambitious and ever-reaching angles searing across the vast portion of the earth's soil.

She had feared that she would not make it into the Forum. Throngs of people covered every stone of Rome's narrow Via Sacra in crowds so thick that the guards flanking Kleopatra's litter bearers had to barrel through them, shouting orders to let them through, and pushing people aside to make way. From inside the litter, Kleopatra could see nothing, but listened to the horrible drunken curses hurled at the men as they navigated her through the streets and into the Forum. Released finally from the vehicle, which though lavishly padded seemed to her as an early tomb, she could see that even more people were cramped into the Forum—men of every rank and class from senator to beggar, militia protecting the former while the latter groped the unprotected for coins. Children perched atop their fathers' shoulders to get a better view, and young women dressed in white were pushed forward to the front of the crowd so that they might participate in the festival. A strange energy hovered over the Forum, too restless and unruly for a religious celebration. She had felt that energy before in her own city, when she was trapped outside the palace gates while a mob of disgruntled citizens pelted her father's quarters with flaming arrows and fiery threats. Though there was no sign of trouble, the feeling that hung in the ether was unmistakable.

The fourteenth of February by the new calendar marked the Feast of the Lupercalia. Kleopatra inquired about the origins of the ritual, but no Roman seemed entirely certain. It was an ancient rite, said to have begun many hundreds of years ago to honor the sacred She-wolf who suckled the city's founders, Romulus and Remus, after their father had sent the twin infants to the riverbank to be carried away by the floods and die. Others said the ceremony preceded even those days and was in honor of Inuus, the name the ancient Romans gave to the god Pan, who made the land and the beasts and humans upon it fertile.

Julius Caesar presided over the crowd, sitting on his golden throne, draped in a resplendent purple toga, the color of victory. He sat high on the new Rostra that he had recently built, looking over the assembly. Antony had overseen the construction of the Rostra, and for that, Caesar had his name inscribed on the platform, crediting him for his work. Caesar leaned forward to talk to those who approached him, one arm resting along his knee while he huddled close in intimate conversation with whomever wished to get a word with him.

"Why does he make himself so vulnerable with rumors of plots against him swarming the city like flies?" Hammonius asked the queen. "A powerful man must be ever cautious. A man feared as much as he must respect his opposition."

"He is like a sixteen-year-old boy impressed with his new virility. He thinks himself invincible!" Kleopatra whispered into the burly Greek's ear.

"Old men return to the foolishness of youth," Hammonius said. "I see the tendency in myself, wise as I am in these late years."

"You are not old. I will not allow you to say it."

He laughed. "I am older than I am wise, Your Majesty."

Kleopatra laughed with her Kinsman, but it was a hollow laugh, one that she felt only in her mouth. Caesar, while promising her the world, was daily giving her new causes for concern and doubt. She did not know if she doubted his loyalty to her or his very sanity. She only knew that she must obey the warning chills that shot through her when she heard of his recent actions. Someone—it was not known who—had placed monarch's crowns on Caesar's statues on the new Rostra, and the Tribunes of the People had ordered them removed. The next day, those same tribunes arrested a group of ruffians who were protesting the removal of the crowns by gathering in front of the statues and chanting the word "king." Caesar was so annoyed by the citizens' arrests that he informed the tribunes that they were henceforth removed from both office and senate. But the very next day, an even larger mob gathered in the Forum to protest their removal.

"They simply do not know what they want," Caesar had sighed. "And so I must do what I want."

"Yes, do as you wish, Caesar, but protect yourself against those who disagree!" she had said. "The history of Rome is drenched in blood."

Kleopatra had told him of Servilia's warning, but Caesar said that women were always worried over such things, and that is why, Amazons excepted, they would never be allowed to fight in wars. Calpurnia, too, was always after him these days to watch his back, poor old dear. "I believe it is you three women who are in conspiracy against me," Caesar said, "and not those few ingrate senators who always need something about which to complain."

An astrologer had taken the trouble to warn him that he was surrounded by those planning evil against him, but Caesar dismissed him. "They shall have to march to Parthia to commit it," he laughed, "and fight legions of my men before they might reach me."

To make matters worse, he had recently dismissed the elite Spanish guard recruited in his last war and who attended to him personally, because he did not like to hear their footsteps trailing him. "It interferes with the thinking process," he had said.

"You are pushing Fortune too far," Kleopatra had told him.

"That is an earned privilege," he had answered.

Now he wore a slack smile that seldom left his face as he talked to those Romans who approached the throne. Throne! The Roman people despised the very word and its connotations, and yet the senators had given this privilege to Caesar for all the city to see. Whenever he was before a large assembly nowadays, he was seated like a king upon the gilded chair, raised above all. The same image that inspired awe in Kleopatra's own subjects—that of an illustrious being given power and position above all other earthly creatures by Divine Sanction—inspired a palpable unease in Caesar's countrymen. The dictator and his throne were a busy topic of conversation around the city. It struck Kleopatra that this was part of his enemies' plan; they baited Caesar with the trappings of monarchy and made it appear that he was usurping the powers of his own volition. Hopefully, the drama that was about to unfold would help delineate the wishes of the majority of the people. She wished that she had thought to station spies throughout the crowd today to hear what whispers slid in and out of Roman mouths.

The bright, sharp sound of a trumpet interrupted her worries, and Caesar raised his right hand to begin the ceremony. Three dozen priests of the Brotherhood of the Wolf marched into the Forum, two of them carrying a big white goat whose legs were bound to a stick. The men wore only goatskin loincloths, and had oiled and shaved their bodies so that their skin gleamed. Kleopatra recognized a few senators among them, the highest-ranking men in Rome, who had recently been inducted into the priesthood to pay honor to Caesar. Two of them untied the goat, whose deep throaty cries only got louder, and the crowd began to imitate the beast, drowning out its bleating.

"Baah, baah, baah," they yelled as if mocking the animal.

The high priest—or so Kleopatra assumed because he wore a goat's head as a headdress—held his arms up to the crowd in a request for quiet. As they settled, he called out in prayer: "Inuus, who makes fertile the men and women of Mighty Rome, accept our offering and hear our prayers. Receive the honors we bestow upon you this day as you have for every year since time out of mind. Grant us this day that every Roman man finds his gods-given masculinity, and that every Roman wife shall receive the seed to become a mother. For the glory of the god and for the glory of Rome!"

The throng began to chant the name of the god again, its syllables making a drumbeat that reverberated through the Forum. One priest held the goat by its rear legs and the other slit its throat, letting the animal's blood drain into a silver bowl at Caesar's feet. Though he was several feet above them, Caesar had to draw his long legs back so that his toga was not splattered. The chanting broke into screams so loud that Kleopatra wondered if a riot was breaking out. Her heart quickened. Caesar was alone on his throne, virtually unprotected as always. Her first thought was to jump from the bleachers and throw her body upon his. But Caesar was smiling and did not seem threatened at all. She grabbed Hammonius's arm, and he patted her hand and pointed to the north end of the Forum.

Two lines of men in loincloths came charging up the Via Sacra, running into the Forum shouting the name of the god and carrying goat-hide whips that they flailed above their heads. They must have searched out the most virile among them for the ceremony, for they were mostly as young and taut as Olympians, but without the dignity of those athletes. They seemed to Kleopatra to be drunk, hooting and screaming at any women they could reach and striking them with the whips. The women did not shrink back, but held out their palms, fighting one another to get flogged. Some of the men struck the women on the body, aiming for more sensuous places than their outstretched hands, but the women did not seem to mind. In fact, they offered themselves whole-heartedly to the whip—not just common women but the most digni-fied in all of Rome. Kleopatra recognized Porcia and her sister Junia Terentia in the front of the crowd, their white palms outstretched, their chests raised high, laughing as they received their blows.

"What does this mean?" Kleopatra asked.

"They believe the whipping makes them fertile," Hammonius said. "Every year after the festival, there are wondrous stories of women long past the years when conception is seemly, who find themselves with great swollen bellies. For the women already with child, it is said that the whipping makes their deliveries go quickly and with ease."

"It is a miracle that Calpurnia is not among them, chasing the whip," she said. But Calpurnia remained in her seat to the far right of Caesar's throne, surrounded by women her age who did not participate.

One by one, after the men had performed the ritual, they passed before Caesar and hailed him, and he raised his increasingly regal hand and hailed them back.

The only runner who did not carry a whip was the eldest, Antony. He was heavier than the others, fuller in chest and thigh, meaty even. The young ones had the finer musculature of boys turning into men, whereas Antony had already accomplished that feat and was a keen spec-imen of the sex, or so Kleopatra thought as her eyes followed him. In his hands was a white crown covered in laurel leaves, the diadem of a monarch. He held it high above his head for all to see, showing it to the crowd as if he were trying to sell it. Then he knelt before Caesar, bowed his head dramatically, and offered him the crown.

Suddenly, there was immense silence, as quiet in its magnitude as the noise that had come before it. Kleopatra held her breath. This was the test that they had so carefully planned. Caesar, before every important personage in Rome and many who were not so crucial, would reject the crown. If the majority protested and encouraged him, he would accept it—publicly for all to see, not quietly and as a result of some conspir-acy that his opponents could criticize and challenge.

Kleopatra had supported this plan. "If Rome is a Republic, and if the overwhelming majority of the Republic wishes you to be king, then you must accept their wishes."

"Paradoxical but true, my dear," he had said. Antony had agreed and had invented the particulars of how and when it would happen. When Antony laid out the details, Caesar had said that he possessed the dramatic talents of a Euripides, and Antony had grinned broadly like a boy.

"Take it away, my son," Caesar called to Antony, and the crowd exploded, some cheering the refusal, others begging Caesar to take it. Antony pretended that Caesar had offended him. He pulled his head back and scowled, first at Caesar, then at the crowd, turning far to his right and to his left for all to see the displeasure on his face. He called for three of his associates to lift him on their shoulders. Carried forward as if mounted on some lumbering animal, he approached the Rostra once more and, this time, tried to place the crown on Caesar's head. Caesar waited for a moment and then shielded himself with his hand, turning the crown away. The crowd now began to cheer more and more, chanting the name of Caesar. Kleopatra thought it difficult to gauge their reaction. She imagined that it could easily be construed that they wished Caesar to take the crown. And she wished he would accept it just to see the reaction. After all, if the response was negative, he could always give it back. "If the majority objects, you can take it from your head, fling it to the ground, and stomp on it!" she had told him.

But Caesar was acting conservatively. Antony proffered the crown once again, and this time, Caesar shook his head slowly and dramatically in the negative for all to see. Then, according to plan, he called out to Lucius Cotta to have the event recorded in the public records.

"Let it be written that on this day, the fourteenth of February, before the people of Rome, Caesar was thrice offered the crown of a monarch and thrice he refused it."

Even to the ear of a queen who wished to hear otherwise, the Roman people unmistakably cheered his words.

The Vestal Virgins, the High Priestesses of Rome, keepers of the flame of the hearth-goddess, Vesta, that lit every Roman fire and burned day and night atop her temple, were not above the bribe. In addition to this duty, they also vaulted in their temple all official Roman documents, holding them in safety and secrecy. Hammonius had made contact with one of the youngest, Belinda, whose bitterness at her family for forcing her to forsake the love of a man and honor them with her position made her amenable to betrayal. She feared for her life, so that his discretion was mandatory. He swore it on all manner of gods and principles, and, to the best of his ability, made the queen swear the same, though he was but her servant and unable to enforce anything upon her. "Please swear it on the memory of your father," he implored her. "For the young woman will be flung into the Tiber if she is found out."

And so Kleopatra promised it, knowing that the information she gleaned would have to remain private.

Caesar had made a will. He retired to a country estate to document his final wishes, and he refused to reveal its contents. "I am not so very *old*," he told her, "that we should concern ourselves with the advent of my demise. But I am planning a two-year campaign, and the gods may have it that it is my last. I do not wish my estates to be challenged. Rome does not need to fight more internal battles over money and property. And besides, I have already told you that it is illegal according to Roman law to leave property to a foreigner, which, regrettably, until we can change the law, our son must be regarded as such."

"And that is that?" she asked.

"Yes, my dear, that is that."

He promised that as soon as he was able to declare victory over Parthia, his friend and supporter Lucius Cotta along with a group of others would put forth the bill that Caesar be given the special privilege of marrying any number of wives he wished in order to produce an heir. And no one, not Cicero, not Brutus, not the most strident of constitutionalists, would contest it if Caesar had added the vast and thus far unconquerable territory of Parthia to the empire.

"It is the most expedient solution, Kleopatra. I will not have to alienate my countrymen by putting Calpurnia away. You and I will marry in Egypt, and there I will be your king. I will remain Rome's dictator until someone has a better idea. Our son will be legitimate, you will be my wife, and we will proceed from there."

She knew that anything more in her favor was impossible, but she wanted a guarantee of some sort, which neither Caesar nor the gods could give. She would have to take yet another risk in a lifetime whose path looked like one long backbone of risk upon risk.

"My darling, you look at me most pitifully, as if our son requires my money for his daily bread," Caesar said. "Unlike you, I have no title that I might pass to him. It is merely a question of some money—much less than you yourself possess. Please be reasonable. This is the best we can hope for at this time."

Still, she wondered if he was covering up something, so she gave Hammonius a purse heavy with gold to pass quietly to Belinda, who reported the contents of the will. That maiden informed Hammonius that the Roman people were Caesar's primary heir. He was leaving a massive portion of his fortune to the individual citizens of Rome. His secondary heir, who was to receive virtually everything else was Octavian, the malnourished nephew.

"It's only money, Your Majesty," said Hammonius, and Kleopatra agreed. "And your son is a king, with a king's treasure. Money is the single ingredient of his power that he need not acquire from his father."

Marcus Lepidus had the finest mansion in the city of Rome—or the finest one paid for with his own money and not stolen in the war, Antony joked. Kleopatra was a guest in that home for the week so that she might enjoy more time with Caesar in the days before he left Rome. Little Caesar remained behind at the villa under Charmion's supervision, and Kleopatra wished that she might have used those final days together to further imprint the affection of father upon son, but Caesar did not want the boy to stay in the city, where he might be vulnerable to foreign diseases and to the dictator's own enemies.

They were gathered around ten large round tables, the men reclining on couches and the women sitting in chairs as was Roman custom. It was the fourteenth of March, the month of Mars, the Roman war god, and Caesar was to depart in four days to launch the greatest campaign in Rome's seven-hundred-year history. Lepidus had gathered Caesar's most faithful friends and supporters to honor him at a dinner. It would certainly be two years before they saw the great man on home soil again.

"Marcus Brutus is conspicuously absent," Kleopatra whispered to Caesar and Lepidus. "In fact, none of Servilia's clan is here."

"Oh, it is more fun without Brutus's somber countenance to rain on our fun," Lepidus replied.

"He is serious by nature," said Caesar. "It is not an easy temperament to disguise for the sake of socializing."

Antony was festive throughout the meal, proposing toasts to the future, and lavishing the attention he had previously given to Kleopatra upon his wife, Fulvia. She was a tall woman, fair-skinned and striking, with almost black eyes and dark hair hennaed to a deep red. Kleopatra noticed the respect she commanded from Antony's peers. She spent the evening in deep conversation with one senator or another, whispering in emphatic tones about policy and civic affairs. Her opinion was sought, even courted. Despite the respect given her, and the smiles and caresses she received from her handsome husband, she was prone to frowning. The single line in her face cut across the space between her eyebrows like a deep canal, ruining the symmetry of her beauty. It seemed that she was as serious as Antony was playful, and he went out of his way to keep her in good humor.

A few nights before, Caesar had commented to Kleopatra in the privacy of their bedroom that he did not quite understand a man like Antony—a man who commanded legions of men, but was so susceptible to a woman. "When Antony was under the influence of the actress, he was debauched. Now that he is married to Fulvia, a taskmaster if there ever was one, he is a model statesman."

"Perhaps women have greater influence than Romans give credit," Kleopatra had answered, wondering where Caesar placed her influence over him in the realm of his life.

"It makes me think of the ancient rituals where men dressed in women's clothing to steal some of their mysterious and life-giving powers," Caesar had said. "That was surely what Clodius was doing when he was caught with my wife Pompeia at the festival of the Good Goddess. He had donned women's clothes, sneaked into the festival, and had his way with my wife on the couch. I believe he was trying to either steal her power, or steal mine through her."

"The goddess gives life to all," Kleopatra had said. "It is not a mistake to seek her wisdom and strength in the mortals of her sex."

"My dear, you do not have to convince me of that fact."

Tonight, after the meal, Antony worked his way around the room to Kleopatra's table, whispering in her ear that he must talk to her.

"Would you like to take the air in the garden, Your Majesty?" he asked her aloud.

Kleopatra noticed that Fulvia's gaze had followed Antony around the room and straight to the queen, who gave him her hand and allowed him to escort her outside, aware that the two black spies of Fulvia's eyes did not leave them until they disappeared from the banqueting room. He led her into the small garden, for no mansions within the city limits had the sprawling manicured outdoor spaces such as she knew in Alexandria. But there were rows of potted citrus trees offering lemons and oranges, and ambitious climbing roses that crawled up the garden walls, mingling sweet pleasant smells. Antony led her to a secluded spot.

"What is it, Antony? You look so glum. What serious matter is causing you to interrupt your fun and risk your wife's suspicions?"

Antony let himself smile again, but he had clearly not brought her into a private area just to play with her attentions. "Did you notice that Caesar didn't eat a morsel of food?"

"He rarely does these days. I suppose the details of planning the campaign and the details of leaving Rome in secure hands have left little room for an appetite."

"It is more than that. I believe he is far too ill to leave the country, but he won't listen to me. I was hoping he might listen to you."

Kleopatra grimaced. She had hoped that her own worry over Caesar's condition was ill-founded, the result, as he so often suggested, of her natural womanly concerns. "I have in my entourage the finest doctor in Alexandria, a medical genius. I have asked Caesar many times to be examined by him, but he refuses, no matter how I beg or cajole. He says that illness is caused in the mind, and if the mind of Caesar refuses to entertain the thought of illness, the body will not get the idea to be sick."

"He is sick nonetheless. A few days ago, I brought an assembly of senators before him to discuss certain burning issues. When we approached him, he sat back in his throne holding his head, barely acknowledging our presence, as if he was on the verge of another of his spells. The men were mostly insulted that he didn't even rise to greet them. Others could see that he was sick. And that is worse indeed, for they will surely find ways to use weakness of any sort against him. Some of the men left that meeting saying that Caesar was now so regal that he needn't rise to meet his peers; others have spread the word that he is ill and incapable of leading either a war or an empire. Either way, the incident has worked in his disfavor."

She did not dare tell Antony of the most recent telltale sign of Caesar's failing health. For the first time, in recent days, he had been unable to make love. Caesar put it down to fatigue, and Kleopatra ascribed it to worry, but privately she wondered if it was but another sign—along with his yellow complexion and his lackluster smile—of a physical decline of a more permanent nature.

"But what are we going to do? He listens to no one." She could see that Antony was frustrated, perhaps because he shared her position. All that they planned depended upon Caesar. What would happen to them if he failed, either in health or in war? The unasked question hung in the air between them.

Antony spoke in hushed urgency, bowing his head so that their faces were close. She could smell the touch of wine on him, though he hardly seemed intoxicated. "I believe, madam, that he might listen to you. What will happen if I am in Macedonia and you are in Alexandria and Caesar—may the gods forbid it and forgive even the utterance of these words—falls ill on his journey? What happens if he dies? Do you know how many factions would war with one another for his power? The world would be in turmoil."

"And where would you stand?" she asked pointedly. "With me and my son? With Brutus and his ilk? With Lepidus and his money?"

Antony moved even closer to her so that she could feel his warm breath on her face. "I find that women's minds are always the quicker. You are bold, Your Majesty, and far more favored by the gods than my wife, who should be in the senate, but had the misfortune of being born a woman."

"I will thank you to remember that a queen is not lucky, but chosen by the gods. Fulvia is not unlucky, merely unchosen."

"Have I insulted where I only meant a gracious compliment?" Charm fell from his smile, coating his words.

"You have not insulted, but you have also not answered my question."

"Should anything happen to Caesar, I must contrive to be Caesar— though no man will be able to fill that singular position. And in that contrivance, I will have to take over any *number* of his most important duties."

When she realized what he meant, she stopped breathing. He took her hand, swallowing it whole in his two huge ones. His skin was hard and hot against her cooler flesh.

"Should Caesar face either defeat or death, I will always protect both you and the prince. No matter who else I take as my ally."

"I am relieved to hear it, Antony, and I will take you at your word." She withdrew her hand, for she did not know how many bargains she was making in that caress.

"And you, Your Majesty, will you keep our alliance? Or will you skip over your friend who will be so very far away in Macedonia, and run to the senators most anxious to call your country's money and resources their own?"

That was an interesting question. How far would their alliance carry their dreams and ambitions without the might and genius of Caesar to direct them? Only the gods could say, and though she silently prayed for it, Kleopatra was not receiving any direct word of counsel from them at this moment. All she had to guide her answer was Antony's penetrating stare, his history as a great warrior who could control many thousands of men, his florid oratory that could twist ornery opponents to his way of thinking, and the sense that whatever happened, he was destined to be a part of her future. When she thought of those who might try to assume power in Caesar's wake—Brutus, Cassius, Lepidus, Cicero—she could not imagine that she could forge any lasting alliance with them. Though the lot of them were polite, they hated and feared both her and her son. But here was Antony pledging his loyalty and only asking for hers in return. Whether he would make good on his promise she did not know and could not foresee. Men made many vows that were broken with the changing tides of Lady Fortune. Perhaps Antony would try to assume Caesar's place in her bed only to sell her out to his Roman allies. It was a chance she would have to take until a better option presented itself. But she believed that Caesar's observations about Antony gave credence to her decision. If he were so easily molded by the woman in his life, then why, at some juncture, should that woman not be herself?

"In all of Rome, Marcus Antonius, you are my only true friend and ally. I intend for you to remain as such no matter what the future brings us."

He took her hand again. The mischief in his eyes reawakened as if from a hard slumber. He kissed her hand, opened her palm, and drew a line across it. "Kleopatra, I should like to exchange blood with you as my schoolmates and I used to do when we made boyhood pacts. But I cannot send you back to Caesar dripping in blood, now can I?"

When they returned to the banqueting room, they were met with dozens of pairs of eyes, though no one commented on their absence. Caesar was eating a pear and drinking a cup of wine. He looked better than he had in days.

"General, was it my absence that brought back your appetite?" Antony asked, laughing, and everyone joined in.

"All of your appetites shame those of other men, my son," Caesar replied, and everyone laughed harder, especially Fulvia, who threw her head back so that Kleopatra could see the sculpture of her teeth.

"We were just playing a game," Fulvia said. "We are going around the room and everyone must answer this question: What is the most preferable kind of death?"

"What grim game is this, madam?" Kleopatra asked. "In my country, conversation at dinner, though often philosophical in nature, takes on a livelier tone."

"You shall see the fun in it, Your Majesty. Marcus Lepidus wishes his heart to fail while deflowering a fine young virgin. Lucius Cotta would like to fall from his favorite horse after a gallop at dawn."

"I see. Well, for myself, I should like to live to be a very old woman, and then ascend into the heavens, flying on the swift wings of Pegasus."

"That is a death for a deity, Your Majesty," Fulvia said.

"That is correct, madam," Kleopatra retorted. "Except for the fact that the gods are immortal."

Antony quickly interrupted the exchange between the women. "I should like to die making love to my wife, an experience unequalled by any other, making all the rest of life seem so very tedious by comparison. That is my wish."

He kissed Fulvia on the nose, which had the immediate effect of relaxing the crevice in her forehead and restoring a smile to her face, while Kleopatra wondered if what he said was true. She felt an unexpected twinge of jealousy, doubting the intensity she'd felt from him moments before when she'd been the object of his attention.

"And you, Caesar?" Fulvia asked.

Caesar hesitated not one moment. He turned his palms upward, making wings out of his arms. "The method hardly matters. The best death, my dears, is a sudden and expedient one."

He walked alone to the senate meeting. Calpurnia had been unwell that morning, sick with dark dreams the night before, begging him to stay and give her solace. She held the hem of his robe as he left the house, saying that the grim skies were inauspicious enough, that he should stay indoors until the sun broke. But he would not give his opponents another reason to criticize him, to interpret his absence as meaning he thought himself too high and mighty now to even attend the meetings of the senate. He would not falter. He was too close to his goal, too close to departing Rome in a state of glory with the greatest army ever assembled. Too close to amassing as much turf for the empire as Alexander had added to his. It would be a long journey, but when he was done, no one would be able to level criticism against him again. His supporters had dug up an old line from the Sybilline Holy Books prophesying that only a king could defeat the Parthian menace. And so the senate had decreed that Caesar might be called king as long as he was away from the capital. That was the first in a short line of steps ascending to the heights he intended to reach.

Still, he was weary this morning, as if the night's sleep had not cast its refreshing dew upon him. So odd for him to be unable to shake the fatigue. He had not slept well in so long. Whenever he closed his eyes and drifted away, he went to a place he did not know, and *she* was there, asking him about his plans, if he was sure that he had prepared long enough and well enough. Of course I'm sure, he always replied, staring into her deep blue eyes until he was dizzy with her power. For she was the woman they all sought, the woman of beauty, of strength, of life itself. All flowed from her, and here she was, visiting him every night. His lifelong love.

He thought of Calpurnia's foolish worries. What was a black sky when Venus herself was the eternal sunshine that hovered above him?

He passed Antony in the alley beside the chamber, embroiled in a heated discussion with Brutus Albinus, a long-winded man. Caesar did not know whether to encourage Antony to remain in the conversation, keeping the dull Albinus from further sullying his own day with one of his endless diatribes on the senate floor, or to interrupt Albinus and save Antony from the dreary duty of listening to him. He chose the course of least resistance, waved to Antony, and moved on.

He entered the chamber, adjacent to the theater Pompey had built. The senate had demanded to meet there today, and he wondered if this was symbolic on their part; would he have to sit through another long exhortation about restoring the Republic, during which they would endlessly revive the memory of Pompey and all the old values for which he had stood? The Republic was as dead as poor Pompey, and no amount of verbiage from a bunch of deluded old men would bring it back. Not in their lifetimes, nor in Caesar's lifetime. Yet there was Pompey's statue, tall and stately like the man himself, rising from its pedestal as if to greet him. Caesar raised his right hand at his old friend, remembering happier times when he and Pompey each held the hand of Julia and wished for eternal happiness and alliance.

The senators stood upon his entrance, immediately surrounding him and wasting no time in issuing their petitions. Tillius Cimber, whose brother was in exile, thrust into Caesar's hand a request for his return, accompanied by a verbal argument reminding Caesar of his own renowned mercy. The others were gathered around him, too, shouting their demands so that Cimber was drowned out.

"Gentlemen, please!" he shouted, annoyed. Their voices rang in his ears; it was intolerable. He clutched his head. "Not today." He wanted nothing more than for them to go away. He felt light in the head, and he did not know if he was succumbing to a spell or whether he had simply forgotten to take his breakfast, what with his urgency to get away from Calpurnia's histrionics.

Cimber retracted his arm and put the proposal in his pocket. He stared at Caesar, and then with great determination pulled his toga down away from his neck. Caesar wondered if Cimber was going to resign his position in protest against his brother's exile. He had little patience at that moment for such dramatics, and he hoped Cimber was not going to start something.

Silence fell upon the senate—a merciful silence as far as Caesar was concerned. One of the Casca brothers, Publius Longinus, approached him, and Caesar hoped it was not another petition, for Casca was nervous and sweaty and reaching into his *umbro*, probably fumbling for the piece of paper that declared his demand. Caesar put his hand up to stop him before he could speak. But Casca's trembling, freckled hand produced a glinting thing, which Caesar could not quite see, and thrust it into Caesar's neck. He felt the pain—agonizingly sharp, like the worst wound he had ever taken in battle—and he saw the blood spurt from his neck. He put up one hand to defend himself from another blow, and with the other grabbed Casca's dagger, wet with his own blood. He looked into his assailant's frantic eyes. Twisting his arm as hard as he could, he demanded, "What evil is this?"

Despite the pain and the blood, he realized he was not badly hurt, and he looked past Casca into the room to see who would first apprehend this madman. Every face looked on in horror, but no one moved to help him.

"Brother, help!" Casca called out, and suddenly Caesar saw a host of daggers fly at him. He took a knife in the leg, another in the gut, several from behind, stabbing his back and making him throw himself forward into another blow. He turned away from each one only to meet another. He was nothing now but an animal hunted, with no odds in his favor. He took a blow from Cassius, who stabbed him with a cold, determined, slit-eyed look. Caesar took Cassius by the hair and pulled his head toward him, biting his ear until he had a piece of it in his mouth. He spat it out, elbowing someone behind him who had just thrust another dagger into his back. He fought like a wild beast, looking everywhere for Antony, but not finding him. The face he saw instead, not inches from his own, was that of Brutus, who grabbed him by his robes and held him close. Was Brutus going to save him? Caesar looked straight into the tense eyes and saw his own death. "You, too, my child?" he asked him in Greek, the language in which they communicated. Brutus's face was full of terror, his bushy eyebrows wild like weeds, his mouth skewed into a contorted gaping hole. Caesar saw Brutus's confusion and smiled at him, which seemed to set the man on a deadly course, as if the father had mocked the threat of the son. Brutus let out a little cry, and Caesar felt the deepest cut of all in his belly.

Caesar gagged on his own pain, a throaty lamentation into the air, acknowledged by no one. Surrounded by men he had known all the days of his life, he was utterly alone.

Through the window he saw a ray of sunlight swell through a black cloud, making a crucifix of light. The light grew taller and wider, taking over the scenery around it until it was all that he could see. No longer could he hear even the cries of his own pain, though he was aware that his body was in agony and his voice still cried out for someone to help him. He could hear nothing at all but that familiar silent hush of his spells. He could not stop looking at the light, whiter than anything he had ever seen, whiter than the clouds that covered the Italian mountains like collars of fur. Whiter than snow, and with a shimmer of gold at its edges. He left his body entirely behind on the senate floor and walked toward the glittering shaft. Out of its great gleam, suddenly *she* emerged, more beautiful in this radiant manifestation than she had ever appeared before. She was huge now, taller than him, taller than any mortal, and the light spread about her as if a part of her being. She carried it with her as she moved to Caesar, drenched in it as if in some glorious bath.

Do you like the light of heaven? she asked him, all smiles. Here was the fickle beauty who had given him great Fortune and safe harbor all the days of his life. He knew that she was not toying with him as she had done in the past. She was finally ready to unite with him forever in perfect and divine union. *Come with me,* she seemed to say through her smile. *Take your place with us at last.*

Caesar looked back at his body, still twisting and turning against the blows of the senators, and he made his last conscious choice for that self he was leaving behind. The last human gesture of Gaius Julius Caesar, dictator of Rome, was to cover his body with his cloak and let them finish him off, because that was the only way to leave the pain behind and to walk into the exhilaration she offered.

Are you ready to be rejoined for all time with your fellow gods? she asked.

Finally, the proof. He was so pleased to see that he'd been right all along, that he had indeed been a god, descended from a goddess. They had doubted him, but as usual, he had the last laugh. "So I have been right?" he asked.

Oh yes, she explained. For not only was he a god, but so were all mortals gods in disguise, divorced from their divine lineage, their true identities shrouded from their earthly selves. That is what she now revealed to him: He had been one of the rare humans who had not forgotten the connection with his divine self, and had lived like a god all of his mortal life.

Caesar stood with the goddess at the entrance to the chamber, where he could see Antony still trying to disengage from Albinus. At least that son was a loyal one. Octavian would have Caesar's money, and Antony his power, and all would be as it should. The goddess instantly read Caesar's thoughts. *One possibility in a world of endless varieties of possibility,* she said. She cracked the sky, revealing to him the many layers of possibilities that represented the futures of those he was leaving behind. He watched in awe, with a multiplicity of vision he'd never known in his mortal life, all the possible variations of the same drama he was leaving behind. He saw that the drama shifted and the stories changed as the players made decisions, turning their lives one way or another, each action affecting themselves and those around them. *You see, Great Caesar,* she said, *this is the way in which mortals retain the power of the divine—in every earthly choice they make.*

"But it's a paradox," he said. "Human beings are in control of everything and nothing at all."

Yes, she answered, her coy smile spreading joy across her lovely face. *It is that simple.*

Caesar brought his attention back to the present moment, which now seemed an awkward lump in the straight arrow of earthly time—time he would soon leave behind forever. He realized that he was to join *forever,* to be a part of the very idea of it; that he would now attain the immortality that he had so fruitlessly sought on earth.

Inside the chamber, the statue of Pompey presided over the murder, watching it all from his pedestal, staring down remorselessly at Caesar's bloody body. The men were still stabbing frantically, white cloaks splattered with his blood, as if they were afraid to stop, for then they would have to face the consequences of their actions. Like puppets driven by some master who was divorced from his own reason, they continued to pour wounds into a lifeless body.

"It hardly matters, does it?" he said, turning to her and letting any sadness he felt melt away in her radiance. And she agreed. *Yes, Caesar, it all melts away in the ether. Shall we go? There are those on the other side who are most anxious to see you.*

"Julia?" he asked hopefully.

Oh yes, Julia and so many more. You shall have a triumphal parade the likes of which you have never known. But this time, the victory is sweet and uncontested, and there are no enemies. All is honor.

He felt light and giddy, pulled irretrievably away from all that he had known, but then something yanked him back to the corporeal world. Suddenly, at the house of Marcus Lepidus, where Caesar had dined the night before, he saw Kleopatra standing on a balcony staring at the same strange crucifix of light, an expression of stark fear on her face. He could hear his murderers begin to yell in the streets. *Liberty! Liberty!* Kleopatra heard this, and he knew that she knew in that instant what had happened. How he wanted to hold her, to send her this great love that he felt, and the knowledge that all things of this earth fade into the luster of heaven.

"But we haven't finished yet, she and I," he protested, hoping that the goddess would allow him this final gesture to the woman he was leaving to her own Fate.

Oh yes you have, my darling. Time has another agenda.

Caesar sighed, letting the sight of Kleopatra slip away as the goddess took his hand and gently led him home.

Kleopatra felt a chill slip into her body, making ice of her blood. She breathed deeply and then shuddered, holding herself tighter, a look of panic spreading across her worried face. She was engulfed by the very scent of him, the gentle essence of eucalyptus his manservant rubbed into his shoulders and arms in the morning after his bath, and the deeper smell all his own that lay underneath the aroma of oil. She opened her arms to clasp him, hoping that some part of him would come to her, would hold her, would take her with him. But her embrace was empty. She had felt him for a fleeting moment, just as surely as she had held him night after night in their bed. It was unmistakably him, but in seconds he was gone, leaving her to confront the future without him. Now she could barely sense her own body. Frozen, arms wrapped about herself, she felt her knees buckle, and she fell to the ground. She put her hands on the cold tile, and yet her flesh was colder still. She tried to bal-

ance herself, but could not, and rolled to her side so that she lay like a
baby on the rigid floor, curled about herself, biting her hand and feeling nothing.

She heard the cries in the streets escalate. *Liberty! Liberty! The tyrant is
dead! Long live the Republic!* People screamed in horror, anguished moans
wailing in response to this news. She wondered who exactly it was who
had liberated the earth of Julius Caesar. Which son was it who had slain
the father to collect his inheritance? She did not have to ask the question twice, for she knew which son was prepared to murder for an ide-
ology. And if he had taken such a cold-blooded step, killing the man
whom he called father, the man who had mentored him all the days of
his life, who spoke to him in loving tones in Greek over philosophy and
poetics, who had forgiven him for joining Pompey's war against him,
who had honored him even after his betrayal—if Brutus could manage
that, then would he not at this moment be wiping his dagger clean of
Caesar's blood to use on her and her son? If they had killed the father,
would the true son of his blood not be the next target? If the son was
to die, then so too his mother, so that no one would be alive to take
vengeance. Son and mother to be wiped out, leaving no one to threaten
the claims of the assassins.

And what of Antony? Kleopatra could not imagine that anyone
could harm Caesar while Antony was around—unless Antony was in on
the conspiracy. She let herself ponder this evil for a moment, until she
thought she would retch. But she did not have the luxury of being ill
now, and she breathed deeply until the desire to empty her insides sub-
sided.

She lay on the floor for a long time, unable to move, shivering against
the cool morning air and the tiles still damp with the morning dew. She
knew that action had to be taken, preparations made, safety sought, but
she could not imagine what to do. She remembered that she had felt this
way before, been a player in this kind of predicament, and had survived.
When her father had died, she was left alone, without the sanctuary of
his power, a teenage queen with hostile factions against her. Was there
not one safe place in the world? Was there no person to whom one could
turn for protection? She clenched her hand into a fist and bit it even
harder until she could once again feel pain. She let her teeth sink into
her soft skin, breaking it, until she could take the infliction no longer.

No, there was no such being anywhere on the earth, no person of such power and magnitude that he might direct events in her favor. *We come into this world alone and thus we leave it.* And in the interim, there was little respite from that solitary fate. Henceforth, she realized, it was but herself and the gods—no father, no Caesar, no mortal individual in whose power she might rest. No mortal could accomplish for her what she must petition from her own strength and from the gods. And so she appealed to them, for they were the solution to every grim situation.

Mother Isis, Lady of Compassion, once again you have taken away the source of my power, leaving me alone on this earth without mother or father or husband. It is only I who can protect the kingdom of my ancestors and my tiny son, the true prince of Egypt and the only true son of Caesar. Once again I ask you to restore my power to me so that I may carry out your purpose on earth, not in the body of another, but in my own person, where only you and I may guide my actions and declare Destiny. I ask you this as your humble daughter, in all sacredness. Let me survive.

Hot tears came falling down her face, cutting warm little rivers over her cold cheeks. She should not cry now, not when there was so much to be done. She would weep later, much later, when she and her son were safe and back on Egyptian soil. She forced herself to sit up, wiping the tears from her eyes. Wobbling, she stood, holding the wooden rail for support.

Under the noise in the streets, Kleopatra heard an unmistakable, rhythmic beat. She had heard it so many times before that she knew it was the pounding of the sandaled feet of Roman soldiers marching toward the center of the city. Now there would be war, and she was miles away from her son. *Mother, please, he is but a little child. Help him!* She had neither the energy nor the imagination to elaborate on her prayer.

A tall man in a tattered peasant's cloak rushed onto the balcony. She shrank from him, but he pushed his hood away from his face and she saw that it was Antony. He put an arm around her. "Quickly," he said. "You must go inside." She had not the strength to question him, nor the need, for she knew very well the chain of events that had brought him here in disguise. She was relieved to see him, not just because he represented a friend and ally of both herself and Caesar, but because his presence exonerated him from participation in the terrible crime.

"You realize what has happened?" Antony asked.

"It is being shouted in the streets," she said.

"And you realize what that means? We must get you out of Rome."

"Tell me what happened," she said, choking on her words. "Was it Brutus?"

"Not now, Kleopatra. There is no time for talk. Lepidus has called his troops stationed on Tiber Island and they are marching on the city."

"You are going to war with Caesar's murderers?"

"No. I am going to negotiate with them."

Kleopatra was shocked at the news. "But how can you?"

Antony's face was lit with an energy that she had yet to see in him. He was entirely calm, though marvelously alert. He was glowing, as if driven by a light within. "There is no time for emotion. War must be averted, power seized. The greatness that was Julius Caesar is dispersed in his death."

"Just tell me, was it Brutus?" She wanted to know. She had warned Caesar, and he had ignored her. He must have wanted this death, designed it somehow, with an unspoken will. Why would he leave her?

"Yes, Brutus. And many others. But they were scorned, not praised, when they ran through the streets shouting their news. People threw rocks at them and chased them away. Apparently they had no plan of action. I suppose they thought they would be thanked for their crime." Antony smiled bitterly at the irony. He took Kleopatra's face in his large hand, his fingers very warm and gentle against her cold cheek. "No tears now. We will all cry later. I must go now, first to Calpurnia, and then to the assassins."

"To console her?" Kleopatra asked in a strange voice that she did not recognize as her own.

Antony smiled again. "She has control over Caesar's private papers and a large fund that he used to pay his soldiers. Whoever has those tools has Caesar's power. Lepidus and I already have the loyalty of his troops."

"What do I do? My son is at the Janiculum villa with his nurses."

"You'll go back to Egypt and wait to hear from us. Arrangements are already being made for your voyage home, or so I am told by a Greek man who is at the door. He is detained by the guard until we verify his identity."

"Hammonius?" she asked. "Is he old and fat?" Her old friend and

Kinsman come once again to help her. Was there no end to his goodness and loyalty?

"No, he is young and slim and handsome for a Greek."

When she saw Archimedes, she saw not the lover of her womanhood, but the friend and protector of her youth. All that had passed between them—her betrayal in the name of politics and his bitterness at the loss of her—vanished in the sight of his familiar expression. "Cousin! Thank the gods it is you." She moved to put her arms around him, but something in his manner stopped her. He did not smile. She composed herself and stood still at Antony's side.

"Cousin." Archimedes bowed formally. The two soldiers who stood at his side fell back.

"He is your Kinsman, then?" Antony asked.

"Yes, he is my Kinsman," she said, smiling at him. For all that I have done to break his heart and wound his pride, he is still my faithful Kinsman. She felt tears well up again, and though she tried to check them, they ran freely down her face for him to see.

"I do apologize," Antony offered Archimedes. "I did seem to remember you in the king's service, but it has been so many years since I was in Alexandria."

"I appreciate your precautions," Archimedes said.

"I must go, Kleopatra," Antony said. He embraced her, not as a man embraces a woman, but as she had seen him embrace Caesar many times, in a kind of fraternal hug. "Our alliance is not broken by this tragedy. You will hear from me shortly." He took her elbows and looked at her one last time. Then he pulled her close and whispered in her ear, "The sons of Caesar shall have their revenge." He released her, signaled his men, and rushed away.

It was dusk in the Forum. The day's black sky turned to the color of the sea at midnight, pink clouds hanging like rosy anvils over the square.

Kleopatra stood with her cousin, dressed as one of his guard, wearing a short chiton, thick leather sandals, and a white cloak bordered with a Greek pattern of gold. She had forced Lepidus's maid to chop off her hair, and now it hung about her ears and forehead in little ringlets, making it exactly like Archimedes' cut. She had lost weight during the last months of constant anxiety, and she looked like a fifteen-year-old boy, going to honor the fallen dictator with a young uncle.

People poured into the square from all entrances, carrying gifts to lay at the body of Caesar. Soldiers came with the arms they had used under his command. Women brought their family jewelry and the amulets that had protected their children. The poor brought simple household items, well-worn pots and kettles that were undoubtedly the only goods they had to offer, while servants of the wealthy carted bronze goblets and bowls, silver chalices and wine bowls, and statues of their household gods.

Hammonius had already left the city for Janiculum Hill, where he would secure Caesarion and the entourage and see them safely to Ostia. There they would board a vessel for Alexandria that would leave in the morning. Archimedes had arranged with Antony for a guard to wait at the port until the boat was safely at sea.

But Kleopatra had heard that the citizens of Rome were outraged at the death of Caesar, and had already begun a fire in the Field of Mars, where, years before, they had taken the body of his daughter Julia, stolen from the house of Pompey, and cremated her for all of Rome to behold and to honor. Groups of mourners had gathered in the Forum, making public speeches and sacrifices, grieving, and waiting for Caesar's body to arrive so that they could make a spectacular funeral pyre to his glory. And she—lover, partner, ally—would not leave the city until she witnessed the spectacle and said good-bye to him along with his people.

"I thought I had ended my days of arguing with you against your unreasonable demands," Archimedes said without the slightest trace of emotion or humility. "Is your lust for adventure and intrigue so strong that you'll risk leaving a motherless son?"

"Caesar would not wish me to run off like a frightened child," she said. "There is always a way, Cousin, to be safe in the face of danger. I need not appear in the Forum as myself."

He smiled for the first time. "You're still the little girl who dreamed of running away with the slave Spartacus. You never change."

Now flocks of people—Romans and foreigners alike—poured into the Forum, each mourning Caesar according to their own custom. Jews in long black robes and wearing skullcaps walked slowly to the tune of their women, who took turns crying lamentations in their strange and guttural language. Blond-haired Gauls and Britons whose legs were wrapped in a fashion called trousers held gold breastplates to the skies as they let out short shrieks.

Roman sentinels on horseback trotted up the Via Sacra, blowing trumpets and crying, "Make way for the body of Caesar! Make way for our leader!" The throngs parted. Led by Antony and his soldiers, a procession of magistrates carried Caesar's body on an ivory funeral carriage. Trailing them were musicians playing a mournful tune, wearing the very clothes Caesar had donned in his triumphal parades. Kleopatra knew this because they had been on display in his office and he had shown them to her. The long procession walked slowly and solemnly toward the Rostra, where they laid him down. The body was cushioned by fabrics of purple and gold, and at the head hung the torn and bloody clothes in which the dictator had been murdered, blowing now in the breeze, billowing as if inhabited by Caesar's ghost. Four men carried a tall statue of Mother Venus from the temple to preside over the funeral, just as it was whispered throughout the crowd that the statue of Pompey had presided over the murder.

Antony climbed onto the Rostra and called for silence. He was in his senatorial robes, looking more like the solemn statesman than the fierce warrior. He raised his arms until the crowd was quiet.

"Many of you have asked me to speak tonight, to honor our fallen leader with a eulogy." Antony's voice was as powerful as his body—deep, intense, resonating until it hushed the emotional crowd. "But perhaps the greatest way that I may honor Caesar, and that you may know how deeply he loved the citizens of Rome, is to share with you the contents of his will, read to me today by his grief-stricken widow.

"Citizens! Who is Caesar's heir?"

Many shouted, "You are, Marcus Antonius! We will now follow you!"

Antony laughed, shaking his head. "No, my friends, I am not Caesar's heir. But you are! All of you. For our benevolent and all-knowing Caesar has left every Roman citizen, rich and poor alike, three pieces of gold from his personal fortune."

A huge cheer went up, but a woman standing near Kleopatra clutched her small son to her and began to cry. Antony called for silence once more.

"That is not all. He has also left us his lands by the Tiber to use as public parks for our pleasure and in his memory."

Now the mob chanted, *Caesar, Caesar, Caesar! Death to the assassins!* And people were shouting at Antony, begging him to help them kill those who had killed their leader. Even the soldiers, who until this moment had stood at absolute attention, began to yell. *Vengeance for Caesar! Vengeance for Caesar!*

Antony shook his head as if to agree with their desires, but he did not move to join the cause.

"Remember, citizens and soldiers, that Caesar was not a man of vengeance. He was a man of mercy. He had already forgiven once many of those who raised their daggers and drew their swords upon his undefended body after they had joined with Pompey against him in the war. Those men he might have slain, but he did not. He forgave them and he prospered them, thinking that mercy and forgiveness would breed the same.

"But let us talk more about Caesar the man. Citizens, he fed you, did he not, with his own money that he might have used to make his pockets all the heavier? Instead, he shared each and every victory and treasure with you. He gave you corn, oil, wine, and money. Not just his favorites, but every man, so that every man might take a small part of Rome's glory home with him and feed his family."

The Romans around Kleopatra were crying now, and she wanted to cry, too. Archimedes stood beside her, not touching her, watching in perfect stillness the eulogy of his rival, the man who had caused him so much pain. And yet Archimedes was there, always there, when she needed him. Before her father, he had taken the oath to protect the Royal Family, and despite what she had done to him, he had not reneged. Kleopatra could not reach out to him, so she wrapped her arms around herself for comfort.

Antony continued: "Friends, Gaius Julius Caesar was born fifty-six years ago into a Rome that was for the most part a league of Italian states. The Rome that he leaves us is an empire beyond the dreams and expectations of mortal men. Now Rome is everywhere, and that is because Caesar marched across the world and gave these countries Rome's name. And in his mercy and his wisdom, he did not trample upon those whom he had conquered, but raised them up and made them citizens and senators and statesmen. He did this in opposition to his enemies in the senate, those men who today poured their hatred into his body. Why? Because they feared his ambition.

"Friends, Julius Caesar made the common man a king, though on this very spot, he turned down the honor himself for all of Rome to see. And yet they did this to him. Citizens! Who are the assassins of Caesar?"

The mob chanted the names of the killers—*Brutus, Cassius, Casca, Cimber.*

"Yes, we know them by name, but who are they, I ask? They are those who most benefited from Caesar's victories, from Caesar's labor, from the many times Caesar put his person in jeopardy in yet another foreign land. Those are his slayers. They slew the body that in so many ways guaranteed them life.

"Citizens, our father is dead. The man who ended our civil wars, who imposed peace upon a nation at war with itself, a man who conquered the world in our name and for us, is dead. Caesar was our solution, and now our solution has been murdered. Citizens! Let each of us mourn him as we would our own father, because that is what he was. Not merely the Father of His Country, but a father to every Roman citizen.

"Young men, shed your tears, for you will not have such a father to bring you to manhood. Women of Rome, beat your breasts in grief, for you no longer have the father to protect you. Old men! You among all are the most melancholy, because you have seen Rome's greatness rise through the relentless efforts of Julius Caesar. Your lives have seen so much war, the wars that Caesar brought to conclusion. What will happen now?

"Citizens, I have met with Caesar's assassins."

Now the mob began to jeer and boo Antony, calling him a traitor, charging that he should have killed them and done so in the name of Julius Caesar and all of Rome. Antony responded to the shouting with the same slow, knowing shake of his head, offering empathy for their feelings but not agreement.

"Citizens, Caesar's assassins, our *liberators*, are foremost among those who mourn his passing." A rumble began at this unexpected news, and Antony once again demanded quiet.

"Why do they so mourn the man whose life they ended by their own swords?" Antony smiled broadly, as if about to deliver the punch line of a long joke. "They mourn, citizens, because every one of them was appointed to his post by Caesar. In killing Caesar and in calling for the repeal of his government, they have—according to the constitution— invalidated each and every one of their own positions. If Caesar's measures are repealed, so are the posts he appointed."

Antony let the irony sink into the minds of those who listened. Kleopatra could see men explaining the situation to their sons and wives, with either sad smiles or outrage breaking out across their faces.

"Citizens, we have come to this," Antony continued. "In order to keep their posts, Caesar's assassins, our *liberators*—now argue to allow Caesar's legislation to stand." He shook his head sadly. "Strange that they did not understand the wisdom in Caesar's appointments *before* they murdered him.

"And where does that leave us, my friends? That leaves us with Caesar's legacy, given to Rome's history by Caesar in his greatness, and held in place even by his own assassins. The only difference is that we no longer have Caesar himself to guide us.

"He was not a young man, nor was he a healthy man, but in three days' time, he was to take his leave to conquer once and for all in the name of Rome—in your names, citizens—that great barbarian land of Parthia that has threatened the safety of our empire for so many terror-filled decades. For Caesar wished for all the earth to be Rome, for every free man to be a Roman citizen, for every baby born on this earth to add to the glory of the empire. No less were his ambitions for you, citizens. And now we know that his ambitions were born out of his great love for us all. Citizens, the man whom the Holy Books proclaimed would defeat the Parthians has been murdered!

"Now those of us he left behind must set about his tasks in his memory, but without his leadership, praying to the gods to be gifted with just a portion of the wisdom, the strength, and the *genius* that they showered upon Caesar."

Kleopatra grabbed Archimedes' arm. "He is naming himself Caesar's successor."

Archimedes withdrew his arm and shot her a cold look. "I wonder, Cousin, in how many ways you will support that claim?"

She was about to chastise him for his insolence when something bright and swift and gleaming shot across the sky like an arrow from a warrior's bow. All heads lifted to see the cosmic wonder streak above, a shimmering white tail slashing the black of night. Two augurs rushed to the Rostra. Antony bent low so that they might deliver him news. All eyes were now upon him, and no one spoke until he broke the silence.

"I have just been informed by the Holiest of Holies that Caesar has ascended into the heavens and taken his place with the gods."

The citizens of Rome gave a collective gasp at the news of the dictator's ascension. Antony looked at the skies as if for another sign, another appearance from the spirit of Caesar, but darkness prevailed.

"I, for one, shall pray to Caesar," he said. "Not for myself, for Caesar knows my heart. No, I shall pray for his assassins. I shall pray for them that as he sits among the gods, Julius Caesar will demonstrate the same mercy and forgiveness he did when he was mortal and among us."

After a moment of silence, people began to pour forward to the funeral carriage, heaping their gifts upon Caesar's body. Men stormed the arenas where the magistrates met, tearing the judges' benches and spectators' bleachers from the ground to use for the pyre. Antony stepped aside as soldiers with torches set fire to the mounting heap around Caesar, and it rapidly took the flames. There was no order as people trampled one another to add to the mound of treasure dedicated to Caesar.

A young boy from the provinces carrying a farmer's tool jostled Kleopatra aside, dashing past her to offer his humble gift.

"We are getting out of here," Archimedes said, taking her arm and pulling her away. "No arguments, Your Majesty. Or I shall use force against you and face the consequences in Alexandria."

Kleopatra knew that to leave was to abandon every hope, every plan that she and Caesar had made together. As soon as she turned her back on the fire, all that she had built in her life would be dashed to shreds and she would once again be at the very beginning, the future a blank map upon which she must once again forge a path for herself, her son, her nation.

"I cannot go," she said. "Take Caesarion back to Egypt and wait for me."

"Yes, Your Majesty," he said with restrained mockery. "And as you have no enemies either in Rome or at home, I am certain both of you will be terribly safe."

She knew that he was right, that she must let go of all her dreams, or at least of this set of them, and return to her country to plan anew. She let him lead her through the crowd, staying close to him, letting his body be her shield against the masses that pushed against them to get to Caesar's body. She could barely breathe as he dragged her by the hand away from the spectacle. They pushed on through the throng, past the basilica dedicated to Julia, which the citizens were now tearing apart for the pyre, past the temple of Venus, where Kleopatra's statue stood. How long would it remain there now? she wondered. She imagined it being taken out and melted on the fire, the gold gilding Caesar's body, as if she were being cremated with him. Archimedes brought her to the Forum's exit. No one was leaving but them, and they stopped for a moment and looked back at the Rostra, where Antony stood watching his countrymen turn the funeral pyre into a spectacular theater of flames, burning upward and outward like a star on fire. Though the mob was out of control, destroying the Forum, battling one another to make final offerings to Caesar, and shouting demands for vengeance, Antony stood among them, fearless, in control, not flinching from the growing heat—all at once and for the very first time reminding Kleopatra of Caesar himself.

Part II

Alexandria:
the 8th year of
Kleopatra's reign

Kleopatra paced nervously across the deck of the ship. Only one day into her mission, the weather was inauspicious—no clouds overhead, and all the sky an unbroken sullen gray. If a storm swept across their path, it would be swift and deadly.

She did not feel well. Her stomach revolted against any and all kinds of food no matter how bland, and she was thinner now than when she was a girl. She did not know if it was because of anxiety, or because there was no man in her life for whom she wished to be womanly. She ran her hands down her sides, feeling the jut of her hipbones. She worried over her weight now. She could not afford frailty. Her son was still a baby, his father dead. What would become of the boy in the treacherous swarm of world politics if his mother perished?

Surely the events of the last year had taken a toll on her health. She had returned from the tragedy of Caesar's death to a country of plague, pestilence, and famine. The Nile had not risen that year; the crops had not grown. In the rural areas, there was widespread starvation. In the city, the plague, which had been threatening the harbor area for years, unleashed its black destruction, creeping into every corner of Alexandria. All over the city, bodies oozing with inky sores were thrown into hospital carts and burned in a perpetual pyre outside the city limits. Day and night that flame burned, fed with the blood of Egyptians,

Jews, Greeks, whose flesh mingled in the fire, defying the burial customs of each of those cultures, so many thousands of years old.

Egypt was in the grip of darkness, and yet deeper woes lurked at her borders. Antony had run Caesar's assassins out of Italy, and now Marcus Brutus and Cassius were at large in the eastern territories, threatening Kleopatra's kingdom. Cassius, hiding out off the coast of Egypt, had had the nerve to send a messenger demanding that Kleopatra release the legions Caesar had left in Alexandria to aid his cause. He had said that if the queen denied his request, he would march on Alexandria. Moreover, unless she gave him the full support of her army, navy, and treasury, he would back her exiled sister, Arsinoe, as queen of Egypt.

Though she did not have the forces to face his legions, Kleopatra decided to hold out against him, ignoring his demands, sending him a message that posed a simple question: "Is it wise for Caesar's assassin to ask the mother of Caesar's child for support?" Then she placed all her confidence in Antony, who had also called for her aid. Sailing now to him in Asia Minor with sixty warships, she had cast her lot with finality, and she hoped that she had chosen well. After Caesar's death, all civilized people—and the queen of Egypt was no exception—looked on in anticipation to see who would emerge the victor in the mad fray over Caesar's succession. The whole world was splitting apart, and it seemed that the only man who might hold it together was Antony. She was sure that her faith in him was justified, and yet she was so weary of Rome's fist squeezing the life out of Egypt and forcing her own hand. Here she was, sailing to answer a Roman call for aid at the risk of her own life, her own fleet, her own nation.

For over one year she had been watching the astonishing scramble for Caesar's power from Egypt's troubled shores, and she was anxious to see an end to it. In the interim, however, all the players had revealed their true character, but none as clearly as Caesar's heir, Octavian. Antony and Lepidus had taken a clear stance against the dictator's murderers, while Octavian, who proclaimed himself the New Caesar, danced on both sides of the fence. He sold all of Caesar's possessions and used the money to bribe Caesar's soldiers to join him. He paid each citizen the money promised to them in Caesar's will, using the rest of it to stage lavish games in Rome, allegedly in honor of Caesar, but the true purpose of which was to promote himself. On the other hand, he also aligned with some of Caesar's enemies and assassins, paying particular attention to Cicero, appealing to that old man's vanity and treating him as a mentor.

Kleopatra and her advisers had a difficult time sorting it all out: Caesar's second in command was now at war with Caesar's heir, who had aligned with Caesar's assassins, all the while presenting himself as the New Caesar. It was a puzzle. Finally, they heard that the assassins, with Octavian on their side, had squared off against Antony's forces at the battle of Mutina, after which Antony appeared defeated.

But Antony had rebounded by raising the biggest army Rome had ever seen. When Octavian realized that Antony could not be defeated again, he sent his mother, Atia, to Antony's mother, Julia, to secretly negotiate an alliance. At the Po River, with the mothers as mediators, Antony and Octavian met clandestinely and declared a new Coalition, in which they also included Lepidus for their bankroll. Antony sealed the alliance by marrying his stepdaughter, Clodia, to Octavian. Then Antony marched into Italy with ninety thousand men, scattering the assassins to the east.

Antony and his fellow triumvirs took control of the city of Rome, issuing a long proscription list against all those who had betrayed Caesar. Among the first to be executed was Cicero, who was decapitated by soldiers as he tried to flee Rome. Despite the fact that the old man had lavished his support on young Octavian, his head and hands were cut off and nailed to the Rostra in the Forum—all with Octavian's blessing.

And now Kleopatra was sailing with her fleet to answer Antony's call for reinforcements in Asia Minor and Greece. She had been informed that Cassius had sent ships plus a legion from Cape Taenarum to intercept her, but she had made up her mind to proceed, undeterred by his threat. She had no idea how the legion left to her command by Caesar would react if faced with fighting another Roman legion at sea, but she had spoken to the men herself, reminding them that they were Caesar's legion, and that Cassius had thrust a dagger into their commander's body, ending his life. The men had said that they were eager to aid the great Mark Antony, and she hoped that their word back in the comforts of Alexandria would hold out against the sight of their fellow Roman soldiers aboard Cassius's ships.

"Your Majesty," said her admiral, "I believe this is the first time a woman has commanded at sea since Artemisia, the Persian queen, led her navy against the Greeks."

"I wonder if the weather threatened to defeat her plans as well," answered the queen, looking up at the ominous skies. The wind had picked up speed, moving through Kleopatra's hair, blowing her dress and cloak behind her, making her shiver. The admiral caught her arm so that the sudden rocky waves did not knock her off her feet. She steadied herself, but as she watched the ululation of the flanking vessels on the choppy waters, she felt light in the head and queasy in the stomach.

"Are you unwell, Your Majesty?" asked the admiral.

As far as Kleopatra could see, his skin was turning an unhealthy yellow too, but his voice remained steady and he did not flinch as he held her arm.

Kleopatra felt a fat drop of water fall on her nose. She looked up into the glaring metallic skies, and another drop fell straight into her eye. Before long, the skies opened and sheets of rain began to beat the planks of the deck. The admiral quickly escorted her to shelter.

She lay on the bed in her cabin, clutching the sheets as the waves made the warship into a child's seesaw. Blood rushed from her head to her feet and back as the boat dipped into the sea, riding its violent rollers. There would be no sleep this evening. The last time she had looked, the skies were purple, a hideous bruise of a color, making it impossible to know if it was day or night. The lamp flickered as the boat rocked, its oil sloshing over the sides and onto the cabin floor.

Kleopatra roused herself and put on her cloak, but she was soon thrown to the floor. She waited for a moment of stillness and stood again, slipping on the spilt oil, but quickly reaching for the cabin door. Steadying herself along the walls of the narrow corridor, she made her way to the admiral's quarters.

"Your Majesty, I was just about to send you a message." His pupils were so large as to obliterate the rest of his brown eyes, which were encircled by deep olive moons. "I do not believe we should proceed. The winds are as violent as I've seen off the African coast. I'm afraid too many of the crew are taking ill."

"And yet we cannot turn back, Admiral. What will the general Marcus Antonius think if we simply do not come? He has asked for our aid."

"We will send a message that the weather has defeated us. He is a man of war, and all men of war understand the precariousness of weather."

Kleopatra did not want to say what she was thinking, that it might be preferable to perish at sea than to let Antony think that she had not heeded his call for help. She had Antony's pledge of support, but too many Romans had reneged on too many promises to the Egyptian throne in her family's history. If she was seen at all as being cowardly, or as trying to sit out the battle until its victor was decided, she would never recover her privilege with him.

"Can we not ride out the storm?" she asked. "What is your estimation of damages if we do?"

"I have discussed it with my officers," he said. "I believe that if we do not turn around and ride the winds back to Alexandria, we may lose the entire fleet, including this vessel."

Kleopatra nodded weakly, releasing him to send his command for retreat, and then she went back to her cabin and worried over her decision.

The sons of Caesar shall have their revenge. Antony's oath. Antony's promise. She believed him. At this moment, she had no choice. Caesar himself had more than once staked his life on Antony's loyalty. But still the question loomed in her mind: To exactly which sons was Antony referring?

Syria: the 10th year of Kleopatra's reign

Kleopatra let the great palm leaves offer a rhythmic respite from the deadening August air along the Syrian river. The barge moved slowly, as if its prow must slice the heat itself to navigate the way. She closed her eyes against wisps of hot breeze that escaped into her garments, cooling her skin. Sweat would not do, not at this crucial time when she must appear to be above such mortal vulnerabilities. A goddess, Charmion had insisted, does not perspire. At the last moment, as they were leaving Alexandria, packing the treasures, the gold and silver plate, the gilded couches, the jewels, the great trunks of costumes designed and sewn in a hurry by dozens of Royal Seamstresses, Charmion had had the brilliant idea to include the Cupids—twenty boys under the age of twelve, armed with palmetto leaves as tall as themselves and painted in bright and variegated colors, with which they fanned the heat away from the queen.

Preparations had been hasty but meticulous. She had waited a very long time for this moment when she would again meet the man who had emerged victorious from the struggle over the power relinquished in death by Caesar.

Rome's civil war was finally over. Cassius and Brutus had met Antony and Octavian in a final confrontation at Philippi in Thrace, where Antony commanded the army and Octavian showed his true character.

A novice in battle—and a coward as well, Kleopatra suspected—he was chased out of his camp by the enemy, and barely made it to the safety of Antony's encampment. There he feigned illness so that he would not have to engage in any confrontations.

Antony led the army to an overwhelming victory against the assassins, and both Brutus and Cassius committed suicide. Antony, in the manner of Caesar, draped his own purple cloak over Brutus's body and gave him a proper burial. But before the body could be interred, Octavian had its head severed and sent to Rome to throw at the foot of one of Caesar's statues. Upon hearing of her husband's disgrace, and perhaps in anticipation of the humiliation she would incur upon Octavian's return to Rome, Porcia, Brutus's wife, also committed suicide. Kleopatra was saddened to hear of Porcia's death, but also believed that she was not wrong in her estimation of Octavian's character. It was reported to Kleopatra that Octavian had played cruel games with his political prisoners at Philippi, forcing a father and son to choose which of them would die, making them draw straws for their lives. The father sacrificed himself for his son, but the son, distraught at seeing his father die, committed suicide. Antony and most of the men, it was said, were sickened by Octavian's twisted behavior.

Kleopatra could not understand why Antony, after leading his army to so clear a victory, did not claim the entire empire for his own; why he continued to share power with Octavian and Lepidus. Octavian's character was apparent, and Lepidus was not a leader of men. She wondered if Antony's sense of loyalty worked to his detriment, and she hoped that when they met, she would be able to mine his thoughts and discover his motives. He had always seemed to her a straightforward man. Or did he only appear to be that way?

It was a more formidable Antony Kleopatra would face in the Syrian city of Tarsus: He had taken as his portion of the empire Macedonia, Greece, Asia, and the kingdoms of Asia Minor, and Syria, leaving Octavian Italy and Lepidus Africa. Then he had traveled to Ephesus, where he summoned the leaders of all his nations and instituted extraordinary financial and trade policies that would enable the territories to prosper despite the large amounts of money and resources extracted by Brutus and Cassius. For his leadership, Antony was deified by the people of Ephesus, who called him the New Dionysus, the same title that had been held by Kleopatra's father. The Ephesians proclaimed him God Manifest, son of Ares and Aphrodite, and Savior of all mankind. He was also called the Giver of Joy, for his good nature and goodwill, and for his love not only of his soldiers, but of all people. He appreciated their cultures, attended their theaters and lectures, engaged in dialogue with their philosophers and scientists, and praised and patronized their poets. Thus, Kleopatra could not help but to notice, while Octavian went back to Rome calling himself son of the Divine Julius, Antony went to the east and became a god himself.

Now, with his prestige beyond compare, Kleopatra was sure that Antony was turning his energies to completing Caesar's great mission of conquering the Parthian empire, of settling the vast half of the eastern world for Rome, and toward Kleopatra and the role she would play in his plans.

In the eyes of the world, he had taken Caesar's place, and so she must acknowledge that. She must impress him in a manner larger and more grand than she had done with Caesar. Antony did not possess Caesar's nonchalance, but delighted in worldly things. She would dazzle him, demonstrate to him everything she might offer with her alliance— including herself. She had not forgotten his insinuations; in fact, in the absence of any sexual companionship, they had become part of her daily reverie.

Antony was married, true—and not to a passive political pawn like Calpurnia. Fulvia was beautiful and brilliant and had shown forceful political sway. Her likeness was stamped into Antony's coinage, and as far as Kleopatra could tell, no living Roman woman had ever before had that honor. The Roman senators said snidely of Fulvia that her ambition was to rule those who ruled. Finally, Kleopatra thought, she had a formidable rival. And yet was she? A Roman woman who could hold no official role in her government? Whose fortune, no matter how vast, was safeguarded by male relatives? Who had virtually no legal rights? Fulvia could not cast a vote in her country, while Kleopatra's very word was law in hers. Let Antony experience a woman of real power. Then would he be so satisfied with his wife?

Julius Caesar had seen the possibilities in a union between himself and the queen of Egypt, and Kleopatra was certain that Antony, a quick study, had already calculated what union with her was worth. Had the three of them not made their secret alliance while Caesar was alive? Antony's ambitious plans were made obvious in every move he made, and Kleopatra had been following those moves carefully. In the eastern territories of Rome's empire he had issued coins with images of himself as the sun god, whom the entire Graeco-Egyptian world worshipped as the ultimate Divine Ruler, so that each hand that passed the coins spread news of his ascension. The golden rays that haloed his head, the eagle of Zeus at his feet—looking ever so much like the Ptolemaic eagle, Kleopatra thought—told the whole world that as the new god came east, he would bring to the people all the riches that man and nature might offer.

But crucial to the distribution of those promised blessings was access to the riches of Egypt. And to procure those riches, this new beneficent god would have to position himself with that country's queen. Let him come, thought Kleopatra. I look forward to the negotiation.

For almost three years, Kleopatra had not been touched by the hand of a man except for the tiny one of her five-year-old son when he reached out for her. Archimedes had remained in Alexandria to advise and serve her, but he refused to come to her bed. Knowing his pride, she had withheld the invitation for months on end while she mourned the loss of Caesar, both personal and political. She had attended with a widow's restraint to her son and to her duties of state, casting aside all human emotions and focusing entirely on the good of her people. She had brought brilliant physicians in from all over the world to administer to those with the plague; she had made a trip down the Nile with engineers to redirect waters to dying crops; she had redistributed the grain crop so that the people in provinces whose harvest yielded nothing did not starve. She had staved off the demands of Caesar's murderers while attempting to send aid to Antony and his allies. And she had sat in meeting after meeting with Archimedes, more aware every day that she was staring into his mournful brown eyes for some sign of, if not forgiveness, then understanding, watching the curve of his beautiful lips as he spoke, wishing to put her arms around him and make amends for the suffering she had caused him. But as soon as she confessed her feelings—one year after Caesar's death—he stopped her flow of lovely words.

"Kleopatra." He held up one admonishing finger as if to shush her.

"It is over. I lost you once, and I will not risk repeating the episode. I cannot be your king, and I refuse to be your plaything."

"But Cousin, I can marry no one. My brothers are dead, and any choice I make at this juncture is fraught with political implications. As you told me once so many years ago, if we cannot be married, then why can we not be together as a man and a woman should? Why must we deny ourselves that pleasure? That love?"

But he looked at her stony-faced and said without a trace of humor, "You can command many things of me, Kleopatra, but even you cannot command my penis to rise."

After that, she left him alone, hearing the rumors of his exploits with the women of Alexandria, who were most anxious to experience this beautiful man rumored to have once been the lover of the queen.

"Many women are paying for what you did to him," Charmion admonished. Not that Charmion wished for Kleopatra to have chosen Archimedes over Caesar. She wished that Kleopatra had never entered into the affair with Archimedes at all. Kleopatra sighed. She supposed that she must allow Fate this episode of irony. She had, after all, broken his heart.

Though Kleopatra was making her way to the most important political negotiation of her life, the scent of sensuality hung in the air. It had arrived with Antony's first letters, delivered by Quintus Dellius, a scholarly man who was nonetheless a hedonist of infamous pluralistic sexual tastes. Antony's choice in messenger was not lost on the queen. He might have had any somber diplomat deliver his demands, but he sent Dellius, whose every sentence was laced with sexual overtones. "The Imperator would *delight* in your presence at Tarsus. He wishes to share in the same *favor* you so graciously and wisely showed to Caesar. Unlike Caesar, he is a man in his *prime*, and able to return that favor tenfold."

Kleopatra accepted the offer to meet with Antony in Syria, and then sent his messenger to the Alexandrian brothels, from which he did not emerge for one week. He would return to Antony intoxicated and confident that the queen of Egypt was, so to speak, in Antony's pocket.

Then she made him wait. She was scheduled to appear immediately, but she did not like the idea that anyone, even Antony, could summon her. If she rushed off to meet him, she would be playing right into his hand. He would have her alliance, her resources for his war on the Parthians, access to her army and her navy, and her body—for she was certain he would demand to take Caesar's place in her bed. And she would have—what? The privilege of giving him all those things. So she waited and she made preparations to meet him on terms that were her own. He may have been proclaimed the New Dionysus by the people of Asia Minor, but she was unimpressed. Her own father had held that title for most of his life, and he did not have to win a war to earn it. She had been consorting with gods-on-earth all her life. She herself was the earthly representative of Isis and Aphrodite, and the lover of the mortal man who was descended from Mother Venus. Not to mention the mother of his son. She would go to this New Dionysus, but not as a beggar holding out her hand for the favor of Rome, all the while opening her legs for him. She would to go him as his equal. If he was Dionysus, then let him negotiate with Aphrodite, the Greek Venus, the Mother of All Life and Creation. The significance would escape no one. Egyptians, Greeks, Romans, Syrians, all who saw her would know that she, living incarnation of Lady Isis, had come to meet with the conquering god—Osiris to the Egyptians, Dionysus to the Greeks, Bacchus to the Romans—in a sacred union not only of nations, but of man and woman, of god and goddess, to spread peace and beneficence over the earth.

"It shall be the greatest event the world has seen," she told Charmion as they hastily sketched the costumes for the dressmakers. As she made her plans, she felt herself shed the widow's sadness, along with the constant pain she endured from Archimedes' rejection and from his renowned conquests of other women. For the first time since Caesar's murder, she felt truly alive.

In a month's time, she orchestrated the entire spectacle. The Royal Barge, dormant and in storage since her Nile cruise with Caesar, was refitted with a golden stern, the oars dipped in silver, and new sails made, not in traditional nautical white, but in deep, royal purple.

"I want my vessel to be a celebration of light," she told her engineers. "By day, it should capture the power of the sun with gold and silver and reflect it back to the people, and by night, I wish to dazzle every eye with my lamplight." She could take no chances on her hour of arrival. If the sun was already set, she would not grope her way up the river in darkness, but sail into the port at Tarsus like fire in motion. The light must seem as if it was the sacred illumination of the gods. For it must be made plain that when Antony and Kleopatra reveled together, it was a divine celebration of peace and cooperation not only between two nations, but between all nations and all peoples. It must be emphasized and understood that the gods themselves sanctioned, indeed arranged and orchestrated, this alliance—that the union of Aphrodite and Dionysus on earth would bring security and prosperity to all those who honored it.

She lay now on her chaise of golden fabric like the goddess in repose. Her body was draped in folds of white linen woven with tiny shimmering metallic threads. Her hair was simple, pulled into a knot at the neck as the goddess was always depicted, with curls escaping at the temples, framing her face. She wore a giant amethyst upon her ring finger, the stone of the god Dionysus. On her right hand she wore her mother's ring, the ring of the Bacchant depicting the god in revelry—the same revelry in which she and the New Dionysus would soon engage. About her neck hung a long strand of pearls the size of marbles. Iras had pinned smaller white and black pearls into her hair in straight rows that clustered in a net, keeping tight her coiffure. Her appearance was paramount, for not only was she meeting a man who was as susceptible as any on earth to the charms of a woman's beauty, but the insecurity left by Archimedes' refusal to rejoin her as a lover stabbed at her like a secret wound.

Was she no longer desirable? She did not think that was the case when she examined herself in the mirror. She was as fit as she had been before she gave birth to Little Caesar. In the last months, her appetite had come back, and she had regained her womanliness. Now it had merely ripened into an elegant sensuality. Despite the responsibilities that kept her up late into the night and awoke her before the sun every morning, her face was unlined. When she regarded herself now, she no longer saw the shining enthusiasm of her youth, but an expression well-defined by wisdom and experience. Iras had raved over her appearance as he helped her dress, but she took little comfort in the praise of a eunuch whose tastes were exclusively directed toward those of his own sex. She knew that as a queen she must not rely upon the opinion of others but rest in the knowledge of her own charms and abilities. Ah well, all that would be tested now.

The sun was beginning to sink into the river's mossy waters when the captain informed her that they were not half an hour away from the port. She had sent messengers ahead to spread the word through Tarsus—and eventually, of course, to Antony himself—that Aphrodite had come to mingle with Dionysus for the good of all of Asia, and apparently, the message had been heard. Townspeople were running down the banks, pointing to the spectacular vision of the queen of Egypt afloat on the river Cydnus, looking for all the world like the goddess of love. Her attending women were draped in glorious white and stationed at the rudders and oars as if the Graces themselves were piloting the vessel. Below, the real work was done, but Kleopatra had wanted it to appear that her barge was powered solely by Divine Energy. From giant smoldering vats, the sweet scent of jasmine perfumed the river's air, as if the barge floated in a heavenly effluvium.

The late afternoon light was lazy enough to warrant illuminating the lamps. One by one, the women dipped their torches into the fire, lighting up the geometric festival of circles and squares that Kleopatra had designed. In the center of the design was something that should please Antony—the Nemean lion, the symbol of his astrological birth sign and the symbol of Herakles, the god he claimed as his direct ancestor. Kleopatra could hear the chatter of the people as the lights were lit. She was certain that never had they seen such a lavish sight, and she hoped that word would spread to the Imperator hastily, while the lights were at the height of their fire and she was at the height of her appearance. Her makeup was impeccable, her dress without wrinkles, her breath sweet, her hair undisturbed by the breeze. Her women were still fresh and lovely. She wished that she knew of a god of timing, for that was the deity to whom she should direct her prayers at this moment. Instead, she closed her eyes and spoke silently and swiftly to Isis, the goddess to whom Fate bowed.

She opened her eyes as the crew was dropping anchor at Tarsus. A large crowd had gathered about the docks. By their dress, she recognized both Syrians and Romans of all classes, some bedecked in the robes of government, others in workers' tunics. It seemed that rich and poor alike had come to see her arrival. She saw the uniforms of Roman soldiers, the lavish robes of wealthy merchants, the bright linen dresses of Syrian women, but she did not see the Imperator. Was he angry at her for the delay? Was there a chance he had moved on in his tour of the eastern provinces? Had she staged this entire drama in futility? There would be no recovering from such a blunder.

Kleopatra tried to maintain the mien of a goddess while her stomach churned. She smiled, waving gracefully, if languidly, at the people who stood awestruck before the golden vessel, which glimmered wildly against the still, dusky sky. The river reflected the lights, making a pool of luminescence around the boat. Where is he? she asked herself again and again, searching every face on the dock while trying to appear detached. Finally, she saw Quintus Dellius slinking toward her, swishing his hips from side to side like water in a moving goblet. He threw out his arms to the ladies-in-waiting, who helped him board the vessel.

The Cupid boys parted their fans to give him access to the queen. He bowed dramatically before Kleopatra, rising slowly, as if his blood rushed to his head. When he stood erect again, his eyes were wide. Perhaps he was drunk.

"Your Majesty!"

She could not tell if he was mocking her.

"How nice to see you, Dellius," she said. "And where is the Imperator?" She could not make small talk. If Antony had left Tarsus, she would have to make a hasty plan as to her next move.

"Why, he is in the marketplace hearing the local cases, though I imagine that at this point, he is very much alone. As you can see, the entire community has come to greet you."

"But not the Imperator?"

"Oh, he expects you this evening at his lodgings. He is most anxious to see you."

No, that would not do. Kleopatra remembered the awful time long ago that a Roman dignitary, Cato, had summoned a king—her father—to his lodgings. It was an indignity then, and it would be an indignity now. If only out of respect for the memory of her father, she would not go to Antony. If he wished to negotiate, he must come to her. He must see how a queen arrives to do business with a Roman general. No longer the girl in exile who rolled herself in a rug to meet Caesar, Kleopatra was in full command of herself and her nation. Her throne was unchallenged. She would sit on this chaise and act like a goddess until he arrived.

"But Dellius, I have prepared so very diligently for the Imperator's entertainment. I will not allow the burden of hospitality to fall on his already overencumbered shoulders—broad and strong though they may be," she said with just enough innuendo for Dellius to take back to Antony as enticement. "He must come to me and reap the rewards of my attempts to amuse him. He won't regret it."

"I shall tell him directly," Dellius said. With a slight hop, he turned from her and went away quickly.

The sky had grown dark. Kleopatra remained on the chaise, holding her position, hoping her cosmetics had not begun to smear. The air was cooler now, but the boys continued to fan the insects away from her face. When would he appear? She wanted to slip below into her cabin, wash her face, eat a small meal, and go to bed.

She heard his voice before she saw him, talking loudly and coarsely to his companions. The flat sound of Roman sandals on the deck was unmistakable, as was the laughter in Antony's voice. The voices and the footsteps grew closer and suddenly stopped. Silence hung in the air, the whooshing of the fans the only sound breaking the quiet. Then he laughed as only Antony laughed, not from the throat, but from the great cavern of his being, as if every organ, every ounce of oxygen and blood was in on the joke. She heard the footsteps quicken, rushing toward her. She did not move.

"Your Royal Grace!"

The lady-in-waiting who had rehearsed announcing the Imperator tried to say his name but was interrupted.

"No need to announce such an old friend," he said, rushing the chaise but stopping short at the sight of her. His eyes grew wide. He forgot to bow, standing very still with his mouth open and his lips frozen. Whatever he had intended to say was swallowed in the astonishment at her image, or so she hoped.

Finally, he recovered. "It is as they are saying in the marketplace. Aphrodite has come to Tarsus."

"To revel with the new god," she replied, sitting up.

She did not invite him to be seated, but enjoyed the awkwardness of him standing before her.

"Is this the vessel that astonished Caesar with its luxury?" he asked.

"Yes, but it was so old and in disrepair when he sailed with me. I've had it renovated for you, Imperator, in honor of your great victory over Caesar's assassins. It was the very least I could do to show my gratitude to you for vanquishing the enemies of my son's father. I tried to guess at your tastes, but time was short. You must forgive my delay in answering your summons. You see, I was in the throes of trying to please you."

She had never known him to be without words—millions of words, flowery, hyperbolic, ribald—whatever the occasion called for. But now he stood quietly, his thick brown eyebrows asking questions, making three deep wrinkles in his high and fine forehead. His curly hair was clean and free of pomade, hanging loosely about his face and ears; his body was wide and full, muscles rippling from the recent labors of war. As always, he belted his tunic very low like Herakles, and a broadsword hung at his side. He was as superb a specimen of the human male as the species had to offer, she thought. Not slim and elegant like Archimedes, whose beautiful masculinity held a touch of feminine refinement, but rather someone entirely masculine. She invited him to sit beside her, and he took his place almost gingerly, sweeping his cape aside. She recalled when she was a girl of fourteen and had met him for the first time. Then, too, he had swept his cape over his shoulder, revealing his powerful arms, and she had been taken by the beauty of the gesture. He sat very near her and she smelled his musky scent.

"We have many things to discuss," he said. "The world has changed since we last met."

"Yes, and we have changed with it. Will you and your men dine with me this evening? I've had my cooks prepare a twelve-course meal to serve forty."

"Forty? There are but fifteen of us here," he said.

"But do your men not like the company of women?" she asked, looking at her ladies in white, each chosen for her beauty and ability to converse.

"Do you mean to have them enchanted?" he said.

"I mean to alleviate their boredom while their leader discusses the business of state," she replied without any coyness.

"Caesar always admired the many variations of your personality, Kleopatra. He used to say to me, 'Antony, she is not a mere woman, but she is all women.'"

"It is simply a necessary element of being a queen. Most women must enthrall only one man. I must have that power over an entire kingdom."

"And have you any objections to turning the full force of your attentions on one man?" he asked, sitting so close to her that she could feel his heat and smell the wool in his clothes. He looked down at her, gazing quickly over her body, taking in her face, her breasts, her legs, her feet. Then he looked back into her eyes.

"It depends, Imperator," she replied. "On whether I have the power of his full attention in return."

"And what is it that commands this exclusive attention?"

She smiled at him. It was time for levity. "Shall we start with dinner?"

How many pheasants, quails, doves, boars, lambs would have to be roasted, braised, boiled, before her terms were accepted? How many fish would have to be procured, skinned, and cooked in sauces? How many heads of lettuce washed and salted? How many dates and figs harvested, how many cheeses sliced and served, how many enormous jars of wine emptied into gold goblets and spilled down Roman throats before Kleopatra had exactly what she wanted? Her cooks had brought ample food to feed a legion of men, or so they thought, but now, on the third day of the festivities, Kleopatra sent them into the Syrian markets to bargain for the town's goods, paying exorbitant prices and shouting down the local shoppers to procure yet more delicacies to appease the Roman contingent.

How many sets of gold and silver plate, with bejeweled goblets to match, would have to be given away as souvenirs of the evenings? Last night, at the end of the third feast, Kleopatra had surprised her Roman guests with her most extravagant gift yet. She had produced litters made of ebony, inlaid with mother-of-pearl, cushioned with the down of baby geese and draped in red and gold silks, to carry each Roman guest home. She had told each guest that she was making a gift of his litter. He was welcome to keep it as a token of her friendship. But as they were Romans and terribly cruel and greedy, she had to make a point of telling them that the Ethiopian torchbearers who lit the way home were to be returned.

It seemed they would never tire of her hospitality, and why should they? For she was undoubtedly the most lavishly generous host they had ever seen. She had heard stories of the opulence of the court of Darius the Persian, but she believed she may have outdone him. Tonight, having given away the crates upon crates of precious cargo she had brought from Egypt, she spent in excess of one talent on rose petals, which were presently being strewn over the dining floor so deep that they cushioned the sandal. It was a more delicate touch than the Romans might appreciate; yet they seemed to grow more accustomed to Graeco-Egyptian refinement with the passing of each night.

For the past three evenings she had sat with the Imperator, picking at her food while he gobbled great masses of his, sipping her wine cautiously and trying to keep up with his massive appetites, all the while bargaining for her kingdom. He had surprised her by immediately putting her on the defensive. There were those who said that she had not been a victim of a storm when she set off with her fleet to send him reinforcements in the war against Caesar's assassins, but had invented the problem so that she would not have to take sides in Rome's civil war.

She could not believe that he dared suggest such a thing, and turned on him with a fury that was not contrived. "How can you think I would conspire with Caesar's murderers? Three times Cassius demanded my support, and three times I turned his messengers away, even when he threatened to march on my city!"

"I was sure that was the case," he said. "But I did want to put to rest these rumors."

"Why would I come to the aid of the men who thrust the daggers into my son's father? Their victory would be my son's death."

"I understand, Your Majesty. There is no need to get angry with me."

She dismissed everyone from their table so they could talk alone. Antony's men, accompanied by her ladies-in-waiting, took chairs on the deck of the vessel, where they could continue their drinking and flirtations by the light of her lamps.

"We made a pact, Antony, do you not remember? A pact between the three of us. You affirmed it once again after Caesar's death. Or were you just serving up words to pacify me?"

He smiled and took her hand. "The New Triumvirate. The triangle of power. I do remember, Kleopatra, and I meant every word. And so did Caesar. Of course, I have had to join a *Roman* triumvirate in the meanwhile. To keep the peace, you understand."

She did not know if he was mocking her. "How much has changed in the triangular configuration, Imperator? One angle, two angles, or all three?"

"Caesar is dead, and conditions have changed. Let us just say that new actors are assuming leading roles. We must go with the times, Kleopatra, but that is no reason to forget the original plan. To continue with our little theatrical metaphor, the words remain the same, but take on new meaning when performed by new artists."

"If two players remain the same, that leaves a third role to be cast. Do you think your new partners might fill that role, or do you think they wish to recast the entire production?"

"They may wish for an entire new cast, particularly one of them, the younger one, who wishes he might rewrite the very words the actors say. But he may not. I won't have it. I do believe that once the little fellow reconciles himself to his subordinate role, he will be satisfied and will read the lines written for him. And then you and I might simply continue with the plan we made with Caesar. I see no reason not to carry on his ambitions. It would be a tribute to his greatness to subdue Parthia in his name, and to honor the alliance he made with you."

She did not know this Octavian, this new corner of their triangle. She did know Lepidus. The man was not a leader, but was willing to throw his money and his troops behind whoever he believed would prevail. Octavian's motivations were less clearly defined. He was young, one and twenty, and physically unimpressive. But that did not mean that he could reconcile himself to a world in which one of the three most powerful people had a rich kingdom in a strategic location, and a son who was also called Caesar.

"I would like to make an offer to you, Imperator. To establish the strength of our alliance, I suggest you set up your eastern headquarters in Alexandria. I shall furnish whatever you require for the war on

Parthia—men, ships, food, horses, saddlery. You may even take a legion of Egyptian whores if that is what your men need on the campaign. But your permanent center of operations in my country will let the world know of our partnership."

"I have always regretted cutting short my visit to your city all those years ago. It's a splendid location to organize the campaign. Done. It's so easy to be magnanimous with you, Kleopatra, when you offer so much in return. What else?"

"I would like you to ask the Roman senate to recognize me for my efforts to help you in the civil war, and you must ask them to recognize my son as the son of Caesar."

"That will require a little more finesse, but I don't see it as a problem. Is there anything else, Your Majesty? Because I have a few additional demands of my own."

She hesitated. She had promised Hephaestion that she would not return to Alexandria until Antony had agreed to eliminate her sister. *In matters of state, let your blood run cold.* Hephaestion had used those words again when they spoke of this or any difficult matter. It was not always easy to allow one's blood to run cold, but Hephaestion's philosophy had always proved right. Yet it was not so easy to ask for the demise of one's own blood. But Egypt was full of malcontents ready to back a rebellious rabble-rouser's claims to the throne. Renegade Ptolemies always found supporters in one region or another, with one faction or another. Between the Egyptians who hated the ruling class, and the Greeks who loved to take sides, someone like Arsinoe could always find enough support to cause grave trouble.

But, like Caesar, Antony was loath to execute a woman.

"I am a generous man," he said, "and determined to follow my mentor's example of mercy."

"May I point out to you that Arsinoe urged the governor of Cyprus to join with Caesar's assassins in the civil war. The two of them, along with the high priest of Ephesus, who is sheltering her now, have repeatedly declared Arsinoe the true queen of Egypt. Would even Caesar have been merciful under such conditions?

"I don't think you fully apprehend the danger. Arsinoe is not like some Roman citizen who happily changes allegiance with the shifting tides of power. She's a traitor, a deceiver, and the daughter of Thea, the traitor who usurped her own husband's throne while he was in Rome pleading for his kingdom.

"Are you aware," Kleopatra continued, pacing the floor with her argument as if she were prosecuting a case, "that Arsinoe turned on both Caesar and myself in the Alexandrian war, slipping out of the palace against Caesar's orders, and joining with the eunuch Ganymedes against Rome's attempts to restore order to the Egyptian throne? She had deceived our brother, Ptolemy the Elder, into thinking she was his ally, all the while conspiring against him. And she used her younger brother as her agent against me until the Prime Minister did away with him.

"She will not rest until I am dead and she is sleeping in the state bed," Kleopatra concluded. "Some evenings, I feel her menace in my dreams, as if she is already testing out my mattress for her back."

"It seems to me she is merely a spirited girl, powerless but vocal," Antony replied.

"Do you so underestimate the power of a woman's voice?" she asked. "I hear that in Rome, those at the highest levels of government and society cling to your wife's every utterance."

She thought she might have insulted him, but it seemed impossible to insult this good-natured man, who relished a good laugh at himself even more than he enjoyed taunting others. He smiled at her words and leaned very close to her. "And men of all nations cling to yours. But what man would not want Her Majesty's sweet breath whispering in his ear? It may be soft and perfumed, but it causes shivers and quakes in every crook and cornice and shaft of a man's body."

She merely smiled. She had grown accustomed to Antony's coarse innuendoes. He was the type of man—open, lusty, exuberant—who could get away with such things without seeming insulting.

"Even when that sweet breath carries a request that the man considers unpleasant?"

"Especially so. The paradox of a bloody demand transported by something so sweet confuses the senses."

"I am most sorry to have confused the Imperator," she said.

"I am most delighted to have experienced the confusion," he replied. "May it be the first of many."

"It shall be as you wish, Imperator. But there are, of course, considerations."

"Of course. But I cannot see my way just yet to agreeing to proscribe your sister."

She allowed—and very sweetly—that she respected his position. But when the evening drew to its end—just as the morning light was coming up—she refused to let him come to her bed. "I am just a woman, Imperator, and therefore weaker than you. I won't be able to negotiate so well on behalf of my people if I have fallen for your manly charms."

With one finger he tipped her chin, raising her face to meet his eyes. "That argument is best made by a man, Kleopatra," he said. "I doubt that any man's charms would influence your negotiating strategies."

She was very glad that she was exhausted, because she wanted him badly. He was thrillingly tall, broad-shouldered, and intelligent. She thought he always smelled of sex, and she did not know how he accomplished that. Everything about him evoked the sensual in her. She remembered how, at fourteen, she could not even look at his naked calf without blushing. Now she had the same problem with his face, his chest, even the curly brown hair on his chiseled forearm.

But at the evening's end, she exercised all discipline and descended to her cabin, leaving him stunned and alone. Or so she thought. She found out that he had quickly ordered two prostitutes from the town to tend to his needs before he fell asleep at nine o'clock in the morning, waking three hours later to hear court cases in the town's forum.

She walked now among her rose petals, supervising their placement on the floor, the banqueting tables, the dining couches. Each footstep released more of the flowers' sweet scent into the room, and once crushed under heavy studded Roman sandals, the smell would become intoxicating. She hoped that the petals distracted from the simple table settings, borrowed from a city official's kitchen. With a little luck, her guests, inevitably drunk, would not take them home at the end of the meal. She did not wish to slight them, but in truth, she had not foreseen that the feasting and the negotiating would last for days, and she'd already given her guests every plate she'd brought from Egypt. No matter, she thought. It was no time to worry over funds, or over a civil servant's cheap pottery. The conclusion to these events would have repercussions that could last through her lifetime and that of her son.

All that I do I do for my son. She said these words to herself as she strolled among the petals. There was no limit to what she would do to secure his life and his kingdom, to see that he grew to manhood and assumed the dual mantle of power endowed upon him as a birthright by his mother and his father. How different Caesarion's life would be, she thought, remembering the many obstacles she had to surmount to arrive at this moment when she, queen of Egypt, was entertaining the greatest Roman of his day. Her father had overcome his illegitimate birth, his seditious wife and daughter, and Rome itself, which had extorted so much money from him that he began to feel it as blood draining from his very veins. He had survived his treasonous family only to have the Romans murder him slowly and treacherously, by bleeding him of his money, his spirit, his dignity. Kleopatra had taken up where her father left off in the family battle for the kingdom. But she had exceeded her father thus far by making an alliance with Caesar that was based on more than the total sum of her treasury. And because she had the foresight to do this, her son would not have to fight the battles she and her father had fought. He would have others, for no monarch of a great nation remained in power without a struggle. But his struggles would serve a higher cause—the unity of the world.

All that I do, I do for my son, including call for the execution of his cunning aunt. If Arsinoe ever got into power, the first target of her revenge against Kleopatra would be Little Caesar.

Whatever she must do to ensure Arsinoe's demise, she must do and do swiftly. The girl had a way of evoking sympathy. She was both smart and conniving. Had she not played her brothers for fools? Had she not captured the hearts of chilly Roman matrons and turned them against Kleopatra? Had she not won the high priest of Ephesus—a man of great sway—over to her cause, so much that he addressed her as queen? If Kleopatra had to go to Antony's bed prematurely to get him to promise that he would end Arsinoe's miserable life, then she would do just that. But she must not make a miscalculation. Antony's men joked about his exploits with Glaphyra, the princess of Cappodocia, who had tried to boost her political position by hopping into Antony's bed. But apparently, Antony hopped right out of both her bed and her country, having given her no more territory to claim other than the inches from the base to the tip of his organ. Or that was how his men laughed about it.

Kleopatra was more vulnerable with Antony than with Caesar and she knew it. Not only was Antony's power not as solid as Caesar's; the fact remained, Kleopatra wanted Antony in a way that she had never wanted her late lover.

Antony's demeanor this evening was different. He was less relaxed than at previous dinners, when he had made long and flowery speeches praising every detail of the banquet, holding up pieces of meat until a cook was summoned from the kitchen to explain every step of their preparation. He would drink goblet after goblet of wine, telling jokes and stories as if he were not the Master of the World on a tour of his empire, but rather a loquacious vagabond who had nowhere else to go and nothing else to do.

But this evening he merely looked about at the tables of food around which the rose petals were disseminated, and with the briefest nod of approval, sat down and began to eat—not with his previous gusto, but methodically.

"Is all to your liking, Imperator?" Kleopatra asked, flinching at the insecurity that crept out with her words. Was he tiring of their game?

"Quite so," he said perfunctorily.

"You seem not yourself."

"Like you, Your Majesty, I find that I must be not one man but many. My duties are pressing. I shall not long be in your company."

"Where are you going?" she asked. She knew that she sounded both surprised and afraid, and she cursed herself for not being able to summon up every morsel of her powers to disguise her emotions. She felt like an insecure girl again, in the days when only a small flame of intuition and the hotter burn of desire told her that she had what it took to be queen.

"There is incessant trouble in Judaea. I must settle it and confer power upon my allies in that region. There is no present governor of Syria, and I must see to that as well. And, as you know, I must also begin preparations to march on Parthia."

He spoke to her as if to a stranger. He had shared with her every detail of his planned attack on Parthia, and she was to play a very definite strategic role in the campaign. Now it was as if they had not had that conversation. What had changed?

"And when do you leave Tarsus?" she asked.

"Day after tomorrow."

"I see. And when do I anticipate your arrival in Alexandria?"

Antony did not look at her. He put the last piece of quail on his plate in his mouth, dipped his fingers in the water bowl, cleaned his hands with his napkin, and drained his goblet, slamming it down on the table forcefully so that it captured the attention of his men.

"Dinner is over, gentlemen," he said. "The queen and I have business to attend to, and so you must forgive us for asking you to take your leave."

The men murmured and muttered, but no one was going to challenge Antony's demand. Kleopatra did not want to give them any cause to think that it was she who had arranged this unceremonious dismissal of their company, so she stood and smiled at them.

"Gentlemen, please forgive us for putting country and kingdom over pleasure." She could see the disappointment on their faces—and Roman disappointment always turned to bitter tongues. "As a token of our lovely times together, I wish to make a gift to each of you of the gold dining couch upon which you have lain these many glorious evenings. If you require help in transporting them back to your quarters, my staff is available to serve you."

There was great applause at this, and the men excitedly jumped off their couches, examining the details of the curved legs and overstuffed pillows and glimmering silk fabrics as if they had not been lying on them for four nights, but had never seen them before.

Antony said nothing until they were alone. Kleopatra awaited him, realizing all the while that she was completely unprepared for whatever it was he was going to say.

Finally, he spoke. "I have seen my way to accommodating the last of your requests."

She did not answer him, did not demonstrate a reaction at all, because she did not want him to see how grateful she was.

"I was thinking of your son, Kleopatra, and of my sons. We must do what we must do to protect our sons. I have come around to see that your sister's very life endangers your son. And so I will go against my policies of clemency for your sake."

"I am grateful to you for it," she said quietly.

She looked at him and saw something dark flash across his face.

"What troubles you, Imperator? Is it the quality of my entertainment?"

"There is trouble in Rome," he said. "I've just received a very disturbing dispatch from my wife." Fulvia's letter informed Antony that while he attended to the business of settling the empire's eastern territories, his alleged ally, Octavian, was trying to usurp his supporters in the city itself.

"How is he accomplishing that?" Kleopatra asked.

"The traditional way. Bribing the soldiers," Antony replied.

Fulvia was so concerned about the state of things that she marched her children through the ranks of Antony's troops, reminding the men that it was Antony to whom they had pledged their loyalty. "She's in an awkward position. One of the conditions of alliance with Octavian was that he marry Clodia, Fulvia's daughter by Clodius. Now Fulvia says there is great tension between Octavian and herself, which puts her daughter in jeopardy."

"This Octavian? What sort is he?"

"No one knows, really. He is whatever he needs to be to your face. He probably thought that with me out of the way, he could easily usurp my legions. He didn't count on Fulvia's tenacity—or her audacity."

"Your wife is quite a woman," Kleopatra said in what she hoped sounded like a respectful tone. "In other circumstances, she might have been a queen."

"There is nothing I wouldn't do for her," he said.

Kleopatra did not know if he was trying to convince himself or her. "I am sure of it," she replied, wondering if she had miscalculated Antony's interest in becoming her lover.

"Do you know why Cicero's head was displayed in the Forum?"

"Because he had your stepfather executed on false charges of conspiracy?"

"I did hold a grudge for a long while over that. He caused my mother no end of financial woes and shame. But that is not the reason."

"Because he spoke against you before the senate?" she answered. "I would have executed him myself had he leveled such outrageous accusations against me."

"I don't begrudge him that. Those were merely political speeches. I ordered his body disgraced because he never tired of speaking ill of my wife."

"Your loyalty does you credit, Imperator," she said all too formally, feeling her heart sink. He had negotiated with her, allied with her, and now he would close those negotiations and send her away. He had toyed with her as women so often toy with men, using his charms to strike a favorable deal when he had no intention of satisfying her deeper, personal longings. Now she would be relegated to Friend and Ally of the Roman People, like her father before her. No more; no less. When Antony required something of the Egyptian purse or the Egyptian army or wished to claim a portion of the Egyptian granary to feed his men as they trampled over her land to reach Parthia, he would send a letter of demand to her as he did to any other eastern potentate over whom he held inexorable power.

"I'm afraid I've disappointed her," he said. "Her letter was quite harsh, and rather sarcastic. She closed it by saying that she hoped that her news wouldn't disturb the enjoyment of my triumphs on foreign soil."

"And will it?" Kleopatra looked him straight in the eye.

"No, Your Royal Grace, it will not. I have a few more triumphs to make before I leave." He stood up, scooping her in his arms as if she were a baby, lifting her off the dining couch and holding her close to him.

She was sure that the stunned look on her face was what provoked his first laugh of the evening. "You're as light as a feather, Kleopatra. I believe it is only your brain that carries any weight at all."

She opened her mouth, either to chastise him for so handling the body of a queen, or to tell him to be discreet, that servants were watching. She had not made up her mind about what she would say. But he covered her lips with his, kissing her hard, blotting out any concerns she might have of observers. Before the dawn's light, every member of her staff would know anyway. There were no secrets in a queen's life.

She opened her mouth wider to take his tongue, sucking on it wildly, as if it gave her nourishment. And it did. It had been so long. She felt like an infant at the breast as she circled his tongue with hers, grasping at it with her lips, sliding it in and out of her hungry mouth. She wrapped her arms tighter around his neck, turning her body into his, greedy for all that was to come. She wanted to lose every thought, every responsibility, every worry, in his solid mass of flesh.

Silently, kissing her all the while, he carried her down the stairs and into her chamber. The body servants crept away like mice when he entered the room, rolling themselves into obsequious balls. He slammed the door shut with his foot and put her down, backing her against a wall, pulling up her dress. At the same time he put his tongue in her mouth, he put his fingers inside her so deep that he lifted her in the air. She wrapped her legs around him, amazed that he could raise her body so high while she pushed down on his hand. He held her against the wall with the strength of his thighs, and before she realized what he was doing, had replaced his fingers with something larger, hotter, harder. She cried into his mouth as he thrust into her, grateful that his lips muffled her sighs to curious ears that might be at her door. He tore at her belt, sending its jewels skittering to the floor, and lifted her dress over her head, leaving her naked and shaking. She clung to his shoulders, letting him enter her, feeling as if she was being slain over and over, and as if the wounds were so sweet that she could not die enough times. Fear seeped into her ecstasy; at some point soon, tonight, within this very hour, this would be over, and life and all its pain and uncertainty would once again creep back in. But for now, she was not Kleopatra but the receptacle of this man's passion, and she let her own rise up to meet his. She concentrated on her own mounting pleasure, biting into his neck, hugging him harder, letting him go deeper and deeper into her body, like an explorer who was helping her mine the secret gems in the abyss of her own body. His hands were beneath her and he moved her up and down rhythmically as if she were a musical instrument and he the musician, playing her pleasure. It was completely new for her, this surrender. She had been the object of her lovers' desires, but never had she so thoroughly put her pleasure in a man's hands.

When he felt the spasms of her orgasm, he carried her to the bed and put her down like a baby. He removed his own clothes, his penis still huge and jutting at her as he stepped out of his sandals. Little scars covered his chest like a constellation, white and jagged against his tanned brown skin. He was broad at the middle, and she could see where he would be fat in his later years, but now that weight sat on him handsomely, making his large body seem so much more substantial than that of some lithe boy. A gash, badly repaired, shot like a lightning bolt across his left side.

When he lay beside her she traced it with her fingers.

"Taken in the service of our Caesar," he said. He took her fingers and put them in his hot mouth, sucking them gently. "We had some very bad seamstresses in Gaul."

"You should have had a Greek doctor," she said, smiling at him.

"So much finer than a coarse Roman physician?"

"Precisely."

"Ah, Your Majesty, back to your imperious ways so soon?" He pulled her to him and rolled on top of her, pushing into her quickly, searing her with quick, hot friction. "We must humble you again."

Ephesus:
the 10th year of
Kleopatra's reign

Arsinoe did not know where she was going, but she knew she had to leave the temple precinct immediately. The high priest had found out that her death warrant had been signed by the Imperator himself, and there was no escaping it unless she fled in disguise. Where could she go? She was under guard, followed everywhere she went, even to her daily offerings at the temple. She was sure the Romans would have joined her in her prayers if they knew that each day she beseeched the goddess to do away with her sister, the Roman's whore. The orders left for her care by Julius Caesar were more compassionate than she would have believed possible from a Roman; she was to be kept under house arrest, but left unharmed. Unharmed. Everyone knew what that meant, even the soldiers who lasciviously eyed her body as they fell behind her wherever she went. They were not to defile her. They wanted to, of course, and she could not imagine why Julius Caesar had given such an order. What had he cared of her safety? He had marched her in chains in his disgusting victory parade. Well, he had shamed himself in the act more than he had humiliated her. She was sure of that. The Roman matrons who visited her regularly in prison were horrified that a princess—young, regal, educated, of illustrious lineage—should be paraded like a savage, an animal. She made sure that those tongue-wagging women knew exactly who was responsible for her treatment. Not Caesar. No, she told them, the poor aging general was bewitched by her sister, who worked through the dark nights with conjurers while all decent people were asleep to put spells and enchantments on all those she wished to control. Poor Caesar was just one of her many victims. Did he not become frail in his later years, with the strange falling-down sickness? Either Kleopatra had caused those spells by her alchemy, or she had taken advantage of Caesar's weakness in order to manipulate him. Their cherished late father, Kleopatra had duped with her dark magic all his life. She probably had had a curse put on him, the true cause of his death, once he had made her queen. Did they not know that she had also murdered two of her own brothers? Arsinoe loved watching the disgust on the faces of the Romans, so concerned with filial ties, when she told them stories of her sister's crimes. No matter what happened to her now, she would at least know that she had done as much damage as possible to Kleopatra in the eyes of those whom she wished most to impress—the citizens of her beloved Rome.

But now Julius Caesar was dead, and the orders against harming Arsinoe no longer stood. Now her sister was in the bed of the swaggering hulk whom Arsinoe had seen in Rome—all beef and bluster, that one. Was there no limit to Kleopatra's harlotry? She, Arsinoe, would rather be dead than to find herself under the pernicious bulk of these shark-toothed monsters. She had made that much clear to the cretin Helvinius, who, despite Caesar's orders, could not take his eyes off her breasts. She thought his eyes would fall out of his head with the force of his staring. He had tried—one time only—to sneak into her chamber when he thought everyone was asleep. He had crept onto her bed and tried to stick his penis in her mouth, but she gripped it, jerked it up, and bit with all her might one of his testicles. She had never heard anyone scream so loud. Within seconds, the priest was rushing into her room, followed by the other Roman sentries. Helvinius was carried away, still hunched over his balls, and assigned to a new post. Her only regret was that she had broken the skin, and tasted his salty blood on her tongue. She could not eat for a week. But at least she had tasted spilt Roman blood. That much was gratifying.

Three short knocks on the door was the signal. Arsinoe covered her head, said a last-minute prayer to the goddess, and wrapped herself in a long shawl. She and her most loyal man, the High Priest, would slip away into the night and take a boat for Cyprus, where the governor would give them shelter, at least until the Romans found out where they were. Then—who knew? If necessary, she would disguise herself as a palace slave and scrub the governor's floors until the proper time when she might once again raise support to win back her kingdom. As long as whichever Roman was calling the shots was in her sister's grip, she was not safe.

She opened the door. The High Priest was in the custody of two Roman sentries whom she had never before seen. One was taller and stockier than the other, but the shorter one had his sword drawn and looked meaner. The priest could not meet her eyes. The shorter of the Romans grabbed her arm gruffly. "Your friend here has given you up in exchange for his pardon," he said.

"That is untrue, Your Highness," the priest insisted, still not able to look her in the face. "We are both sentenced to die."

"But only one of you will," the Roman countered. "Isn't that interesting?"

He pulled her arms behind her back while the taller, silent one tied them with a coarse rope.

"What are you doing?" she screamed, trying to pull away from them, falling forward into the priest, who leapt backward as if she carried the plague. "What are they doing to me?" she demanded of him, but he shied away from her.

"I won't be a part of this," he said to the sentries, walking away. But the shorter sentry grabbed his arm and jerked him to a stop.

"You are a part of this, whether you like it or not. You defied the orders of the triumvirs of Rome, you sided with the assassins of Caesar, and now you will pay for it."

The priest stood still and looked at Arsinoe for the first time, summoning up his dignity. "Your Highness, I will have the privilege of dying with you."

"No you won't," said the taller Roman, breaking his silence. He spoke as if he regretted his words, whether because he did not like what he had to say, or because he did not like what he was ordered to do, Arsinoe did not know. But he spoke evenly and bitterly. "We are under orders to spare you. Someone—who knows who?—has pleaded for your life. Perhaps your position at the temple has saved you."

"But you will witness the death of the one you call the queen of Egypt," said the other. "And you will remind yourself of your part in her demise. You are a holy man. You should have delivered better advice."

The Romans pushed Arsinoe and the priest down the hall, torches on the wall making black shadows on the floor ahead of them, and into the brisk night air. Arsinoe's shawl fell to the ground and she stopped, looking at one Roman and then the other to retrieve it for her. "You won't need it where you're going," the short one said.

The priest picked up the shawl and wrapped it around Arsinoe's shoulders. "If you die tonight, you die the rightful queen of Egypt," he whispered in her ear. "And if I live, I shall spend the rest of my days making that known."

"The rightful queen of Egypt lies in the arms of Marcus Antonius, Imperator of Rome," said the short guard. "If you had better sense, you might have been in her place."

Arsinoe looked about her, but there was no one there to meet them but the columns of the temple precinct, so beautiful by day, but now stony sentries to her disgrace. She thought of Berenike at the moment of her death. What did her sister do but look with scorn, hatred, even pity, at those who condemned her, right up to the second when the sword met with her neck? Arsinoe would make Berenike proud. She would not disgrace the memory of her sister by showing fear to these Romans. They might take her life, but not her dignity.

She walked right up to the short Roman and stared straight into his eyes. "I prefer death as a lover to a Roman," she said.

He swept his right arm across his chest to backhand her in the face, but the taller guard checked him. "Stick to the orders," he said. He turned Arsinoe around and marched her forward. "You're just dragging things out."

Arsinoe squared her shoulders, looking ahead. At the end of the courtyard, behind the sacrificial stone, stood a Roman centurion. Arsinoe could not quite make out his features, but saw that he was a large man, standing with his feet apart, making a long triangle of his legs. Was she to be sacrificed on the same stone where animals were offered to the goddess? No trial, no witnesses to her death but these barbarians and the betrayer of a priest? The sentries pushed her forward, out of the shadows. It was then that she recognized the face of Helvinius, his smile broad, and his sword drawn and gleaming in the light of the moon goddess along with his straight, white Roman teeth.

Alexandria: the 10th year of Kleopatra's reign

Kleopatra wondered if, true to the philosophers' warnings, her reason and intellect would die an expedient death-by-drowning in pleasure. "I've succumbed to you, Imperator," she told Antony, "mind, body, and kingdom."

"And I to you, Your Royal Grace," he answered.

They had just made love—again—in her bath. When they finished, she moved to go to her bed, but Antony called for dinner. "At midnight?" she asked.

"Time must subordinate itself to a man's desires," he said. "That is all there is to it."

She hoped the cooks had obeyed her orders to have fresh and sumptuous meals ready to serve at all hours of the day and night. Antony was completely unpredictable in his appetites. The only guarantee was that he would have them. Where, when, and for what was always a surprise. Kleopatra had never seen a person with such passion for work and for life. Antony spent the major part of his days preparing with his military staff to march on Parthia. He took meeting after meeting with cavalry officers, weapons specialists, siege builders, and mapmakers, attending to the tedious details of assembling a war machine.

In the afternoons, Antony did not rest, but demanded to be entertained either with sport, lectures, theatrical performances, or sex—and sometimes those pursuits in combination. Before dinner, he met with visiting dignitaries and heard their concerns. In the evenings, he and Kleopatra gave long dinners for Alexandria's wealthiest and most interesting citizens and for the Romans in Antony's entourage. The Alexandrians adored him, calling him the Inimitable Liver, a man whose love of life knew no bounds, who lived with style and passion, who literally gobbled up experience, both visceral and esoteric. He was cherished in the city for his generosity, his sense of humor, for his love of all things Greek and Egyptian, and for the fact that he had made their queen a partner in his enterprises. Those who had watched her father grovel before Roman leaders were amazed that their queen was not only financing a large portion of Rome's war with Parthia, but was clearly orchestrating its strategy with the Imperator. After their guests would leave—often at dawn—Antony and Kleopatra would take horses from the stables and ride into the wild country south of the city, just as she had done so many years ago with the desert girl, Mohama. After a brisk ride, Kleopatra would sleep a few hours while Antony bathed and began his day, catching fifteen-minute naps between activities. Though he was tireless, he was caught more than once falling asleep during a presentation by one of his staff.

This evening, they ate alone in one of the small dining rooms where her father often shared a late dinner with one of his mistresses after he had supped with his wife. Antony lay on the same couch of purple silk that Auletes had so loved, and Kleopatra marveled at the symmetry of things, that both men who had singled her out to share their power loved lounging and eating in this small room. Antony cut a figure more pleasing to the eye, however. His bronze skin was pink from the bath and his face flushed with hot food and warm, spicy wine. His months away from war and dining in royal style had put some bulk on his body, but Kleopatra still found him beautiful. Somehow, each pound added more masculine appeal. Kleopatra sat in the crook of his body, curled against his thighs and facing him. Occasionally, after a sip of wine, he pulled her to him and kissed her with hot, well-seasoned lips.

"Of all the philosophies I have studied, Imperator—the Platonists, the Aristotelians, the Epicureans, the Stoics—none recommend this sort of indulgence in the passions," Kleopatra said, licking her freshly kissed lips. She picked up a tiny pheasant wing and nibbled at its delicate flesh.

"And so they do not," he said, nonchalant. "Their goal is detachment from all that one lives for—food, drink, friendship, war, love. I studied with them myself in Greece, and I am proud to say that I could not be argued out of my desires. One crumpled up old sophist called upon me to 'confess' my wicked desires and rid my soul of their torment. 'I've no desire to rid myself of my desires,' I told him. 'I adore my desires, and they me.'"

"But do you not think that extirpation of the passions is crucial to rational decision-making?" She was goading him, of course. She loved the time she spent with Antony, hunting, riding, feasting, laughing, making love. She had not had even a glimmer of such fun since her youth. She was not about to abandon these pursuits in favor of philosophical restraint. But was it possible to continue to live life on this grand and relentless scale, recklessly gobbling up time and experience?

"How bookish you sound, Kleopatra. It's very erotic."

She knew by the lascivious look on his face that he meant what he said.

"Don't flirt with me, Imperator. You've already used me up this evening like the commonest of whores. You'll get no more play from me."

She smiled at him, grateful that her strategy to lure him to Alexandria had paid off. When he had made love to her at Tarsus, she had been entirely swept away by the experience, taken over in a way that had never before happened to her. She had worried that she would not be able to hold her own with this man, who could obliterate her very consciousness with the ferocity of his sex. It was intoxicating, but it would not do to become just another of Antony's whores. She remembered fretting over the same problem in those days with Archimedes when sex was new and overwhelming. But it was even more so with Antony. She had no power over him as she had had with Archimedes. She must not become so vulnerable that she was in Antony's control. Politically, she was dangerously close to that fact. If she succumbed so utterly to him sexually, she would be lost.

On their last evening together in Tarsus, he had insisted on entertaining her in his quarters, taking up the challenge to match her in lavishness. When she arrived, he announced that because Her Majesty had bought up all the food and luxuries in the region, his staff was forced to prepare a simple Roman meal. They ate together in smaller company than on previous nights, and when he dismissed his few guests and presumed to carry her off to his bed, she protested that she was weary and would leave to prepare to set sail before dawn. If he desired the pleasure of her sexual companionship again, she suggested he make haste to Alexandria as soon as his business in Syria was brought to a satisfactory conclusion. This time, she left him stupefied, and there was no report of his calling for whores.

It was a risk, but she had taken it and it had paid off. Here he was, indulging his feral Roman appetite at her table as he considered what she said about the dichotomy between philosophical reason and sensual passion. He sucked the last of the fat off a bone, washed it down with a long swig of wine, and wiped his hands on a napkin before reaching for a cluster of purple grapes. "You've forgotten the Cynics," he said.

"Ah, the Cynics. Do you ascribe to the philosophy of the Cynics, Imperator?"

"I seem to care little for money except to lavish it foolishly on others. Isn't that one of the virtues the Cynics sought to cultivate?"

"Yes, but that was only to realize that there is no value in material things."

"And so I realize it. There is no value in material things, so we may as well throw them away as enjoy them. What does it matter in the end? Yes, I do believe I am an exemplar Cynic."

"Yes, my darling, you are its most perfect paragon. Did Diogenes not say that Herakles was the model of the perfect Cynic? A simple soldier who lived hard and trained hard?"

"And do the people of your nation and mine not say that I am a great likeness to the god?" Antony turned his face upward so that Kleopatra could admire his fine profile.

"Oh yes, but you are far from a simple soldier, though you fool others with that persona. And secondly, I hate to tell you this, but Diogenes was mad."

"He was not. He simply rejected rules and regulations so that people who love such things *thought* he was mad. They always do, you know. Those who love rules simply cannot abide those who do not. We frighten them."

"But Crates, his disciple, was surely mad."

"No, he wasn't mad. He was a clown, a performer who taught wisdom through comedy." Antony poured Kleopatra another cup of wine and held it to her lips. "Here, have some more. You are entirely too moderate."

"Yes, moderate in the Aristotelian sense," she said. "It's no accident, but part of my philosophy."

"But our Crates would not have approved of your restraint. He used to make love in the open air with his wife, Hipparchia, regardless of spectators. Now that's freedom—freedom from rules, from shame, from inhibitions."

"What a time they must have had," Kleopatra said. "Hipparchia the aristocrat traipsing through the streets with her lunatic, hunchback, philosophizing husband, Crates, knocking on the doors of the good people of Athens, giving philosophical instruction, or just playing pranks. Imagine having such freedom."

"People have freedom because they take it, Kleopatra. I thought you knew that."

"What is the difference between freedom and hedonism? Between freedom and insanity?"

"Well he was all of those things. A hedonist, yes. But he merely indulged his passions; he was not ruled by them. He gave away his money and her money just to show people that simplicity and love was all. Just like myself, don't you think?" Antony puffed out his chest and waited for her approval.

"But it is not all, is it?" she asked. "Bring *that* philosophy to your senate. The verdict upon you will surely be madness."

"No, no, the senators all pose as Stoics, but privately live like Sybarites." Antony smiled wickedly. "But we are not in Rome, are we?"

Before she knew it, Antony was pulling her by the hand, dragging her across the courtyard past astonished guards and into the stables. He burst into the dormitory shared by the stable boys, who were fast asleep, rousing them from their beds, throwing them onto the floor and demanding that they shoo. The lads looked at Kleopatra quizzically as they gathered their nightshirts about them and fled their beds, and she returned their glances with equal curiosity, for she had no idea what mischief was in Antony's head. He herded them out the door, rushing them with his arms as if they were chickens. When the last of the boys was gone, he shut the door, lit a lamp, and demanded that the queen take off her clothes.

"Not *here*," she said. Not with ten bleary-eyed stable boys at the door. She had her limits.

"No, not that," he said. He opened the boys' trunks, rifling through their habits. He pulled out a short chiton and a cloak with a hood and threw them at the queen. "Put this on," he said, as if commanding one of his soldiers. He continued to look through the trunks, lifting the clothes to himself for size. When he found a costume long enough, he began to strip. Kleopatra clutched the clothes to her body but did not move until Antony, naked and laughing, pulled them from her chest, stripped her, and dressed her in the sacklike work clothes of the stable boy.

"Perfect," he said, pulling the hood over her head.

"What evil plan are you concocting, Imperator?" she asked.

"Hipparchia." He put the big brown cloak over himself and hunched his back, looking back at her, she thought, with the eyes of a lunatic. "And Crates. Let us go out and meet our disciples."

Antony stood in the open-air carriage. The night air was warm for autumn. Stars glittered in the black sky, a celestial backdrop to his theatricality. He drank from the leather pouch as the vehicle rolled down the stone streets, spilling wine on the queen and laughing at her fastidiousness as she wiped it away and admonished him with her looks. He was more playful than her seven-year-old son, who sat for hours at his studies, his knitted brow a seriousness inherited from both mother and father. Antony, the son who had seized Caesar's power, was like a boy who had inherited the whole world for a playground.

"Here, stop here," he commanded the driver. The carriage came to a halt, and he hopped out, offering his arms to help Kleopatra. His men had followed behind on foot and had caught up with them, snickering, waiting to see their general's latest mischief. Antony leapt up the white marble stairs two at a time to the house. He knocked loudly on the door. A footman answered, and quickly drew back when he saw the large, beggarly-looking man.

"Tell your master that Philosophy is at the door," Antony said dramatically.

Kleopatra put her hand over her head. "You have chosen the most serious man in the kingdom for your antics," she said. "He will think us mad! He has no humor."

Hephaestion. The Prime Minister. The loyal eunuch who had accompanied the queen into exile, risking his life and reputation to secure the throne for her. The man whose motto was *in matters of state, let your blood run cold*. As much as she loved him and was beholden to him, Kleopatra believed that his blood ran cold at all hours of the day and in all situations.

"Precisely," Antony said, turning back to her. "He is the citizen in most need of comic relief." Antony threw the hood over his head and hobbled like a hunchback up the stairs.

Hephaestion appeared at the door flanked by his guests, the high priest of the Mouseion, and a thoroughly beautiful young man of about eighteen years of age, undoubtedly a prize-winning athlete that the men had agreed to either fight over or share. Kleopatra groaned, tightening her grip on her hood, hoping against all hope that they would not be recognized. But who else would take to the night like this, drunk and delivering philosophical discourse, with the Imperator's Roman militia in attendance?

"Prime Minister!" Antony's voice rang out. "The god of mirth has sent me here on a special mission."

Hephaestion exchanged looks with his guests. He cracked an almost discernible smile. "And what is that sacred mission?"

"To make you laugh."

The priest raised an eyebrow, but Kleopatra saw the boy stifle a giggle.

"It has been decreed by the gods that your philosophy is lacking in humor, and that although you have served queen and country well, you have done so without mirth. The gods won't have it."

"And why not?" asked the priest. "The gods are not known as jokesters."

"They fear that gloom is contagious, and may infect them all the way up on Olympus."

Hephaestion looked at Kleopatra, who shrugged. The Romans laughed. Antony walked right up to the boy. "Why, you're the discus thrower. I saw you compete in the games at Ephesus." He pinched his cheek, and the boy blushed and laughed. "You mustn't stay here with these serious old men. It's bad for the health and the humor. Tomorrow you'll wake up and your spleen will be sour and your balls all shriveled! No, boy, come with us. Come into the streets and help us spread our word."

The boy looked at his host. "I give you leave," Hephaestion said.

"No, no, you're all coming with us," Antony insisted. "Come on, get your cloaks. There's no future here. It's past midnight, and you're all sober." He looked back at Kleopatra. "It's a pathetic state of affairs. They must be helped."

Antony hustled Hephaestion, the priest, the boy, and the queen into the streets, pouring liquor down their throats as they walked. Hephaestion scowled as if he'd never drunk from a pouch, awkwardly opening his mouth wide so that nothing would spill on his impeccable garments. But the priest took Antony's arm, calling him the New Diogenes, Man of Philosophy, and sharing his flask as if the two had been stationed together on a savage frontier and were celebrating their survival. Arm in arm they walked to the next home, where Antony banged on the door demanding to see the head of the house.

"Sir, we are here to resolve your philosophical dilemmas," he announced when Cleon, Minister of Finance, arrived at the door, his eyes puffy with sleep.

The man looked puzzled enough.

"My apologies, Cleon," said Kleopatra. "The good philosopher here was anxious over the state of your soul."

"Well, what are they?" Antony demanded. "What's wrong? Cat got your tongue?"

"I have no philosophical dilemmas, sir. My mind is at peace, as was my body, until you came to my door."

"Let me put it to you this way. If a man is wrested from his bed in the middle of the night and offered the opportunity for mirth, should he make a rational decision, based on the hour at which he must rise in the morning or the duties he must attend to the next day?"

"One should not count the queen's money with a laggard's mind," Cleon answered.

"Oh, that is the excuse of an old man! Let's say a chord is struck in the soul, Cleon. Looking into the eye of his seducer, he remembers how his heart used to soar in his youth, before he became a Learned

Philosopher or an Important Man. Before he extinguished his passions and took up the ways of Reason and Duty and Money. Let's say there is a sudden stirring in his body. A memory of lost youth takes hold of him, and he wants to run into the street with his friends and drink and laugh with them until dawn. What should such a man do?"

Cleon threw his arms up in the air. "What if the man has responsibilities to his government that must be attended to in the morn?"

"Does dry action alleviate human suffering? Does the good man, the virtuous man, let Duty throw water on the fires of Passion and Longing?"

"Answer carefully, Cleon," Kleopatra called out. "There are those here who will report you to the queen."

Cleon threw his outstretched arms around Antony. "He does not, Brother!" And Antony lifted the Minister of Finance up, threw him on his back, and carried him into the streets.

On like this they went for hours, tumbling through the streets of the city's finest neighborhood adjacent to the palace quarter, dragging diplomats, rich merchants, landowners, and high-ranking officials from their homes to join their ragged band. Antony invaded their kitchens, confiscated their wines for his flasks and his men, slapped their serving girls' behinds, made naughty comments to their wives, and brought the whole party—thirty in all—back to the palace. He opened the kitchens and was pleased to find eight boars roasting in anticipation of his appetite and his unannounced guests. He did not know that Kleopatra had sent a messenger ahead hours earlier to alert the cooks.

"Your kitchens are not kitchens, but enchanted places where feasts are conjured up by magic out of thin air," he exclaimed to Kleopatra, his eyes glowing as he looked over the guests, who were laughing and drinking and eating a meal as the sun came up as if it were the most normal thing in the world.

She smiled, and decided to let him think that was true.

"Look at your Prime Minister, in earnest, drunken conversation with that boy. I do believe he is actually smiling," Antony said.

"Even he has had enough wine to crack open his somber frown."

"Yes, the wine has made him believe in his good fortune. He looks absolutely certain that he is going to take that discus thrower to his bed."

"See what your recipe of mirth has done for my subjects? The most pessimistic among them have turned romantic."

Antony took a tendril of her hair from the nape of her neck and wrapped it around his large index finger. "I am very much at home here, Your Majesty. More so than in my own land. Why is that?"

"Because you are Greek at heart, my darling. You are more than Greek. You are like me; you are all nationalities at once. You love what is best and most beautiful in every land and in every kind of people."

"You know what they say in Rome, Kleopatra? They say your court is decadent, concerned with all the wrong things. Well I say you are concerned with all the right things. Is love of life and all its beauty and all its pleasures decadent?"

"Your countrymen would say so. But life is not so simple as they would have it. The Egyptians are concerned with deciphering the mysteries of death, and the Greeks are devoted to the mysteries of life. For the Romans, there are no mysteries! There is only conquest and domination. And money."

Antony laughed. "Very succinct, Your Majesty."

"You belong to us because you love all that we love."

"All the world should have what we have here. Sumptuous foods washed down with sweet wines."

"And poetry to help the digestion."

"Athletes as swift and graceful as the gods, and actors whose voices sing the wisdom of the ancients."

"Yes, and statues everywhere to our glorious ancestors and our illustrious gods."

"And beautiful bejeweled women wrapped in silks and the sheerest of linens."

"Ah yes, your world would not be complete without them, would it?"

He cuddled her very close to his chest. "No, Your Majesty, that would be the poorest of worlds. Not even the waves of the great green sea could cheer a man in a world with no beautiful women."

"You see why you are at home here, Imperator? Because all that you see, you love, and all that you see loves you. It is that simple."

Antony's wide smile closed into an cynical grin. "For you, Kleopatra, it is that simple. But for a Roman to be so in love with life's more aesthetic offerings, I am afraid it is not simple at all."

Rome:
the 11th year of
Kleopatra's reign

Julius Caesar had never feared fighting a war to find out who his friends were. Oh, it's worth the trouble, he had assured his adopted son. Most men are happy to join with their fellows in honoring you at the ceremonies, or to lie about on your dining couch and shower you with words of loyalty and admiration while they eat your food and drink your wine. But none will expose his breast to the sword to demonstrate a false loyalty.

Makes sense, the boy Octavian had replied.

War is so very helpful in so many ways, the uncle had said. It draws the lines of loyalty, puts money in the pockets, staves off monotony, and invigorates the blood.

Now, so many years later, Octavian recalled that moment when the uncle and father had imparted one of the many gifts to his nephew *cum* son in the short time they shared.

Octavian let himself feel a moment of nostalgia for his dead bene-factor. How nice it would be to have him here today at his wedding. How proud Caesar would have been at his nephew's maneuverings. Yet he realized that if Caesar had lived, he, his heir, would not be here in this grand mansion, marrying this exquisite girl who made his very blood shiver as it ran through his veins. He would still be at military school in Greece studying strategy, rather than having put to the test all that his uncle had tried to divulge to him through their few but long talks and by his lifelong example. Now, at twenty-four, Octavian had not only inherited his uncle's money by power of Caesar's will, but had also gained his fearsome army and his great mass of allies by power of cunning and bribery.

Octavian was certain that his uncle—a god now, inhabiting that ether world where divinities lived—was pleased with him. He had taken Caesar's advice and fought a war to determine his friends, just as he had played into the hands of Caesar's assassins and had let them hang themselves in the end. That had worked well enough, so well that he was rid of all of them now, thanks to his mother's convincing him to make an alliance with Antony. It had been simple enough to ally with his uncle's man; logical, even, to put aside his tender young ego and let Antony think he could control their alliance simply because of his advanced years and experience. Octavian had manipulated Cicero, his so-called mentor, to his own advantage, and Cicero was a genius. Why could he not put on the same show for the blusterer Antony? The mask could be worn as long as necessary.

So that when Lucius Antonius, Antony's ridiculous brother, took up arms against him under the command of Antony's wife, Fulvia, Octavian pondered long and hard before he took action. He did not know if Fulvia had lost her senses and acted without Antony's blessing, or if there was some secret correspondence between husband and wife in which Fulvia was charged with breaking the alliance with Octavian so that Antony would not have to take the blame. Octavian had already openly broken with Fulvia—General Fulvia, he called her, to throw into sharp relief the ridiculousness of a woman heading an army—and had returned her whimpering daughter, Clodia, to her untouched. Oh, he wanted to touch her all right, but her whiny cries that she was frightened, and her constant reminders that she had been sacrificed to him by her mother and stepfather, caused all the blood and semen to take flight from his prick. If called on it, he could explain all that away man-to-man to Antony, who would understand.

Octavian had quickly took as a new bride Scribonia, old and ugly but politically well-connected. He held his nose and impregnated her, and just before he left to fight Fulvia and Lucius, she had given birth to a very fetching little infant girl, Julia, who he was pleased to say looked just like himself and not the old witch who incubated her in the womb. When he saw the child, he laughed at his own foolish fears; he had anticipated the baby being born with its mother's scowl and wrinkles, not realizing that it had taken a lifetime of bitterness to carve those atrocities upon Scribonia's face.

But the sight of Livia Drusilla had instantly wiped Scribonia from his mind like a clean cloth sweeps away a stain. The circumstances under which the courtship and marriage had taken place were highly unusual, but they accomplished his goal—the goal of having her. He saw her first in the city of Perugia, where he had starved out the allies of Fulvia and Lucius in a devastating siege. Finally, after three months of famine, the renegades opened the gates to the city and let him in. Livia was with her husband, a longtime supporter of Antony who had gone over to Fulvia and Lucius. She must have been forty years her husband's junior. As soon as Octavian saw her, with her clear pale skin drawn over her conspicuous cheekbones and her dark brown eyes sunken into a face that had lived on less than a modicum of food for months, he knew that he must rescue her from this paunchy, grandfatherly figure she had married, and take her into his young arms.

She was the essence of all that was Rome. It was not just the noble and ancient Etruscan features, but the carriage of her tall person. He couldn't place it exactly, but something about her reminded him of Caesar. Behind the feminine beauty, he discerned a restless and questioning mind, which saw all but commented on nothing. She had the reserve that Caesar could call upon at any time, whether in the midst of battle or in the most grueling negotiations. Livia wore that same mask that Caesar had so successfully donned and which had served him so well. Octavian knew it as soon as he saw her dark eyes darting about when he entered the city. He had met those eyes, and something deep inside himself had responded. He had lost his uncle too soon, long before the mentoring was over. He had not had an opportunity to probe the mind of Julius in depth. Not that anyone had. For who really knew his uncle? If Caesar was a correct witness to his own relationships, then the one in Egypt, the one presently making a bedroom and war-room alliance with Antony, was the only one in whom he confided utterly. But Octavian doubted that Caesar had given anyone, much less a foreign queen, open access to his thoughts, even if he so claimed.

The very instant Octavian saw Livia was prophetic. He had entered the walled city of Perugia with his men on the Ides of March—as if that was not in itself a message from the god Julius—and immediately all the sniffling cowards who had deserted him and joined his enemies began to appeal to him for mercy, heaping all praise and adulation upon him for his skills, crying that they had underestimated him for his youth, allowing that he was the very soul of Caesar and that they would remain loyal to him to their deaths.

What would my uncle do, he wondered? Then he remembered Caesar's exemplary record of mercy. Should he imitate his uncle's nonchalant generosity and let them all return to their homes? How his beneficence would be talked about through Italy! But then he also remembered his own needs. Caesar's troops had still not received recompense from Caesar's war against Pompey and the Republicans. They had backed Octavian in this present conflict because he promised to deliver not only money but land. He had taken great pains to settle some of the soldiers, but the vast majority were still standing before him with their hands out. Where was he to get this precious, promised land?

Octavian looked at the faces of his enemies, Romans once fat from the lavish lifestyles they enjoyed in Italy. Their eyes, sunken deep into their sockets, implored him to believe that their treachery would not be repeated. As he scrutinized their faces for signs of sincerity or treachery, he tried to calculate how many hundreds of thousands of acres they must own among them, and how nicely those acres would be divided among thousands of soldiers. Then he calculated how long it would take the angry and weary soldiers to turn on him should Antony decide to leave Kleopatra's bed and return to Italy to avenge the defeat of his wife and brother. When Antony returned, these same men who were now imploring him for mercy would turn against him in a heartbeat.

With all of this in mind, he gave his answer to his enemies: "If you are prepared to be true to me until death, then even you shall pass this test of fealty, gentlemen, because all of you must die immediately." And then he turned away to avoid the look of horror on their faces.

Oh, it wasn't what Caesar would have done, but look where Caesar's mercy got him. Twenty-odd blows of the dagger into his merciful and forgiving flesh, delivered by many of those same men who had enjoyed his leniency. Besides, Caesar, more than Octavian, could afford to be

merciful; Caesar had never been in the position of having to face
Antony's wrath.

Octavian ordered his men to march the captives to the sacrificial
altar. There he gave a short speech about the god Julius, and how those
who took up arms against his rightful heir were in a sense murdering
him again, and how, on this anniversary of his death, they would be sacrificed to placate him.

Then he instructed his incredulous men to sacrifice three hundred of
their fellow Romans—senators and aristocrats one and all—right then
and there in a ritual offering to the Divine Julius Caesar. Many of those
soldiers who had served Caesar tried to protest, but enough of them
had put together the same formula that Octavian had already come up
with: Every one of these men was a holder of great parcels of land that
would pass to the state—hence to the soldiers—upon their death.

With that motivation, the ceremony began. Unarmed and too weak
from starvation to defend themselves, a few tried to run. Most went to
their deaths screaming at him, cursing him, condemning him, but that
did not bother Octavian, because as soon as he looked into the eyes of
Livia Drusilla, all ambient sound was vanquished, and the only thing he
could hear was the pounding of his own heart. She looked back at him,
not with anger or bitterness or even judgment of any kind, though her
husband was one who was slated to die. He could not guess what was
behind those eyes, but he knew that he had to find out, and, whatever
it was, claim it for his own. He couldn't describe the impact of her look,
but he knew that he must act quickly to secure her for himself. When
the death sentence was announced, she was standing next to her husband. He closed his eyes, accepting his Fate, but she reached out her
long, thin arm and placed it—strained palm facing outward—across his
chest, like a sentinel protecting a charge. It was a simple gesture, but not
to be challenged. Behind her, a governess held her infant son, clutching
the child and weeping over the impending death of its father, but Livia
did not move. She just stood there with her arm across her husband's
chest forbidding either his movement or the soldiers from taking him.
Octavian thought at that moment that she might be a goddess, or if not
a divine being, then one inspired by those heavenly ladies. No mortal
woman could have made his very will a prisoner to her eyes.

He walked right up to her, mesmerized by her gaze. "You may follow your leader to Greece," he said, for that was where Fulvia had fled when she knew her quest for power was lost. "And you may take your family with you. But you must return to Rome within the month, or there will be a price to pay."

The girl said nothing but squinted her eyes against the sun that lit Octavian from behind. Her husband, Tiberius Nero, remained silent, confused, perhaps, as to why he had been granted this reprieve. But he was a rich man and probably thought that had something to do with it. Only the governess wailed her thanks to Octavian and to the gods as she held the baby up to the skies, proclaiming him the most blessed of children.

"Do you understand me?" Octavian asked Livia. She did not remove the barrier of her arm that separated her husband from him, nor did she say one word of thanks.

"I do indeed," she replied.

But she hadn't understood, not really, because when Octavian came to them back in Rome with his demand, they were stunned. It was simple. She was to divorce Tiberius immediately and marry him. Octavian had already put Scribonia away, and had convinced his allies in the senate to hurry along the process by lifting the imposed amount of time before remarriage. It would not be a problem, he explained to Tiberius and Livia, and hardly a big demand to make in exchange for their lives.

"But she is pregnant with my child," Tiberius said.

"Yes, I've thought of that," Octavian replied. "If it's a boy, I'll send him to you to be raised in your household."

"I don't know what to say," Tiberius said.

"The death sentence was not commuted without condition," Octavian replied. "Just because we are in Rome does not mean that it won't be carried out. We made a bargain, if you recall."

"*I* recall," Livia answered. "Do you guarantee the safety of my children and their rights to bear their father's name and to be reared in his home?"

"I do, Madam," Octavian said. "I do, indeed, on my word and on the memory of the Divine Julius Caesar."

"Then make arrangements right away for our wedding. We shall have it right here in my husband's home with his blessing."

Tiberius quivered and twitched but did not protest. Octavian was heartened by her words—thrilled, truth be known—but he did not suffer the illusion that she said them in the spirit of love. She seemed at that moment more the general than Fulvia had ever been. Fulvia had emotions that ran high, despite her ability to calculate and maneuver. There was no emotion in what Livia had said, merely the acknowledgment of a business deal. Whether she closed that deal out of fear, duty, or ambition, he could not decipher.

Now Octavian's bride sat next to him stiff as stone and puffed up with pregnancy. Occasionally she looked in his direction and offered up a half-moon of a smile, but it looked painted on her face rather than animated by a feeling of happiness. Six months along, still, no one said a word about her condition. In fact, despite the odd circumstances of the wedding, everyone ate and drank and celebrated the union with pleasure, even Tiberius Nero, the father of the seed that grew inside her belly. Well, Octavian *would* do what was right. He would send the child to the father after it was born, particularly if it was a boy. A girl might only be a burden to Tiberius, and would make a good companion to his little Julia.

Perhaps people talked behind Octavian's back. But the only gaffe made at the wedding was by a ten-year-old serving boy, dressed in white, cheeks rouged to recall Cupid, who informed Livia that she was sitting with the wrong husband. That provoked a snicker or two, but it did not matter to Octavian. He was very proud of his manipulation of the circumstances. His uncle would have felt the same, for was it not Caesar himself who had gleefully reported the secret schemes he concocted with his comrade Clodius, defying law, constitution, and even nature?

Octavian breathed a deep sigh of pleasure and satisfaction. He had the woman of his choosing at his side, and she would learn to love him. He had Caesar's army. General Fulvia was gone to Greece, thanks to the military genius of Marcus Agrippa, one of the two young men whom Caesar had handpicked to serve as Octavian's advisers. His enemies were dead by his own hand. The only outstanding problem was Antony. Was Octavian up to a confrontation with Antony? What would Antony do when he found out that Fulvia had started a war in his name and had broken his alliance with Octavian without Antony's blessing? Or so everyone said. Was Antony really ignorant of his wife's actions, or did he sanction them from Kleopatra's bed? Was Fulvia so ambitious that she would wage war on Antony's behalf while he was entwining himself with another woman? A woman who would stop at nothing until she was Antony's partner—his empress—in Rome's eastern empire? Perhaps that was their secret arrangement—Fulvia would defeat Octavian so that Antony would have no obstacles to total authority in Rome, while Kleopatra would furnish him with the resources to command all the countries of the east. Was Antony's enchantment over women so great that he could manipulate both Fulvia and the queen into doing his bidding? Octavian pushed that thought aside. He did not want to think his rival so formidable. At any rate, did Antony really think he could make an alliance all at once with Caesar's chosen heir, and also with the woman who claimed to be the mother of Caesar's only true son? Antony's next step would answer that question. Octavian did not believe that Caesar's army would take up arms against Antony, the man who had led them into battle time and again. No, he would have to think of some other way to manage Antony. He did not yet have the plan in mind, but he was sure it would soon occur to him.

Then he remembered that he was not alone. He remembered the calm with which Livia Drusilla, ignoring her husband's protests, had agreed to their marriage—her subtle but emphatic closing of all questions on the issue, as if she had worked it all out in her mind. Someday he would make her tell him the thought process that had led up to her decision. Someday, but not this evening. This evening, after he consummated the marriage, he would take up the matter of Antony with his new bride and find out what thoughts were swimming about behind that beautiful, impeccably smooth brow.

Alexandria: the 20th year of Kleopatra's reign

The light is harsher this morning, cutting a hot white slab across her desk. Kleopatra holds a vase in her hands. It is a cheap one, hastily spun on a pottery wheel and crudely painted, manufactured in quantity by order of Octavian and offered for a few pennies so that anyone at all might afford to have something that mocks her. But it is a poor likeness. The figure is huge and shrewlike, and she is taunting the god Herakles with her size and power. She has confiscated his stick and club and holds it in her greedy, grasping hand. In the harridan's other hand is a bowl of wine, held out to the humiliated god, demanding that he pour her another serving. Herakles, with Antony's face, is small and sullen, cowering before his female master. The message is clear: Kleopatra has emasculated Antony and has assumed his power.

Is there a truth she might construct to palliate the lies now circulating all over the known world? In her kingdom, she is called Kleopatra VII Theas Philopater, Neos Isis, Father-Loving Queen of Kings, living incarnation of our divine Lady, and Pharaoh of the Two Lands of Egypt. To her children, she is known by a single word—Mother. In her time, she has been called by her regal name, the Queen of her Sons who are Kings, and, for her deeds to the people over whom she rules, the Savior, just as her forebears were honored with that title. But now, new monikers have been invented by the evil one in Rome—monster, prostitute, seductress, mortal enemy of Rome.

She wonders which image will survive. The succubus on the vase? The destroyer of the living Herakles? The monster Octavian created and fed to the people? When she dies, her first mission in the underworld of the shades will be to confront Caesar for his choice of heir. She will make him answer to her, or her soul will never rest.

She takes the vase to the fallen Titan sitting alone, staring over the sea, the Great Green as he called it in happier days, following the habit of the native people. She shows him the thing, carefully watching his face as he takes it in his big hands and stares at it, holding it a little farther from his eyes so that he might see it more clearly. She is hoping it will spark a dialogue between them, hoping this measure of Octavian's cunning, this assault on his masculinity, will rouse his ire. Instead, he laughs. A good likeness of us both, he says, and turns away.

She is stunned quiet. Not because of his reaction, but because she remembers that this is not the first time he has turned his back on her.

She feels the memory of it all creep up on her like an intruder in the dark, and she is helpless to stop its invasion. For years, she has put aside that dark period of her life, the only time in a lifetime filled with conflict, challenges, and adversity, when she had lost hope. For so long, she has forbidden herself to recall those times, those years when she had to go on without Antony. For so long, she has told herself that those were the years in which his loyalty to Rome shone most brightly; that he had only sacrificed their love and ambitions for circumstances that he believed would bring world peace. She has reminded herself that she, too, has more than once chosen country over love. She has always concentrated on how horribly Antony was deceived by Octavian, not how horribly she was deceived by Antony.

But now, in the wake of Antony's dismissal, the memory of it all sneaks back in. She feels the glorious rush of love in which she had lived that entire first winter with Antony fill her body. She remembers how Antony had received no word from Rome because the Artesian winds prevented the delivery of mail, and how their love thrived in isolation from Rome and its problems. She remembers her disappointment when the weather cleared and they learned that the Parthians were attacking Roman provinces and had murdered a Roman governor. And she remembers the sorrow and hope she felt as Antony set off with his army, whispering in his ear the joyous news: She was once again pregnant. She remembers him taking her into his great arms and whispering in return that now the son of Caesar would have a son of Antony with whom to play.

She remembers his broad back—the same one she is staring at now—as he walked away, departing with a considerable amount of her money, her army's horses, and Egyptian grain, leaving her to build ships to strengthen his naval forces

and recruit mercenaries from nearby territories for the final encounter with
Parthia. But then it all changed. With one letter, and in one instant, once again,
everything Kleopatra had worked for and believed in was gone. Somewhere around
Tyre, Antony received the devastating news about Fulvia's uprising: Fearful of
Octavian's growing influence in Rome, and seeing firsthand his betrayal of the
treaty he made with both Antony and Lepidus, Fulvia and Antony's brother
Lucius had waged a bloody war against Octavian's forces.

Fulvia. What courage it must have taken for her to act. Was she so in love with
Antony that she was willing to lay down her own life? Or did she have such confidence in Antony's popularity and in the men left to her command, and in her
own ability to command them? But the hundreds of senators and statesmen who
fled Rome to join Fulvia's cause were slaughtered on a sacrificial altar used for
offering animals to the gods. This Octavian had done in Caesar's name. Caesar,
who was renowned for his extraordinary mercy. If there is judgment and
vengeance in Hades' dark land, perhaps Caesar would avenge his name against the
deeds of his heir.

As Perugia fell, poor starving Fulvia had fled to Greece. Antony, upon hearing the news, made for Athens to meet her. There he found a broken woman.
Starvation, defeat, and the demise of her friends and supporters at Octavian's
demonic hands had ruined her health. Antony chastised her greatly for her efforts,
and she—perhaps because she was too weak—did not adequately defend her
actions.

Since then, how many times has Kleopatra reprimanded Antony for his treatment of Fulvia? How many times has she said to him that Fulvia was prescient?
That she knew Octavian would never honor the terms of peace with Antony, and
had attempted to put him down before his influence spread?

Suddenly, Kleopatra feels herself getting dizzy. She has never let herself believe
she is reliving Fulvia's experience, but the comparison has now made itself manifest and sits like an unwanted guest in her mind. She does not let herself dwell
on the possibility that history is repeating itself, as it so often does. No, that will
not do. She has no time for such meditations. She closes her eyes, cracking the whip
on her mind, forcing it to move on.

What happened next? Antony left his grieving wife behind and hurried to Italy
to assess the situation. Arriving at Brundisium, he found himself persona non
grata—the effects of Octavian's influence. The local officials did not give him leave
to dock. He disembarked nearby with his men and waited. Soon enough, Octavian
arrived, encamping directly opposite him.

Antony was ready to strike. Oh, why did he not? But the soldiers who had served both commanders were reluctant to choose, and so they forced their generals to renew their alliance. Octavian pledged Antony twenty thousand soldiers for the Parthian campaign, and also a pardon for Fulvia. But before Octavian had agreed, word came that Fulvia had died in Greece.

It was then—before Fulvia's body was cold, much less cremated—that Octavian made the proposition that struck through Kleopatra's heart like one of the daggers that killed Caesar: To demonstrate conviction for their alliance, Antony must wed Octavian's sister, Octavia. Anxious for peace, Antony readily accepted, giving Octavian leave to install a most loyal spy and operative in Antony's very bed.

And what of Kleopatra, who had subsidized Antony's military efforts, and with whom he had made far-reaching plans that he had sworn were paramount to his ambitions and desires? What of Kleopatra, who had just given birth to his twins? What of Kleopatra, who loved him fiercely? He ceased to answer her letters.

Kleopatra now wallows in the very misery she spent years forgetting. She remembers how she watched from afar as Octavia usurped her position in Antony's life. How she prayed to the goddess that Octavia would be a wife like Caesar's Calpurnia, taken for political alliance only, a silent mouse of a spinning Roman housewife who stayed home and worshipped Hesta while her husband ran about the world dancing on the heads of his enemies. But it was not to be. Antony—though he denied it, still denies it—fell in love with Octavia. He brought her to Athens with him and honored her as Athena herself, the goddess who presides over the city.

Kleopatra is desolate remembering this, as desolate as she was when she realized that Antony had brought his Roman wife to Greece to show the people of east and west alike that he had rejected the alliance with Aphrodite, the Mother goddess, the goddess of love, in favor of the chaste Athena. And how the Romans approved of that notion. Though they are most barbarously crude in their sexual proclivities, they still like to appear as chaste and restrained as Athena herself. Goddess of War, Abstinence, Childbirth. What better model for a Roman matron? How many times did Antony later swear that he was just putting on a show? And how much of her intuition did Kleopatra have to deny to believe him? The evidence was to the contrary: coins issued with Octavia's image, coins with them costumed as Athena and Dionysus, making a mockery of his love with Kleopatra. Fabulous games hosted by him and Octavia in Greece, for which they received much praise.

The worst evidence of all: Quickly, very quickly, she became pregnant with his child, and the world rejoiced. The poet Vergil even wrote a verse about it that was circulated around the world. It proclaimed that either the child of Antony and Octavia or the child of Octavian and Scribonia would be the New Messiah, the Bringer of a Golden Era of Peace and Joy. Of course, by the time the poem was in print, Octavian had already put Scribonia away and was conspiring to take Livia away from her husband. But the Romans were anxious to produce a New Messiah of their own, because the Golden Child who most fitted the descriptions in the prophecies was the son of Kleopatra and Caesar, Caesarion.

Grief buried long ago descends upon her like a shroud. The astrologer she had attached to Antony's circle tried to console her with the notion that the baby was the work not of Antony's semen but Octavia's magic. She remembers smiling at him, though she saw the lie. She had known Antony's passion; she did not believe that Octavia, even if she was just her brother's spy, could or would resist him.

They were husband and wife in the eyes of the world, and Kleopatra was alone with her heartache, praying that the people of Egypt would accept any of her bastard Roman children as heirs to the throne.

Still, Antony continued to amass forces to march on Parthia. As he moved east with his wife, Kleopatra did not know if the two of them would come to Egypt together, and if she would have to receive them. Or if he would come by himself and demand more of her grain, her money, and her troops. Or if he would merely march into her country with his men and declare the land of her ancestors a client kingdom that he would rule himself, with Octavia his eastern queen.

It was not impossible.

Syria: the 15th year of Kleopatra's reign

If Antony thought that Antioch was neutral territory, he was mistaken. She knew what he was up to. He had his Roman wife, his Roman children, his Roman army, his Roman half of the empire. She had spent the better part of the last few years wiping him from her heart and her mind. Finally reconciled to life without him, she was annoyed that he was "summoning" her to him now. And if he thought her appearance would come without a price, he was dead wrong.

She was tired of being summoned—by him, by Romans, by men. This would be the last time she answered such a call. Queens summoned others; they were not summoned themselves. But when Capito came to her so respectfully on Antony's behalf—at least he had not sent the debauched Dellius again—Kleopatra talked it over with Hephaestion and they agreed that she should respond.

She was elated that he had chosen Antioch, a city founded by Seleucus, the companion of Alexander and of her ancestor Ptolemy. At the mouth of the Orontes River, at the crossroads of two major trade routes, the city resembled Alexandria in many ways. It had been settled by a Macedonian general; it was full of libraries, parks, Greek and Asian statuary, crowded markets with every luxury, tall white mansions, and wide boulevards; its large Jewish population lived harmoniously among the Syrians and Greeks. Kleopatra spoke all the languages of Antioch—

Greek, Syrian, Hebrew, and the Arabic dialect of some of the merchant class. She not only had visited the city frequently in her youth, but her family held a palace there. It was the capital of Syria, of the Seleucid empire. Caesar had liked it so well that he made it an autonomous city even after Pompey had annexed it to Rome. Her father had spent much of his youth there with his mother, and there he had also met his first wife, Kleopatra's mother. Kleopatra decided she would go directly to those lavish quarters where her parents had once lived and "summon" Antony to her.

She did not enter Antioch quietly, but was met at the seaport thirteen miles from the city by a royal Syrian entourage. For her own transportation, she ordered a white Arabian steed, decorated in the finest bejeweled saddlery the local craftsmen had to offer. With flaming red plumes dressing the animal's head and a saddle and reins of studded rubies, Kleopatra and her retinue rode into Antioch in the middle of the morning when the markets would be most crowded. Pipers brought from Alexandria announced her presence so that people flocked to the streets to see the queen on her snowy, high-prancing mount. She welcomed the animal's haughty gait; it was how she would have walked into town herself if she were on foot.

He needed her. She knew why; knew about Antony's army of one hundred thousand men who would take the Parthian empire for him once and for all. She knew how much it took to clothe, arm, and feed such a horde of human beings; how much it cost to feed and maintain the horses and dogs; how much it cost to dress and heal the soldiers' wounds; how much food it took to make those soldiers strong enough to fight and to bury their dead on the battlefield after the day was won. Would it not be convenient if food and money flowed freely from the neighboring country that just happened to be world's largest producer of grain?

Kleopatra knew all too well what Antony required and where he intended to get it. She was prepared for all his tricks, for the facile charm that he could muster without effort, for the poetry that flowed from his lips as if he were the scribe of Euripides, for the smoldering looks that could melt a woman's heart, make her knees weak, and extinguish her will. She had spent four years without those niceties. She had trained herself not to miss them one bit. After Antony's long absence, she knew, finally, what his flattery and his lust were worth in the end. Nothing.

This was a business meeting and the topic was money.

This time, neither party kept the other waiting. Antony arrived promptly at the palace at the appointed time with Capito, who stood stiffly by his side. Perhaps he was present to alleviate the need to address the consequences of their former intimacy—unrecognized children, and a woman's abandonment. Apparently there were to be no games, no theatrical presentations, no divine costumery. Kleopatra was dressed sedately, though she had taken every effort to make herself solemnly beautiful. Since the birth of the twins, she had been soaking in donkey's milk from Aswan to revive her body's skin. No longer a peanut brown coltish maiden tanned from long days on her horse, she was paler, rounder, more serene than the last time he had seen her. Truth be known, if asked, she would have said that though she was thirty-four years old and the mother of three children, she was at the height of her physical appeal. She liked the new roundness that had come with the twins; her breasts were fuller than ever before, and any wrinkles that may have been tempted to appear were smoothed by the extra pounds. She felt more solidly ensconced in her own body, more real, more vivid. She was still athletic. Her thighs were still columns of muscles, her arms long for her height and free of fat, and she could still manage a stubborn horse as well as any man she knew. All the pretense of youth was gone. She no longer needed to assume costumes and personae to present herself as she wished to be perceived. She had become what she had always hoped she was—a woman whose natural charms and ferocious intelligence were made exponentially apparent as the sole and sovereign ruler of a great nation.

Antony, too, had changed. Kleopatra had steeled herself against his charisma, but found herself disarmed by his presentation. He had aged. A deep line slashed his formidable brow from hairline to nose, the kind that only came from wrinkling one's brow in worry. He had put on weight as well, but Kleopatra did not think the new pounds sat so attractively on his physique. Somehow, with his new imperfections, she found herself liking him better. His godlike features were now tempered with the weight of his humanity.

"Your Majesty." He did not move toward her, nor did he smile.

"Imperator."

She was so focused on controlling any emotion that she did not notice what language they spoke. But emotion she felt. His eyes dislodged her composure, though she prayed she did not reveal it to him. She was completely unprepared for the fact that his eyes were identical to the eyes of their twins—brown and deep, as if one could fall into them and swim straight to the underworld, losing oneself forever. So many times she had looked into her children's eyes, fascinated with the expression, not realizing—or not allowing herself to remember—that they were Antony's. She waited for him to speak.

"We have many things to discuss. Are you prepared?"

To whom did he think he was speaking? she wondered. She had no intention of resuming their intimate rapport before she had everything she wanted. She saw that she would have to set the tone of dispensing with small talk. She invited him to sit down. Then she asked Capito to leave.

"I believe the messenger has accomplished his mission," she said, nodding in his direction. She was pleased to see that he did not ask Antony's permission to depart, but took Kleopatra's dismissal as an order.

"Now then," she said.

"Kleopatra," Antony began. But she cut him short.

"Imperator, I know why you have called upon me. I have been watching with great interest your doings on my borders. Very clever. You've set yourself up brilliantly."

"How do you mean, madam?" he asked formally.

"You have given power to the kings and princes and noblemen whom you think you can control. Not because you are generous by nature, but because you realized that you must have strong and secure countries in Asia Minor and the Arab lands to prevent Parthian invasions. Herod, you have made king of the Jews. Not a strategic move in the long run, but I do understand why you did it. You've propped up Artavasdes of Armenia so that you'll be able to follow Caesar's strategy of invading Parthia from the north. I don't think you'll be able to keep him loyal. The man is notorious. The king of Media is a more intelligent risk. Monaeses—well, you've given him too much of Syria. But he is more interested in trade than in your wars and is a man easily bought and sold. Now let's see. The kingdom of Cappodocia. You've entrusted the land all the way to the Parthian border to Archelaus, son of the bastard prince who married my sister Berenike and fought with her against my father. Do you think he'll really be loyal to you? Oh, but he is under the influence of Glaphyra of Cappodocia, is he not? And you secured her loyalty in her bedroom, so she will not be tempted to betray you. That is the way with your women, is it not?

"And now, the missing link in your chain is Kleopatra of Egypt. That is why you are here. To judge her resentment for your desertion of her and to negotiate."

"I see that your intelligence operations are still intact, Kleopatra of Egypt." Antony smiled. "As well as your intelligence."

"What did you expect? I am not finished. I have also been informed that you have given large tracts of land in Asia Minor to a couple of crafty Greek planters—what are their names? Polemo and Amyntas? Do they not sound like characters in a play by Aristophanes?"

"What is your point, Your Majesty?"

"My point is that the queen of Egypt shall not be made to settle for less than your plebeian upstarts, or less than Herod, whom you made a king. I was born from a great line of kings, I will thank you to remember. I did not need a Roman to appoint me to this throne. I know what you require from me, and as always, when you ask something of a woman, you will get it. Here is what I require from you in return."

Kleopatra called for her scribe. "The map, please."

He returned with a thick scroll, which he unrolled and laid before Antony. Antony said nothing, but raised his eyebrows.

"This is a map of the empire of my ancestors. The black borders represent the countries chiseled away from us through the years by the greedy appetite of Rome."

"Thank you for this instruction in history and geography, Kleopatra."

"I want it restored to me."

She could not be sure, because he was not meeting her gaze, but she could swear that he had rolled his eyes. He took another long look at the map, collected himself, and spoke. "I know that has been your ambition all along, Kleopatra, but now is not the time to ask for such things. When we succeed against Parthia, then you'll have the lands of your grandfathers once more."

"We, Imperator? I do not believe I am going to war, nor do I believe that I shall be queen of Parthia when you are done."

Antony put his hands on the arms of his chair and leaned toward her. "Have you forgotten our ambitions, Your Majesty?" He was almost seething, not in anger but in intensity.

"I have heard nothing of such ambitions for many years. Perhaps they were the reveries of foolish lovers. But those two people are gone, and *we* are here in their stead. I will reiterate my demands. You have given great power to those who rule the lands on my every border. You have weakened me. Here is what I require. Please look at the map. I want the northern frontier of Syria. It was held by Ptolemy Soter and it is rightfully mine. I want Ptolemais Ace and I want Ituraea. Believe me, if you give me Ituraea they shall hail me as queen in Damascus, that much is guaranteed. Going south, I want Hippos and Gadara and the lands surrounding them. You can let Herod keep Gaza, but I must have control over the date groves. They are very lucrative, and were taken from Egypt long ago. I also need more control over the Red Sea. Do you see the plan, Imperator? I want the seas that surround me. It is imperative if I am to support your war. I know that your ally in Rome is not your ally at all, and I will not be vulnerable to his invasion while your back is to him in Parthia."

Antony shook his head. "I see that you have had too much time to think."

"Ample, Imperator."

"Dare I ask about the health of our children?"

"Children are not the subject of these negotiations. If you are inquisitive about your issue, you must come to Alexandria sometime."

"Kleopatra, don't be cruel."

"Do not dare speak to me of cruelty."

"You think that your informants have kept you apprised of everything, but even they do not have access to a man's heart."

If she did not know that Antony was a consummate performer, she might have pursued this line of dialogue. She might have let herself begin to hope for more than the restoration of the empire of the Ptolemies. She might have hoped for a restoration of their partnership, their dreams. But he had a Roman wife who was pregnant again with their second Roman child. True, he had just sent her back to Rome, but that did not mean that he was ready to switch his loyalties. As with the unfortunate Fulvia, Antony required a loyal female to watch over his interests in Rome. Who better than the sister of his rival? Who would have access to more information? Who would be better to follow the machinations of her brother? A female. Loyal, but vested with no real power, so that she would never be as threatening to Antony's interests as a man.

"Your heart is not part of these negotiations, Imperator."

"That is where you are mistaken."

"Where was your heart when you ignored the letters of our children's birth? When you turned your back on everything we had so carefully planned? You have no heart. What beats in your chest is the drum of ambition."

She had pushed too far. Emotion had sneaked into the room and made itself palpable. She tried to retract the feeling, the anger, the bitterness, but it had escaped and was now on the loose.

Antony leapt from his chair. She did not know if he was going to attack her and she shrank back, but he threw his arms in the air. He stood over her like a huge animal.

"You frighten me, Imperator. Please sit down."

He did not sit but dropped his hands and stared at her. "I wonder what you might have done under the circumstances, Kleopatra. You, who hold paramount your ambition to preserve your throne for yourself and your children. I wonder what you would have done if you found out that the person you trusted the most had broken that trust over her own ambitions."

"I know what I would have done, Imperator, because that is precisely what happened to me. And yet here I sit willing to negotiate again with that person."

Antony took a deep, exasperated breath. "There is no winning an argument with you. I won't explain myself, then. I won't tell you the horror that Fulvia's actions brought down on our friends and allies. Poor woman. I won't go into that at all, how her defeat broke her courage and how my anger murdered her. All right. That's extraneous here. And I won't go into the story of how I was manipulated into marrying a shy, smiling Roman matron as part of a peace treaty. Do you know what peace means to the people of Rome, Kleopatra? Do you know how many years our conflicts have gone on? How many of our friends and relations we have watched die? My grandfather was murdered and beheaded, my stepfather executed, my mentor Julius Caesar assassinated. How many faces across the battlefield have I once called friend?

"The world yearns for peace. I believed that by my alliance with Caesar's nephew, and by my marriage to his sister, that I could bring peace. I believe it no more."

"What do you believe now?"

"I did nothing that you would not have done to secure your own future and position and that of your people. I have seen the risks you are willing to take. And you have told me of the difficult decisions you have had to make. 'In matters of state, let your blood run cold.' I did not invent that phrase, Kleopatra, but I took your advice, believing that you above all persons would understand."

"I see that you know me too well, Imperator, and that is my own fault. You seem to know me through and through, and yet I do not even know where your alliances lie. I do not know this heart of yours that you speak of so freely."

Antony paced, hands on the belt that was slung low on his hips. She noticed that he did not wear a sword. "I have reason to believe that my partner and ally plans to betray me, has betrayed me, and works to sabotage the war against Parthia. As part of our agreement I promised him one hundred and fifty ships to fend off Pompey's son Sextus in the Mediterranean. I delivered the vessels before I left Rome. Octavian, for his part, promised me twenty thousand troops, four legions, for the war. He has yet to deliver despite all my demands. It's clear that he's trying to weaken me. Either he cares not for his sister and turns a deaf ear to her pleas for peace between us, or she is in league with him at every turn. I have no way of finding out the truth, and so I have decided that the question is moot. She does not matter. Marriage to her has secured no peace and no loyalty. I sent her home so that you and I might resume our former strategies, everything we planned when Caesar was alive, and everything we planned after his death."

He finished his speech and waited for her reaction, but against all desire to question him more, she remained silent and solemn.

"Do you accept?"

This was no drama staged for her benefit, Kleopatra could tell. For

Antony the actor always had a spirit of play about him. This Antony, the Imperator, was the straightforward soldier, the plainspoken man whose authenticity won the hearts of his men. Though she had no guarantee that he would not again change his mind, she also knew that he was correct on one point—she would have acted as he had if presented with the choice. She had turned her back on Archimedes after he had gone into exile with her and prepared her for war against her brother. She had had no choice, but she knew that the gods would eventually exact a toll, and they had, when they sent Antony back to Rome and gave him a fertile and beautiful Roman wife. After Caesar's death, she had had little choice but to align herself with Antony, and she had little choice now. Stability for the kingdom superseded all other matters. And so it was with Antony. He had decided from his broad range of options that she was the best choice for alliance. She tried to suppress the hope and the swelling of victory that rose up inside her, but after so many years of desolation and uncertainty, she found that her Stoicism broke down entirely. Still, she must not appear so vulnerable. She tried to look as stern as possible.

"I have issued my request, Imperator. I accept your terms only if you accept mine."

Antony looked again at the map. "It is premature, Kleopatra, but given the circumstances, I accept. It will be difficult to explain to my colleagues what I have done."

"Imperator, you have no colleagues. You must get used to that notion. When we are victorious in Parthia, you will have no equal."

Antony knelt beside Kleopatra and took her hand. "No equal but you."

She did not resist.

"Now come, tell me about my children. Have they inherited my fine appearance?"

"I have told you that if you wish to know of your children, you must come to see them for yourself. They are most curious about you."

His face lost the worried look that he had worn into the meeting and he smiled at her, looking once more like himself, or the self that she had held in her mind the last four years.

"Then go home and prepare for my arrival." The old smirk returned. "I must be well cared for before I go off to war."

Alexandria:
the 20th year of
Kleopatra's reign

A sunrise meeting with the War Council. Kleopatra searches the room for the
one face whose presence will have meaning, but that face is probably snoring into
the ear of a whore. She smiles at the irony. She has absolutely no control over the
man whom the Romans claim she controls utterly. The faces before her, however,
are full of optimism. Canidius Crassus, most faithful Roman friend, and
Hephaestion, most loyal Prime Minister, update the queen on the progress of the
plan to escape by the Red Sea. I do not wish to escape, she wants to scream at them.
I wish to fight. They have every possibility of raising an even larger army than the
last time, but Antony is not up to the effort, and Kleopatra knows that the majority of his Roman soldiers—especially the commanders crucial to victory—will
not go up against another Roman army for an Egyptian queen. Blood, after all,
is blood, and sometimes, in the course of human history, prevails even over money.
This, Kleopatra believes, is one such circumstance. She has money to pay, but the
Romans have been facing one another on the battlefield for so many years now,
since Sulla's days, long before Julius Caesar crossed that little Italian river, spilling
Roman blood on Roman swords. Kleopatra has walked through the ranks of the
soldiers herself—despite the objections of certain Roman officers who cannot bear
to see a woman in power—and has spoken to them in their native tongue. Some
have been fighting all their lives and are old men. They want money, land, peace—
all the things promised to them by Julius Caesar, but he did not live to settle his
debts.

And so Kleopatra lets her advisers tell her of the lightweight ships being con-
structed for her escape. They will be loaded onto massive trailers—also being con-
structed—and hauled by an army of slaves a mere twenty miles to the Red Sea,
where the queen and her family and entourage will sail away. But sail where? she
asks them.

Do not lose sight of your goals, Your Majesty, they tell her as if she is a child
who must be reminded of her lessons. She needs no reminder of what she has done.
Once again, she has tried to protect herself and her family. She has taken great
pains to strengthen her alliance with the king of Media. They have made a secret
negotiation, which Antony does not know about. But the queen realizes that she
must have a fallback position. She will never quit Antony, but he shows every sign
of quitting himself. And what is she—some slave girl who is supposed to offer her-
self up for sacrifice when her ruler dies? No, she will prevail, even if Antony
graduates from the oblivion of alcohol and sex into the oblivion of suicide. She will
escape to Media, marry the king, and together they will crush the Parthians and
found a kingdom that will sweep from Egypt to Arabia to India, the empire envi-
sioned by Alexander. An empire that in the coming years might challenge Rome
and win. Media has only one demand to solidify the alliance: execute Antony's
prisoner, the king of Armenia, whom the king of Media hates for many reasons,
not the least of which is that they share the same name, Artavasdes, and he is sick
to death of the confusion. Shall it be done, Your Majesty? asks Hephaestion. But
he is the Imperator's prisoner, she answers, trying to uphold her husband's author-
ity. Shall we ask him, then? Hephaestion politely asks. She sends to Antony for
permission to execute the prisoner and receives a scornful reply. Kill whomever
you like. Why not start with me? The War Council falls silent, pitying her, she is
sure. She sighs, signs the death warrant, and sends Diomedes, her secretary, away
to put the deed in motion.

She spends the rest of the day in image-making. She takes her morning meal in
the Common Room at the Mouseion. Throughout her life she has taken comfort in
this house where knowledge is mined and dedicated to the Muses. She enjoys break-
ing bread in the company of the men of learning as she has done from time to time
since she was a girl under their tutelage. It is the custom of her family not only
to patronize, but also to maintain a certain intimacy with the scholars. Could
Eratosthenes have included such colorful stories of Arsinoe III in his autobiogra-
phy, which her own children still read, if that great queen of the past had not dis-
pensed with queenly formalities and invited him to share in the contents of her
mind? No, this is the manner in which her family indulges its passion for liter-

ary and scientific matters. And now, at this crucial time, it is important to uphold all traditions, to maintain the semblance of normality.

The queen is given a nervous reception. Rumors of her desertion of Antony and of their cause have spread in her city. She does not announce her arrival, but bounds into the room unaccompanied as she did when she was a girl, bursting in on their quiet conversation. Upon her entrance everyone jumps out of his seat, a few dropping bread to the ground, and young Nicolaus spitting out his milk in greeting her. Mouths full, hands shaking, they stand long after she sits, until she gently commands them to take their seats, trying to restore an atmosphere of casual dialogue. She uses the opportunity to calm them by relating the actual events of the battle at Actium, and assuring them of her many plans for ultimate victory. She realizes that she should have done this weeks ago; undoubtedly they have been ruminating among themselves about the consequences of the battle. She imagines that many of them are already arranging new posts for themselves at Rhodes or Athens, while others are wondering how long it will be before they are kissing Octavian's ring. She is sure the letters to their Greek colleagues begging for the specifics of the battle at Actium have been sailing out of the port since the day she returned, if not before. No one adores the details of failure or the pleasures of gossip like an intellectual.

She sees that she has surprised them with her extraordinary good humor. They have been listening to the servants' stories of Antony's condition, and they must have expected to see her in that same state of mind, particularly after hearing rumors of her "defeat." They behave toward her as one acts in the presence of sick persons and the recently widowed. Cautious and overly solicitous. She smiles at young Nicolaus, who is spied wiping the spilt milk from his beard, and then at old Philostratus, a teacher of her youth. He is grateful. He has probably been waiting for a private audience, such as in the old days when she would solicit his advice. But these days, she finds his grand speech-making and pithy way of speaking otiose and unnecessary. She has little patience left for aphorisms. But Philostratus is old; he reminds her of the days when her father was alive, when she had the king and his authority to depend upon, and her affection for the philosopher returns. She forces herself to show courtesy to Arius, one of Caesarion's tutors whom she neither likes nor trusts. But she tolerates him for Caesarion's sake. The son of Caesar appreciates Arius's work categorizing schools of philosophy into logic, physics, and ethics. The boy has inherited Caesar's intellect, but not his cool judgment. Ah well, did Caesar not patronize that vain fool, Cicero, who betrayed him so many times, who vocalized his objections over Caesar's ambitions until the senators took up *their daggers? Caesar had placed the intellectual discourse the two shared above loyalty, and Kleopatra senses that their son shall do the same. How to gift someone with the ability to judge character? She wonders if such a thing can be taught. She wonders if she, too, has fallen short in this area by aligning herself with the man who sits in his mansion by the sea, whose once great virility as a warrior and conqueror now shows itself only to paid courtesans.*

Kleopatra finishes chatting up the philosophers and leaves them so that all might prepare themselves for the ceremony at noon, the idea for which sprang to her mind as she sailed into the harbor of her great city. First, she gave orders as they docked that poets be paid lovely sums to write songs of her victory and glory. The first men off the ship swiftly carried her wishes into those quarters where such tributes might be efficiently written. Another idea occurred to her as soon as she and Antony received news of some of their soldiers' defection to Octavian. At that moment, she watched every muscle in Antony's face droop, his chest sag, his arms hang limp at his side as if he were a sick monkey and not the commander of the greatest army the world had ever seen. And she knew in that moment that she must hurry the cycles of Time. For Time would surely dictate that the sons usurp the power of the father. Antyllus and Caesarion are young men, fourteen and sixteen, but no younger than Alexander when he squashed whole cities that his father, the great warrior King Philip, had not been able to subdue. Perhaps the combination of Antyllus's confidence and effrontery and Caesarion's sharp intellect might combine to make the leader their father could no longer be. The two are more than brothers; they are two sides of a great personality, like the twin souls of Plato. There is never a conflict between them; together they comprise a whole and great man. The blood of Caesar and the blood of Antony mixed with the blood of Alexander and the Ptolemies. How can they fail? She has explained all of this to them at length. They eat up her words with the enthusiasm of young men, each eager to assume the mantle that their mother is placing on their young and strong shoulders. Antyllus, courtly and brash, promises the queen that he will lead his father's men to victory in her name. He kisses her hand, and then stands over her as if she were his own little mother and kisses her forehead, and she wishes for a moment that things were different and that she could start all over with this young man's courage and energy propelling her plans. Her own son, King of Kings, is gracious, accepting the Fate that was assigned to him when his august father coupled with his regal mother. He does not even smile, but bows formally, the long arm of Caesar sweeping out from his body like the branch of a young tree in the wind.

Canidius has promised that he would have the Imperator dressed and propped up for the occasion, and on this point, he has delivered. Antony appears, shaven, oiled, costumed in a general's magnificent purple, and—for all who do not know him as intimately as the queen—sober. Kleopatra cannot look at him without her heart sinking. His fine features are drowned in bloated flesh. His eyes—eyes that she once had to discipline herself to look into because they caused such a shudder in her body—stare straight ahead in a flat brown gaze. Two withered mushrooms have moved in where the bold eyes of a hawk used to be. He takes his place next to her. I know why you are doing this, he says. You have forced my hand, she replies. I would rather uphold the father than the sons. But the father is gone and has left a beggar in his bed. He says nothing in reply.

The weather is mercifully cool for a September day. The sea breeze participates in the ceremony, dancing in through the windows in the gymnasium, ruffling the toga virilus, the robe of manhood that is presented to Antyllus by his father. Caesarion lowers his head to accept the pharaoh's crown from his mother, signaling his true coming of age. And in a singular moment the two boys make the elusive transformation into men. And that is that, Kleopatra thinks as she sees the joy on the faces of her subjects at the sight of the vigor and virility that will lead them into the future. Youth is hope, and her people lock onto that hope in the face of every wild rumor being circulated about town that Antony is finished. Her plan is working. The people ignore the father's slump and paunch for the potent, erect posture of the sons. Before he turns away from her to return to his debauchery, Antony takes his wife's arm. Give me time, he says. You are not very good at that, Kleopatra, but that is what I need. Despite herself, she feels the thrill of hope, of the possibility that he will become again the man he was not six months prior when they celebrated the execution of their plans for a Golden Empire at Samos. How could the soul of the man disappear so quickly? She wishes to carry that hope with her, but though his voice is sincere and sounds like Antony, his eyes are pools of death. She smiles gently, pats his hand, and walks away.

Phoenicia: the 16th year of Kleopatra's reign

Charmion held the bowl for the queen as she leaned over and retched. Kleopatra thought that she was immune from seasickness, but she had never traveled on such tumultuous seas so soon after giving birth.

Ptolemy Philadelphus, so named after his great ancestor but called Philip by the family, had inherited his father's size. He was the biggest of Kleopatra's four children, ten pounds at birth, with a head wider than a discus. She thought she would die as she pushed the future prince into the world, calling upon every god to hurry the process, and when that failed, putting expletives in the place of prayers. The reluctant baby remained in the birth canal, so she began to talk to him in a panting and desperate voice, assuring him that he would one day be king over all that he saw if he would only agree to come out into the world and see it. Through the lancing pain, she explained to him who his ancestors were, from which gods he was descended, and of his father's great deeds of war and soldiery. It seemed that only when she promised him that he would inherit the entire world empire from his older brothers that he made his appearance. As he crowned, the midwife exclaimed, "What a head the future emperor has! And what hair sits upon it!" The baby was born with Antony's brown curls in place on his giant head as if he had already visited Antony's barber. He seemed to have inherited his father's appetites, too, because he howled from the moment he was born, all the way through the ritual cleansing, until the wet nurse was dragged out of her bed and he was in her arms and at the tit.

Kleopatra was still exhausted from the delivery and heavy with milk when she received Antony's desperate message. Her breasts were rock-hard and full of pain. She demanded to nurse the baby herself to get rid of some of the milk, but the midwife assured her that she would be encouraging its production. Better to suffer the pain for a week or so until the body got the message that the milk was not needed. It had been three weeks, and the body was still resisting the message, as much as it resisted healing its lower half from the excruciating delivery. The other three births were, if not exactly painless, then at least expedient. She had healed quickly, and was on her horse in two weeks' time. She did not know if the trouble this time was caused by her age or by the baby's size, but the factors mingled to make a very difficult experience—one that she could not afford at this crucial juncture.

Antony's message was simple and to the point: One-third of the army is dead; the other two-thirds require clothes, shoes, and food. Please come at once to Leuce Come on the coast of Phoenicia, north of Tyre.

Did he think she was a magician? How was she to produce food and clothes for sixty thousand men *at once?* And what chink in their battle plan had created this disaster so early in the war?

Nonetheless, she pillaged the supplies of her own army, of her own estates and granaries, of the country's factories that produced leather and woolen goods. She had three ships loaded with the effects, and coaxed her beleaguered body onto a fourth.

Thank the gods that there was no protest against her actions in the city, even though her subjects would be footing the bill for Antony's failure. Her careful strategy had worked. When Antony had returned to Alexandria after their reunion in Antioch, she had married him in a grand ceremony in the style of her ancestors. Except that this time, it was no brother or cousin or fat Ptolemy at her side, but Rome's greatest general. The Alexandrians celebrated wildly after the ceremony, matching the queen's new husband's Dionysian capacity for wine goblet for goblet. The wealthy sent Antony fabulous gifts of gold, jewels, statues, and manuscripts of his favorite poets and philosophers. The poor offered him the tops of their heads in solicitous devotion. They loved Antony anyway, ever since he had marched Gabinius's army into Egypt twenty-one years ago to restore Kleopatra's father. They remembered that he had convinced the king to spare many of the Egyptian rebels, and was merciful in victory. For all that, Kleopatra could not be certain that her subjects would be behind his war effort, especially since she would have to tax certain goods and luxuries if she intended to finance it through to total victory. Therefore, he must be, if not king, then at least the queen's consort, a king of sorts who was perceived as fighting as much for Egyptian interests as the interests of Rome. Kleopatra believed that her marriage to him, as well as his public acceptance of their children, would make a convincing case for this.

She was right. After the marriage ceremony, the new names of their twins were announced—Alexander Helios and Kleopatra Selene, Brother Sun, Sister Moon—and the subjects cheered wildly. The meaning was not lost on anyone, for the boy, Alexander, was not only the namesake of the greatest king who ever lived, but now he was also Ra, the Sun itself, the divine force that made crops grow, that warmed the cities and the fields, that obliterated the frightful dark chill of Night and illuminated the earth. Kleopatra Selene carried the weight of her mother's name and that of all Queen Kleopatras who came before her. She was also the moon goddess, the force that shed light into the dark night and was keeper of all the mysteries of the world. Antony's enemy, the Parthian king, called himself Brother of the Sun and Moon. When Kleopatra got the idea to enhance the children's names, she and Antony had laughed at how their children's new monikers usurped that power and bested it.

After the celebrations, when they were alone, Antony made a great ceremony of his own giving her his wedding gift, a strand of gigantic creamy pearls from the Caspian Sea that hung to her navel. She claimed she had never seen pearls so large, and he said that none existed, that oysters had obeyed his command to mold themselves into pearls worthy of a goddess's neck. He demanded to see them as he had imagined them on her when he bought them. She asked him to place them around her neck, but he would not do so, and made her guess how he wished her to model them. She teased him with different coiffures and gowns until he scolded that she was not quite as smart as she appeared. Only then did she slowly let her dress fall to the ground. She stepped out of it, and he placed the jewelry over her bare neck. He ran his fingers down both strands all the way to her belly and stopped there. He cupped her stomach in his hands.

"Again?" he asked, smiling, disbelieving.

"Yes," she answered.

He pulled the pins out of her hair and smoothed it around her shoulders. "You are as fertile as the Nile itself, Mother Egypt," he laughed. He picked her up, put her on the bed, and made gentle love to her—not his normal way, but out of fear and respect for the baby growing inside. Every night thereafter, he would put his lips to her stomach and talk to the baby, apologizing that he would be off to war when the little creature came into the world. He told the baby stories of gods and goddesses, of war, and, in case it was a boy, he said, dirty stories of nightlong orgies with prostitutes. "A man must know these things," he told Kleopatra.

"And what if it is a girl?"

"Then she will be haughty like her mother and turn a deaf ear to me."

Kleopatra did not turn a deaf ear to Antony's stories but let them be a catalyst to her own desire—and her desire for this man never ceased. She did not let his four-year absence fester like a wound but let it heal in the passion of their reunion. She had even consulted Hephaestion, though he was not one to discuss personal matters. But this matter transcended her heart; her kingdom and the future of her children depended on Antony's maintaining the level of trust with which she endowed him.

"I know that you consult me as a political adviser and not a philosopher, Your Majesty," the eunuch answered. "But I believe that the life you are making with the Imperator is a calculated risk with acceptable odds in your favor. Besides, Your Majesty seems, how shall I say it? Happy?"

She *was* happy, happier than she'd ever been. Everything contributed to her growing affection for Antony: his playfulness with his young children; his loyalty to anyone to whom he gave his word, be it a fine shoemaker whose station he promised to improve or king of a nation; his light sense of humor as he sped through his day readying the very highest and the very lowest of his men for war; and finally, his unwavering vision of an empire that united all the peoples of the world.

Before he set out on his long march to Parthia, he and Kleopatra issued a coin with both their images. On one side, it was dated in the traditional way, the Fifteenth Regnal Year of Queen Kleopatra, and on the other side, it was dated the Year One. It was meant to signal the first year of a Golden Age of Joint Rulership between the Egyptian queen, who was the dynastic successor of Alexander, and the Roman general, who was the king's spiritual scion.

"The foundation is laid, my darling," Kleopatra said when they were shown the impression of the coin for approval before it went to the Royal Mint. "Our empire will celebrate the highest and best in all the civilizations of the world."

They explained it to their children, not expecting the small ones to understand, but to begin to make them see that they were to be a crucial part of something that was greater and bolder and more beautiful and important than themselves. Antyllus accepted everything that was said with hawklike interest, but Caesarion, the philosopher, asked Antony if he thought it would always be necessary to go to war to make peace.

"The strong do as they will while the weak suffer what they must. A famous expression, one that Caesar used to say often. But it is no less true for its overuse. If we are weak, we have no power. The only way not to be weak is to be the very strongest. And there will always be those who wish to take that power from us. So that the only way to maintain the peace that we hold paramount is by maintaining absolute and resolute strength. Julius Caesar also used to say that there simply must be a master. Otherwise there is chaos. Rome's recent history is the most blatant example of his wisdom."

"And why is it that we are to be the masters?" Caesarion asked, his twelve-year-old face as worried-looking as an old man's.

"Because our bloodlines and our experience give us the divine right," Kleopatra answered. "Because we uphold the principles of Alexander that will make the world and all its inhabitants great: harmony among nations, respect for all the gods and religions and people of the world, devotion to the Greek ideals of Knowledge, Virtue, Science, and Beauty."

"And what will we do to make that the law of the land?"

Kleopatra wondered if Antony felt as she did, that the boy was like a tutor who was testing his star pupils. Antony answered: "A few years ago I held a conference with as many of the leaders of the world as I could assemble. And I determined at that time that the best and most humane system of administration in the territories of the Roman empire under my jurisdiction was to continue to allow the people to govern themselves. Instead of imposing a Roman governor upon them—a man whose own greed might incite him to invoke hardship on the native people—I gave the power back to the existing governments. Now they have more incentive to remain loyal to me, and not to raise nasty rebellions behind my back. And yet they have all the force of my power behind them should they require it."

"It's a brilliant system," Kleopatra added, "and perfectly faithful to the ways of Alexander."

"I see, Father," Caesarion said. He had asked permission to call the Imperator his father, and Antony had replied that he would be honored if the son of the man whom he himself called father called him such. "And what of the other man who calls himself Caesar? Will he wish to govern this empire with us?"

Antony and Kleopatra exchanged looks. They had agreed not to frighten their children with anxieties over the duplicitous Octavian. Besides, they hoped that when they had defeated the Parthians and had gained control of the land from the River Indus to the western borders of Egypt, from the Sudan to the northern territories of Greece and the Balkans, that Octavian would begin to see the wisdom in cooperating with them.

"He will be in charge of the city of Rome and the Italian lands, and those countries on the western side of the Mediterranean Sea," Antony replied. "Those are very far away and need a closer hand to govern them. We shall live here in Alexandria and take care of the east."

"I shall strive to make myself a worthy heir to your efforts, sir," Caesarion said. Kleopatra smiled; it was the sort of thing she would have said to her father, in the same overly earnest tone.

"Oh, come here, boy," said Antony, grabbing the thin young man and ruffling his hair. "You are far too serious for your tender years. Why don't you go have some fun for a change?"

"I'd like to go to war with you, sir," Caesarion said, straightening his chiton. "I would like to be there when you take the ancient city of Phraaspa, where the Parthians hide their national treasure!"

"In due time," the Imperator replied. "In due time, all my sons will be called upon to serve with me. And at that time, and that time only, will they truly be able to call themselves men."

"You won't be prejudiced against me, sir, because I am not so fit for soldiery as my brother?" Caesarion said, looking at the larger, more muscular Antyllus. "He defeats me every day at swordsmanship and in races. If I weren't his brother, he would kill me!"

"Let me tell you something, my boy," Antony said. "Never was there a finer, fiercer man in battle than your father. And never was there a thinner and less healthy man. Caesar taught us the greatest lesson of war—that a man's finest weapon is his mind. You have inherited that mind, and like him, you will learn how to use your physical characteristics to your advantage. I am sure of it."

Caesarion went away from the encounter full of confidence. Just like any one of Antony's men, Kleopatra thought. No one was exempt from Antony's charm, no one left his presence less than he was when he entered it. It was a gift. Just as Caesar's gift was to inspire awe for himself, Antony's was to inspire confidence in others. Kleopatra admired both talents, but remained uncertain as to which was of greater use to her cause.

⌂ ⚊ 🐆 𓏏 𓏏 𓊹 ⌐ 𓂀 ◇ ⌐

When Kleopatra arrived with supplies in the village of Leuce Come, Antony put his head in her lap and sobbed like a baby. She was disturbed at his despondency. Here was the man in whom she had placed her life and her future, weeping over the thousands of men lost, either from the menacing Parthian arrows or from the treacherous snow that plagued them in Armenia. Most of the men were from warmer climates, he said, and had never faced such conditions. Not only that, they had been betrayed by Monaeses, who changed his allegiance and turned on the baggage train full of siege equipment when Antony and the majority of his legions took a swifter road to Phraaspa. When they arrived, the city had been fortified, and the siege equipment needed to take it was destroyed. They tried to build their own fortifications with the timber and rocks in the area, but it wasn't enough. They failed to take Phraaspa, so they turned back, finding themselves confronted by snowstorms in the mountains, Parthian archers, and a scarcity of food.

Antony wept now at his own bad judgment. "Their deaths are on my head. If only I had made the decision to set out earlier, when victory might have been taken before winter set in."

"But you did not know that this year the storms would be worse than in decades," Kleopatra offered. "There is no way to predict such a thing. And you had to wait for Canidius to negotiate with Media and to secure the regions for the march. You were correct in your strategy, Imperator. One does not just go sprinting off to war!"

Antony was not appeased. If only he had not made the decision to leave the heavy baggage behind, so sparsely guarded.

"But you had no choice, Imperator," she said. "You couldn't very well slow down the entire army with the baggage, especially when you were trying to beat the weather."

"Perhaps," he said. "But I made the treaty with Monaeses. I was convinced of his loyalty, if only because it served his interests."

To this she had little consolation to give. It was true that no one could be counted on for unswerving loyalty. Betrayal had orchestrated its wickedness through her own family's schemes for control of Egypt. Why would a barbarian king behave differently?

"Caesar made such mistakes," she told him. "How many alliances had he made with the chiefs in Gaul, only to have them turn against him as soon as his back was to their village?"

Still Antony blamed himself.

"As I blame myself when the river doesn't rise and the crops don't grow and there is hunger and suffering among my people," she said. "But this is nothing from which you won't recover."

She tried to cheer him with a report of Philip his son, who was born in his own image, but Antony only replied that he was glad the baby was just an infant and could not comprehend the disgrace his father had brought upon him.

"I have had a lengthy conversation with Canidius Crassus, who claims that your leadership was an inspiration at every turn; that you made the most of impossible conditions and turns of fortune, and that had you been less a leader, every man would have fallen either to the enemy, to starvation, or turned loyalties to avoid those things."

"Then I should have Canidius flogged for his lies."

But after he had cried enough and chastised himself enough and paced and moaned enough and hit the wall enough times with his fist, he changed moods and began to talk of future victories. He was so unlike Caesar, so unlike any of the Romans Kleopatra had known. His emotions ran high, as high as a Greek's, but as he let his temper loose, he also seemed to dispense with his grief. A few hours later they were sipping wine with Canidius and planning the next step.

"Are the men comfortable in their Syrian winter quarters?" Kleopatra asked.

"They will be when they have been presented with your generous supplies," Canidius replied.

"Good. Then the next step shall be decided in Alexandria."

"I cannot face your people," Antony said. "I promised victory, and I have delivered humiliation."

"Then we shall declare it a victory, Imperator. You are alive and well. That is victory enough for me."

"Kleopatra, thank the gods that you answered my call for help."

"What was I to do? You are my husband," she said. "Whatever I have is at your disposal."

He looked very bitter. "Would that my other partners had the same sense of honor."

"Enough grief over Monaeses' betrayal, Imperator!" she said. "A man like that has no sense of loyalty but does the bidding of whoever's pockets he can reach into. You were simply out of his range at the time."

"I mean my wife."

Kleopatra's heart thumped loudly in her chest. Had someone started rumors about her meant to sabotage Antony's trust? "What on earth do you mean? Am I not here with everything you requested, even though our baby is barely out of my womb?"

"My darling, I apologize. I was speaking of Octavia."

"Octavia has betrayed you?"

"Or her brother. Or the two of them. When I returned to the Syrian headquarters, I received a letter from Octavia. She was in

Athens, on her way to meet me in Syria with two thousand troops for my war effort."

"I see," Kleopatra said, feeling more ill by the moment. Was she expected to receive Octavia?

"No you don't. Octavian pledged *twenty* thousand troops. He is sending one-tenth that amount. He means to undermine me."

"What did you do?"

"I wrote her back and told her to take her troops and go home. I'm not a fool. I see exactly what he is doing."

"And what is that?"

"He is breaking our alliance, but he is not man enough to do it directly."

"We knew it was coming," Kleopatra said.

"That is not all. He has dismissed Lepidus from our coalition without consulting me. Can you imagine the audacity? He's taken the entire domain of North Africa away from Lepidus and claimed it for himself. I sent word immediately to Rome demanding an apology from him and my share of the confiscated lands. Do you know how he dared to answer me? He said that he would be delighted to share North Africa when he receives his portion of Armenia."

"After you've spent a grueling year and lost so many men in the service of Rome? He is depraved."

"Yes, a man can be dishonest to the point of depravity. He's not even twenty-five years old, that little sniveling, pale catamite of a creature. He feigns illness in every battle, did you know that? As soon as the fighting starts, he takes to his tent with a sudden high fever!" Antony's whole body shook as if he were trying to slough off his disdain. "If he didn't have Marcus Agrippa to lead his armies, he would be nothing."

"Then that is the key," Kleopatra said. "We must send an assassin after Agrippa. I wonder if Ascinius is still alive." She remembered the man with the grim countenance who had easily dispatched twenty of her father's enemies one chilly morning in Puteoli. Even at twelve years old, she had recognized that his efficiency was extraordinary.

Antony turned his anger on her. "Do you really think I would be party to the murder of a Roman general who has not declared himself my enemy? What kind of man do you take me for? That is an action worthy of Octavian, not me."

"It may take adapting his tactics to best him. It is not always the honorable man who triumphs. What about negotiating with Agrippa?"

"It's worth a try, but I don't think we'll be successful. Caesar himself bound Agrippa to Octavian. He gave his family money and position in exchange for the loyalty. I believe the two are in solidarity for life."

"Why did Caesar yoke us with this menace?" Kleopatra said quietly. "I have prayed for an answer to that question, but I have none."

"I thought I knew the man, Kleopatra."

"I thought I did, too. But I was not privy to that portion of his mind."

Antony's face tensed, his eyes narrowing into cold slits. Kleopatra thought that he might be trying to contain the hurt he carried at Caesar's slight to him of naming the frail underage nephew his heir, and not the man who had fought with his very soul at Caesar's side, whose courage and bravery and daring had been responsible for some of his most celebrated victories. It was something they shared that bound them together in a way that no vow of marriage could—they had both been loved by Caesar and betrayed by him in death.

Antony broke the silence. "I have made my peace with Caesar's memory by choosing to believe that he did not for a moment think that Octavian would pose a threat to either of us or to your son. I cannot believe that he knew what dark possibilities lay inside the mind of that boy."

Either that, Kleopatra thought, or else he identified them, and decided in the end that he admired them and wanted to give them free reign.

Rome:
the 17th year of
Kleopatra's reign

What was the queen, some kind of magical Egyptian cow? How could she produce sons at will? Surely she must be a student of the dark magic known to be a common practice in those wicked lands that lie far to the east, those places where fat potentates ensorcelled their populations and lived lives of decadent luxury off the backs of their poor, bewitched subjects. First, she had used her magic to give Julius Caesar a son—proof of her collaboration with dark powers. Caesar had bedded hundreds and hundreds of women in countries all over the known world, and never had anyone claimed to have given him a son. He had produced only one child, a girl, and then his semen had turned bad.

Octavian wondered if Caesar's homosexual affairs had diminished the potency of his semen, and if so, would the same thing happen to him? Octavian had only done what he had had to do, and who would have made a different choice in his position? It was a small price to pay for what came after, and, truth be known, not unpleasant at all, especially for one's first sexual encounter. Caesar was an old greekling, no doubt about that, loving every art form, every mode of philosophy, every piece of drama and comedy, and every tradition that had come out of that small country. No doubt he was thinking of Plato and the Symposium when he took Octavian into his tent in Spain and explained the proper way for a man of stature to pass his power along to the boy of his choice, to groom him for his duties in society. Octavian was amazed at the proposal, but he also had been told by his mother that he must appease Caesar *no matter what*—that disobedience or making himself unpleasant or unliked in any way was not to be. "Julius is your future," she had said plainly. "His patronage will raise you above all men. If he chooses to place his generosity elsewhere, you shall be on your own, with only your talents and your abilities to take you into the future." And then she gave him the look that made him understand that this latter notion was not a very good idea, considering the gifts he had demonstrated thus far in his young life. Ah well, he laughed to himself, so many have given so much more for so much less.

But Kleopatra, not content producing one bastard to challenge Octavian's claims to power, had now given Antony not one son but two. Antony already had two other sons, Antyllus and the younger Antonius, the big handsome motherless boys who lived in Antony's Roman mansion with Octavia. Why should the gods gift him with two more? Unless it was not the work of the gods at all but of *her*, the bold queen who claimed to be Isis on earth. It was no accident that the senate had to squash the worship of Isis every so often. The goddess made women crazy. They prayed to her to fulfill their every desire; to fulfill wishes that their husbands, sons, and lords of government would not give them. Things that decent honest women did not need and should not want. Things to which the sterner Roman gods would turn a deaf ear.

I am Isis. I control Fate. Destiny bows to me. That is what those women chanted in her temples. Any right-thinking person could see how that would not do.

Octavian turned his attention to the animal games. The sun was high, beating a relentless heat into the canopy under which he sat with Livia. At his signal, the leopards were released into the Circus. What trouble it was to procure wild animals for these spectacles. It cost a fortune to have the beasts hunted and captured in Africa, caged, fed, and shipped all the way to Rome. Those who could handle the creatures were rare, and often did not last. A lost hand, a mangled foot, and alas, their careers were over. Octavian sighed. No wonder Caesar had grown weary of the details of administration. How tedious it must have been for a man of war. Yet Caesar had stressed the importance of celebration; in fact, it was Caesar who got the idea to take the gladiatorial games out

of the realm of ceremony for the dead and make them events of celebration and triumph. Himself, he did not care for the spectacle. Caesar
preferred spending his time with intellectuals and artists, but he assured
Octavian that the games were a necessary vice. He had been right; the
people were wild for it. In some quarters, women were demanding to
attend along with their husbands. Octavian would discourage that. He
did not think it proper. Women had no control over their passions if
given the least opportunity for error. If chanting to a goddess incited
wildness in females, what would the spilling of so much blood make
those creatures do?

Octavian turned his thoughts from the passions of women to the
passions of the one whom he considered the worst example of her sex.
Oh, she paraded herself through Antony's territories as if she were
already empress. Little did she know how effectively Octavian had
begun to interfere with her plans. After Antony's disaster at Phraaspa,
Octavian made a mournful little speech to the senate. Poor Antony! he
cried. How can we rescue our great man from this wicked woman? He
is so bewitched by her that he put off his campaign for months and
months so that he might lie in her arms! He preferred to face the white
death of an Armenian winter rather than lose a moment in his lover's
bed. Then, after his setback at Phraaspa, instead of waiting through the
winter and attacking in the spring, he called for her, so anxious to once
again be near her that he summoned her to Leuce Come! He could not
even wait to travel all the way back to Alexandria to see her once more.
Pray for him, senators! Pray for the expedient return of his senses!

Octavian was quite pleased with the effects of his speech. Soon all
Rome was bemoaning Antony's Fate, contrasting his adulterous days in
Kleopatra's luxurious bed to the restraint and fidelity practiced by
Octavian with his sedate but beloved Livia.

Despite Octavian's efforts, Antony and Kleopatra quickly rebounded.
Kleopatra had taken Antony back to Alexandria, nursed his wounded
ego, and rebuilt his forces. In the spring, she escorted him—rode with
him as if she were his co-commander! another Fulvia!—into Syria, and
then left him to invade Armenia. Then she spent the summer strutting
about the globe with an entourage, he was told, of hundreds of Greeks
and Egyptians, whom she feted lavishly along the way, giving money and
jewels and granting all sort of promises and favors to all whom she vis-

ited. She went to all the cities established by Seleucus, reminding every-one that her ancestor, Ptolemy, was a commander and a successor of Alexander. Apamaea, Emesa, Damascus. She left no city untouched by her presence and decadent largesse. Finally, she went to Judaea, where she tried to bully Herod. She had stolen his most productive farmlands, and practically landlocked him. Then she demanded—demanded!—that he appoint his brother-in-law High Priest. It seemed that Herod's mother-in-law, Alexandra, was a dictator in the style of Kleopatra, and the two were friends. So when one dictator proposed to the other that her son be made high priest, it was done. Herod had secretly written to Octavian for advice in the matter, and Octavian had given a curt response: If you have no recourse, appoint the boy to the post, and then have him killed. Fear nothing, not even the wrath of Kleopatra. Plans are being made for her demise. And young Herod had swiftly taken Octavian's wise advice and had the High Priest—a boy of seventeen—mysteriously drowned shortly thereafter.

Still, Antony prevailed. Even though Octavian had been secretly nego-tiating with the king of Armenia to prevent Antony's successful invasion of that country, Antony took both Armenia and Media, imprisoned the royal Armenian family, and dragged them back to Alexandria, where they remained his captives. From his new headquarters, Antony sent tri-umphant messages back to Rome. He had claimed Media and Armenia for the empire, and Octavian was forced to hold these very games in his honor. But Antony had made one enormous mistake. Instead of return-ing to Rome—and how could he, really, when he still had the vast expanse of Parthia yet to subdue?—he staged his triumphal parade in Alexandria. When Octavian realized the gift Antony had given him, he was elated. Oh, he would host all the games Antony wished in his honor. There would be no limit to how many wild beasts would lose their lives today in Antony's name. But he would also point out to Antony's supporters in Rome that the Imperator had celebrated his triumph not on Roman soil for the Roman people, but in Alexandria—for Kleopatra. Was that not a direct signal of their sinister ambitions? He had mentioned this idea already to a select few, and he saw the slow outrage break out over their faces. Kleopatra had succeeded in making Antony a traitor. Praise the gods! Antony was still a hero in the Roman mind, a great man who could not be attacked directly. But Kleopatra was another story.

They were on some kind of deluded high, the two of them, but slow-ly, surely, he would bring them down. He had almost succeeded when Antony sent Octavia marching back to Rome in disgrace. Antony had rejected her meager offer of assistance—which Octavian had so prayed for him to do—and he had petitioned to divorce her. Octavian seized the moment, and despite his sister's protests, insisted that she play the part he wrote for her, the bereaved and humiliated matron.

Octavian made a great public show of demanding that Octavia leave Antony's house, but he quickly realized that he had made a tactical error, that he could make much more use of dragging out her humiliation. So he convinced her to publicly repudiate his orders and insist before as many senators as he could gather that she would remain true to Antony, her lawful husband. After all, he was the father of her two baby girls, and he had charged her with the care of his two sons. It had been a mar-velous scene.

No, Octavia had said, I will not leave those motherless boys! Octavian had to encourage her to go on; her lip quaked and her eyes fluttered and he did not know if she was capable of finishing the per-formance. Then she pulled herself up to her full height and said, My husband has a weakness for women. But I pray to the gods that he will regain his composure, leave the bed of the queen, and return to his true Roman wife. Little tears fell from her eyes, and all the men lowered their heads in deference to her pain. Then they began to rouse themselves against Antony, and against the wicked woman who had tempted him away from this noble Roman girl.

Was there any more precious treasure than a sister's love?

Many of the senators sent strong letters to Antony demanding that he break his alliance with Kleopatra, but Octavian knew that he would not. Why should he, when she had so much of the world's gold in her treasury; when most of the earth's grain came from her shores? When she was constructing a navy for Antony that could defy the fleet of Jason? Instead, Antony sent long replies to his supporters explaining his position: The queen was one of Rome's fiercest and most important allies, and crucial to the eastern campaigns. He invited all of them to come to Alexandria where they might see for themselves how useful the queen was to his enterprises. Octavian did not successfully intercept all of those letters, but enough of them so that many of Antony's staunchest defenders were left without any reply from him whatsoever. Soon their puzzlement turned to anger. It was not a complete victory, not yet, but it was enough for the moment.

Octavian sent a tiny prayer up to Apollo, thanking him that he was made of a chillier flesh than Antony. In the early days of their alliance, Antony had rushed to claim the territories of the east, and Octavian had allowed it. He didn't mind if Antony wanted to be heir to all Rome's failed campaigns in Parthia. He knew that any victory in that savage place would also be fraught with horror. Caesar had told him that. Sometimes Octavian wondered if Caesar hadn't walked into his own assassination just to avoid being killed in disgrace with Parthian arrows and having his head passed around like poor old dead Marcus Crassus. So Octavian was pleased when Antony insisted that he resume the cause in Parthia. Octavian would wait and watch from home, where he could control the flow of information in and out of the city, as well as the number of troops recruited on Italian soil and sent to Antony.

Octavian realized that all eyes at the games were waiting upon him. It was time for him to signal the commencement of his favorite part of these events, the pitting of different animals against each other. Animals that would never encounter one another in their own environments were thrown into confusion at the strange sight of a foreign beast, and then their survival instincts would manifest themselves with a vengeance. What went on in their animal brains? he wondered. What wondrous intuition must they draw upon to defend themselves against the strange pursuer? It was never boring.

A crocodile was released into the Circus. The animal seemed slightly stunned at his freedom. His great claws were perfectly still, almost as if he were already dead. The crowd was eerily silent. Lulled by the quiet, the animal began to creep across the grassy surface into a patch of sunlight. Slowly, as if in a dream, the sun lit up his body inch by inch, turning his craggy brown skin a shimmering gold. Finally he stood fully illuminated, looking about as if he were all set to enjoy an afternoon in the sun. But the poor ignorant fellow had no idea of what was coming. Two trainers on horseback rode into the Circus holding by metal chains a great lion, pale brown like a fawn but with a head larger than a bear. The beast pulled fiercely against his leashes, his angry roar filling the arena. The crocodile did not react. The trainers gave the signal, releasing the lion into the center of the Circus, and quickly rode out of the arena. For a long time, neither animal moved, and Octavian wondered if the lion was going to lie in the sun with the crocodile and go to sleep. Then gladiators would have to come into the ring and taunt them into action. If they wouldn't fight each other, the men would have to incite them by throwing raw meat into the ring for them to duel over. If that did not do the trick, the gladiators would have to come in and slay them with their tridents, or hack them to death with axes. But a gladiator with a weapon inevitably was the victor over a beast. It was just not as entertaining.

The crowd grew restless and began taunting the lion, who started prowling nervously. This will simply be no fun, Octavian thought. The lion, so large, so fast, so revered, will surely make a fast meal of this reptile. The lion was so clearly agitated by the noise of the crowd that he began to roar back, an angry retort to their contempt. He seemed insulted by their jeers, shaking his head at them, baring his feral teeth in their direction. Oh, he was a formidable creature. The crocodile, on the other hand, refused to move. Slowly, however, his tail wiggled ever so slightly, almost like a snake. The lion, disturbed by the slight motion, hurled himself upon the creature, and Octavian's heart leapt. Finally, some action, even if it was to be short-lived and, in the end, so unevenly matched. The lion fell upon the crocodile with a vengeance, so that all that could be seen of the reptile was his tail. He is done for now, Octavian thought. But then the lion threw back his head. The crocodile had the beast's neck in his great gaping jaws, the lion's hot red blood spilling out onto the green grass, almost making a crimson watershed over the reptile. The crocodile—could he weigh half of what the lion weighed?—threw the big cat over on his back. Tightening his jaw, he crushed the lion's throat, and the poor beast died gagging on his own blood.

The crowd went crazy. Rarely had a lion been defeated in the ring. Octavian must find the clever fellow who thought of pitting those two mismatched creatures against each other and reward him. It was so rare to be treated to a surprise at the games.

Alexandria: the 17th year of Kleopatra's reign

To Kleopatra, this was the crowning moment of her dreams and ambitions, the achievement of all that she had begun to put into motion with Julius Caesar so many years ago. She hosted the Declaration of the Eastern Empire in the giant hall of the Gymnasium. It had been only days since Antony had marched into Alexandria in his triumphal parade after his conquest of Armenia. But for Kleopatra, that triumph was merely the beginning. The purpose of the Declaration was to demonstrate to the people of Egypt the wisdom of their queen in her alliance with the Roman general and the Roman dictator before him. Kleopatra had always known that she was acting on behalf of her nation in aligning with the Romans, but her subjects hadn't always agreed. Her father had been chased out of his country for his patronage of Rome. Now she could show them how she had elevated Egypt and all its inhabitants by this association.

At the ceremony of the Declaration, Antony and Kleopatra sat high upon golden thrones on solid silver platforms, flanked by their children, with the exception of Antyllus, who had been sent back to Rome to resume his studies. They displayed themselves as Aphrodite and Dionysus once more, and with a massive portion of the Alexandrian community looking on, Antony gifted Kleopatra and the children with the territories of their ancestors that had been chiseled away from the vast empire of the earlier Ptolemies.

"By all the powers invested in me as Imperator of Rome and General of the Eastern forces of the Empire, I declare Kleopatra VII Ptolemy Queen of Kings and Queen of her Sons who are Kings." Antony was an orator by nature and by inheritance; his grandfather had been one of Rome's most renowned speakers. His voice rang through the hall, reverberating in the cavernous hollow of the massive ceiling. He possessed all the authority of a god, she thought, and that was how the people responded to him. Everyone stood and repeated Kleopatra's new title so joyously that it sounded like a song written especially for the occasion: "All hail Mother Egypt, the Lady of the Two Lands, and ruler of the island of Cyprus and Koile Syria. Queen of Kings! Queen of Kings!"

Kleopatra went through the ceremony slightly dizzy and distracted. She assumed a demeanor of solemn dignity for her subjects, but in her mind, she was watching all the pieces of the puzzle she had dreamed of assembling begin to come together. Caesarion, thirteen years old and in a particularly gangly phase under his purple ceremonial robes, was crowned King of Kings. "Come forward, son of Caesar," Antony exclaimed. The boy bowed to his stepfather as Antony placed the golden crown upon his head, wiping the strands of the stringy hair he had inherited from Caesar away from his eyes as he raised his head. Alexander Helios, "my son," Antony was careful to say, was proclaimed king of Armenia and Media and all the eastern regions of Parthia. Kleopatra Selene, "my daughter," was made queen of Cyrene. Just six years old, the twins were very tall for their age and solemnly accepted their new imperial titles, bowing and waving just as Kleopatra had instructed them to do. They were dressed in the costumes of the regions they had just been granted and were flanked by soldiers in uniforms from those lands. Ptolemy Philadelphus, not even three years old, won the hearts of the crowd in his bright purple cloak and tiny golden diadem, wearing a very small replica of the Macedonian boots seen on the feet of Alexander on all his statues throughout the town. He was named king of Syria, Phoenicia, and Cilicia, his bright eyes glittering as his name was chanted, aware only of the fact that much of this pomp was for himself, and delighting in it. And with that proclamation, the picture was complete, and every inch of the ancestral empire of the Ptolemies was restored to Kleopatra, their rightful descendant, and secured now for her descendants. Not only had she restored the greatness of Egypt's most glorious days, she also now controlled much of the former empire of Seleucus, companion of Alexander and friend to Ptolemy I. She had succeeded beyond the dreams and achievements of each and every Ptolemy who had come before her.

She thought of her father, so long dead now, his jolly disposition and his good health eviscerated by the tyranny and greed of Rome, which had lost him the goodwill of his people. He had made her queen on her eighteenth birthday, had believed in her loyalty and her abilities, and had elevated her above all women. She promised him on his deathbed that she would always honor the meaning behind her name, *glory to her father,* and on this day she delivered the ultimate evidence of her vow. The single element that prevented her joy from being complete was his absence. But honoring one's ancestors was as important in the eyes of the gods as honoring the living. Honor aside, she missed him and longed to hear the lilting melodies of his flute in her court. Was ever a king such an artist? Since his death, no musician could please her. He was mocked by Rome for his artistic ways and for his fervent patronage of the god Dionysus, just as Antony was mocked in his own country now for demonstrating his love of the ways of the people of Egypt and the eastern territories he governed. Her father was fat and effeminate while Antony was muscled and manly, but she had not realized until this very moment how many similarities they shared, including the willingness to acknowledge her capabilities and govern with her.

She did not even realize that she was crying until she felt the coarse skin of Antony's finger wipe away a tear.

Finally, after all her efforts and all her struggles, she had fulfilled the promise she had made more than twenty years ago at the temple of Artemis in Ephesus, the city she would soon return to as Queen of Kings and of her Sons who are Kings, and the exulted partner of Rome's greatest general. Just as she had promised the goddess on that day, she had not stooped to the humiliation and subjugation of her ancestors before the monster that was Rome. Instead, she had put herself and her kingdom in a position of equality with the Romans. The Declaration of the Empire of the East was the moment that represented the culmination of her entire life's efforts. It was all she had ever wanted, and now she had it.

Weeks later Kleopatra found out how little Rome welcomed equal partners. Octavian distorted every one of Antony's actions, making it appear that everything he did was a signal that he was stealing the Roman empire to slake Kleopatra's thirst for conquest.

"But you have done nothing for me that you have not done in one form or another for any of your monarchical allies," she had protested to Antony.

"That is correct. If I have given you more, it is because you have given me more."

Much more, she thought. More money. More troops. More ships. More grain. She had lain her country's resources at his feet. More to the point, after the failure in Parthia of so many Roman generals past, Antony, like Caesar, figured that he could not win that war without her. Was she not supposed to enhance her own prestige for her continued efforts to help Rome subdue its most menacing foe?

But that was not the story circulated by Octavian. He used Kleopatra's assistance in building up the eastern forces as evidence that she was planning her own full-scale war against Rome. He put this idea into circulation so successfully that Kleopatra began to think that she no longer had any choice but to do it. Antony had made dozens of attempts to make peace with Octavian, but it was clear that Octavian did not desire peace, at least not peace between himself and Antony. Antony had sent numerous letters to Rome explaining the logic of his alliance with Kleopatra, and listing her many efforts on behalf of the empire. Somehow, those missives were never read before the senate as intended.

On Antony's fiftieth birthday, he decided that he must make a will. He named his Roman children his heirs in Rome—for legally, he could do nothing else—and made separate provisions in Alexandria for his children with Kleopatra. He had the will drawn up in Rome by a Roman solicitor and filed, according to custom, with the Vestal Virgins in Rome, the holy temple considered a sacred depository for private documents. But Octavian, who now went everywhere with a bodyguard, burst into the temple and took Antony's will by force from the High Priestess. He made a great show of reading it to the senate, although what he read bore no resemblance to what Antony had written. He declared that Antony had disinherited his Roman children in favor of

Kleopatra's children, and that his fondest wish was to be buried in Alexandria so that he never again would have to leave the queen's company.

Octavian began to send letters to Antony "accusing him" of sharing Kleopatra's bed. In letters and pamphlets and speeches, he asked the question over and over—did Antony not realize that this sexual liaison was against the Roman moral code? Antony was furious and wrote to Octavian asking why he had waited nine years before he decided that it was morally wrong to sleep with the queen, and then listed Octavian's many mistresses by name.

"The man's staff goes about Rome tearing girls away from their families for his sexual delight," Antony told Kleopatra. "He is remorseless in this, as if he's a brothel master! This, after breaking up a perfectly good and legal Roman marriage that had produced two male heirs and forcing the man to give up his wife! Serves him well that she remains barren."

"After producing two sons with another man?" Kleopatra asked. "Livia is not barren. She despises Octavian, and takes secret herbs to prevent conceiving his child."

"Interesting," Antony said. "Do such potions exist?"

"If one is schooled in the old ways of medicine," Kleopatra said. "Greek doctors know nothing of these remedies. The old women keep the ingredients secret and pass them down to their young apprentices only by word. They also say that sometimes a woman remains barren if she is unhappy."

"Then I take it Your Majesty is fiercely happy," Antony said, and they both laughed. "But if you were forced to divorce your husband and leave your sons, would you not be unhappy?"

"Yes, but there is not a man on earth who is able to make me do that," she replied, taking his face into her hands and kissing him. He had let his beard grow again for the winter, and she ran her fingers through its fuzz. "Either his wife is punishing him, or the gods are punishing him. I cannot decide which. But whichever the case, it is not punishment enough for his evil."

To: Kleopatra VII, Queen of Kings
From: Hammonius in the city of Rome
Dear Your Majesty,

I am writing to inform you that I will sail with this letter away from the city of Rome for good. I have been here for many years now serving the needs of your kingdom and those of your father before you. While I have successfully operated as an importer of goods, many here know my true purpose. It is no longer safe for one who serves the queen of Egypt so closely to rest on Roman soil.

And so with Your Majesty's permission—for I am so certain it is coming that I am leaving Rome today—I will sail to the port of Piraeus, make a short pilgrimage to Eleusis where I shall be reinitiated in the Mysteries, and then I shall make for the place of my retirement, an olive plantation outside the city of Athens. I will not be lonely there, for it is the home of Archimedes' father-in-law. Archimedes has married at last, a lovely young Greek girl who cannot yet be twenty. When he enters the room, she regards him each time as if he is a hero returned from the Trojan War. I am certain they will have an enormous brood of very fine children who will sit on my lap in my old age as you used to do when you were but a girl.

Your Majesty, I am seventy years old and still fat, healthy, and enjoying the pleasures of love whenever I may, but soon I shall be old and blind and bent over a cane. I hope that I have served you well. Archimedes and I are bound by oath to protect and serve you until we breathe our last. But now, you are under the protection of the great Marcus Antonius. With such a man as your husband and ally, and with an army of one hundred thousand at his command, what more might two poor Greeks—one elderly, the other now middle-aged and in search of peace in his life—do in your service? And yet if there is such a mission you wish us to undertake, we are at your command.

After all the many covert means by which we have corresponded over the years, I must now ask you to reach me by more mundane methods. I may be found at the plantation of Demosthenes of Brauron, that sacred town founded by the children of Orestes. There I shall eat olives and drink wine in the sun while young maidens—they are all named Iphegenia there—worry over my health, or so Archimedes has promised.

I hope to see you again before you find yourself staring at the flames of my funeral pyre. I will offer a sacrifice in Eleusis in your name.

Your eternal and humble Kinsman and servant,
Hammonius

Ephesus:
the 18th year of
Kleopatra's reign

N eos Dionysus!" shouted the Ephesians gathered at the harbor, chanting Antony's divine moniker as soon as he appeared at the bow of the *Antonia*. "Queen of Kings! Queen of Kings!" Kleopatra heard the people shouting for her as she hurried to Antony's side.

Antony and Kleopatra had sailed into the Great Harbor of the city of Ephesus in Asia Minor with their entire navy. Eight hundred ships from all over the world had come to join them in their cause, two hundred built by Kleopatra and flying the Ptolemaic standards with the red and white colors of Egypt. The *Antonia*, their flagship, led the aquatic parade, a pageant of power that took one's breath away. Kleopatra knew that on this day, every spectator would rush from the docks, spreading the word of this mighty force that had landed on their shores.

She and Antony alighted from their vessel and walked together up broad Harbor Street under a prescient blue sky unmarred by clouds while the citizens of Ephesus threw rose petals in their path. She had once walked this street at night, when its fifty lanterns cast gigantic columnar shadows from the colonnades across its big square stones. Ephesus was one of the region's holiest spots, the location of the temple of Artemis, and therefore a good place to secure the absolute favor of the gods before going to war. Blinding white columns along the route both welcomed foreigners into the city and warned them to wash before entering its gates. Strangers were welcome; their diseases were not. Ephesus was a marble city, and it shimmered now in the noontime sunlight like some divine desert mirage. Only the barren fig trees and the tapered cypresses stuck like spears into the ground made the city seem earthbound.

The royal procession continued through town. Looking up, Kleopatra could see the theater built by Lysimachus into the slopes of the mountain. Straight ahead, at the end of the street, a huge statue of a boar, the mascot of the city, opened his chasm of a jaw. The porticos along the streets were jammed with people spilling into the avenue to catch a glimpse of the divine queen and her Roman consort. A little boy with two goats trailing him had become the unofficial leader of the procession. He scampered ahead of Kleopatra's party, swatting the bottoms of his animals to keep a few steps ahead of her guard. The crowd stayed with them until they reached a great corridor of pines that were taller than the temple. There they boarded the carriage that would take them to their winter quarters, a Greek-style palace in the slopes above the city with a view of the sea so that they might look out upon their navy.

It seemed to Kleopatra at this moment that all the world was with them, and today even the heavens showed approval for their cause. They had sailed in perfect weather with the most favorable winds and landed gently on the white sands of the ancient city. Not only the populace had been there to greet them. Many Roman senators, outraged by Octavian's actions, had fled their own country to join with Antony and Kleopatra and were now headquartered in Ephesus.

"If it's war Octavian wants, it's war we shall give him." Kleopatra was resolute, standing on tiptoes to whisper these words in Antony's ear, though she was smiling and waving at the throng.

Without the courage to declare war on the great Antony, Octavian had been waging a war of slander, propaganda, and sabotage, inventing wild stories and poisoning minds that lacked the discretion or the knowledge to think for themselves. Through some loudmouth poets, Octavian had spread the word that Kleopatra had taken to ending every sentence with the oath, *As surely as I shall dispense justice on the Capitol!* She had laughed to Antony when she heard that. "Firstly, it is a cumbersome phrase with which to end a sentence," she said.

"And secondly," Antony added, "Even if you were so inclined to make that your ambition, you would never be foolish enough to say it."

How low was the level of the Roman intellect that they would believe such ridiculous tales? Not only accept such strange fantasies as truth, but react with such enormous outrage? The latest stories invented were the most foolish, and yet they were accepted and circulated by Antony's Roman enemies with the ferocity of a hurricane. It was now said that Antony's appetite for Egyptian luxury had grown so great that even Kleopatra chastised his extravagances. It was said that he only pissed into golden chamberpots—the least serious charge leveled by Octavian, but interestingly, the one that solicited the most ill-will among the Romans. Rumors had also spread that at banquets, Kleopatra melted priceless pearls in vinegar and drank the potion to Antony's health; that Antony anointed Kleopatra's feet as if he were her body slave; that he had robbed the library at Pergamum to appease her unquenchable thirst for stolen manuscripts; and that the two wrote one another love letters on priceless tablets of onyx and silver. Kleopatra wondered if the most ignorant and superstitious servants in her palace would have believed the kinds of ridiculous things propagated by Roman aristocrats. The stories had all the elements of cautionary fables written to frighten little children into obedience. She supposed that made sense; intellectually— with rare exception—the Romans were less sophisticated than little Greek schoolboys.

But the rumor and innuendo secretly disturbed Kleopatra's peace of mind. Had she and Antony made tactical errors? She had asked herself that question as they sailed toward Ephesus. She did not share her concerns with Antony because he allowed what were mere questions in her mind to shadow his moods and humor. He preferred utter optimism, and so that is what she presented to him. But privately, she reviewed the choices they had made. Nothing was irreversible as far as she was concerned. What had been said today might be taken back tomorrow. Or at least that seemed the Roman way. Antony planned to proceed from Ephesus to Rome to set the record straight on Octavian's lies. Kleopatra was to wait in Ephesus with the army and the navy, for surely her presence in Rome, after Octavian's propaganda against her, would pose too much of a threat.

That was the plan, until Octavian took the final step in breaching with Antony forever. He declared Kleopatra Enemy of Rome. Now there was no question of Antony going there peaceably.

"Of course he could not say such a thing of the Imperator, who still has the support of at least half the senate, the eastern forces of the army, and a good number of the country's monied classes," said the senator Ahenobarbus, one of the many who had fled Rome and joined Antony and Kleopatra in Ephesus.

Kleopatra sat with Antony and his War Council as Ahenobarbus reported Octavian's recent exploits. "With no constitutional authority, he has denied the Imperator the consulship—an elected office—and he has declared that the great Marcus Antonius is no longer a Roman officer, but a mercenary in the service of a foreign queen!"

"The insult to Your Majesty will not go unpunished," Canidius added.

Kleopatra wondered how much of Ahenobarbus's fury was genuine and how much had been called up to make a show of his loyalty to Antony, who did not join in the fray but sat calmly listening to the reprehensible actions of his enemy. He had a look of incredulity on his face, as if he did not quite believe he had to take these bizarre actions of Octavian seriously. Kleopatra, too, wondered how Octavian managed to get away with his actions in a country that supposedly had slavish love of its constitution. The Romans had murdered Caesar over what they considered violations of that sacrosanct document. Now they allowed his pale nephew open interpretation of five hundred years of inalienable law. Octavian was cagey, however, and while he played fast and loose with the constitution itself, he adhered publicly to the strictest Roman forms. Very clever, the queen noted.

Calling upon all the Roman traditions he could summon up, Octavian staged a drama in which he cast Kleopatra as the evil predator and magician who had bewitched Antony and many of his supporters. Himself he portrayed as the upholder of the constitution and the Roman Republic who would vanquish the Egyptian menace in the names of the gods.

"He put on his priest's robes and marched into the Field of Mars, where he dipped a sword in blood and threw it toward the east," Ahenobarbus said. "There were those who remarked that he could not throw very far, so frail is he. But he declared the war against you a holy war, Kleopatra."

Kleopatra did not like the way Ahenobarbus made use of her given name, which was reserved for intimates of the queen. It made her suspicious of him. If he could not address her by her formal titles, what was his true opinion of her partnership with Antony? But she said nothing, encouraging him to supply more details.

"Then he set about Italy with a large army, making the population swear an oath to him."

"What sort of oath?" Kleopatra asked.

"The typical sort of thing a Roman is made to swear to a general. 'I will hold my loyalty to the Son of the Divine Julius Caesar above my loyalty to family, children, and friends. I declare the enemies of the Son of the Divine Julius Caesar to be my enemies and I swear to fight to vanquish them.' Oh, it goes on and on, but that is the gist of it."

Kleopatra had no control over the way her body cringed when she heard that Octavian referred to himself as the Son of the Divine Julius Caesar. Perhaps because her son was the only true son of Caesar. Maybe it was motherly protection, but every time she heard the phrase, she shuddered.

"He frightened people into signing it by saying that the Imperator and the queen wished to destroy the city of Rome and to make Alexandria the new capital of the world."

Antony still had said little. He looked at Kleopatra. "Perhaps that's what we should do."

She laughed. "Destroy the city of Rome?"

"No, set up a new Rome in Alexandria. We've got enough of the Roman senate with us to make a case for having Rome itself. What is Rome? A piece of geography? Is it not the families who have made it great? The scions of those families are here with me. The ones who are not are with the shopkeeper's son—a boy who is elevated only by adoption. And I am convinced that Caesar named him his heir while in one of his dizzy spells."

"Sir, you can't be serious?" Canidius spoke softly.

"About Octavian being the son of a shopkeeper? His grandfather made unguents for the people of Aricia. That is his fine lineage."

Kleopatra could see Antony's temper rise. It was a point of pride, having to fight this boy after he had won so many battles over more formidable opponents. Once, drunk and angry, he had told Kleopatra that Octavian was Caesar's last great joke on them all.

"No sir. I mean that you cannot be serious about moving the capital to Alexandria."

"I am perfectly serious. Rome is the senate and the constitution and the nobility. The senate is here with me. It is not I who have broken the constitution by preventing an elected consul to serve his term. And if I may claim descent from Herakles through my ancestor Anteon, while Octavian descends from a purveyor of liniments, then I ask you in all seriousness—who is Rome? Octavian or me?"

"Would the senate support a new capital?" Kleopatra asked. She and Antony had always intended to make Alexandria his eastern headquarters, but they had never discussed making it the capital of the Roman empire. Why not? she thought. Was it not a more fitting location for the center of a great empire than the noisy, chaotic, violent city on the Tiber?

"Sir, you go too far," cautioned Ahenobarbus.

"Shall we ask them?" Antony replied. He was very calm. He chuckled, turning to Kleopatra. "Perhaps we should just take everyone home to Alexandria and show them their new quarters."

"It isn't advisable, Imperator," Canidius said. "It is too extreme."

"How is anything in this matter too extreme? My opponent goes for the throat, practicing every kind of extreme, while my supporters and advisers caution me to act prudently. Where is the wisdom in this?"

"Octavian will use it as more evidence that you have abandoned Rome and act on behalf of the queen. You have too many supporters still in Rome to take such a drastic measure." Ahenobarbus spoke as emphatically as Kleopatra had ever heard anyone speak to Antony. She decided to stay out of the discussion. She did not quite trust Ahenobarbus, and was certain that anything she said would be misinterpreted and sent directly back to Octavian.

"I see. Then I will take a more conservative measure. All the kings and princes of the eastern territories must swear an oath of loyalty to me, similar to the one Octavian has solicited in Italy. To these men, and to my Roman supporters, I will vow to destroy Octavian in a war that will accept no compromises. Then, six months after the war, I shall return my triumviral powers to the senate and the people of Rome."

All of Antony's advisers approved the measure, giving him a mixture of hugs, bows, and hails before leaving the meeting to carry out his plan, until only Kleopatra and Canidius remained in the chamber with him.

"Imperator, what you promise is impossible," Kleopatra declared. "Who will govern the eastern empire if you lay down your powers? The senate? That is what started so much chaos to begin with."

"Yes, I realize that, and it will never happen, of course," Antony replied. "But with Octavian promising to restore every vestige of the Republic, what else can I do? Remember what happened to Caesar? He expanded the empire beyond Rome's wildest dreams and then was assassinated for fulfilling their ambitions."

Even Caesar had failed to reconcile Rome's global greed with its self-definition as a nation of simple, land-loving, austere farmers.

"Though I despise him above all men, I almost admire the way Octavian plays both sides of the political fence," Kleopatra said.

"More and more, he presents himself as a simple man who cares for nothing luxurious," Canidius said. Of all Antony's Roman supporters, Canidius had become her biggest confidant. Her own staff she had left behind in Alexandria to administer the government. She had longed for someone like the cool-headed Hephaestion to confide in during these difficult times when emotions ran high, factions changed often, and decisions had to be made quickly. But Hephaestion was indispensable at home, and Canidius shared with both Antony and Caesar the quality she had found lacking in virtually all other Romans—willingness to accept a woman in a position of authority.

"Of course, he is trying to contrast himself with our own Imperator, whom he has portrayed as a man despoiled by the riches of the east," Canidius added.

"They say that the home he shares with Livia in Rome is no finer than that of a humble tradesman, and that poor Livia is made to do all her own housework to demonstrate that she is an old-fashioned Roman girl. Are these stories true?" asked the incredulous queen.

"Yes, but it's all part of his grand theatrical production of himself!" Canidius exclaimed. "Behind closed doors, he held a grotesque banquet with himself and his closest associates costumed as gods—the very thing he cries out against the Imperator for doing in Alexandria, where it is actually expected of those in power."

"I thought there were food shortages in Rome," Kleopatra said. "How do the people feel about their leader hosting feasts when they themselves have no bread? I remember how they reacted in my country when my late brother did the same."

"Word got out about the feast, and he was humiliated. People said snidely that the gods had eaten up all the bread, and that was why there was starvation in the city. So Octavian denied what he had done, and from that point forward, Livia was made to wear even simpler gowns. All her family jewelry has been locked away, and she may not even have pearls in her hair anymore."

"The poor woman," Kleopatra said. "First, torn from her husband and children, and then made to live like a beggar."

"The man is infuriating," Antony said. "He made a big show of laying down his powers and becoming a private citizen, and at the same time he bullied the senate into giving him all kinds of powers that are normally reserved for a dictator."

Canidius threw the stick he had been using to refer to the maps across the table. "And yet he stands before the senate daily and swears that his only goal is to restore traditional Roman values. Simplicity! He is as simple as a spider's web."

And he is wrong if he thinks I am going to be one of his little flies, Kleopatra said to herself. Her conversation with Canidius had given her an idea, the kind that came with a chill and a rush of blood to the head. That night, she revealed it to Antony.

"Imperator, Canidius informs me that food shortages in Italy are causing people to cry out against Octavian. Is that not the case?"

"Yes, praise the gods, it is true, but it isn't enough. They should slay him at his table."

"Then why do we not take this opportunity to do just that?"

"What do you mean, Kleopatra? Are you thinking of employing your father's old assassin, Ascinius, because if you are, please do your arithmetic. He will be either hobbling with a cane or serving as the assassin to the gods by now."

"Let me tell you something about arithmetic. Mine tells me that we have eight hundred vessels at our command, seventy-five thousand men ready to march as soon as you give the word, and another twelve thousand on horse who would take to the saddle tomorrow at the behest of the great Antony. When you are not looking, Imperator, I walk among them and speak to them in their own languages. They are men of war and they are anxious for it."

"Thank you for rallying the troops," he said sardonically.

"If Rome is weak and we are strong, then what are we waiting for? We must attack Italy now, while people are disgruntled with Octavian and his ways."

"I have thought of that, Kleopatra. I have even discussed it with the generals. The Roman generals, that is. We have come to this conclusion. Caesar marched against his own countrymen on the soil of his fathers and their fathers, and the people used it against him until the last blow of the dagger went into his back. I miss him, but I do not wish to join him. I will not attack Italy."

"But you did so at Caesar's behest. You will not do so for yourself?"

"I was under his command. Now I am under my own."

"I do not understand you. Do you not wish to triumph over your enemy?"

She did not like the look he gave her. Since their earliest days together, he had never slung so much as a hint of suspicion her way. Their trust in one another was paramount. Yet now he turned his head away as if to hide his private sentiments. She did not like looking at the back of his head when she knew so much was going on in his mind.

"Perhaps Ahenobarbus is right." He did not turn around.

"Right about what?"

When he did turn to look at her, his eyes were soft again. "My dear, the Roman generals wish you to return to Alexandria."

This was nothing she hadn't anticipated. She saw the looks of disdain on their faces for the presence of a woman in a War Council meeting. Once, she had gotten fed up with their hostile silence and reminded them that she had raised and commanded an army herself before she was twenty; that she had ruled a kingdom for eighteen years; that men lived and died by her word. And that she had built many of the ships in the harbor waiting to fight their enemy. She was the monarch to whom at least half of the troops stationed in the camps—many of whom would die for the ambitions of these generals in the tent—had pledged their loyalty. She had silenced them for the moment, but as she now saw, not for long.

"And which generals were for this?"

"All but Canidius, who gave a most eloquent testimony to your intelligence and your many assets."

"And what of the Imperator himself? What is his position on this issue?" The betrayals of the past lurched out from the place in her memory where she had locked them away. Would the man who had turned his back on her and Egypt for four years return?

"I weighed the question." He spoke slowly, while she despised her own anticipation, a terrible reminder of how vulnerable she was to his goodwill. "And I decided that to send you away would be too much a grand victory for Octavian. It is what he wants, and he will turn it to his advantage. Because if I am not a mercenary in the service of a foreign queen, then I must be starting another civil war. And there is nothing the Roman people want less than another civil war. I won't be a scapegoat to that."

"Well, at least you have thought the situation through. I commend you." She felt so much hurt in her body that she thought she would faint, if only from trying to hide it from him. With great effort, she held her face perfectly still. The slightest movement would release a storm of emotions. She bit the insides of her cheeks until she tasted the salty metal tang of her own blood.

"Besides, if you leave, I am certain that half the army will turn around and follow you."

"Then thank the gods that you have decided that I might still be of service to you, Imperator."

She turned to leave the room but he caught her arm. "Kleopatra, keep hold of yourself. This is not a bedroom quarrel. This is a discussion of wartime strategy."

He was right, but she resented the knowledge that if he chose to, he might send her away like a servant who had displeased the master.

"I have made my position known to all men. What kind of general sends away his greatest ally? His most brilliant adviser? His wealthiest supporter?" He said this last with a broad smile. "Or the woman he loves and treasures above all things?"

"All right, Imperator. I have once again fallen for your charms, whose powers seem to have no limit." She pulled away from him. "But I believe we were discussing the attack on Italy."

"I will not be the man who decimated his own country. The last two wars for control over Rome were fought on Greek soil. I prevailed with Caesar in the one and with Octavian in the other. I will prevail on Greek soil again."

That was the last word on the subject. Kleopatra feared that pursuing the topic of pressing his advantage on Roman soil—though she was sure it was the right strategic move—might move Antony to believe some of Octavian's propaganda against her as the woman determined to bring Rome down. As Antony would not give Octavian the satisfaction of sending Kleopatra home, so Kleopatra recognized that it was indeed possible for her to give Octavian a victory by playing the part he had written for her. Antony was the general in charge of all the forces of the eastern empire. Let him command as he saw fit.

Samos:
the 19th year of
Kleopatra's reign

There was nothing left to do now but fight. Antony and Kleopatra had left Ephesus with their army and navy and sailed to the tiny Greek island of Samos to hold games celebrating the unity of so many kings and nations under their command. For weeks now, the theaters had been filled with athletic games, theatrical plays, and music, all of which were followed by feasts both public and private. Every prince of state had sent players and musicians for the festival and had donated oxen for the sacrifices. Music played day and night through the island, and people from all over the world came to see the festivities prepared for them by the new masters of the world.

"Has ever there been such a celebration of victory *before* a war?"

Canidius sat in a place of honor next to the queen in the theater at Samos. "We are not celebrating victory, Canidius. We are showing the world what life will be like after we have won," the queen replied. "We will feed every man, woman, and child, body and soul."

Kleopatra was joyous that so many Romans of ancient and noble lineage had made such a show of support for Antony, but she also realized that it was she who would be feeding them while they were in her camp. She had hurried meetings with those in charge of the kitchens, making sure that more food, wine, plate, dining couches, lavish tents, servants, oil lamps, candles, and linens were sent from Egypt to their headquarters. "And they are Romans, so remember to order double what you would need to feed civilized people," Charmion reminded her.

Now she looked out over the assemblage of those who had marched across the world to Samos to join in their cause. How could they lose? Almost every king, lord, prince, vassal, and chief had come with his army to fight for Antony. If he had not come, he sent a high commander with troops, cavalry, weapons.

Following Caesar's ambition that all the world be given Roman citizenship, Antony had issued massive numbers of coins in honor of every nation that had joined his cause, showing the country's banners side by side with the Roman eagle and standards. Each man who risked his life did so for citizenship in the great Roman empire. Those coins were now in the pockets of every man in the theater, a special assurance of his loyalty.

Kleopatra and Antony stood to salute their allies. King Bogud of Mauretania, Caesar's great supporter, had been chased out of his country by Octavian, who confiscated his lands when he expelled Lepidus from Africa. The king and his men were bedecked in gold tunics, bright in the sun against their deep ochre skin. Tarcondimotus, the prince of Cilicia, had come bearing a trunk of coins that heralded Antony friend and benefactor of his nation. From Asia Minor, Archelaus of Cappodocia had arrived with the same sort of formidable force that his father had once raised to defend Kleopatra's rebel sister, Berenike. Antony had a long-established friendship with Archelaus's family, though they were the bastard heirs of Mithridates, the famous enemy of Rome. Antony had always maintained that Archelaus would not let him down despite his father's relations with Berenike, and despite the fact that he had died in that rebellious girl's attempt to steal the throne. Antony was not wrong. Today, Archelaus saluted Antony and the queen. Surrounded by his men, he was tall and beautiful. Berenike had always made much of the father's good looks, and now Kleopatra saw that the son had inherited his impressive height and features. From Paphlagonia, Pontus, Galatia and Commagene, every prince of Asia Minor was present and making a great show of color. National and tribal standards cast a rainbow across the amphitheater. The tall, fair men of Thrace made Kleopatra think of her childhood obsession with the Thracian slave Spartacus. She had to laugh to herself. How she had lusted for stories of the gladiator's exploits, dreaming that one day she would meet such a warrior as he and the two of them would join forces. She had exceeded the dreams of childhood; she was not united with a rebel slave but with a man whom the whole world heralded as Imperator.

Every faction was assembled for these games, as if the world was already celebrating how beautiful life would be after their victory. It would no longer be beholden to cruel Roman governors, to crippling taxes and tributes, to hostile Roman armies marching across their lands, destroying their crops, recruiting their sons, raping their daughters, and pillaging their temples and treasuries. The world would be united under Antony and Kleopatra. The spillage of rivers of human and animal blood in the arena that the Romans so favored would be replaced by what took place here in Samos—games that celebrated not cruelty, domination, and death, but art, music, poetry, athletic prowess. All that was high and good and beautiful in, of, and from humanity.

From Arabia, Iamblichus, prince of the holy city of Emesa, and his men wore the billowing black robes and turbans that protected them from the sun and wind of the desert. When Antony saluted them, they stood in unison like an army of falcons, drawing daggers and pointing them in the direction of Rome. The sun slapped the scimitars' metal, bounding a streak of light back into the air, and all the other soldiers from the other nations jumped to their feet and cheered. Armies from as near as Pontus and as far as Judaea and Media all stood in unison, paying tribute to Antony and the queen.

"Not since Alexander has so much of the world united behind one man," Kleopatra whispered to Antony.

He took her chin in his hand and turned her face to his, and a few men were moved to respond with a soldier's taunting whistle.

"And behind one woman," he added. "Alexander may have had such an army and such a navy, but even he did not have you, Kleopatra."

Patrae:
the 19th year of
Kleopatra's reign

We shall form a chain of naval outposts along the Ionian coast, one for every pearl in your necklace." Antony had said it in his most courtly voice as they were moving their theater of operations to Patrae, one of the most key of those seaside bases, for the remainder of the winter. Near the opening to the Gulf of Corinth, Patrae was just one of the pearls of the sea where Antony set up operations. Beginning with Corcyra in the north, Antony stationed his legions in a curving impregnable strand through the island of Leucas to Zacynthus, down to Methone, and around the southern tip of Greece, all the way to Crete and Cyrene. He showed Kleopatra on the map how they would be invincible to attack by land or by sea, and how their supply vessels could continue to reach them from Egypt without being threatened. Now all they had to do was wait until Octavian and his forces crossed the sea. Subject to its rigors, they would lose many.

"They will have traveled through the winter, crossing the sea at a most inauspicious time. I made that trip for Caesar, so I know what I'm talking about. There's a food and money shortage in Italy as it is. They'll be half mad with starvation by the time they reach shore. We'd better make provisions for them because they'll undoubtedly begin to desert Octavian as soon as they are on Greek soil, and they'll want to be fed." Antony's confidence was as high as Kleopatra had ever seen it. So great

was his power, and such awe did it inspire that his friends in Alexandria
had stopped calling him the Inimitable One and had begun to call him
the Invincible One. "When Octavian's foot soldiers begin to desert, we'll
swiftly attack the navy—there won't even be a need for a land war—and
by summer, we'll be sitting on the terrace in your palace in Alexandria,
sipping our lemon drinks while the sea breeze cools our faces."

"May you be as prescient as you are powerful," Kleopatra answered.

He looked again at the map, tracing the naval bases with his finger,
making a slow, sinewy curve. "It's the most precious necklace I've given
you, my darling, and how well you shall wear it. The world is yours."

He said all of this privately, of course, because any public affection
between them now was made to be a sign of his disproportionate
solicitousness of her. She should have learned her lesson at Caesar's
side, she thought. He was severely criticized whenever he had associat-
ed himself with the rights and privileges of a king, though he had
made the conquests of a king and had a king's army. But Kleopatra
was not assuming the mantle of a queen. She *was* a queen. Why did
that threaten these Roman generals so? Would it make any difference
to those who criticized her if she were a king, a man? In Rome, the
power of a woman was confined to how well she could boss her husband. Fulvia had been crushed like a bug when she tried to step outside that narrow definition of power. She had been criticized more
vehemently for taking action without her husband's permission than
for the wisdom in the measures she took.

The Romans had never seen a woman with powers as strong and as
far-reaching as those of Kleopatra. She believed that the very assets she
thought would win their admiration, like her resources and the loyalty
given her by the troops from her country and from countries east of
Egypt, were the very things that made them turn against her. The longer
she spent encamped with Antony's Roman friends, the more she realized how terrified they were of her monarchical authority. They were
fascinated, too, but they covered their awe in a veneer of fear. Sometimes
that fear took the form of disdain, as in Athens, where Antony almost
attacked a man for his insult.

They had stopped in Athens on the way to Patrae. Kleopatra had not
been to that city since the funeral of her lady-in-waiting, Mohama. She
visited that monument again after so many years, wiping a speck of dirt

from the stone as an unexpected tear escaped from her eye. She had insisted upon erecting the memorial to her murdered companion, and she smiled now, remembering the crooked priest who had taken her money, and the shoddy craftsmen in his employ. Not thinking she would come back to see the fruits of her coins, they had completely garbled her instructions for the epitaph, naming Kleopatra, who paid for the monument, the little Libyan Princess, and not naming Mohama's origins at all. Kleopatra had been eleven years old. Twenty-seven years had passed. Mohama, forever sixteen, would have been over forty years old now. Kleopatra could not picture the desert girl a woman. If there was beauty in untimely death, it was in preserving eternal youth. Mohama, so strong and fierce, so sensual, would never age. Her beautiful brown skin would never wither into the wrinkled chestnut shell that inevitably covered the dew of youth. The taut skin of her breasts and belly would never be slackened in bearing children.

Kleopatra wished she could summon the dead. She had never felt fear when she was with Mohama. What would Mohama make of the Queen of Kings and of her Sons who were Kings? And what would the men who now challenged the authority of the queen have made of her if she still had as her constant companion the dark-skinned siren who wielded a scimitar with the skill of a Scythian warrior? What stories Mohama's presence would have spawned. The generals would have all tried to sleep with her, all the while spreading stories of Kleopatra's terrible Amazon. It would have made fine gossip back in Rome.

Kleopatra turned away from the monument to her girlhood companion, but not before she saw Charmion put a hand on the stone and whisper, "Good-bye, desert girl. May the gods be with you." And that made the tiny tears in Kleopatra's eyes swell into pools of sadness. Charmion put her arms around the queen. "You are crying over the loss of your youth and the carefree days you enjoyed in her company. They ended forever on the day of her death."

Charmion was correct; on that day, the little princess who used to love to put on disguises and run through the streets of Alexandria put away her costumes and her childhood adventures for good. "But Charmion, it was as if the gods had sent Mohama to me to prepare me for my later years. The adventures we pretended to have I have had in actual experience. My days with Mohama were like a rehearsal for my true duties as queen."

"The gods are good to those who honor them. You and your father honored the gods, and you have been blessed above all women for your attentions to them."

In honor of Kleopatra's arrival in Athens, a statue of her in the robes of Isis had been placed atop the Acropolis, the holiest spot in the city, where Athena stood in her magnificent temple. Kleopatra was sure that the city wished to redeem itself for the honors it had heaped upon Octavia, whom they had lauded as an earthly incarnation of Athena. Now the streets were practically littered with coins honoring Antony and Kleopatra. There were so many statues of them that everywhere they went, they ran into themselves. At all events, Kleopatra was hailed as Queen of Kings and was honored as the first queen of Egypt to grace the city with her divine presence. A huge assembly of officials and priests had met her at the harbor with poems written in her honor. Athletes, actors, singers, and philosophers dedicated their every endeavor to her majesty. Little Athenian maidens threw flowers in her path wherever she walked, and the serving women were made to wear Egyptian dress at formal dinner parties she attended.

Antony, though he was called Imperator, was given all the honors of a visiting king. Kleopatra wondered if the Greeks, so fiercely attached to democracy, were sending the signal that they would welcome a Greek-inspired monarchy over Roman rule. And why not? A Greek monarchy would honor the glory of their country, whereas the Romans only wished to rob its temples. At night, after all the festivities, when they were finally alone, she and Antony talked over the details of their vision of a Graeco-Egyptian empire, ruled jointly by themselves, and governed locally by the native people under their supervision. The only exception would be Rome itself, in which the Republican forms would be preserved as an appeasement—at least until the people lost their sentimentality for bygone days.

Kleopatra felt as if the two of them saw from the same set of eyes. She had been Antony's friend, his ally, his benefactor, his lover, his wife, and the mother of his children, but now she believed that she had transcended all of these roles and the two of them had become one being with a singular mission. Together, they were greater than either of them could possibly be apart. Together, she prayed, they were invincible.

Two arrivals from Rome, however, cracked her pool of joy like great thudding rocks. One of these was Antony's son Antyllus, who had been "returned" to his father after Octavia had finally displayed enough humiliation and quitted Antony's house. The younger Antonius was returned to relatives in Rome.

"Octavian is very good at returning sons to fathers," Kleopatra said, recalling how he sent Livia's son back to his father after his birth.

Antyllus was happy to be in his father's company again, but was full of stories of Octavia's kindness. "She treated me as a son," the boy said, an innocent unaware of the pain his words caused the queen. "She is as honorable a woman as has lived. And she is terribly upset about the trouble between her brother and her husband."

Kleopatra had not seen Antyllus in several years, and she was disturbed to see that he was so thoroughly smitten by Octavia. "Your friend and brother Caesarion longs for your company," Kleopatra said. "And the twins talk of you all the time to the smaller brother whom you have not even met."

Antyllus thanked her formally, as if he had forgotten every affection between them, as well as all the time he had spent with Caesarion, the two of them tramping about the palace all day long. Antony saw her disappointment and sent his son to bed. "The boy has been in Rome, Kleopatra, spending his days with our enemies. Who knows what lies he has been told about you? We'll send him to Egypt for safekeeping."

Kleopatra agreed, hoping that when she returned home, her own children would not be full of stories of the lovely Octavia. Someone would have to enlighten the boy—in the struggle between Antony and Octavian, Octavia had long ago chosen sides. Her kindness to Antyllus was purely a matter of form, or so Kleopatra wished to believe.

Antyllus had been escorted to his father in Athens by Gaius Germinius, a thin, arrogant man. Kleopatra could not see how Germinius would have been charged with the care of Antyllus without being an agent of Octavian, or at the very least of his sister. She shared this concern with Antony, who said, "I wouldn't be surprised. He is pale and thin and looks like one of them. Put him at a table far away from us at dinner tonight, and we'll rid ourselves of him tomorrow."

The mood was light and jovial at dinner. Kleopatra kept her eye on Germinius, who barely sipped his wine, watching everyone's good humor with a sour look on his face. After dinner, he sent a footman to Antony announcing that he had brought a message from Rome and required an audience.

"What did I tell you?" Kleopatra hissed as the man walked to their table. "He is bringing some poisonous words from Octavian."

"What is your message, Gaius Germinius?" Antony addressed him without greeting him or inviting him to be seated.

"Perhaps I should save it for a more sober occasion," Germinius responded, looking at Antony's bowl of wine.

Kleopatra was outraged. How dare this creature stand before Antony with insinuations of Cicero's old accusations of his drunkenness?

"Perhaps you will not live to see a more sober occasion." Antony put both hands on his bowl of wine and squeezed it hard. "So you'd better deliver your message and be gone."

All conversation in the room came to a halt. So many eyes were on Antony, while others, too afraid to see the countenance that matched the seething tone, looked down.

"The message is this. The supporters of the Antonian cause in Rome remain faithful so long as you send the queen away from your camp."

"Who sent you here?" Antony asked, not acknowledging the message.

"I am a representative of the Antonian factions in Rome. I was sent here by your friends, who will not long be your friends if you do not respect their wishes."

Antony stood, thrusting his chest at the man, and Germinius fell back, but Antony grabbed him and raised him so that his face was inches away. "You are a representative of man's evil daimon. You and your friends are no friends of mine. Now get out of here before I torture you to death."

He threw Germinius aside. "Go."

The messenger did not dare give Antony the same insulting look that he had worn into the room. Tripping on his own cloak, Germinius ran scrambling from the hall.

Antony said no more about it, but the incident had shaken Kleopatra, and she left Athens depressed despite the honors that had been heaped upon her. Half the world had minted coins hailing Kleopatra their queen. Even the Roman provinces of Macedonia and

Achaea had boldly placed Kleopatra's face on bright silver, demonstrating to all the world that she was entitled to once again rule the birthplace of her ancestors. Yet these Romans could not tolerate her authority.

She worried now that her presence was becoming increasingly detrimental, but what was she to do? How would her own country react if she left Antony and returned to Egypt? If she was thrown out of the war? She could not leave all her resources behind, and Antony would be half as strong without them.

She also knew that if she left, with no one to represent her interests but Antony, she would have to make great concessions at the end of the war to those who had stayed and fought until victory. It was the way of the world. Antony would owe more to those who remained and fought with him than to her. Personal obligations would subside as the realities took over. Just days ago, she had fused herself and Antony into one being. Now she was faced with the reality that love had no place in this conflict. That much was plain. Had he not said it himself? *What kind of general sends away his greatest ally?* He had used those words to comfort her, to let her know that he was not so foolish as to ignore her worth.

Now she had an answer to the question he had asked: What kind of general sends away his greatest ally?

A general who determines that his ally is no longer an asset. The conundrum was, was Antony that kind of a general?

Alexandria:
the 20th year of
Kleopatra's reign

*T*hey slip quietly into the streets hand in hand like a pair of young lovers. They have hooded themselves in drab cloaks against the winter winds, with only two men carrying the secret of their identity along with brightly burning torches. They have not done this for many years. But her hand feels as it has always felt in his—small, soft, protected. They have had wine together and the taste of it lingers on her tongue. She pulls him to her and kisses him. She is so happy to taste those lips again. They meet hers almost hungrily, and she feels a long-absent thrill shake the deepest part of her.

It is the twenty-fourth of December, a special night of celebration to greet the Sun Child, whose birth brings the winter solstice, the lengthening of days, the welcoming again of the light. On the eve of this great night, the goddess has gifted her with a dream, a dream of him when he was young. It is so lovely to visit the warmth of his love again that when she wakes she sees that he is not beside her and she weeps. She cries through much of the day, and only at the end of her festival of tears does she realize that through every ordeal, she has refrained from weeping. She has stored a year of tears, and now she lets them flow until the last drop falls.

She puts on a simple dress, not something magnificent to make him feel small, but a plain linen shift. She leaves most of her hair down, only pinning back the side with tiny silver combs. She puts a hint of red on her lips and cheeks to make him remember the flush of her younger days before anxiety made her wan. She is

as thin as a girl again because she can no longer eat. When she looks into the mirror, she sees the self of many years ago. She wonders what it is that had brought
back the visage of her youth and she realizes that the ingredient is hope.

She goes alone to him without a plan of anything to say. No speeches, no
recriminations, no threats, no gifts, no whores. And she finds him alone, too, and
sober, looking at the giant red ball of the sun as it sinks into the sea. She stands
behind him, laying her head on his back, not speaking a word, staying very still
and quiet, just resting against him, pretending that nothing of the last six months
has passed. Pretending they have never left Alexandria, never raised an army or
gone to war, never had an ambition beyond feeling one another, skin against skin.
She does not want the moment to end so she says nothing but hopes that she is back
in her dream; hopes in fact that she is already dead and this is the afterlife where
they may be together for all time with no wars to fight and no kingdoms to govern.

It is almost dark before he speaks. I have let you down, he says in the last violet haze of twilight, his words going straight out to the sea. You and many others.
I won't do it again. He turns around and without looking at her envelops her in
his arms, squeezing her so tightly that she has to hold her breath. She gasps a little
and he loosens his arms, but she does not want to move. Is she dreaming? She has
kept hope at bay for so long that she wonders if the day she has just lived is merely part of her reverie. Wonders if she will have to wake once more and realize that
the bed is empty, the war is lost, and their plans are in ruin. She will have to wake
up all over again and cry more streams of sadness. But she does not think she can
do that because her body has wrung itself of tears and left her drained, as if someone has punctured a hole in her gut and let out all the wrenching anxiety. In its
place, though, an odd peace has settled over her.

Finally he takes her small face in his hard hands and looks at her. Like a ghost,
he has come back from the dead. Grief has marked his face, but it seems that the
anger and humiliation have left and he, too, shares her strangely peaceful state.
Without leaving that place of calm, they make love. There is nothing of the desperate passion of the past. They are driven neither by lust nor by ambition nor by the
thrilling, encroaching drumbeat of war, but by some odd bliss. Without force or
struggle, without drowning in pleasure or desperately grasping for satisfaction, they
simply couple like two innocents who come to the act in a state of wonder, learning its mysteries step by step.

She has no idea how long they make love, nor how long they stay in each other's
arms. Time has stopped, and there is no talk. It is very dark, and no one dares

enter the chamber to light the lamps. Moonlight slips gently through the window, turning their warm skin a cold white. She clings to him for warmth, throwing her leg over his belly while he holds her to his chest. She twirls his chest hairs around her finger like a child plays with her curls. She does not want to cover the nakedness. She has missed the sight of them together like this for so long.

It must be just before midnight because they hear singing in the streets. The worshippers are leaving the temples and are pouring into the avenues crying, "The Virgin has given birth! The light has come!" In their voices ring gladness and joy, and it rouses her and makes her want to be a part of the celebration of her people.

Come into the streets with me, she says. It has been too long.

She puts on her simple dress and he a plain Greek chiton and they cover themselves with cloaks. The Feast of the Nativity of the Sun is a quaint ceremony, and they do not wish to interrupt it with the regal formality of their presence. Besides, they have not run about the streets at night since the burden of war has taken them prisoners. Two guards follow them with torches. Light dances under their footsteps, and they try to step into it as it moves forward, laughing like children at their game, catching up to the Procession of the Sun Child, the infant chosen to represent the son of the great goddess Astarte, worshipped in the far-off eastern lands. The little babe chosen this year has a wizened face. He does not cry as they usually do, but sits wide-eyed and in good humor upon his tiny litter like an infant king as he is paraded through the streets, lit by the flambeaux of the worshippers. She thinks: How beautiful my city is at night. How white the columns and walls and houses against the black midnight sky. She thinks for a moment that she catches the little baby's eye, and she is reminded of her first look at each of her own children, and of the visions she had at their births for their futures and the parts each would play in the future of the nation.

All around them people's faces are full of joy. She does not know if she and her husband have been resurrected on this holy day as a gift from the gods, or if their reborn love is so great that it has spread its joy to the people. She thinks that such events are orchestrated by the mysterious wills of the gods, and, if the astrologers are to be believed, by the arrangement of the stars. She does not know what will happen tomorrow, but tonight their desires are in alignment with the heavens, and it seems enough.

The Procession ends at the temple of Serapis, the god of east and west created by her ancestor Ptolemy the Savior. Serapis was Ptolemy's gift to the people. He discovered the worship of such a god in both Delos and Egypt, saw that Serapis was loved by both peoples, and appreciated the opportunity for unity. The people saw it, too; they made Serapis the consort of the Lady Isis—mother goddess of healing and creation, warrior, Lady of Compassion. The union was a happy one. Ptolemy the Savior united people everywhere through his understanding of the power of the Divine. No temples were destroyed, no worshippers persecuted when the successor of Alexander was made king of Egypt.

Unity. The dream of Alexander, of Ptolemy the Savior, of Kleopatra and Caesar, and of Kleopatra and Antony. Honor all the gods of the world and unite the people under their worship. That vision has been handed down to her through so many generations, and despite everything she has suffered, she realizes that the dream of unity is still alive.

She thinks of her discussions with the philosophers who suggest a theology in which all gods, including the singular, fierce one worshipped by the Semites, are but one Divine being, and she wonders if her ancestors did not invent this concept. Her father, though a devotee of Dionysus, leaned toward this theology. She remembers when as a child of nine her father took her to the temple of Serapis and had the priests demonstrate for her the science behind the magic of the temple. She was shown how magnets and wires moved the god into the arms of the goddess, how siphons were used to make water appear to turn into wine, and how the great blaze at the altar was created by fire machines. All these spectacles were recorded by Polybius in his histories, who had been appalled at the way the priests used magic to frighten the native population into fearing the gods. But Kleopatra thinks it is not a way of creating fear but a form of appeasement, a physical confirmation of all the magic of the gods that the people feel in their hearts and know to be true.

"The god has no power to perform miracles?" she remembers asking her father, grim-faced and indignant. Auletes said, "The people call it a miracle; the scientists call it invention. But invention is miraculous, is it not? You must never deprive the people of their belief in the power of the gods, and you must never deprive yourself of it either."

Kleopatra holds Antony's hand as she meets the gaze of the little child in the Procession. His eyes are two black bowls of wisdom. Looking into them, she is neither queen nor goddess but a mother praying for safe and secure futures for her children. A humble worshipper inspired with an awe that she does not understand but accepts.

Actium, the coast of Greece: the 20th year of Kleopatra's reign

Though Antony had forbidden her to do so, Kleopatra walked among the dying men, talking to them in their native tongues, assuring them that she would see that they were cared for, or in the worst cases, promising that their mothers would be informed of the day of their deaths and the details of their funerals. Antony was furious with her for risking her health, but she never contracted a disease. Besides, she thought she actually detected looks of admiration on the faces of the Romans for her willingness to give sympathy to the sick. She was more courageous than they were; no healthy soldiers of any rank dared come near the diseased.

They had been blockaded into the Gulf of Ambracia for nearly four months. Death by dysentery was protracted and grotesque, and when combined with the fevers of malaria, it was doubly long and horrible. It had hit their rowers two months ago, the third in a series of abrupt and unanticipated disasters that had toppled them into despair. Kleopatra held a scarf over her nose and mouth to protect herself from the stench of death. The hospital camp was overcrowded, and the blockade had made it impossible to call in more doctors or to receive the necessary medical supplies. She walked among them now, if only to witness the extent of the damage. They had lost half their oarsmen; others who might be lucky enough to survive would never again be strong enough to row. The result was inevitable: They would have to either burn half their fleet or leave it for Octavian to add to his navy. So they remained encamped in the marsh.

"How is it, after all our planning and all our advantages, that we are now the ones who are planning a retreat?" she asked Antony. She knew as well as anyone what had happened, but she believed that if they went over the details again and again, some previously unseen solution would manifest.

"I have tried to engage him in a land war. He would not be budged."

It was true. Antony had crossed the gulf twice in the last two months, once to bait Octavian into battle, the other to cut off his water supplies. Both efforts failed. Octavian and his legions sat upon high ground and would not come down from their camps.

"There are those who whisper that the gods have left me," Antony said in a low voice. He mocked the idea with his tone, but Kleopatra thought that deep in his private thoughts he believed it.

Kleopatra hoped that Caesar had not willed Octavian the thing he considered his most priceless asset: the patronage of Fortune. But she feared that when Caesar died, Fortune had frantically looked about for someone to whom she might attach herself, and she had found Octavian. Perhaps Fortune believed that the boy, so seemingly devoid of natural assets, required her attention far more than someone like Antony, who already had so much on his side—age, experience, renowned bravery and courage, statesmanship, craftiness, articulateness, and beauty. Perhaps Fortune considered Antony, but decided that he had been blessed enough. So she turned her favor on the unimpressive boy whom Caesar had elevated by the terms of his will. Fortune had been so devoted to Caesar until that moment when she stepped aside and let his enemies stick their daggers into his flesh. She must have been a little lost without his demands, like a mother whose only son is sent away for schooling, and finds herself with nowhere to place her great love.

Even if Octavian did not have Caesar's direct relationship with Fortune, it was clear that she had sent him Marcus Agrippa. Agrippa had Caesar's strategic genius, coupled with his willingness to take sweeping risks. No one liked him, but it did not seem to matter. He was austere and by all accounts without charm. He was the antithesis of Antony, who veritably commanded by charm.

"I don't know if it was luck or wisdom, but Agrippa's strategy was brilliant," Antony said. "Attack Methone in the south so that our naval forces will have to leave the northern base of Corcyra to help, freeing the sea for Octavian's voyage. He cut off our supplies and landed his own forces all in one swoop. Did he know our minds? Then we rush to the Gulf of Ambracia to meet Octavian, and Agrippa takes Patrae in our wake! I do not believe it was planned. Octavian cannot be so clever. I believe the gods favor him."

Agrippa had taken a circuitous sea route with a small navy and surprised King Bogud, who commanded Antony's forces at Methone. Bogud was ambushed and killed; once their king was dead, the men were thrown into confusion and hastily surrendered to Agrippa. It was only one victory, but Agrippa had risked all to capture the base that was the gateway to Egypt, Antony's source of money, food, and supplies. For months now, food had had to be carried over steep, narrow paths on the backs of local Greeks whom Kleopatra heard that the soldiers lashed with whips to keep them at their labor. She was not surprised. Hungry men are not known for their patience or their kindness. The swampy land where they were encamped was infested with insects. The men were weak from lack of nourishing foods and easily fell prey to the diseases that incubated in the marsh.

"Well then, we must act swiftly to get the favor of the gods back," she said impatiently. She did not want to discuss the will of the gods—it was disheartening enough to entertain her own private thoughts on the matter—but the will of her general. "We should have attacked earlier, before we gave them the chance to attack us!"

"You are very good at saying what we should have done after you've seen the results of what we have already done. You would have had us give credence to Octavian's claims that you would not rest until you were standing on the Capitol like some kind of mad goddess of war? Is that what you wanted, Kleopatra? Has that been your secret mission all along? To march into Rome with an army behind you and bring it to its knees? Do you think the Roman soldiers would have followed you into their own country?" He was very harsh with her at times now. The anxiety that accompanies setbacks had erased many of the niceties between them.

"Then you should have left me behind and attacked on your own."

"Don't think that wasn't discussed," he said. "But it was not practical. You have the treasure and the fleet."

"Thank the gods that I still have some worth."

He must have seen the pained look on her face because he softened his tone. "Kleopatra, we both know that these men would not have willingly attacked Italy, at least not the Roman legions, and without the Roman legions we do not have a full army."

"It appears we have caught ourselves in an untenable position. You cannot win this war with me, and you cannot win it without me," she said bitterly, knowing that she had just spoken the truth.

"That is not quite correct. There are other factors. You see how the men are since Octavian's army has arrived. They had much too long to think about fighting. That much I concede. I did not think of it in advance. But for months, they sat in their camps and thought about the fighting to come, and of the cousins, brothers, and friends whose faces they would inevitably encounter on the battlefield. It weakens a man's heart for fighting."

"We have sat here the winter and watched their will for confrontation dwindle along with the food source," Kleopatra said bitterly. "Did you hear Dellius last night at dinner, complaining over the quality of the wine? 'Why must we drink this sour stuff, Your Majesty, when even the pages who wait upon Octavian have in their cups the finest Italian vintages?' He will be the first Roman in history to change his allegiance for a better quality of wine."

They were in their private quarters, he on one side of the room and she on the other, squared off as if it were the two of them who were at war. Kleopatra knew that they must unite themselves again before they faced anyone else.

"But he will not be the first to change his allegiance, now will he?"

Nothing depressed Antony like loss of loyalty. He lived for his men's adoration, and when they took it away, he became like a dejected child deprived of the attentions of his playmates. In fact, nothing at all soured Antony's spirits but this. And this was the one thing over which Kleopatra had no control.

"My husband, are you still smarting over the desertion of that fat Greek peasant?"

Antony had sent Dellius in co-command with Amyntas, whom he

had not so long ago elevated to landed nobility with large tracts of farmland in Pontus, to Macedonia to raise more troops. Their covert mission, however, had been to distract Octavian's army so that Gaius Sosius could break Antony's navy through Agrippa's blockade and out of the Gulf of Ambracia. Amyntas had two thousand horsemen under his personal command, but the mission was soon aborted. Dellius returned to Antony with the story of how he and his men watched as Amyntas declined to take the road to Macedonia, instead leading his men straight to Octavian's camp. An incredulous Dellius looked on as Amyntas shouted, "Come, Dellius, let us go with the winners."

"I had thought that my generosity would not have been so soon forgotten," Antony said.

"Then we must remember not to give such generous donations to men of low character," she answered. "We must now forget about Amyntas, and we must rouse ourselves. Whatever action we take, even if it is wrong, will be better than continuing to allow ourselves to be blockaded in this bog watching our men die of malaria. Even the officers are taking ill. Have you seen Ahenobarbus as of late? He hides the day long in his tent, but I have seen him sneaking to the latrines. He is as green as the gulf. And he weighs nothing."

"I thought you did not like him," Antony said. "Perhaps I should take ill. Then your sympathies for me might be aroused again, too."

Kleopatra lost all patience. "Why are you turning against me, who am your friend, your ally, your wife? Why do you not turn your hostilities north toward your enemy? Isn't that where they might do us some good?"

Antony froze. She hated these moments when his flow of emotions was stopped. It was only in these times that she feared him. He was so like her father, who was never frightening when he was screaming and flailing, but who made his coldest decisions when he was silent and calm. She thought Antony might lunge at her as he had lunged at the messenger Germinius. But he did not move. She had insulted his manhood, she knew, and she wished she could take it all back. Without meaning to, she had accused him of attacking a woman because he had not been able to attack a man. She would pay for this, either in a loss of his affection, or in the damage done by her words. She decided to refrain from apologizing, but to turn to him for wisdom.

"Antony, what shall we do?" It was a simple and sincere question. She realized that she was not used to asking questions of others without already having arrived at the appropriate answer herself.

"We shall call a War Council. And we shall all have our say. I want to listen to everyone. I do not want to risk more desertions. Then we will decide what to do."

She did not like this. She believed that the two of them must always present a united front; that without making a show of their unbending unity, her position with the others would be weakened considerably. She knew this was true, but she also knew by the look on his face and by the chill that seemed to emanate from his usually warm body that he would not change his mind.

Kleopatra listened to the reports of the generals in the War Tent, each summary of hardship and defeat taking away a chunk of her flesh. But no matter. As for herself, she knew that she would survive any amount of bad news and rally. She was unsure about her husband, though he coolly listened to each report.

"The legions stationed at Crete have defected to the enemy, sir."

Antony did not reply to this. "Has anyone a report from Cyrene?" he asked. "Did the legions there follow their neighbors into Octavian's camp?"

"They have remained loyal, thanks to the leadership of Lucius Scarpus," Canidius replied.

Antony looked about the room. "Where is Ahenobarbus? Is he too ill to attend a War Council?"

Canidius and Sosius exchanged a quick furtive glance that did not go unnoticed by Kleopatra. Sosius spoke. "Sir, this morning, Ahenobarbus stole a small boat and rowed himself over to Octavian's camp."

"He was very ill, sir," Canidius added. "I believe the fevers got to his mind."

"The last time I saw him he was too weak to salute. Now you say he has rowed himself across the gulf?" Antony seemed more incredulous than angry.

"That is correct, sir."

"Well then, good riddance to him. We don't need another sick man to care for. Send a skiff after him with his baggage, with a message that it comes with my compliments."

"Is that necessary?" Kleopatra asked.

"I do not want him to think he is missed," Antony snapped at her. "Do as I say," he commanded to one of his secretaries. "See that it is done and done now."

Antony looked around the room, including Kleopatra in the faces that he met. "Now, does anyone else wish to join our colleagues across the bay before we discuss strategy?"

No one moved, but Antony's question left a palpable degree of discomfort in the air. "Quintus Dellius, is the quality of the wine sufficient to keep you here, or will your lust for fine vintages hurl you into the arms of our enemies?"

"Better sour wine than sour grapes, Imperator," Dellius replied, smiling, trying to make a joke of his cryptic retort.

Antony made no reaction but let the comment stand.

"That was tactless, Dellius," Kleopatra said.

"It was a joke, Your Majesty," he replied coldly.

Clearing his throat, Antony called the meeting back to order. "It is obvious that we cannot remain encamped here in this bug-infested hellhole. We must break out, even if it means great sacrifices."

"Imperator, I have been studying the maps, and making a count of our forces," Canidius began. "Why do we not abandon the fleet in the gulf, and engage Octavian on land? We are evenly matched in foot soldiers, and there is no man who is a greater commander of cavalry and infantry than yourself. Octavian's legions have been fighting at sea for eight years against the pirate Sextus. His rowers are healthy and his men disciplined. We will not win a sea battle. But on land, he will never defeat you. He is neither experienced nor wily enough."

Antony did not immediately respond, but Kleopatra knew he could not agree to this plan. What Canidius did not know—what none of the men knew—was that Kleopatra had brought a massive treasure with her aboard her flagship, the *Antonia*. Five hundred pounds of gold, sacks of diamonds and jewels, and twenty thousand talents sat in locked trunks in boarded staterooms on her main vessel, under the watch of her loyal Macedonian guards from Alexandria. Kleopatra would trust no Roman save Antony with the knowledge of what she had in her possession, nor with its safekeeping. The men who watched the treasure were from families who had served the Ptolemies loyally for generations, handpicked personal guards from the Royal Macedonian Household Troops. They were the queen's men; of this she had no doubt. Many of these same guards had been at her side since she was forced into exile almost twenty years ago.

There would be no abandoning the ship containing the treasure, so there was no abandoning the navy. But Antony could not tell his commanders why.

Canidius pleaded on. "Sir, at least half our oarsmen are dead. The rest are not well. There is not enough food nor enough medication to revive them. Who will row the ships?"

"Imperator, we are having difficulty understanding why a man of your experience is unwilling to fight on land. Is it some newly pledged loyalty to Neptune that keeps you inured to engaging the enemy with the navy?"

Dellius had said this in such a way that even Antony laughed. When he did, some of the men joined in. Kleopatra was now deeply suspicious of Dellius, but she welcomed the modicum of levity that he had injected into the room.

Dellius continued. "Julius Caesar used to say you were his own lucky charm on the battlefield. He respected you above all men in matters of war, or at least that was always my own impression." Dellius sent his most pointed look in Kleopatra's direction. "Of course, I was never Caesar's intimate as some were."

Canidius was quick to jump in, averting any retort the queen might make. "Sir, there would be no shame in abandoning the fleet. The enemy is in control of the sea. But to abandon your land forces, or to fritter them away in useless naval skirmishes, would be a crime. A land war it must be. And it must be said—with all due respect to Your Majesty—that the queen's presence would not be an asset in a land war." He turned to Kleopatra, her loyal Roman champion, and in a low but firm voice said, "It would be better for Your Majesty to escape by land over the Peloponnese, or to attempt an escape by ship once we withdraw from the gulf."

Kleopatra waited for Antony's response.

"It is for the best," Canidius added, looking not at the queen but at Antony. "Morale among the Roman legions would improve greatly. If you are going to ask the men to endure, you must make some concessions to their desires."

"And what of the half the army that is not Roman?" Antony asked.

"What of their desires? If the queen leaves, many of them will go with her. Besides, she is our ally, and we do not send our allies away."

Yes, if he sends me away, he sends away his money, Kleopatra thought. He is trying to say this to his commanders without actually uttering the words. But they will think that he avoids a land war out of deference to me. She knew that she must say something to alleviate this idea, to stop the spread of poison before it left the tent.

"Canidius Crassus, if we abandon our navy, then the enemy will have complete control of the seas. He will be able to blockade us in wherever we go. It takes time and money to build ships. Do you really wish to be an army without a navy? It would leave us indefensible."

"The queen is entirely correct," Antony said. "We will not abandon one of our greatest assets. It is my assessment that no war should be waged from this vantage point. Our men have grown weak. Morale is low, the disease and defection rate high. We have resources to regroup and to win, but we must get our army out of this mire. I move that we withdraw from the gulf, and take the winter to gather new armies and supplies. Let Octavian remain encamped in Greece. Let his army and his navy suffer the same indignities we have endured these last months. Our best plan is to escape and fight another day."

"And how does the Imperator suggest we escape?" Sosius asked. He had taken a back seat at the meeting and he did not look happy. "We are blockaded."

"Remember the disaster at Phraaspa, gentlemen? We were in severe and desperate conditions. I called a retreat. You spent a very comfortable winter in Syria, drinking and dining on the queen's purse, and we went back the next year and were victorious."

"History shall repeat itself," Kleopatra promised. "I believe you shall all find accommodations in Alexandria to your liking."

"Leave the details to us," Antony said, referring to himself and the queen. "We shall escape this place within the week."

All summer long Kleopatra's mind had been weighted down with the heat and humidity that pressed on the Gulf of Ambracia like some invisible anvil. She longed for escape from this place. Every moment was lived in anticipation of a time when her ships would break free from the double pressure of the soggy atmosphere and Octavian's vessels that kept them imprisoned in their encampment on the shores at Actium. She did not walk about in the hazy malarial stupor that had descended upon most of the troops. She felt rather as if the power was being squeezed out of her body by unseen forces. If she might only escape this place, she could breathe again and think once more with clarity.

They had waited for a harbinger of good weather, clear skies and winds from the east that would bring the westerly afternoon breeze known as the Maestro. Finally, after what seemed an interminable time spent watching the skies, she and Antony stood under a blood-red sunset—auspicious for sailors—and he announced that tomorrow would be the day they left this place for good.

That night, Kleopatra watched as two hundred of her ships—the ships for which she had bargained for the very timber, supervised the planning and the construction, and paid for the finest rowers to man them—were destroyed in titanic flames. The sailors had soaked the polished Cypriot beams in flammable oils and then lit them with torches. The army stood on the shore, the shadows of the flames dancing on their red, sweaty faces, and watched their mammoth warships burn. There were no men to crew them, and it was far better to destroy them than to leave them for the enemy. Kleopatra knew that Octavian was watching and hoped he was not aware of their plan.

"Once we are safely in Egypt, we will begin again," Antony said, feeling her sadness as they watched the navy they had so carefully constructed become great black hulls that would be left to ghost the shores. "We'll rest and restore the men on good Greek food and wine and sunny Egyptian skies, and we'll begin recruiting once more."

"I will order timber for new ships immediately," Kleopatra said, turning her face away from the blaze, but the fire lit their camp as if it was the middle of the day. "And as far as recruits, they are being born every minute. We shall send all the way to India if necessary. Some of the spices we import are from as far away as that land. Why can we not import men if we can import cumin? We will make it worth their while."

"And they will teach us those mystical ideas that so fascinated Alexander," Antony said. "It is said that they harbor great secrets that bring a man and a woman in touch with the very gods during coupling."

"That is surely knowledge worth paying for," she replied, trying to smile at him in the old way that meant that in minutes they would be escaping to their quarters, arms and legs wrapped about each other in a tangle of lust. She wanted to respond to his efforts to bolster her, but she thought her voice sounded hollow.

Since they had decided to flee and regroup, Antony's spirits were high. He brushed off the betrayal of Ahenobarbus and Amyntas and was once more looking to the future. He was a man who thrived on a soldier's freedom, Kleopatra reminded herself, a man who would remain by one's side forever as long as he did not think he was required to do so. The confinement the naval barricade had imposed upon him must had been overwhelmingly difficult, more so than he had revealed to her or to his men. If he had prowled about their quarters moodily like a caged lion, she must forgive him, for that was what he was in these circumstances.

The sky was a seamless blue on the morning of the flight, and the heat of the summer was swept away by the cool autumn winds arriving from the north. They could not have commanded the sky god to have furnished them with more auspicious weather.

"If only we could have had more days such as today," Antony remarked as he dressed for sea battle. His trunks were already packed and loaded onto Kleopatra's flagship. Charmion had removed all valuables from their tent the day before. Nothing of consequence was left behind. They were staking everything on their success. "We would not have had to bury so many this summer."

"The gods choose who lives and who dies, my darling," she replied.

"Perhaps. But the burden falls too often on those whom the gods choose to command other men," he said. "It is not always pleasant to share these responsibilities with the gods."

They said a hasty good-bye away from the sight of others, but as Kleopatra's escort came to help her board her flagship, Canidius Crassus requested entrance to their quarters.

"Sir, there is grumbling among the men." Canidius was clean-shaven, with little red nicks on his neck. Even the barbers' razors were wearing thin, Kleopatra thought.

"Are you sure it isn't the rumbling of their stomachs? Do they not know that we are moving them out of here and toward lavish meals?" Antony was in a hurry and in no mood for a disruption of his plans.

"Sir, the land forces are not a problem. But the legionnaires who have been assigned to the ships know that you've ordered the sails to be stowed away on board. They know that can only mean one thing—flight. And yet they have been instructed to engage the enemy in battle."

"Yes, we are going to fight our way out of here like soldiers. Do they think Agrippa is going to give us an escort to the opening of the gulf?"

"No sir, but half the men wish to stay and fight. I've heard them swear that if they think they can win the day, they will do so. No one wishes the war to drag on another year."

"Are you telling me that my orders are going to be defied?" Antony spoke quietly, but there was menace in his voice. Kleopatra realized that he could not tolerate one more day in the present situation. He had set his sights and his soul on escape. Anyone who threatened the success of that would surely die.

"Not exactly, sir. But there is confusion in the dual purpose of the mission."

"There is no dual purpose!" Antony roared. "We are little more than two hundred ships against Agrippa's four hundred. Those are not good odds, Canidius, even for me. The naval orders are to engage the enemy until the queen's sixty ships escape, and then turn around and follow. Isn't that clear? The army marches north through Macedonia, on to Syria, and then to Egypt. What could be simpler?"

"Ships will be lost."

"For the sake of the gods, Canidius, of course there will be losses. It's a damned war!" Antony was beyond patience. Kleopatra did not like to see him so upset before such an important maneuver, one that would require all his calm and his cunning.

"I am simply reporting what I hear in the ranks to you as is my duty."

Kleopatra could not dislike Canidius even though he, too, had turned against her involvement in the war. He was dignified and loyal, as loyal as a eunuch, she mused as he patiently withstood Antony's anger. It was not a trait she perceived in many Roman commanders. Canidius had filled the role Antony had played with Caesar. Had Caesar lived, Antony would forever have been contented to remain Caesar's second. But circumstance and Fate pushed Antony to take on Caesar's position. Canidius was one of the few men capable of commanding in the first position, but he would never thrust himself forward. How rare. Kleopatra wondered if this Marcus Agrippa who was responsible for

Octavian's victories would remain loyal to his commander, or would Octavian, like his uncle, soon meet with the Roman daggers of his so-called friends?

"I am not going to alter my plan for a few disgruntled soldiers," Antony said. "I will be in the very visible position of commanding the right squadrons. I am personally taking on the task of facing the portion of the flotilla under Agrippa's command despite the fact that he has me severely outnumbered. I am asking nothing of the men that I am not demanding of myself—despite my advanced years." He smiled at Kleopatra. "We shall fight until we have weakened their center. Then, Kleopatra's squadrons shall hoist sails and catch the afternoon breeze out to sea. At that point, I shall retreat from the enemy and escape. As many ships as are still afloat will follow me."

Kleopatra knew she still claimed Canidius's respect. She no longer addressed Antony in a personal way when Romans were present, but she was not afraid of Canidius's judgment. She grabbed Antony by the cloth of his cloak. "You convinced Gabinius's army to make a monthlong march across a waterless desert to restore my father to his throne. Surely you will have no difficulty inspiring your own men today."

Antony gave her a light kiss on the lips. He took her hands and freed himself from her grip. "I'll join you in Cape Taenarum. May the gods be with us both."

As her ship left shore, Kleopatra looked out over the lush green mass of land they were leaving, with its patches of brown left by the hot summer sun and the abuses of the soldiers. Shepherd boys with their small flocks had come out to the sloping hillsides to watch the action, and Kleopatra could see one of them resting in the noonday sun in the stalky shade of a cypress tree. He looked as if he was taking his lunch while his sheep, indifferent to the looming confrontation, helped themselves to the thick blades of grass on the hills. She had forgotten to eat, and she wished she could leave her ship and join the shepherd boy in his meal of bread, grapes, and cheese, washed down with sweet peasant wine. Antony's army had lined up along the shore in the event that the enemy navy pushed his ships back to land. It was ready to engage if that were the case. Octavian's army, following suit, had lined up on the opposite shore. Like pieces in a board game, they faced each other across the water.

Antony waited until he felt the first stirrings of the Maestro before he gave the signal to move. Slowly, his three squadrons of one hundred seventy ships eased into the gulf, the wings moving forward before the center, to tease Agrippa's ships into an identical motion, and leaving the middle free so that when given the command, Kleopatra's squadron could quickly sail straight through the fighting, out of the gulf, and into the open sea.

Agrippa did not take the bait but spread his line longer, moving his south flank toward the open sea as well, blocking any quick escape of the treasure-loaded fleet that lagged behind the action. Kleopatra worried that Agrippa had uncovered their plan; either that, or someone had uncovered it for him. But it was too late to worry over betrayals now. Antony's vessels were quickly outflanked on the north and the south by Agrippa's greater numbers. Kleopatra had not anticipated how difficult it would be to remain out of the action, watching as their navy took blows and assaults from Agrippa's warships. They were so outnumbered that many vessels were attacked by multiple ships. Before long, twelve of their boats were surrounded and forced to surrender.

How could she refrain from engaging? Could her sixty ships, armed with men and weapons, not save some of their navy? Kleopatra ran the length of the vessel to find Eumenes, the Graeco-Egyptian commander of the squadron, defying Antony's orders to remain either below with her staff or safely out of sight at the ship's rear.

"Admiral!" she yelled to him above the creaking rhythm of the rowers. "We must reinforce the front line! We've already lost a dozen vessels. If we cannot escape, then let us at least die fighting with honor."

The admiral merely shook his head. "The Imperator anticipated Your Majesty's will to join the fighting. He assured me that if I disobeyed his orders, he would execute me with his own hands. He was not speaking lightly."

Kleopatra wanted to rip Eumenes' fine black beard off his face. "But can you not see that the plan is falling apart? You might be executed anyway for your reticence while our men are dying."

"Your Majesty, I assure you that the Imperator has already calculated these risks. Please. He will get us out of here. You must not allow the small defeats to test you. They are a grim but necessary step to victory."

He was patronizing her, and nothing infuriated her more. But she also knew that he was right, that she was not of a temperament to simply watch men die in the service of her plans. The Romans were quite skilled at this, as perhaps were all men of war. She wondered if bearing four children had erased this particular instinct from her character and made her softer to the horrors of bloodshed and death. But she knew she must steel herself for the day ahead. She had not seen the last of death and dying on this day.

"As you wish," she said. "But we cannot wait forever. If the center is not clear for escape by the afternoon's end, we *will* join in the fray. And if you refuse me, *I* will execute you with my own hands."

"Your Majesty." He bowed. If he had any plans to defy her later, he did not demonstrate them now.

Kleopatra returned to her safe place at the back of the ship, panicking when she realized that she no longer had Antony in her sight. He was not on his own flagship, but commanded from a smaller, lighter vessel. He knew that his ship would be the first the enemy tried to board, for if they captured Antony, the war was over. She saw now that his strategy was correct. Two of Agrippa's vessels, battering rams readied, were making haste to the flagship, sliding up against it. Archers stationed in tall towers aboard Antony's ship began to shower the rammers with arrows, but Kleopatra saw that the rams had not moved. Replacements ready to take the positions of the dead or wounded held those shimmering timbers in place as the two metal prows of the ships collided. On the leeward side, Agrippa's second ship rammed the flagship, whose crew tried to hold off the soldiers from the other enemy vessel from boarding. Like ants, the Roman soldiers pushed one another in a straight line onto Antony's ship, tumbling onto the deck, swords drawn and thrusting as they landed. Antony's ships were larger than Agrippa's, and Antony had taken advantage of this asset by putting as many foot soldiers aboard as possible. If they were lacking in the number of vessels, they might compensate by having larger forces to fight once the enemy boarded. Antony also had figured that their greater numbers of men might easily overwhelm any enemy ship they were lucky enough to overtake and board.

But men were pouring onto the flagship from either side now, two

legions of well-fed Romans who had been drinking Octavian's fine
wines all summer and not suffering from the illnesses that had drained
the will to fight in Antony's camp. Still, this was Antony's flagship, with
some of his best and most loyal men aboard. But from the distance, the
men's bodies were but a jumble of thrashing metal and flesh, and
Kleopatra could not gauge which men were theirs, much less who had
the advantage. She looked north, where Octavian's ships were closing in
on their front line, sailing just close enough to pummel the vessels with
missiles and then retreating to reload. They were lighter than Antony's
ships and easily fell back into the empty waters behind them. The south
end fared better. This was under Antony's direct command. His
squadron of fifty ships had managed to engage Agrippa's flotilla in
more even numbers. From their turrets, the archers sent well-aimed
arrows into the helpless men on the decks.

Kleopatra ran again to the bow to plead again with Eumenes to aid
the right flank. Antony himself was aboard one of those vessels. Even
though he was outnumbered, he and his men were holding their own,
that much was clear. But how long could they last? Were they to let
them fight to the death while they watched like spectators at a gladiatorial match? She was about to open her mouth to yell at the admiral
when she followed his eyes out to sea. The meticulous drawings
Antony had sketched in their War Tent were now drawn upon the sea
itself. Agrippa's entire naval force of four hundred vessels or more was
completely engaged by Antony's one hundred seventy ships. The middle of the gulf was a great blue void of endless lazy waves. There was
no longer a center line protecting Kleopatra's squadron, and there was
nothing to prevent them from hoisting their sails and catching the
wind straight into the open seas.

"Sails!" yelled the admiral to the riggers, who were hustling the white
canvases to their launches. He took Kleopatra's arm. "Your Majesty,
please go below. The winds are picking up. You risk being hit in the head
by a careless and excitable rigger."

"Where is the Imperator?" she demanded. "We cannot leave him
engaged in the fight."

"Your Majesty, the Imperator knows what's best. He's made the
clearing for you to flee. He will follow as soon as he can disengage from
the enemy."

Kleopatra's heart sank at the idea of leaving Antony without know-ing his Fate. How easy it had been to make this hypothetical plan, and how difficult it was to carry it through. Antony would be furious if she did not take advantage of the winds and escape. His soldiers would be roused against her if by her fault they were once again trapped in the gulf. They might even overwhelm their commander and murder her. And there were no provisions to care for the sick and the dying, little food for the hungry, and nothing with which to boost their wavering morale. There was nothing to do but carry on and secure the treasury.

"If I must leave the Imperator in the gulf, please do not ask me to turn my back to him as well," she said to Eumenes. "I will stay here with you. Aboard what ship is Antony?"

"He is jumping from ship to ship to encourage his men and to avoid capture." Kleopatra could see the admiration in Eumenes' eyes. "He is much too sly to be taken prisoner and much too strong to die."

The sails cut giant white triangles in the clear blue sky, the wind puffing them up like rising dough. Kleopatra looked from ship to ship for a sign of Antony—his standards, his closest commanders, the bright metal of his breastplate stamped with the Nemean lion, or the flash of his sword high above his head to get the attention of his men. But in the commotion, she could not decipher her husband. She was still search-ing for some clue of his whereabouts as the wind took her through the straits and into the choppier waters of the Ionian Sea.

Cape Taenarum, the coast of Greece: the 20th year of Kleopatra's reign

"When I looked back and saw Agrippa's ships close in on those left behind, I had a moment of unequaled despair," Antony said. He sat glumly on the bed in Kleopatra's stateroom. A tiny shaft of light shot through a single small portal. The room was dark, though it was only late afternoon, and Kleopatra had run her servants away before they could light her lamps. Antony's shoulders were slumped, and he refused all offers of food, wine, and touch. His elbows rested on his thighs, and he looked up at her in sorrow. "I am ordinarily the last to retreat from a fight, not the first."

"My darling, you succeeded where any other man would have failed," she said pacing before him. "You managed to get us out of a disastrous position. Concentrate on the lives you have saved. You rescued many of our ships, the treasury, and *me*. Our casualties were minimal compared to what they might have been under the leadership of a less courageous man."

"If we do not count those who were forced to surrender."

"We knew that was inevitable. It was the only way out."

"My dreams are haunted by the faces of my commanders in Octavian's grip," Antony said, turning his face up and into the ray of light so that she could now see the full scale of his remorse. His eyes sagged at the outer corners, as if they might slide off his face in disgrace. "They're some of my best men. And he is not known for his mercy."

"Perhaps he will be inspired by the ghost of the one whose name he flings about as if it were his own."

Antony swung his legs around and lay on the bed. "Come here," he said, stretching his arms out so that Kleopatra might lie next to him and rest on his shoulder. It was a feeling she had known only as a child, this respite in a man's chest, and then, it had belonged to her father, whose judgment she often had to question and override. She was not sure if she was there to comfort Antony or he to comfort her, but she took what solace she might in his strength, in the musky scent of his leather tunic, and in his hot hands that reached around to enclose her in the circle of his grief.

"We did not lose," she said.

"Nor did we win," he answered. "I had to abandon my own flagship, and with it, some of the most valiant men I've known."

"Let us not mourn those who may still be alive, drinking good wine with pockets full of Octavian's bribes."

He laughed a bitter laugh. "You offer grim comfort, Kleopatra."

"You carefully calculated our risks, Imperator. We've fared better than we predicted."

"That is true. But when one loses men, one loses a piece of one's soul."

"My darling, would your soul have fared better watching more of them die of dysentery?"

"My soul would have fared better if we had not been ensnared in that wretched place to begin with."

She realized that he would remain glum for whatever he considered a respectable amount of time. She lay beside him breathing quietly, grateful to have him alive at all, even minus odd pieces of his soul, which she was sure would return once he stopped blaming himself for their losses. He had managed a valiant retreat from a terrible situation. Surely his men recognized that and, like Kleopatra, were at this very moment grateful for their lives. For when she escaped, all did not go as planned, and she thought that she had lost him.

After Kleopatra had sailed out of the gulf her eyes remained on the sea, searching for Antony's ships that she had expected would quickly follow. She squinted into the setting sun until it sank deep into the water, and then stayed on deck until the night air forced her into her cabin. Antony had fought on, and was still trying to extricate himself as Kleopatra was watching the sunset. Because of his greater numbers, Agrippa was able to close in on many of Antony's ships and keep them blockaded into the gulf. When Antony saw that those commanders had no choice but to surrender—were, in fact, in the act of surrendering— he took the opportunity to raise sail and quickly flee the gulf with most of his squadrons following. All in all it was a successful operation, but Antony was not to be pacified with small gains.

He caught up with Kleopatra's fleet the next morning just in time to rebuff an attack from the king of Sparta, who surprised them off the Peloponnesian coast with a shower of missiles from some fifty ships, but Antony's colossal rams were still in position. He battered the Spartan ships mercilessly as Kleopatra watched from her flagship. To protect the queen from direct attack, however, Eumenes was under orders to refrain from engagement. Together, they watched Antony's archers man the turrets in the gusty ocean winds, hitting their marks on the Spartan decks while the sea breeze bent their tall towers. She did not know if it was their training or their anger at having been entrapped all summer in the gulf, but she had not seen men repel an advance so quickly and with such ferocity.

But after the battle, Antony would not board her ship. When they moved into position to allow him entrance, he sent a messenger instead to inform the queen that he would join her later. She could not imagine why he did not rejoin her, and she spent two sleepless nights wondering if he was wounded and keeping it from her. She sent a messenger to his ship to inquire, with orders that he would be drowned at sea if he returned without witnessing Antony's state of being. Breathless from rowing the dinghy, the messenger brought the news to Kleopatra that the Imperator seemed in fine health, was wearing no bandages, and showed no sign of injury or the shedding of blood, not even the usual cuts and bruises that marred one's face and arms after any skirmish.

Eumenes whispered to the queen, "Perhaps it is an injury of the soul that keeps the lion alone in his quarters. The goddess of war collects a heavy toll from even the fiercest men. And the Imperator is such a passionate man." He bowed his head until Kleopatra saw the shiny red spot at the top of his scalp where his thin black hair had ceased to grow. "Forgive my familiarity, Your Majesty. I wish to console, not insult."

"You are forgiven, Admiral, because I suspect you offer a glimmer of insight."

When at Cape Taenarum he finally agreed to join her, Antony greeted her with open arms and the face of victory. His face was flushed and tanned, making his teeth seem as white as the moon. As he and his officers disembarked, Kleopatra heard his men singing a filthy song in Latin about Antony's prowess in slaying his victims, and the stiffness of his mighty sword. All with double meaning, of course. She was used to such ditties. To honor their general's renowned virility, Caesar's men used to sing that he was every woman's husband and every man's wife. Just as Caesar had never minded this—liked it, even—Antony strode down the plank of his vessel, his dark purple cape split at his chest like a giant orchid flying behind him, gleaming scabbard slapping his thigh. His men were still celebrating not only their escape, but their quick and decisive victory over the Spartan fleet. Antony gave Kleopatra a lupine smile, a quick bow, and then took her arm.

Not until they were alone did he share his private suffering. As soon as the door to their quarters closed, shutting out the soldiers' raucous singing, Antony sat on the bed and slumped over, as if someone had let the air out of his leonine posture.

Now they lay on the bed in silence. Kleopatra closed her eyes, sending a prayer of gratitude to the goddess that her general and husband, the father of her children, was safe, if somewhat despondent. She had seen him in similar condition after his retreat from Phraaspa, when he had lost so many men to the snow-covered Armenian mountains. Eumenes was right; Antony was impassioned. The very quality that propelled him to make vigorous love as if he were still a boy, to drink and laugh with his friends or with the lowliest soldiers in his command until dawn, to fight with preternatural courage, to pursue command of an empire—that was the same quality that caused him to retreat like a lion licking his wounds in the face of loss or defeat. He did not have Caesar's nonchalance, she thought, but Caesar did not have Antony's heart. His very mortal, very breakable heart.

She put her hand over his heart and left it there until there was synchronicity in their breath and in the pumping of their blood. His heart beat under her pulse in a dance of camaraderie, not something that might be felt between casual lovers, or between a husband and wife who shared only the domestic realm. This was union of the highest order— of a man and a woman who together had seen life enter the world and leave it, of lovers who had visited the deepest recesses of each other's secret lusts, of warriors who had faced the enemy and prevailed, of friends who simply cherished the presence of one another in a moment of strife. A deep calm settled over her. Her breathing slowed, and with each exhalation the tension stored in her muscles during the long summer siege left her body. She thought she was asleep or in a trance when she heard Antony say, "Help me with this," and he released her so that she could untie the leather laces of his tunic.

The final step in expiating his sorrow, she thought, and she welcomed it. She unlaced the ties under his right arm, releasing his scent into the air, the smell of blood and salt, of the polished timbers of his ship, of the sea, of the almond oil he used to prevent the leather from chafing his body. Antony always smelled like sex to her, like the essence of a man, like conquest. There was power in his scent. Even now, when he was sweaty and unbathed, she could bite the muscle in the pit of his underarm and be aroused by it. *Your Royal Grace Mother Egypt, you are no better than a Fayum prostitute,* she laughed to herself as she traced the muscle around her husband's nipple with her index finger. But Antony had no patience for such play. He was anxious to rid himself of his anguish, which both of them intuitively knew would be released with his semen. He rolled on top of her, pulling her dress up to her neck. He did not bother to touch her breasts, but took a moment to look at them. Satisfied, he clutched the mane of her hair in his hand so that he had utter control of her head. He kissed her hard, covering her mouth with his lips, taking her tongue into his warm cavern and sucking on it until he felt her thighs wrap around his. Sinking his teeth into her neck, he thrust himself inside her. With one hand pulling her hair and the other on her buttocks, he pressed himself deeper and deeper into her. She moved with him, meeting his thrusts, but he whispered in her ear, *just let me fuck you.* He liked this sometimes, when she was not the queen of Egypt or his partner or his wife but a passive pocket for his pleasure. She loosened her legs, opening to him like a lotus flower, letting him explore the deepest part of her. She breathed in his essence, taking all of him into her body, letting his smell fill her nose, letting the sound of him pour into her ears, inviting his sweat to seep into her skin and mingle with her blood—sucking the liquid off his tongue as if she were in the desert and his mouth her only source of water. As her desperation for him quickened, he pulled away, and then gradually reentered her, this time very slowly, like a soldier carefully sheathing a dangerous weapon. She loved that about him, that even in his steady march to his own satisfaction, he could not resist slowing his pace to bring on her ecstasy. Still he had her head in his hand. He held her like a little doll while he brought her to climax, putting his palm over her mouth when she started to scream, for the ship's staff was about in the hall doing their chores. Then he tightened his grip on her hair, pinning her arm to the bed at the wrist, and shoved himself deep inside, moving so fast now she felt a burning between her legs, because a besieged and starving camp on a marshy shore had been no place to make love. With a low groan that sounded almost like a plea, he released into her in one final thrust.

They lay very quietly, sweating in the cabin's hot air. Antony reached to the bedside for a cup of cold water. He took a huge gulp and then poured the rest of it on Kleopatra's belly. She yelped like a shocked puppy, jolting up, their heads almost clashing. But he was prepared for her and quickly pinned her back down to the bed. He laughed so hard at her indignant face that she had to laugh, too, mostly because she realized that his period of mourning for the loss at Actium had come to an end. Now they could sail back to Egypt, kiss the shiny young faces of their children, and begin to plan the next confrontation.

Kleopatra longed for home, where the two of them could once again bathe together in her smooth marble tub with her body servants pouring hot water on Antony's shoulders while he made dirty jokes that sent them into giggles. Sometimes, if they spoke no Greek, he would make Kleopatra teach him what he wanted to say in their own tongue, which would shock them and make them laugh all the more.

Their lovemaking had made them very hungry, and they dressed quickly for dinner, Kleopatra sending a servant ahead to the kitchen to warn of their arrival.

"You have a visitor waiting for you aboard ship, sir," the girl said to Antony. "General Canidius Crassus has only just arrived."

"Bring him to our table," Antony said. "Thank the gods he is safe, but what is he doing at Taenarum?"

Canidius was already seated when Antony and Kleopatra entered the dining hall. He jumped up when he saw them, his face and his hair showing signs of neglect. He had obviously cleaned himself very quickly for the encounter. Kleopatra noticed that there was dirt under his nails, and his usually immaculately shaved face was covered with stubble. Outside of the battlefield, she had never seen a Roman officer of his rank enter the presence of his commander in so disheveled a state.

When Antony saw him, he walked faster, leaving Kleopatra behind. She rushed to keep up with him.

"What on earth has happened to bring you here?" Antony asked without greeting Canidius. "Canidius, have you deserted the men?" The alarm in his voice escalated with each word.

Canidius did not seem to want to answer the question. He looked at Kleopatra with wild eyes. "Your Majesty," he whispered hoarsely.

"What is it, Canidius? Are you ill?" Kleopatra asked.

Antony showed no concern for Canidius's condition. "You'd better speak up," he said.

Canidius stood straight to his full height, which still put him inches shorter than Antony. Looking up into his commander's eyes, he said, "Sir, I . . . I barely escaped with my life. I am here to inform you that the land army was intercepted on our way to Macedonia by a column of Octavian's negotiators. Sir, at first, the men wanted to kill them, but they were Romans, and familiar to so many of our officers. So the men voted to hear them out."

Canidius stopped talking as if waiting for some miraculous reprieve from having to deliver the rest of his message.

"Finish the story, Canidius," Antony said. It was as if Kleopatra felt all the energy around Antony's body freeze. She wondered if fear could make the blood cease to flow, because the room was suddenly very cold.

"After listening to General Octavian's offers of Italian land grants and large sums of gold, delivered by our fellow Romans in the sweet and longed-for language of peace, all but a very few went over to him."

Brundisium: the 20th year of Kleopatra's reign

It was the easiest thing he'd ever done, easier than his examinations at school, where he'd never been regarded as a brilliant, or even better-than-average student. Easier than military training, which required more physical stamina than he'd been given at birth. Octavian found that manipulating the minds of others was easier than any other human endeavor he'd had to tackle. Caesar had had all kinds of gifts he employed to astonish others—he wrote books and poetry, conquered nations, made great speeches, bedded perhaps thousands of lovers. But Octavian didn't seem to need to do any of these things to get what he wanted. He simply had to turn people's minds in a direction that followed his ambitions. All the hard work of his uncle, all the posturing and soldiering of Antony, was really unnecessary. All one had to do was change people's beliefs. Even the slaughter of battles past now seemed superfluous. Once the mind—that most rigid human aspect—flexed itself, physical reality altered immediately. Who would have thought that the mind, which was not a physical thing at all, which was located nowhere, which one couldn't touch with one's hands, would have turned out to be more powerful than corporal reality? How ironic, he thought. If one could gain control over the intangible, the tangible fell under one's control immediately.

The whole world had been behind his enemies, and now, thanks to the way he had altered their image in the minds of their allies, the whole world had turned on them. Except for an obstinate few, those who had followed Antony and Kleopatra across the world, who had heralded them as gods, saviors, emperor and empress, were now against them. They had changed their minds, or rather, he had changed their minds, and now everything was different. Octavian laughed. He would probably never have to take to the battlefield again. Henceforth, all combat was to take place in the mental realms, where he now believed he excelled above all men.

Thank the gods for Dellius's love of luxury and his malleable loyalties. Dellius had changed his mind on his own. He had escaped to Octavian right before Antony led his ships into the gulf and had betrayed Antony's plan. If he hadn't done that, Octavian wondered if he would have had the prescience, the presence of mind, to use Antony's actions against him. Had Antony's plan been made obvious only by his actions, and not by Dellius's treacherous whispers in Octavian's ear, Octavian did not think he would have been given the enlightenment to do what he did. If he had watched Antony fight only to escape and re-marshal his forces in Egypt, Octavian would have sighed and waited out another year, anticipating another war and wondering how on earth he was going to feed one hundred thousand men through a long winter in barren Greece, whose fields and crops had never recovered from the last Roman Civil War. It would have been a year of stealing goats and lambs from sobbing shepherd boys, of taking bread from the mouths of old ladies, not to mention solving the food shortage in Rome itself. But Dellius's betrayal had gifted Octavian with Antony's clever plan, and Octavian was able to swiftly rewrite that plan in his own words.

All he had to do when Antony's navy fled the Gulf of Ambracia was to tell the captured men that Antony had abandoned them in favor of Kleopatra; that all this time they thought they were fighting for their great Roman general when in reality, that general was no longer in control of his senses but enslaved—body, soul, and penis—to the ambitious queen. All this time they thought that Antony lived for the loyalty of his men, would sacrifice himself to save the very least among them, but that was myth. Had he not demonstrated the truth about his unquenchable lust for the queen when he left his own men to die in battle in the gulf so that he could remain in her company? What kind of

man—what kind of *Roman* man—would behave in so thoroughly uxorious a manner? He realized that most of the men had no idea what the
word "uxorious" meant, so he forced himself to be crude and say
"pussy-whipped," and they all snickered.

When he saw how successful he was in quickly changing their minds
about their general, he sent messengers to Antony's army, which was
marching under Canidius Crassus's leadership to Alexandria. Octavian's
negotiators met up with them after just a few days of being free from
Antony's charisma. After Octavian's offers of gold and land, and with
Canidius shouting, "Men! Keep your wits about you!" at their backs,
Antony's army marched in the direction of Octavian's camp.

Once the bulk of the army fell to Octavian, the rest was child's play.
There was only one remaining problem. There *was* no land in Italy, and
there was no money to pay the soldiers the exorbitant promised
amounts. Soldiers without pay often turned to the first man who dan-
gled gold in front of them. Given a little time, that man would once
again be Antony. As it was, they had started riots in Italy when their
demands were not met immediately, and even Agrippa could not quiet
them. Instead of pursuing Antony to Egypt to solidify his victory,
Octavian had to sail to Brundisium, order the confiscation of all the
land and the wealth of Antony's allies, and distribute it to the senior
veterans. The rest he quieted by making personal oaths to them that
they would soon receive their due. To assure them that he was serious,
he put his own lands up for sale, but only after Maecenas assured him
that no one would be foolish enough to buy them.

Octavian would have to act very quickly, while he still had the advantage. Land in Italy would have to be bought from its rightful owners.
There was nothing left to confiscate from anyone who could be clearly
called an enemy. He would not risk another civil war by confiscating the
property of those who were now coming over to his side. Money would
have to be doled out quickly, before the soldiers found a new master or
returned to their old one. Time was now of the essence, and there was
no time to invade lands, levy taxes, or rape temples. There was only one
place in the world where that much money existed in a single, graspable
heap. And it was in that direction that he now turned all his attention.

Alexandria: the 21st year of Kleopatra's reign

May the first, from the city of Hera on the isle of Samos

To: Kleopatra VII, Queen of Egypt

From: Gaius Octavian, Son of the Divine Julius Caesar

Madam,

It has been many months since our engagement in the Gulf of Ambracia, and I have waited long to hear from you. I am in receipt of your letter offering to open negotiations. I realize there is much you have to offer. But I am afraid I cannot negotiate with you until you demonstrate that you are ready to live up to the title the senate once conferred upon you, Friend and Ally of the Roman People. There is but one method of accomplishing this: Surrender Marcus Antonius to the nearest representative of the Roman government, or send proof of his execution. May I suggest my lieutenant Cornelius Gallus in Cyrene to serve as our intermediary in this matter? Once you have dispatched Marcus Antonius in whatever way you deem appropriate, we will begin to forge our alliance, which we might make in the memory of my father and your friend, the Divine Julius Caesar.

Signed and sealed, Octavian, Son of the Divine Julius Caesar

Kleopatra crushes the letter in her hand and holds it to her stomach. How many blows can one deliver in a short message? It is the first open declaration of his long-held agenda; he wants Antony dead. She never believed that he would share power, and now she sits with confirmation of her intuitions in her lap. Octavian waited until he was in Samos, standing on the same soil where she and Antony had held the celebration of their armies, to answer her letter. She regrets now sending the missive at all, but she and Antony had agreed that they must pretend to negotiate while they strengthen themselves for confrontation. Perhaps Octavian sees through their plan and that is why he offers a response steeped in arrogance and innuendo.

It feels to Kleopatra as if eight years and not eight months have passed since that impossibly gray day on which Antony sailed back into Alexandria. When he found out at Taenarum that he had lost his army, he refused to come home with her, sending her away on her own vessel. Kleopatra knew that Antony would have to mourn such a disaster in private. No man would let a woman see him in such grief, especially not Antony. She said all the things she knew to say—that he had saved her and the treasury; that with that money they could rebuild an army even greater than the last; that Octavian was broke, and when his soldiers figured out he couldn't pay them, they'd come back over to Antony, the general for whom their hearts beat. She recited this litany of hope and left. After all, her first concern was to get back to Egypt flying the flags of victory before word of what had happened reached her people.

Weeks later Antony returned, not as she had with her sails high and her ships garlanded, but creeping into the harbor in silent defeat. Immediately, he locked himself in the house on the promontory named after the misanthrope Timon. When she went to him, he explained what had happened during their weeks of separation. He had sailed to Cyrene, where he had stationed five legions under Caesar's man, Lucius Scarpus. He had believed in what she said, that they could quickly rebuild, and he was looking forward to rallying the legions. Besides, he needed to wipe his mind clean of the summer locked into the gulf and the surrender of his foot soldiers. He always had liked Scarpus, and he looked forward to long drunken evenings in which they would relive their glory days as young soldiers under Julius Caesar. But Antony and his fleet were not allowed to dock in Cyrene. He came under attack as he sailed into the harbor, soon receiving word that after the legionnaires heard that Antony had abandoned his men at Actium, they executed

Scarpus and put themselves under the command of Octavian's man, Cornelius Gallus. When Antony heard that, it had taken three men to stop him from thrusting his sword into his belly.

Abandoned my men? Abandon my men? Antony landed in Alexandria chanting the phrase. He repeated it a thousand times, whispering it as a question to the gods, screaming it at Kleopatra, laughing to himself at this awful misreading of his actions, this slander upon his character as a man and as a soldier. He had shut himself up in that solitary villa, his only companion the erroneous idea of his betrayal. He punished himself with liquor and loneliness and living with the shame of what the whole world thought he had done. And thanks to Kleopatra and her misguided attempts to revive his manhood, he was able to spend months mortifying himself between the legs of whores.

But now Antony's penance is over. His sorrow left him months before at winter solstice as he and Kleopatra made love listening to the prayer songs of the Feast of the Nativity of the Sun outside their window. Now he has taken a fleet of forty ships to Paraetonium to block a reported attack on Egypt by that same Cornelius Gallus. His real mission is to win back the legions that fell to Gallus. Antony is convinced that he can change their minds, that he will send operatives before him just as Octavian had done. Those offers, combined with the very sight of him, will win back his five legions. He will need them because the monster who calls for Kleopatra to slay her own husband is reported to have left Samos and is headed for Judaea, where the traitor Herod will undoubtedly furnish him with whatever he requires to march into Egypt. Antony does not believe Herod will capitulate, but Kleopatra knows that Herod has hated her for years, calling for her assassination, trying to slander her to Antony behind her back. She has told Antony this, but she does not press the point. She avoids argument these days.

She is sure that Herod sabotaged her backup plan to escape Egypt by the Sea of Reeds. The Nabataean king Malchus intercepted the ships Kleopatra was carrying over land to the sea. He burned them in retaliation for the concessions of land he had to make to Kleopatra so many years ago. Herod has his own problems with Malchus, but she doesn't imagine that would stop the two of them from uniting to connive against her. Easy escape to the east now seems improbable. Betraying her husband, impossible. She has abandoned the plan to escape to the king

of Media. She would have done so if Antony had not made the vow to
fight back, but now he has.

If Antony is successful in Paraetonium, then what? He will sail back
with his reclaimed men and they will repel Octavian, or perhaps scare
him from marching on them at all. If Herod hears that Antony is
empowered once more, he will remain true. It is a guarantee that Herod
will end up on the side of the winner, for that is the game he plays, even
if it means putting off his plans to destroy her.

Enough rumination. She must go about the business of the day as if
no threat is upon herself or her country. A queen must carry the burden of the future in silence. She asks Iras to apply cosmetics to her face
today, not to enhance her beauty as in days past, but to cloak any seep-
age of her feelings. The smooth pale color he rubs into her hard cheeks
is a mask behind which she might shelter her fear.

She has no adviser at present in whom she confides entirely, not even
her husband. She alternately protects him, and protects herself from
him and what he might do if he relapses into the old melancholy. She
is not entirely sure he will not. Hephaestion still looks at her dead
straight in the eye and says, In matters of state, let your blood run cold.
Hephaestion is not sure she should not do what Octavian urges.
Survival is all, Your Majesty, he tells her. Only those who are alive may
negotiate a future. The eunuch does not understand that the loyalty he
feels to the queen is the same loyalty she feels to Antony. As long as
Antony is devoted to their cause and to her and the children, she will
remain loyal to him. If Charmion and Hephaestion had their way,
Kleopatra would slip him the dagger as they made love. She knows that
it takes all Charmion's restraint not to poison Antony's meals.

There is no giving up, of course. The next morning she takes her
children on her rounds to the departments, explaining to them that
someday they will rule this great kingdom, and they must know its
every detail. She does not tell them of the latest plan that is forming
in her head—her plan to secure the throne for these four curious and
intelligent faces once and for all. She knows she must not reveal her
agenda to them or to anyone else, not even Antony, for he would surely stop her.

Caesarion listens to every word his mother tells her ministers,
instructing his scribe to take notes on everything she says. He will study

her methods, he assures her, so that when his time comes—long into the future, Mother—he will run every aspect of the kingdom with the efficiency she has taught him. "I am more given to reading philosophy than to reading the accounting of our industries, Mother, but given enough time, I shall train myself to be no less diligent a man of business than you."

She gathers all four around her. All operations require careful supervision, she tells them. "Generally, the ministers are out to line their pockets with gold skimmed from government revenue, but it is possible to find good men. My father—your grandfather, may the gods rest and keep his soul—taught me to factor the costs of human nature into all business transactions. Do you understand me?"

All four faces nod in agreement. They are good and dutiful children. She knows that Caesarion would rather be with his scholars reading Lucretius, that the twins would rather be wrestling in the courtyards, that the little one has no idea what his mother is talking about, but looks at her with agonizing seriousness so that he might be thought attentive and smart.

"When is our father to return?" Selene asks with a sad face. "I miss him."

Caesarion snaps at her: "Our father is in Cyrene reclaiming that kingdom for you so that you may rule it when you come of age. He is a general on a mission."

"It is permissible to miss one's father, Caesarion," Kleopatra gently scolds. "I miss mine every day. Apologize to your sister for your harsh tone."

Kleopatra does not like to see a shred of anger between her children. She has never forgotten the poison blood between herself and her siblings. How Berenike tried to have her poisoned. How Ptolemy the Elder sent her into exile. How she had to go to war with him to get her country back. How her youngest brother colluded with Arsinoe to rid Egypt of Kleopatra until she was forced to see the both of them dead.

"I am sorry for my reprimand," Caesarion says, turning the aloof eyes and the superior demeanor he inherited from Caesar on his sister. "But I do not like to hear you whine as if you were just a little girl. You are the daughter of Marcus Antonius and Queen Kleopatra. You must act like it at all times."

Kleopatra watches Alexander squirm through this exchange, his fierce gallantry to his twin roiling beneath his olive complexion. His father's charm and his father's manliness are well-seeded in his young body. He is not yet nine years old, but he is already outspoken and brave. "My sister is a little girl," he says to Caesarion. "And I am a boy but I miss my father, too." He looks at Caesarion with perfect innocence and perfect candor and asks in a voice beyond reproach, "Don't you ever miss yours?"

Kleopatra wonders if Alexander is not more fit to rule a kingdom than Caesarion. He is already a favorite of the tutors, and takes his namesake seriously. He is going to be very tall and handsome just like his father. There is little of Kleopatra in these twins; they look like Romans. Kleopatra is not sure about Selene's prospects of beauty. She, too, is the image of Antony, but the queen is not sure whether the cleft chin and the high, wide cheekbones will make her daughter beautiful or too masculine. She will be tall. She trails her twin brother everywhere, listening attentively when he speaks, letting him choose the games they will play, the books they will read. Kleopatra is not sure she quite knows her daughter. The girl is obedient, respectful, bright, but inscrutable. Alexander is so strong a personality that maybe, Kleopatra thinks, Selene is keeping her own disposition a secret until she is confident enough to challenge him. She adores him. She behaves more like his little sister than his twin. Ah well, Kleopatra thinks, no need for all four children to be chiefs.

She takes her children to the offices of the ink and papyrus factories where they look over the accounting for the month of April. She explains to them that the profits from these exports are so lucrative that they alone might fuel the economy while other resources are used for another military confrontation. "We will put everything behind this next encounter," she says. "It must be swift and decisive."

She muses to herself—for she does not wish them to know how vehemently their mother is despised on the other side of the world—how the Romans' hatred of her does not diminish their insatiable appetite for all things Egyptian. Egyptian oils, fabrics, perfumes, rugs, jewelry, foods are in high demand in Rome and her territories. At the fish factory, she looks at the income from exporting the silurus and is amazed.

"I had no idea people would pay so handsomely for a fish," she says to the minister in charge of the fisheries.

He smiles and tells her that it is a delicious fish indeed—small, sweet, delicate—and he will have three dozen sent to the palace this very day. "But please eat them fresh, Your Majesty."

Through the day, every ledger sheet she reads drives deeper the irony that the Romans are the great market for Egypt's goods. Roman artisans demand Egyptian alabaster; Roman jewelry makers seek Egyptian garnets, serpentine, amethysts, and turquoise. Fortunes are being made copying Kleopatra's rings and necklaces and selling them to the wives of the men who are at war with her. She thinks, When we are successful against Octavian, we will once again have access to certain trade routes that will increase our businesses one hundredfold. She tells her children, "My father had his eye on certain eastern trade routes, but he was never able to negotiate clearance with the Romans. Even Antony's wide sweep of power has not been able to loosen the Roman grip. I believe we can once again monopolize certain goods coming out of the east. We must capitalize on the pirates' devastation to the markets at Delos."

They have no idea what she means, but she talks very quickly, her brain spilling over with ideas for raising capital. She whispers to them as if everything is a secret: "We have not yet properly exploited the abundant wool produced at the mills by the slave girls, but I have plans to introduce those goods to new markets. The women run that business most efficiently, and the quality of the product is excellent. They are the most industrious workers we have."

She thinks to herself, I would like to appoint that sedulous old Parthian woman who runs the dye shop the new Minister of Agriculture. Productivity would double and famine would be eliminated.

She knows she is overloading the children with knowledge, but she must impress upon them what their real duties entail. She tells them every day that all is not wearing crowns and attending ceremonies, or raising armies and fighting wars, but making sure that the government industries turn a profit and that money sits in the treasury. For without profit, there is no loyalty among the subjects, and no political leverage in the world at large.

They say, Yes, Mother, we understand. And they wait for her permission to return to the lives they lead as children away from her counsel.

"You are all dismissed but for Caesarion," she says, and she thinks she sees him wince. He is tired, rubbing his eyes, but he must learn to be tireless. At his age, she was constantly at her father's side. Caesarion has been groomed from boyhood for the duties he will assume when he comes of age. She does not know how to tell him that this may arrive sooner than he wishes.

"It's over, Kleopatra. It is simply over."

Antony's servant Eros is on his knees, hunched over so that his face is hidden while he unlaces Antony's heavy sandals hammered with bronze studs. Antony steps out of them and holds his arms out like a dancer while Eros takes his belt and sword. Kleopatra sees that Eros, who is young and Greek, is trying not to cry. Antony is neither angry nor depressed but looks at Kleopatra with resigned eyes.

"Will you tell me what happened?"

Antony sighs. "Does it matter? It is a scenario we have seen more than once and will see again if we allow it."

Kleopatra waits impatiently. She does not know what Antony intends to do. She has never seen him like this, so acceding to what he now considers his destiny, so devoid of emotion. He is neither depressed nor depraved as he was after Actium. He is like the mummy of Antony, drained of his fiery blood, robbed of his munificent heart. He has the flesh and bones of Antony, but Kleopatra cannot find the anima of the man inside those flat eyes.

"Humor me and tell me the details," she says, trying to ignite their rapport.

"Will you take these dirty things and burn them?" he says to Eros, who is helping him into a linen robe. "The stink of war is indelibly etched upon them. It is a scent I no longer wish to smell."

Eros quietly gathers Antony's shoes, belt, tunic, and cloak, bows his head to his master, and leaves.

"Can you not guess what happened, Kleopatra? Has it not been reported to you that I sailed into the Great Harbor without the fleet I left with? And can you not deduce what that means?"

He acts exasperated, not with what had happened, but with her.

"There was a brief skirmish off the coast of Cyrene. Gallus's navy had been fortified with ships from who knows where. When my commanders saw that we were egregiously outnumbered, they chose to secure their safety and sailed right over to him. And that is that."

Kleopatra is not prepared for such a setback, and yet some part of her must have anticipated this to make her take the drastic and secret action she has. She does not know what to say. She is out of words and out of plans.

They sit together in chairs in a block of silence. The sun is setting, and the red dusk flushes the room, lighting their faces. It is warm, but the twilight breeze is beginning to blow. They are very still, as if they are some mosaic painting of richness and domestic perfection. Just a man and his wife in a room where bowls of fruit are within their reach no matter where they sit, where alabaster statues make monuments of every corner. Where the eagle of Ptolemy hovers over the fluffy brocaded quilts on the state bed. Where the Sun God's presence fills every inch of the cavernous quarters with his divine blush. Perhaps if they do not move, she thinks, they can maintain this fantasy of peaceful luxury.

But she cannot stay silent. She wishes with all her heart that she could just sit with him, perhaps hold his hand, and listen to the ocean's melody outside the window. Instead, she reverts to the old efforts of trying to cheer and rally. "I am told that an army of gladiators has gathered in support of you and marches toward us."

Antony smiles, but it is the shell of a smile, as if a puppeteer is moving his lips. "Ah, for once my information network has exceeded yours. There is so very much you do not yet know. How is that, Kleopatra? Have you been sick in bed and not receiving reports?"

She does not answer but regrets having opened her mouth. She does not want to know anything he is about to tell her, but he continues: "Do you remember our friend Quintus Didius?"

Didius was the Roman Antony had installed as governor of Syria, and in the process, had made very rich. Kleopatra nods her head, but it is an effort. Her face and neck rebel at having to acknowledge Didius, who she knows is going to be the reason for a flood of bad news.

"Didius and Herod have thrown in together. They stopped the gladiators and negotiated with them. Herod went to Rhodes to pledge his support, laying himself and all his kingdom—the kingdom I gave him, mind you—at Octavian's feet. I suppose he is just an ordinary man after all, trying to stay alive. A condition I no longer find so desirable."

Kleopatra took Gaza from Herod long ago and now he has made her pay for it. How many times has she begged Antony to disenfranchise Herod, arguing that such an independent power must not sit at Egypt's border? And now the traitor—for all that Antony did for him against Kleopatra's will—has thrown himself behind Octavian, making it possible for Rome to march into Egypt from the east. Oh, she is so tired of being proven right when it is too late.

She feels a numbness come over her. She wants to tell Antony what she has done in his absence but she cannot say the words. If Octavian accepts her offer, she will carry out the terms she set. Only Antony can stop this. "And now?" she asks.

"Kleopatra, I am very, very tired. In the end, it comes to this. Fatigue. There is nothing left to do. Herod is the last straw."

"But Polemo and Mithridates and Archelaus and your other allies? Why are they not here planning to rebuff Octavian's advance?"

"I have given them enough money to hide safely in Greece, or wherever they choose. I have seen enough men die. All I wish for now is a good meal and a long rest."

Kleopatra's first thought is that she does not care who dies as long as Antony lives, but she does not say that for fear of annoying him. She whispers, "There are worlds far away where we might take our treasure and begin again." She tries to inject the old enthusiasm into her voice. She sounds instead like a street performer reading bad poetry for pennies from a crowd, but she continues. "Euergetes, the eighth King Ptolemy, sent a party of two hundred explorers and cartographers to India."

He interrupts her. "Malchus has destroyed the ships that would take us to India."

"Yes, and we will stop in the city of Petra and kill him for his deed. But listen to me, my darling, there are trade routes all the way to the kingdom of Tamil that we might travel in disguise. I have ways of smuggling our money ahead of us. Legend has it that there are whole kingdoms there waiting for kings, and that is certainly what Alexander believed. From a position of power in India, we might negotiate with the Parthians against Octavian."

He turns his eyes on her. They are oceans of age and fatigue. "I am an old Roman soldier, Kleopatra. I simply do not see myself as the king of India."

Must a man reach the pinnacle of his success by a certain age? she wonders. Otherwise, do their wills evaporate?

"What do you propose?" she asks, though she does not wish to hear the answer.

"You and your family have governed this country since the time of Alexander. There is no reason that should not continue. I have reason to believe that Octavia will persuade her brother to be kind to my children; she is not an evil woman and is very soft on the welfare of children. This morning I sent Antyllus off with a guard to meet up with Octavian. He carries a small fortune, and my offer to take my own life in exchange for your safety and your throne. Egypt would no longer be independent, and you would be reduced to a client, of course, but there are worse fates."

Kleopatra's hand goes to her head. She laughs in spite of herself and in spite of the baffled and hurt look on Antony's face. At least he has come back to life enough to be affected by her puzzling laughter at his plan.

"I do not mean to amuse you, Kleopatra. I am serious. I wrote to him this morning."

"My darling, one week ago, I sent Octavian my royal insignia and a small fortune, offering to abdicate and to exile myself to the location of his choice in exchange for the right of the children to keep the throne."

Antony smiles. "What a bitter chain of command we have made."

"Does Antyllus know the terms you are sending by his hand?"

"Of course not. I told him that under no circumstances is he to hear any discussion. He is to carry back an answer in the form of a letter written in Octavian's hand and sealed with his own seal."

Kleopatra wonders if Antony is more anxious to relieve himself from his loss of honor than to see to her safety. "Would you leave me at his mercy?" she asks. "That is where I would be if you took your own life. He is not a man to honor agreements. Haven't we learned that by now?"

"If I were out of the way, there would be no reason for him to harm you, Kleopatra. You govern this country very efficiently. There is no reason he should prevent you from continuing to do so, and there is no reason for you to dress as a camel boy and flee to India. Or to go to some remote island and live in exile. Octavian will trust no Roman governor in Egypt. He will need you. Of course, you would be sharing your wealth with him, but he won't last forever. Soon, another man calling himself Caesar will rise up and strike him down. Your own son, perhaps."

"We have lived together for thirteen years, and we will die together. That is my final decision, and you cannot change my mind. If you take your life, I will follow before your stealthy spirit is fully out of your body." She hopes this threat will forever squelch his thirst for death.

"Kleopatra, you are not reasonable. We have many children between us. Who will protect them?"

"If you are worried about your children, then act to save your own life instead of offering it up as if you were no more than a goat on the sacrificial slab and that creature your god."

His face slackens. He looks more tired still. "Your Royal Grace is wonderful with words, but words have become even more futile than deeds. I will protect you with my last breath, Kleopatra, but you must look beyond that moment, I am warning you. If not for yourself, then for the sake of the children."

She does not tell him she has already received a letter calling for his death. She cannot. She must fight his urge to die until the gods break this dark chain of misfortune. Perhaps there is another negotiation to be made, something that has not yet occurred to her but will if she keeps her wits about her and Antony's melancholia at bay. She hears her father asking the question he used to put to her under the guise of mirth: *What is the one thing the Romans always need, and the one thing we always have? What is it, little Kleopatra? Say the word with me!* She can see her father's big smile pushing his chubby cheeks up, making crescent wrinkles around his eyes, his brows raised in anticipation of her answer. *Come now, child, what is the one thing the Romans always want from us? Let us say it in unison, and may you never forget it.* She sees her father put his lips together to sound the first letter of the most important word in the Roman vocabulary, and they say it together, delighting in each of its syllables: *Money!*

"You will be safe, I promise you." Kleopatra looks at the soft, prince-ly features of her tall son. He has Caesar's impenetrable eyes, brown and narrow, and the long, graceful neck he inherited from Venus, if one believed Caesar's claims. She has helped Caesarion prepare for his long voyage up the Nile River to the Thebiad, where in Koptos, Kleopatra's allies will see him across the eastern desert to the Red Sea. At the port city of Berenike, he will be picked up by Kleopatra's trusted old friend, Apollodorus the pirate. Apollodorus—an old man now but still con-ducting his illicit maritime operations—will hide Caesarion until he receives further orders from the queen. Alexander is to be his travel com-panion until Apollodorus turns him over to a Median guard who will take him to safety in the kingdom of his betrothed, the princess Iotape. King Artavasdes has promised the boy prince sanction until "circumstances permit him to return with his bride to the land of his fathers." Or so the polite and secret missive reads. Alexander does not want to go to his tiny bride. He does not want to be separated from his sister, but Kleopatra will not risk her daughter on the journey. Even if all were lost, no Roman, not even Octavian, would see wisdom in harming an eight-year-old princess. She reasons that Selene would be more at risk of contracting disease on the journey than in Alexandria, even if hostile forces overtake the city.

The boys know that Octavian and his forces have landed at Ptolemais Ace, and that they intend to march from there to Alexandria. If histo-ry is any indicator, he will storm the fort at Pelusium—where she, a young queen in exile, had once faced her brother's army—and if he is successful, he will march straight into Alexandria. And unless circum-stances change in a way that neither she nor Antony can foresee, Octavian will be successful at Pelusium. The numbers guarding the old fortress are not half of what they will confront.

Where is Hammonius? she asks herself. Why is he not here? But she knows. Hammonius is seventy-two years old and living out his last years bouncing Archimedes' little daughter on his knee. He is much too old to serve the queen in the ways of the past, which is a pity, for no one knows the eastern trade routes like him; no one has bribed more greedy merchants along the way, and no one is craftier at hiding a mission of espionage behind a jovial face and a good joke. She would like to call upon Archimedes himself to see her sons safely across Egypt, but she cannot ask him to risk his life for her again.

She would feel much better if she were entrusting the welfare of her sons to Hammonius or even Archimedes instead of the tutor Rhodon who has sworn to protect the king and the prince, but whom Kleopatra does not trust. He wears too much pomade in his hair and is overly delighted with the gifts of jewelry Caesarion has given him. Kleopatra does not believe that scholars should concern themselves with hair and jewels. Besides, Rhodon is a disciple of Arius, another philosopher Kleopatra cannot abide. But the tutor offered to accompany the boys into this hastily planned exile, and Kleopatra wants her sons to have the comforts on this journey of at least one who is close to them. Once the boys are separated, Caesarion will be entirely without familiar companionship. Kleopatra is sending him with a goodly fortune, but an entourage would attract too much attention.

"Why do we not all go at once?" he asks. "Why must Alexander and I be separated from Antyllus and Selene and Philip?"

She does not want to share with him the realities. Octavian's sister is fond of Antyllus, and Antony is certain that under no circumstances would Octavian harm the boy. He is not quite fifteen. Octavian had been courteous to Antyllus when the boy came to him with Antony's offer, though he confiscated the money and sent him back to his father without an answer. Still, if he were going to harm Antyllus, he would have done so then. But Caesarion is the son of Caesar, and Octavian, who now calls himself Caesar, will not look favorably on Caesar's true and only son. The stamp of Julius Caesar is on Caesarion's face, and Kleopatra wants to keep that face out of Octavian's sight forever.

Caesarion waits patiently for an answer to his question, so she offers him one that is slightly less frightening than the truth.

"We must not travel together because if we are intercepted, our family line is ended."

He takes in that information without any expression of surprise. He is sixteen and a king, and has never been protected by the consolations afforded an ordinary youth. "I'm not leaving until I know your plans, Mother."

If only she knew them herself. She has none and a thousand all at once. "As soon as I am guaranteed a clear route, I will join you and we will make the journey through Media to India, where a great palace awaits us. We shall either live there in peace, or we shall wait for the day when we might regain our kingdom, or both."

"And if you do not join me? What am I to do?"

She is anxious for the boys to leave. She will not feel secure until they are safely out of the city, out of reach of the monster. She tries to cover the impatience in her voice.

"You may either proceed in the journey without me, or you may remain with Apollodorus and learn the ways of piracy." She tries to smile at him, knowing she cannot answer his question more directly because she does not possess such an answer. "If I do not join you, you must rely upon your own intuition and your wits. Pray to the gods for enlightenment, and then follow the course they set for you. Even if it frightens you."

She looks him straight in the eye and is hit with a pain in her gut. If only his father were alive to protect him. "All my life I have known fear. But I have acted in spite of it. I urge you to do the same. Your father used to say that it is preferable to die rather than to live fearing death. It was the philosophy by which he lived. Your father was a great man, but he was only able to accomplish great and impossible things because he believed that Fortune would protect him. While you are on that ship, staring into the blue waters of the Nile, think on Caesar's words and let them become a part of you, and let them guide you throughout your life. It is the very best advice I might offer."

She thinks he stands a little taller now. She hopes he has taken her words to heart. She is unsure about Caesarion's future. He has had such an easy life in so many ways. Indoctrinated from birth with the details of his illustrious lineage, he grew up having very little to prove. He is happier reading than accompanying his mother on her duties. He has none of Caesar's desire to conquer lands, none of his mother's ambitions to unite the eastern half of the world under one great monarchy. She feels that if he is handed the throne, he will try his best to be an intelligent and benevolent ruler, but she wonders if these qualities will be enough to survive the challenges of being a king. Perhaps he will go to India and live a peaceful life while Alexander marries the Median princess and brings to fruition all Kleopatra's dreams and ambitions. She allows herself one brief moment of comfort in this thought.

But now Alexander rushes into the queen's quarters with his sister hanging on his travel cloak. She is crying, and he is trying very hard to refrain from tears himself. Kleopatra pries the girl away from her brother and holds her. Selene buries her face in her mother's dress and sobs. "You are going to see the great lands conquered by the man whose name you carry," she says to the boy. It is he whom she must bolster first. There will be time later to comfort Selene. "Are you not excited and proud?"

The boy tries to be strong. "I want to take my sister. Mother, they say that in Egypt for many thousands of years, princes married their sisters. That only you have put a stop to the tradition. Why can I not marry my sister and stay here?"

Odd that Kleopatra had not once thought of this possibility—that her twins would resume the tradition of both the Egyptian pharaohs and the Ptolemies and marry one another and rule together.

"You are a prince, Alexander, and princes may not simply do as they like. Your responsibility is to go to Media and remain betrothed to the princess there. That is what Egypt needs at this hour to make her strong. If it turns out that you do not marry the princess, you may come back to Egypt and do as you like. With my permission, of course."

"But Mother. It is being said that you and Father have pledged to die together. We can't leave you here to die."

Hearing these words, Selene's sobs turn into a howl. What else have her children heard? Rumors about the kingdom are rampant. Octavian is coming to kill Antony and to marry Kleopatra. Octavian is coming to kill them both. Antony has a secret army with which he will vanquish Octavian once and for all. She has heard all of these things.

"Your father and I are determined to keep ourselves and our children safe. You must cooperate with us by doing your duty."

Alexander puts his arms around his sister, and Kleopatra embraces the two of them, holding back her own tears. "My darlings. I won't let anything happen to you, and neither will Caesarion."

But Selene breaks away. "I'm going with them and you can't stop me!"

Kleopatra is almost relieved to see fire in her daughter. She likes the way Selene's eyes quiver with the power of her own words. She is lovely in her defiance, and for one moment, Kleopatra sees a flash of her sister Berenike in the girl's face. She prays that Selene's newfound defiance does not lead her to Berenike's end. "My darling daughter, you must stay here and keep me company and help me soothe the little one. He would be lost without you, but your twin is almost a man. Alexander will happily sacrifice your companionship to his more vulnerable little brother. Correct?"

She knows Alexander will be gallant just like his father. The boy thrusts his small chest forward. He kisses his sister's forehead. "It's just for a little while," he whispers in her ear, and then looks to his mother's eyes for confirmation of what he has just said. She answers him with all the trust she can muster.

"Yes, darling. A very little while."

She sends jewels beyond reason, money, ivory, exotic spices unknown in the west, with the message that she and Antony will go into exile if her children may inherit the throne. He sends back a curt message that he has already put forth the only acceptable terms, and she is free to comply. Antony intercepts the message, has the messenger flogged, and sends the beaten man back to Octavian with a letter saying he is free to flog in retaliation any of the traitors who left Antony and are now in his camp.

The creature is trying to drive a final wedge between Antony and Kleopatra so that he may have the pleasure of saying that in the end, they had even turned against one another. Kleopatra is certain of this, but this game she will not let him win. How he would love to spread the twisted propaganda that Kleopatra betrayed Antony to save her own life. That would the last stroke of false color on the ugly portrait he was trying to paint and put before the world's eyes.

So this is despair, she thinks. This is the darkness she has seen fall over Antony, to which she once believed she was immune. She sits in its black cauldron, and it buffers her against the rest of the world. She knows now how her husband spent all those months in his remote post on the sea, watching the waves and drowning himself in anything that offered relief from the agony of failure. She is sitting in the suffocating vacuum left by hope's departure.

Now it is Antony who tries to cheer her. Her suicide threat has reinvigorated him, and he is full of plans for, if not victory, then survival. He resurrects the memory of Caesar, of their unofficial triumvirate in those early days in Rome when the three of them made plans to divide up the world. He recites her own speeches of yesterday about the lineage of their children; the fickle nature of the Roman senate that will turn against Octavian if he gets too powerful; the loyalty of the armies not to a general but to a paymaster. You could be that paymaster, he tells her. We must only put out the word. He reminds her that the gods manipulate the Fates of men for their amusement and then right the wrongs they set in motion at the last moment. He is certain that is what is happening here. He spins lengthy scenarios of how their fortunes may change, and how she will soon be laughing with the gods at their trickery. It is as if he has memorized everything she has said and now regurgitates it back to her like a pupil trying to please his teacher. He repeats the wisdom of taking his own life in exchange for her safety, and she repeats her threat: My spirit will join yours immediately.

She has energy now only for her last desperate act. She has loaded the entire treasure of her ancestors and of her kingdom into the mausoleum meant as her burial chamber. It is a magnificent Greek temple by the sea, with high windows that will keep out Alexandria's grave robbers, but will allow the sea air to be her companion in death. She has made an inventory of the contents—sapphires, rubies, pearls, bars of gold and silver so heavy that pulley systems are used to unload them. The aromas of saffron, myrrh, and cinnamon dance under the noses of great alabaster and bronze statues of the gods and of her ancestors. The temple is a monument to lavishness. She has added a sinister element as well—timbers, logs, kindling, so that if Octavian refuses her final offer, she might send the entire treasure up in flames. She will time the fire so that he will smell the smoke as he arrogantly walks into the city. He will accomplish his goal of taking Egypt from her, dishonoring the memory of her ancestors, but he will inherit a bankrupt country. Kleopatra would like to die watching the look on his face as he realizes what she has done, but she has not yet figured out how to arrange this detail.

Antony acquiesces to her plan, though he calls it perverse. When you hear that I am dead, Kleopatra, and you are still breathing the sweet air of the city, you will change your mind and choose to remain in the world of the living. Philip will be clinging to your dress, Selene asking you to fix her hair, and you will not be able to follow my example. He says these things and means them. But Kleopatra knows Octavian's plan.

She will not let it be said that she let Antony die so that she might live. She made the vow twenty-five years ago before Artemis: *I will happily face death rather than live a life devoid of dignity. This I swear before She who hears and knows all. Death before humiliation. Death before supplication before the might of Rome.*

All her life she has tried to negotiate with the beast. She wonders if her sisters were not right after all. Should she have chosen a path of war and not alliance with Rome? Should she not have answered the summons of Julius Caesar, instead going in secret to the kings of Parthia and Armenia and mobilizing an army against him? If she had done that, would she be sitting in her palace, dining with her Parthian king while captured Roman slaves served them dinner?

She had thought about it, had she not? But everyone was against it. Archimedes, Hephaestion, the entire War Council. None wanted to back the savage Parthian king. She was not even twenty years old then, a banished queen exiled in a foreign land, watching as Caesar and Pompey squared off for control of the world. Now she thinks that is what she should have done—turned her back on all things Roman and united with the eastern kings. They are treacherous men, but no more so than the creature calling for Antony's death.

She tries to brush away regret, shaking her hands in the air like an old conjuring woman batting away the demons. She has always believed it a disease, an evil spirit that takes hold of the mind and turns it to waste. What good is rumination over the past? She chose long ago, welcoming the sons of Rome into her kingdom, into her treasury, into her very body. It is hard to regret past actions when children—not one but four glorious children—are the consequence.

"Kleopatra, you must give me your word that you will not take your own life without providing for our children."

Antony is right; if she dies, she must die only after ensuring their safety and their futures. Yet there is a sickness in her stomach at living without him. At living in a world in which she is captive to Octavian and his dark will. But her own desires must be sublimated. That is the Fate of a queen and of a mother.

"In those little bodies, great dreams are sown," she says to him. "I will never abandon them."

"No, of course you will not. I know that you're in despair right now," he says in his new matter-of-fact tone. "But I also know that as long as the children live, the triumvirate of Caesar, Kleopatra, and Antony and all that they envisioned for themselves and for the world, is not dead."

The banquet moves in the slow motion of a dream. It is as if they are acting in a theatrical production in which everyone knows the outcome but has agreed not to reveal it. It seems that minutes pass in the time that food is lifted from a plate and put into a gaping mouth. A hand floats languidly in the air to acknowledge a joke. Wine pours from jars sluggishly like clotted blood. Everyone is laughing in a kind of dizzy delusion, but the sound in Kleopatra's ears is hollow. She can make no sense of the spoken words gushing from anyone's lips.

Privately, she and Antony are calling it the Final Performance for the People, and they are playing their parts as splendidly as any Athenian thespians. Octavian's feet are on Egyptian soil, but that grim reality has not been admitted into the dining hall at the palace. A giant roasted boar surrounded by heaps of greens and grapes sits on every table as if it were just another evening among the fortunate few Antony and Kleopatra call friends. Eyes close in delight of the taste, lips smack, teeth grind away like machines. Kleopatra watches wine funnel into eager mouths, throats gulping like plumbing pipes. The boy soldier with tawny eyes who performed so valiantly today still wears the golden breastplate given him by the queen. A woman, drunk, knocks on it and he asks, laughing lasciviously, *who's there?* His table bursts into peals of laughter.

They are pretending that Antony's coup today over a small reconnaissance party of soldiers from Octavian's army at Canopus is a great military victory. They are pretending that they do not know what will happen tomorrow when tens of thousands of Roman soldiers fall upon them; that they cannot hear the inexorable gait of the Roman army as it marches hastily toward their city. They are pretending that Octavian's entrance into the fort of Pelusium was not painless, that troops did not go over to him immediately, and that Kleopatra did not order the execution of the fort's commander and his entire family for the betrayal. But that, too, was just more theater. It no longer matters so much who lives and who dies; the end of the game is at hand.

The single sober dining guest is the Prime Minister, Hephaestion. He whispers into the queen's ear, *Only those who survive will be able to negotiate.* Antony's Fate is sealed because he, a general, will not surrender himself into the hands of the creature, but Kleopatra's is still negotiable. Hephaestion has been in private consultation with Charmion, who also chants the tune of survival to Kleopatra day and night. The two of them, the eunuch and the woman who disdains men, have become an unlikely couple. It is as if they have somehow made a chaste marriage and Kleopatra is their only child.

She feels that she has entered a timeless zone. Was it yesterday, today, or has the time not yet come when she sends Selene and Philip and their governess to the island palace on Rhodos? When she kisses their frightened faces and tells them to enjoy their time with the old aunties on the island? When she says that she will call for their return as soon as she can? When she lets the governess pull Philip from her gown, watching the tears fall as he latches on to Selene, who is as serious as a statue? How could that have happened already? And yet it has.

Antony has already sent Antyllus to safety at the Mouseion, for who would violate the world's temple of Knowledge? The boy said angry words to his father for treating him like a child; for not allowing his fourteen-year-old chest to wear slats of metal or his young arms to carry sword and shield. Antony's great love for his son has squashed the boy's burgeoning masculine pride. His last words to his father hissed through his lips like steam. Still, Antony took him into his arms and held him, squeezing the anger out of him until his body was slack with resignation. If they do not speak again, the boy will always carry the pain of the last encounter. Nothing she will say will allay that grief. Strange to be sitting next to one's husband, encircled in the warmth of his aura, hearing his deep voice ring out with a story she's heard ten times, smelling his woody scent, and thinking to a day when he will be no more and she will be explaining his last acts to those who loved him. But her mind is in such a state that she cannot be sure she has not already done that. Has someone put a potion in her wine? Perhaps she is poisoned, and unbeknownst to her, her brain is in the process of dying.

She will be surprised neither if the evening ends abruptly nor if it never ends; if this is her death sentence, to remain at this banquet for eternity pretending that reality is not reality. But the evening does end, because Antony stands and announces his leave. He has taken his party by surprise—their New Dionysus has never before put an end to an evening's revelry. He is the jokester who orders the servants to close the shutters against the dawn so that the festivities may go on and on. He is the one who shouts, *Why should Helios be the arbiter of day when Dionysus desires the night to remain?* Kleopatra understands that on this evening, he feels his mortality more than ever, and so he must succumb to the quotidian need for sleep. One by one, those who have drunk and dined with him for thirteen years embrace him as if they expect to see him on the morrow. She sees that few meet his eyes, but many turn away in tears.

She walks with her friends to their carriages, begging them to go into hiding. Their names are known. There will be retribution. They must leave this very night—she will give them a vessel to sail to Greece—taking few possessions and waiting to see who will be forgiven. This is our home, they say. And all the earth now sits on Roman soil. There is nowhere to go. Cleon says, *Our lives will feel like death without him wherever we are.* They thank her for dinner, kissing her cheek, her hand, her ring, depending on prior intimacy, as if they hope to be invited back next week to another of her lavish events.

Antony comes to her bed. She takes him in her arms and asks him if he will change his mind. We are past words and wars and schemes, he says. I am to die and you are to live, but which of us is facing the better prospect is known only to the gods. She sighs. Do not quote Socrates to silence me, she says. I will silence you one last time, he answers.

He pours himself over her and into her. They swim together, slick-skinned and silent, like dolphins at sea. His breathing is the most real thing she has heard all evening, every exhalation a nail pinning her to the bed. The more she sinks into the mattress the more she feels her desire rise up to meet him. This is desire's last stand. If she lives to be an old crone, she will never again open this way to a man. If she is forced to give herself to someone else, it will be a hollow act. The love that comes from deep inside her belongs to him alone. She wraps her legs tighter around her husband, trying to send all her desire into his body so that his spirit may take it with him on his journey to the gods. She wants him to have all of it; every last vestige of pleasure her womanhood has to offer must become an indelible part of his soul now. She tries to will all her sensuality, all of her sex, to leave her muscles, her skin, her nose and mouth and arms and hands. She pushes everything she has— breasts, belly, vagina—into him, imagining her soul seep under his skin and into his blood. She sees it now coursing through his veins, filling him up. It will strengthen his spirit and help him to die with a feeling of power and not defeat, with hope and not despair. She clings to him like a baby lion to the breast of its mother as they flee the hunter's arrow. She has given him the best part of herself and is emptying out. He brings her closer to the moment of her last climax, and she squeezes every muscle in her body before she releases, letting the last gush of her sexual self pour into him.

Tears flow like tiny streams down her temples and into her ears. He feels her cry but he does not stop. He moves faster, but not so fast that he finishes. She will lie there and let him do this until morning if that is what he wishes. He puts his hands on her wet face and kisses her, going deep into her mouth, sucking her tongue savagely. It does not hurt. She is beyond pain. *That's it*, she pleads, *take the very last of me*. But she feels herself begin again to quiver around his penis. No, she prays, there is no more passion in me. Take it away. She tries to free herself from that muscle's will, but it will not stop pulsing around him.

Empty me, she says to him. *Finish me.*

You will live on after me, he says, *but tonight, we go together*. She lets him grab her buttocks and move her body against him the way he always does so that she has no choice but to feel the tension rise, no choice but to reach for that final release. It takes her by surprise this time, bursting like a shooting star all the way up her spine and exploding into her head until she sees a cold blackness before her eyes. *I'm dying with you*, he breathes into her ear, and releases himself into her.

She is dizzy and suddenly cold. She clings to him to stop her shivering. She wishes he would put the full force of his weight on her now and annihilate her. This is how she would like to die. But he rolls to his side and stares at her face. She takes a deep breath, praying that he has not deceived her and slipped any of her passion back into her body.

To: Gaius Octavian

From: Marcus Antonius

By the time you receive this letter, I shall have honored your call for my death. I ask that you in turn honor our agreement and show mercy to the queen and to her children. You and I once called each other friend and brother, and yet we have labored long and hard against one another. Remember the Fate of King Eurystheus who refused sanctuary to the family of Herakles after his death. After setting Herakles to twelve labors, the king was not satisfied with either his trials or his death. Eurystheus was not honored for his vengeance, but executed by his people, who were outraged that a family was punished for the crimes of the father. I ask you to follow not in the footsteps of the unforgiving, but rather the example of mercy given by your uncle, whom I served and whom we both loved. Be content that my labors against you brought you no harm, but in the end, lifted you up and made you even more mighty.

The queen is beloved by her people and she lives to protect them. They offered to take up arms against you in the city, inviting slaughter upon themselves, but the queen would not have it. She demanded that they offer you peaceful surrender and welcome into their city. She rules with grace and intelligence. She merely found herself caught in the struggle between ourselves after Caesar's death. I demanded her allegiance because of her wealth and the strategic location of her country. In aligning herself with me, she did not consider that she was making herself your enemy. Remember that she fought against Caesar's assassins when they threatened her borders, even at risk to herself. The children, as all children, are innocent. I ask you to remember that we are bound by blood. My mother is descended of the Julian clan, and is the third cousin of your uncle and father. My daughters are your nieces and will require your protection. Antyllus considers your sister his mother. I ask that my children not pay the price of their father's ambitions, but retain their portions of my estates so that they may fulfill the civic duties set upon them by virtue of their births. Not for myself, but for the honor and memory of the distinguished service of the Antonii clan to the Republic of Rome, I urge you to refrain from bringing shame upon my name and upon my children.

Caesar always said that the fearful governed by the sword, the great by mercy. Surely you no longer have any reason for fear. The queen has no wish for anything but peace, and to live out her years in the kingdom of her ancestors. Like her father, she wishes only to achieve the title already conferred upon her by the senate, Friend and Ally of the Roman People. I give you my word as a Roman that she will salute you.

This is my final request and must be honored according to the wishes of the gods and by our sacrosanct customs.

Marcus Antonius, Imperator of Rome

She awakens alone. It is not yet daylight, but he has crept away without waking her. He has left a note on the bed. *After all we have lived together, what is left to say? I love you.*

This is how it will be now, every day, for the rest of her life. She will wake to see the empty space next to her cold body. There will be no arms to roll into, no shelter from the world's cruelties, no pleasure to celebrate a victory or to palliate a defeat. No scent of wood and oil and musk on the linens. They have made their tragic bargain, and she lost the only argument she ever lost with Antony. When she tried to convince him to change his mind, he drove her mad with his Socratic taunt. *Who is to say you are the more fortunate? I don't envy you, my queen, for you will live in a world ruled by a tyrant while I make mirth with the gods.* Perhaps he is right.

When she asked him if he would sacrifice before battle, he laughed at her and replied, *I am the sacrifice, Kleopatra.* He will fight as long as he might. This is his plan, to fight to the death, to die driven through the belly by a Roman swordsman, probably one trained by his own hand. He has practiced this maneuver over and over in his mind. He does not think he can force himself to make his throat vulnerable, not after all his years of perfecting the art of combat. But casting aside the shield at just the propitious moment and thrusting himself into the weapon, all the while watching the look of surprise on his murderer's face at his rash self-destruction—this he says he might accomplish. He wishes to die fighting and not by his own hand. He who loves life and all its offerings does not believe he has the will to rob himself of yet one more day, for surely each day serves up some small pleasure hidden in its grand doses of pain. For those luxuries great and small he has lived. He has embraced the Egyptian assumption that the dead continue with their lives in the manner in which they lived but on another plane of existence, and like the pharaohs of old, he intends to rise into the next world complete. But it will have to be another hand that sends him to that heavenly kingdom. His will to live is too great.

She worries over this as Charmion lights the lamps in her room and begins the process of dressing her. Iras appears with the tools of his trade, opens his mouth, and is quickly silenced by that lady. He lays out the combs and pins and ribbons and jewels that he will weave into Kleopatra's hair, while in the next room she is sponged by the body servant. Kleopatra goes through the ritual with no awareness of the hands that cleanse and perfume her, nor of those that pleat the folds of her dress or curl the tendrils around her face. Her mind is with Antony as he marches his troops out of the city and into the dawn.

Both she and Antony know what will happen as surely as if they have lived the events. From a high hill overlooking the bay, Antony will watch as one or two captains of die-hard loyalty engage Octavian's vessels. But as soon as the superior numbers make plain the outcome, those more attached to the idea of living will salute their enemies with their oars. The infantry, more devoted to their commander, will undoubtedly engage in skirmish, and this Antony will use to facilitate his death. He will charge into battle with the lowest of his men, and he will cast himself straight into the sword of some shocked legionnaire. Thus his life with all its ambitions and anxieties will end, and she will be left to negotiate with his enemy. She has promised to do this—for the children, for Egypt, for the sake of all they have been through together—but she fears that the lack of variation in the plan, and the dependence upon the actions of others to carry it to fruition, may lead to unexpected results. She has spent many days searching for her ultimate resolve, and no matter what she has promised, she has not yet decided if it is death or survival. Just in case, she keeps a dagger strapped in a sheath to her thigh as Mohama taught her to so many years ago.

She walks through the palace with a small escort, and no matter how hard she tries to take every detail with her, all is blurred. In the halls, the servants are crying. The old Nubian men who squat patiently through the night, on call to answer her every need and to carry her desires to those who may give them quick fulfillment, are on their knees now, wet eyes covered with craggy hands. Some have been at their posts since her father placed them there decades ago. She sees those familiar old hands reach out to touch the hem of her dress as she walks by, smiling at them, as if she is merely going on a long trip.

In the chaos of the main halls, kitchen maids, cooks, lamp lighters, laundresses are waiting to salute their queen. They have been told to stay at their posts, that no harm will come to them, that if the Roman takes over the palace and sleeps in the queen's bed this very evening, he will be kind to those who attend to him. Still, the loyalists are pushed aside by a diaspora of nonbelievers who flee into the streets, carrying full satchels in their hands and babies on their backs. Kleopatra wonders where they think they will go. Some have said they will not wait upon the Romans, that they will anticipate her return and come back. Others, she knows, have stolen what they believe they can get away with and are planning to sneak out of the city. Do they not know that they will be stopped by Octavian's men, who will put them to death for stealing his property?

Except for the lonely patter of the footsteps of the few who are running away, the streets are eerily quiet. She listens for the sounds of war, but only hears the shrill chirp of birds in the acacia trees lining the avenue. It is a short walk to the mausoleum, and she takes in the smell of honeysuckle carried on the morning breeze, still cool though it is the second day of August. The sky is silvery, and the city is a blur of whites and greens. She does not imagine that it will be any different tomorrow. The Romans do not sack great cities, but slowly bleed them. The treasures of her ancestors will not disappear in any noticeable fashion, but slip away one by one on ships that will carry the glorious confluence of Egyptian majesty and Greek beauty to their thieving bastard child, Rome. She wonders if it is better to die today, with the city and the treasury and her pride intact, or to sit on a throne like a puppet, taking orders and cues from a man she disdains. She has lived her life true to her principles. When that is no longer possible, is it better to die?

The mausoleum sits by the sea, next to the temple of Isis. It is very tall, with only one door that has a tiny, secret portal for the queen to receive messages, and windows so high that robbers would have to be winged creatures or Titans to gain entrance. The door locks from the inside, protecting the building's inhabitants. Before she enters, she looks to the lighthouse, its flame burning in the morning mist, guiding the enemy to its shores. She thinks of Alexander in his tomb, cursing her, she imagines, for relinquishing his city to a Roman. Dirt farmers not

worthy of his interest when he was alive. She makes him a silent promise that this is but a momentary humiliation; that if not she, then her
children will rise up and seek revenge in his name. All must be in the
service of that goal.

She asks her chosen companions—Charmion, Iras, Hephaestion—
if they would change their minds. No one is required to entomb
themselves with her. Charmion answers her with a look of utter disdain. Hephaestion only smiles at her foolishness. She hopes Iras will
give in to his fears and remain outside because he is one to need comfort rather than to give it. But you are my life, he says to the queen,
and walks into the building before she can ask him again.

She has had the walls painted in murals of the city, with its temples
and colonnades and glimmering white beauty, brought to life now by
torches, just as the city outside is awakened by the dawn. She wanted to
live in the city in death as she had presided over it in life. She had no
idea when she built it that she would one day be entombed alive.

The tomb is as silent as if its inhabitants are already dead. No one
speaks. Hephaestion reads poetry. Charmion writes letters, and Iras
embroiders tiny diamonds into a comb, as if the queen were this evening
attending a state affair and he readying her hair ornament. Barely a noise
creeps in from outside; it is as if the city has died, too. People have shut
themselves inside their homes. Merchants have not opened their stores;
stalls at the marketplace sit abandoned. Peasant children do not play on
the shore. It is so quiet that she wonders if Poseidon has silenced the
ocean's waves in sorrow.

Finally, she hears the clop of a single horse in the distance, and an
interminable time before someone dismounts and raps at the portal.
Hephaestion opens the small trap so that Kleopatra can see the moving
lips of Diomedes, the scribe she sent to record the details of the battle,
telling her the story she does not want to hear. She watches it play out
in her mind as the dreadful words pass into the chamber.

"There was no battle, Your Majesty. The Imperator watched as his
fleet sailed into the dawn and joined the single line of Octavian's vessels. The ships fit so neatly and naturally in his formation that one won-

ders if they had been expected and their places reserved. The entire navy sails now toward the city as one. When the cavalry saw the rapid desertion of the navy, they rode away from the Imperator to Octavian. The foot soldiers fell in behind the horses and deserted. The Imperator was left standing with only his personal guard. I believe he lost his mind while witnessing his men go over to his enemy."

Though Kleopatra's heart is racing, her body is cold. "And what did he do?"

"He started for the palace. He said that after the morning's events, he expected to find you there in the Roman Octavian's arms."

"Even at this hour he is not above histrionics," Charmion mutters.

Kleopatra ignores her. "He is alive?"

"He is alive, but he has offered his servant a thousand talents to kill him. He is not himself, Your Majesty."

Her husband is pacing about his chamber, a defeated lion, begging a servant to kill him. The Inimitable One, the Invincible One, trying to face his mortality. His love of life surpasses all reason, and he is staring into the shadows of death, unable to walk into its dark, welcoming arms. Torn between the two worlds, powerless to choose, while Octavian marches into the city. Someone must rescue him from this agony.

"Diomedes, go immediately to the Imperator and tell him that I am already dead; that I heard of the morning's events, and I took my life."

No one questions her. These are her closest associates, and they know what she is doing.

Diomedes looks into the portal for the queen's eyes. She reiterates: "Tell the Imperator that I took a dagger to my own breast, and that I died immediately."

Diomedes leaves. Kleopatra hisses at her companions, "Do not speak."

She wants to be alone with her thoughts. She knows that Antony will do one of two things. Either he will follow her example of courage and quickly take his own life so that they will go together to the gods. Or he will hurry to the mausoleum to see if she is truly dead, knowing he will have to keep himself alive to negotiate for the children.

She begs the Lady Isis to exercise her wisdom. *What is best for the higher good of all is what shall transpire*, she prays. But what she prays for is not what she hopes for. She hopes that Antony will hurry to her. When he arrives and finds that she is alive, they will not kill themselves, but tear off their clothes and dress in rags and run away. She has been an artist of disguise all her life. Antony is a natural man of the stage. He once disguised himself as a slave to escape the hostility of those against Caesar. With an actor's aplomb, he put on a tattered hood and hobbled out of the city and into Caesar's camp to demonstrate what degradation he was willing to stoop to in Caesar's service. She will convince him that it does not matter where they go as long as they are alive. Let Octavian have Egypt. He will make himself their children's regent, and when the time comes, he will put them on the throne like little puppets and he will pull their strings. Better the children, who have yet to learn independence, than herself.

She praises the gods for giving Antony this reprieve from death. It was the work of the Divine, she knows. The gods did not allow a battle today because they do not want Antony to die. Not yet. It is a sure sign that they are to live, to prevail. Together they will flee to India, not as king and queen, but as simple lovers. They will meet up with Caesarion along the way, and take the trade routes through the east with a caravan of merchants paid to keep their secret. They will live in her palace in India in peace, waiting for Octavian to be overthrown, probably by his own people. Then they will return and guide their children to fulfill the ambitions of empire spun long ago. If the gods are merciful, then this is what will happen. Antony will read the truth into Diomedes' message, or beat it out of him, and he will come to her.

She knows, of course, that these are fantasies. Antony will never run away with her. A general first, a leader of men, he goes nowhere without an army marching behind him. Which is why he is so lost now. The footsteps of soldiers that have followed him all his life are silent, and he is lost without that driving rhythm.

Charmion and Hephaestion stare at her like proud parents, while Iras, who loves Antony, tends more fastidiously to his chore of making a new comb. They believe they know what she has done, that she has finally taken the step the two cold-blooded ones have urged all along. Rush Antony to his death so that she might live. They think they know her mind, but none can guess her private hope.

Antony does come to her, but he is covered in his own blood. His arrival is announced by woeful cries. She recognizes the voices of his servants asking her to open the door to let him in, but she no longer knows who she can trust. Octavian's men cannot be far behind. She orders Hephaestion to lower ropes through a wide window so that only Antony may be let in.

"He is slain!" Diomedes yells. "He has taken his own life!"

She hears her husband say, "I am tied to the ropes. Take me up."

Kleopatra and her companions pull on two ropes, she and Iras at one, Hephaestion and Charmion at the other. He must have fastened a rope to each of his arms because she can hear him use his feet against the wall to climb. He yells at her to keep pulling, that he is dying, and that she must hurry or he will die alone. She can hear his servants weeping as he uses the last bit of his strength to die in her sight.

Inside, all four of them are pulling, Kleopatra working so hard that with each effort her arms are in searing pain and her head is to the ground. The servants are screaming to them to keep pulling, to not let their master fall, to be strong. That he is dying, that he must see the queen before he goes to the gods, that this is his final wish. Two times, they almost falter. Charmion's hands are bleeding. Hephaestion and Iras, though they have lived lives of little physical exertion, are stronger than the women, but Antony is the weight of two men. She calls out to him to hold on, that he is almost inside. A ladder is placed against the wall, and three of them struggle with the ropes while Iras climbs to the top, grabbing Antony and helping him inside. Antony strives to balance on the sill of the window while Iras swings his legs over for him and places them on the top rung. One step at a time, Antony descends, groaning in pain. His feet hit the ground and he falls into her arms. Hephaestion helps her carry him to a couch. He is still in his armor.

She surveys his body, taking stock of the laceration in his gut. By the stains on his clothes, on his body, on the walls, on the ladder, she knows that he has lost most of his blood.

Holding his face, she looks into his eyes and sobs. "Oh, my husband, my love, my lord, I have killed you."

"You simply helped an old soldier to die."

Antony smiles, and she wonders if he is so far gone now that he can no longer feel pain. "Get me some wine, would you?" He is casual, as if he has just come in from military drills and is thirsty.

"What have you done? My darling, I wanted us to run away togeth-er. I prayed for you to see through my lie!" She helps him out of his breastplate and puts her head on his chest. His leather tunic is damp and smells salty and metallic like blood.

"When they told me you were dead, I begged Eros yet again to kill me, but he turned his sword on himself. It took a servant's bravery and a woman's lie for me to let go of life."

"Because you *love* life, my darling, not because you have no courage." Kleopatra takes the goblet of wine from Charmion and holds it to his lips. Iras props Antony's head with his hands. The eunuch is crying, try-ing to hide his face.

Kleopatra turns to Hephaestion. "Check his wound. See what can be done."

Antony puts a hand up to stop Hephaestion, and then pleads to Kleopatra with eyes. He whispers, "We only have a moment longer. Drink with me, as if we were alone in our room, with no cares but one another's pleasure."

Her hands shake as she takes a sip of the wine. Antony watches her, wincing with pain, but his eyes are bright. "That's it," he says. "Now, let me have some more. You know how I love a good vintage." He tries to chuckle, but the laugh catches in his throat and he coughs.

Now she breaks down, tearing at her clothes, taking a swath of her white dress and covering his wound. "Let me help you," she cries, spreading the cloth, watching it soak up his blood. She cannot bear to see the life seep from his body this way and she throws the cloth aside and tries to stanch the flow of blood with her hands. She realizes she is hurting him, so she lets him take her wet hand, and they both feel his warm blood between their skin.

"My guard has taken my bloody sword to Octavian. My death will buy you smooth negotiations."

She puts the wine to his lips again because she does not want to hear talk of death or of Octavian. Closing his eyes, he sips a very little bit, swallowing with some effort. "I might have died far away from you, slain by some ignoble foreign sword," he says. "It is better this way, tak-ing your face with me to the gods."

But she does not want him to comfort her. She wants him to live. She tears again at her clothes, thinking she might fashion some magical tourniquet. She begs him, "Do not give in so quickly, Imperator. Let me help you."

He stops her again with his hand, and pulls her close to his face so that he is burying his mouth in her hair. "Happier times," he whispers, and the hot air of his breath makes her body go slack. She stays there, with his warm mouth nuzzling her ear until she feels him let drop her hand.

She realizes she has never known grief, not even for Caesar, because it overtakes her with an unfamiliar ferocity. She has seen death before, and she has always remained calm in its wake. But now, when she is most called upon to remain composed, sorrow takes her prisoner and she is no longer in control. She feels Antony leave her, just as if his flesh is walking away. She tries to grab at his ghost but he is too quickly gone, and she thinks he is laughing, not with her but with someone, something else. She wonders if Caesar has come for his Master of the Horse, and if they are sharing a joke. Or has Antony realized so soon death's pleasures? She is furious that he has this quick relief from life's anxieties, jealous that he has expeditiously discharged himself of their woes. She beats on his chest as if she might resurrect him; as if she can hurt him enough to make him come back. But her fists ring hollow against his breast and so she turns on herself. She wipes his blood on her face like a mad Dionysian, ripping her dress open and beating at her chest. She hears her fists pound against her breasts, sees her hands flying in the air and striking her body, but she is numb to her own pain. She tears open her dress and, making animal paws out of her hands, lacerates her skin with the nails Charmion has so carefully painted pale blue. She cannot make herself hurt enough, and she gives up and falls over his corpse, that same body in which she has taken refuge so many times. Now it has nothing to offer.

She hears shouts and screams outside. As heavy footsteps approach, others scamper away. She knows the unmistakable thud of a Roman soldier's gait.

Pounding on the door. "My name is Marcus Proculeius, Your Majesty, and I am sent by Caesar."

Charmion helps her up and away from Antony's body, but this man's words have awakened her, and she remembers who she is and what she has promised.

"Caesar is dead, murdered by twenty-three blows of the knife. But if you promise to deliver me to him, I will happily open my door."

Charmion takes her arm and yanks her to attention. "Marcus Antonius is with the gods and you are with the living." Charmion has never taken such a liberty, not even when Kleopatra was small and rebellious.

"It is time to negotiate, Your Majesty," Hephaestion adds. "The opportunity may not come again."

Charmion does not let go. "Think of your children. And of your father and his father and his father and the many kings from whom you are descended."

Kleopatra frees herself from Charmion's grip and opens the tiny portal. All she can see is the chin strap of a Roman helmet and a square jaw. "What is your message?"

"You must open the doors and come with us."

"And why should I do such a thing?"

"You are to trust in Caesar's wisdom and mercy. He told me to tell you to have courage. Release yourself from your prison, come to him, and let the negotiations begin."

"A moment, sir." Hephaestion closes the portal and whispers, "Do you hear what he says? Octavian only wished for Antony's death. Now is the time to ask for favor."

"Why is he so willing to negotiate, when he has ignored all our attempts? He wants the contents of this chamber." How could one so wise as Hephaestion be so naive?

She opens the portal. "If your master wishes to negotiate, then tell him to come to this door and swear upon the name and memory of Julius Caesar that he will allow my children to retain their titles and their thrones. For myself, I am done with public life and wish to go into exile. Those are my terms."

"And if he does not accept them?"

"Then you may tell him that all that he covets he will have, but it will be in ash."

For one hour, she weeps over Antony's body, feeling the warmth seep away, when a new pair of lips appears at the portal. It is Cornelius Gallus, who had turned Antony's troops against him at Crete.

Kleopatra cannot wait to speak to him, opening the portal herself and breathing venom. "Ah, Gallus, the Imperator's body lies dead, not by your hand but by his own. So you see that in the end, he succeeded where you failed. Have you come to take revenge upon a dead man? Aren't your hands stained enough with his blood?"

Hephaestion stands beside her fanning his arms in an effort to get her to calm down. "Hear him out, Your Majesty," he says loud enough for Gallus to hear.

"I have come from Caesar, with an answer to your offer, madam. He asks that you first leave your shelter. Then he will comply with your wishes."

Kleopatra is disgusted. "Why will he comply with my wishes only after I leave my shelter? Does he think me such a fool? If he has any intention of complying with my wishes, let him come here now and swear it to me. Why does he not come himself but send messengers? Is he afraid to see me?"

"He is settling the affairs of the city, madam."

Her city. "And what is more important to settle than the city's queen?"

She slams the portal shut. "Do you see his method? He thinks he can lull me into opening these doors. Then he will have everything he needs, and I will be taken prisoner or killed. Or both."

"The Imperator believed he would negotiate," Charmion says tersely.

"You did not trust his judgment in life, Charmion. Has he so risen in your esteem in death?" She turns to Hephaestion, whispering, "Prepare the fire."

"Madam, I care nothing for my life, but if you burn the entire treasure, will he not take revenge upon the children?"

Kleopatra sees no way out. Antony lies dead, Iras sponging the blood from his body so that he will not go disheveled to the gods. Through her grief, she is furious that she agreed to be the one to stay alive. Should it not be him, bargaining with the man he knows so well? Romans are notoriously merciful to their fellow countrymen in matters of civil strife. If Octavian had greeted the familiar face of Antony, would he not have capitulated to at least some of their demands? Now it was far too late. Antony's honor is preserved in death, and Kleopatra is left to defend her children, her people, her throne, her dignity. She knows that Octavian only wants her money. Would he trade it for her life? If she opens the door, he will have both and she will have no bargaining power.

She goes to a wooden trunk, opens it, and removes a large emerald ring and a small ruby pendant. She opens the portal and hands the jewels to Gallus. "The emerald is for your general, the ruby, a gift you may give to the lady of your choosing. I repeat my terms. Say to your general that I respectfully request his presence so that we may talk face-to-face. Say to him that I wish no misrepresentations made through the inadvertent mistakes of mediators. Our business is too important and too delicate a matter."

"Madam, I do not believe he will be summoned. He has sent me with his assurances. I beg you to do as he wishes."

"I do not believe I shall."

"He asked me to remind you of the merciful qualities of Julius Caesar, whose every aspect he emulates."

Kleopatra thinks of the many agreements with Antony Octavian failed to honor: how he neglected to send the promised twenty thousand troops for the Parthian war; how he asked Antony to come to Brundisium to make peace and then failed to show; how he refused to answer any of their requests for negotiation, instead confiscating money sent as peace offerings. How he won Antony's soldiers by bribery. She thinks of the stories of how he feigns illness during battle, turning all responsibilities over to Marcus Agrippa; how he has called her every foul name before the senate; how he used Cicero and then sanctioned his death and his posthumous degradation—severed head and hands ignobly displayed in the Forum. How he murdered three hundred of his senatorial colleagues at Perugia, offered up as human sacrifices after his successful siege. How it was said that his lust forced a man to give up his own wife to him; how he turned his agents into whoremasters, procuring young girls for him, tearing them from their homes and families.

He emulates Julius Caesar in nothing. Caesar's victories were won by Caesar's genius; his lovers conquered by his charm. His enemies in war pardoned as if they had done nothing more than deliver a slight insult over a drunken dinner. There is no evidence that Caesar's heir has inherited anything but his money.

"Still, I must ask you to reiterate what I have said. The general may choose his response."

"Your Majesty, you must trust Caesar. With my own eyes I saw him shed tears upon learning that Marcus Antonius had taken his own life . . ."

She will hear no more of these lies. "Why do you not go forth with my answer?" She has lost patience with this Gallus, this messenger. Why does he dally? Does he really think that he, a second-rate commander, may negotiate with a queen? Is this yet one more of Octavian's insults?

Charmion screams. Hephaestion puts himself in front of the queen, making a shield out of his body. Iras cowers behind the couch where Antony lies dead. A Roman soldier is through the window, descending the ladder. Others follow, one scaling the wall with ropes, swords and armor clanking a song of death.

She will not give them the glory of kill or capture. She pushes Hephaestion forward and reaches beneath her dress for the dagger. With a deep breath, she pulls her arm back so that the blow will be deep and fatal. Before she strikes, she meets Charmion's eyes, eyes that have watched over her all her days. Like herself, Charmion has assessed the situation quickly, has seen that once again treachery and not honorable negotiation has always been Octavian's plan. Charmion gives the queen an almost indiscernible nod as if to say, *Yes, this is the proper thing to do.* Kleopatra braces herself for death, and with all her might, brings the vulnerable spot right below the breastplate. But Hephaestion catches her wrist before the knife hits its mark. She screams at his betrayal, and he pulls her close to him, whispering, *Only those who live can negotiate.* And then Roman hands are on her, and the lips she recognizes as belonging to Proculeius are barking orders to make certain that no other weapons are hidden on her body, no vials of poison, nothing that may be used as an instrument of death. "The general needs her alive," he says. To her, he adds, "He wishes the opportunity to demonstrate his mercy to the queen."

Kleopatra refrains from struggle. She will not give them the gratification of using force on her. Charmion and Hephaestion are as stoic as

old soldiers as they are taken captive. Iras cries softly, offering his hands
to be enchained, his eyes still on Antony's body that he does not wish
to abandon. Despite that she is in tatters, chest red and swollen from
her own lacerating nails, eyes puffed up from indignation and tears,
Kleopatra looks Proculeius in the eye. "Do not degrade the body of the
Imperator, I warn you. I am still breathing, and I can still make you pay."

He casts his eyes downward, ashamed, she hopes, of his part in
Octavian's deceit. She is more concerned at the moment of what will
happen to Antony's vulnerable corpse. Now that he is no longer able to
defend himself, she must see to his proper burial, just as he once argued
with her father for the burial rights of Berenike's husband, Archelaus.
As she is led past his body, she sees that the Romans keep their distance
from him, and at least one—could it be one that Antony himself had
once led into battle?—has his hand over his mouth as if to stifle a cry
for their betrayed commander.

⌣⊂🐪𓏏𓏏𓏏𓈖𓏤𓂀◯⌣◯⌣

"Citizens of Alexandria, arise."

He stands on a tall platform erected by his men for the occasion of
addressing the citizenry of the conquered city, in the great Gymnasium
where princes and kings and the Greek elite have taken their exercise for
hundreds of years. Before him, the terrified populace has gathered on
their collective knees, begging for life, for mercy, for whatever he may
decide to give them. It is a sight to which he has grown rapidly accustomed, this subjugation of a large group of people. And he has begun
to enjoy the look of relief on their cowering faces when he announces
that their lives have been extended; that they have his permission to go
home, live their lives, and die in their beds at a ripe old age.

"People of Alexandria, have no fear. I have visited the tomb of
Alexander, whose genius gave birth to this magnificent city, and whom
its citizens and indeed the rest of the world call Great. The city, I am
pleased to say, is no less great than its founder. I have quickly fallen
under its charms. And therefore, I acquit all of its citizens of any blame
in the recent wars between your queen and the Roman empire, and I
welcome all of you into Rome's embrace."

The sycophant Arius who has not ceased clinging to Octavian's cloak

since he entered the gates of Alexandria begins the applause, encouraging
the suppliants to join him. The philosopher had met Octavian at the eastern Gate of the Sun, reminding him of his status at the Greek school
Octavian had attended as a young man, and heaping all manner of praise
upon him for his victory over the oppressor Marcus Antonius. All this
while still in possession of the money he had undoubtedly been given by
Kleopatra for tutoring Caesar's bastard son. Arius was so quick to dis-
claim allegiance to Kleopatra and her heirs that Octavian made a mental
note that here was a man who would do the same to him were the circumstances reversed. So he paid little attention to the hand-kissing and
flattery and got straight down to business with this would-be philosopher and admirer. Where was Little Caesar? Arius, apparently anticipating Octavian's every request, offered that the boy king was on his way to
India with his tutor, Rhodon, who fortunately was in Arius's service.
Fascinating, Octavian had replied. Send a letter to Rhodon demanding
them to return. Say that I have fallen under the queen's spell and am
honoring her request to allow the boy to retain the throne.

Now Arius has worked the citizens of Alexandria into wild applause
for Octavian's bountiful mercy. Rather than continue his address,
Octavian decides to leave them on this high note, before any questions are
asked; before anyone becomes too complacent with his position and asks
about the fate of their imprisoned queen. Let them be satisfied to return
to their homes, embrace their families, and thank the gods for his mercy.
The issue of the queen will be settled quickly, while her subjects are still
astonished to find themselves alive and beyond retribution for supporting her in the war.

Octavian goes about his business in the next few days of claiming the
city for his own, confident of his spell over the Alexandrian people.
From her imprisonment within the palace compound, Kleopatra sends
a letter begging for the right to bury Antony properly. Octavian wants
no repercussions from any of Antony's soldiers who have come over to
him—the men can be so emotional when it comes to Antony—so he
allows it, not dreaming of the grandness of the queen's design, nor of
the adoration the people of the city will unabashedly demonstrate.
Without fear of retaliation, the entire city lines up in the streets to
watch the cortege. Octavian does not attend the funeral of his enemy,
of course. But he receives eyewitness accounts, all corroborating the

enormity of the spectacle. Kleopatra has Antony embalmed in the Egyptian manner, though he is to be buried in the mausoleum she has erected for herself. Her treasures have been removed and catalogued by Octavian's staff, and the queen has the chambers redecorated with statues and other representations of the god Dionysus, the divinity with whom her people identified Antony.

The day is almost over but the funeral procession has yet to end. It is longer than a mile, he is told, and is led by the entire priesthood of Dionysus. Maenads are trailing the priests, beating their breasts and singing the name of the god and the name of Antony. Kleopatra, in the blood-red robes of Isis, rides on Antony's own chariot, driven by an unknown man wearing the mask of Osiris. Even in defeat, she does not tire of representing the two of them as Egypt's greatest divinities. Arius tells Octavian the meaning she conveys: Osiris is the true and original king of Egypt, the husband of Isis; the god who founded and was benefactor of the great cities of the eastern lands; the god who was murdered by his evil brother and was resurrected by Isis's own hand. Yes, Octavian says in reply. Her meaning is most clear to me. But that is hardly all. Antony's golden coffin follows the chariot, drawn by his two favorite white horses, and it is said that when Antony's soldiers see the Imperator's steeds, they weep openly. The entire affair is a parade of tears, the sobbing Alexandrians falling in with the procession and following the body all the way to the mausoleum by the sea. The queen, by all accounts, is as pale as milk, a regal pharaoh, and does not shed a tear, but plays the role of silent, suffering widow without a flaw in her performance.

The day after the funeral, the petitions begin flowing in. *Save the queen. Save the Royal Family. Have mercy on the queen. Here is money in exchange for the queen's life, for her continued right to sit upon the throne, for the safety of her children.* In the gods' names, some fool sends two thousand talents in exchange for not defacing her statues, arguing that she had merely been the pawn of Antony.

Octavian sits on Kleopatra's bed, the sharp beak of the Ptolemaic eagle pointing down at him. How did she sleep in this room without fear that an earthquake would shake the eagle from his perch and spear her in the gut? Yet the mattress is the largest he has ever seen and the softest upon which he has lain. Her quilts are of the finest white silks, and the linens fragrant from careful laundering. He thinks of Antony, brazen enough to make love on this bed where kings and queens have slept, fearless of the beast above—and of the woman beneath him.

Disconcerted, he walks to the window, which opens out to the Royal Harbor. Even in summer's stillness, the air is fresh. The Royal Barge with the golden prow, much discussed in Roman gossip, is not within view. He will track it down in the next few days and perhaps take a short cruise down the Nile, just as his uncle had done, before returning to Rome.

The Kleopatra Question weighs heavily on his mind, much as the Egyptian Question has troubled the Roman senate for a century. What to do with her and with this nation so rich that he would never entrust its government to any of his colleagues? Every Roman consul, every member of the senate, has always known that sending even the most honest among them to be the governor of Egypt was an open invitation to corruption. Look how its riches, embodied in its extravagant queen, had seduced both Caesar and Antony. How might he, Octavian, be different?

He will never set eyes upon her, that much is certain. No matter how many letters and gifts she sends begging him to sit down and negotiate with her. No matter how many rich Greeks and Egyptians and eastern princes intercede on her behalf. She is a Medusa—lay eyes on her and your life is over. She does not turn men to stone, but into her slaves. Caesar used to say, *Someday you will meet her, nephew. Her voice in any of the tongues she speaks is music to a man's ear.* It is music he will never consent to hear. The woman is dangerous, empowered by some demon goddess, and further enriched by her money and the position of her nation upon the earth. The perfect gateway from east to west. The natural intersection of the world's trade routes. The combination of her resources and her womanly gifts is irresistible. Though she is no longer young, she had Antony bewitched until the last. And she still has her subjects in her thrall. He will not risk himself under such circumstances.

But what to do with her? Now that he has her money, he has no further need to keep her alive. But what would the reaction be to executing a woman? Unthinkable. Her golden statue still stands in the temple of Venus where his uncle had placed it. Still there are Romans in the city, in the senate, who sing her praises, who talk of her intelligence and generosity and of her beauty and stateliness. In Alexandria, the letters he receives accent her great love of her people; her queenly benevolence; her illustrious lineage. Even the king of Media is sending gifts in exchange for kindness to the queen. Kleopatra has already destroyed two great Roman men. He will not be the third, and if he has her executed or condemned in any way, her death would surely bring him down. Maybe not immediately, but eventually.

What to do, though? Risking her continuing rule is out of the question. In time, she would just find another man, some fat eastern king with a formidable military and treasury, and seek her revenge upon him. Artavasdes of Media is probably a candidate. And there are others who would prefer conspiracy with an Egyptian queen to domination by himself. Mithridates, that old enemy of Rome, had fathered a hundred bastard sons, all with money and armies now, each holding sway. Kleopatra might align with any one of them, or marry her daughter off to them in exchange for their armies.

He has kept Antony's letter rolled up in the pocket of his cloak. He reads it one more time, feeling the disdain rise. What arrogance! First, sending a missive that equates himself with Herakles, and then having the audacity to remind Octavian of the sorry fate the poet Euripides gave to the mythical king who did not shelter Herakles' offspring. A double effrontery! Pity the fools who love the words of poets and playwrights more than the cold, hard facts of reality. As if Octavian would be stupid enough to put a child of Antony on the Egyptian throne when he would not trust even the most loyal of his men with the riches of that kingdom. Why, he might not even trust Agrippa in such circumstances, and Agrippa has already shown his loyalty a million times over. Any of Antony's children's faces would soon bloom into Antony's likeness and remind any number of people of Antony's ambitions.

Did Antony expect him to be that naive? Or to demonstrate even more naiveté and name king the boy who claims to be the only son of Julius Caesar? Octavian does not even believe that the creature is Caesar's son, so he will not show him any courtesies that he might extend to an actual blood relative. Kleopatra could easily have become impregnated by another and passed the child off to Caesar as his. Caesar had been so troubled by his lack of a male heir. Kleopatra is conniving enough to have arranged the whole thing. But the boy has been told from birth that the blood of Caesar flows in his veins, along with the blood of Alexander and the Ptolemies, and the gods, and whoever else Kleopatra could think of to make him more illustrious. Would such a boy rule with Octavian as his regent? Only until either he or one of his associates got the idea to use his alleged lineage to raise an army.

There is simply no way to honor the queen's requests; no way to allow her to go into exile in a foreign land, and no way to let her children—living reminders of her and Antony—to retain their kingdom. But she will never tire of asking, and already the entreaties are becoming tedious.

Perhaps he might have her secretly killed, an assassination with a prearranged culprit. He searches his mind for a way to arrange this, but no one save himself wants her dead. She has lost the war, and all of her allies have come over to him. She has pleaded for peace. She is imprisoned, and even worse, ill with a fever from lacerating herself in grief over Antony's death. There is no one whom he might credibly blame. It would always come straight back to him. There is no sense in taking a risk and sanctioning some feeble plan that would come back to haunt him. Oh, it was tiring, this mental energy spent on the issue of the queen and her family. But there has to be a way to get rid of her with no consequences to himself. He is learning to be a patient man. He will wait. Surely, a satisfactory alternative to letting Kleopatra live will occur to him.

"It is very painful to receive the son of an old friend in this condition, dear Cornelius." Kleopatra pulls her dressing gown over her chest, hiding the inflamed blotches that wound once-perfect skin. She worries that despite the poultices applied by the physician Olympus, the infection will leave scars across her breasts, ugly tears that look as if she has been mauled by a wild animal. That animal is herself, a lonely caged beast whose mate has perished and whose children remain hidden from her. She has made herself ill, or circumstances have made her ill; she has trouble deciding which, for she who is unused to illness of any kind both resents her body for its betrayal and blames the creature who has taken over her city, her country, her very chambers.

"Who would not become ill in such circumstances?" Charmion has asked again and again, trying to relieve Kleopatra of the self-inflicted anger. And Kleopatra always has the same answer—Julius Caesar. Why can she not better emulate her mentor? She whispers to him late at night when she is alone and unable to sleep, but his voice is thin. Perhaps he is angry or jealous because she talks to him about Antony.

"Caesar had the dropping sickness," Charmion counters.

"Yes, but it did not destroy him."

She is under house arrest, relegated to a room in the palace to which she once assigned lesser guests. She sent a letter requesting her personal belongings, but only one appeared—a golden throne with eagle-clawed legs, sent, she believes, as a mockery of her situation. As if to defy her to sit upon it in her wretched condition. The monster sleeps in her bed, dines at her table, commands her staff, bathes in her marble tub. Selene and Philip, she is told, remain on the island with the crones, but they, too, are under guard. She has asked numerous times to see them and has been refused. In time, she is told. Now she does not want them to see her, not like this. She has heard nothing from Caesarion, and prays that he is making his way to India. No matter what her fate, he has enough money to live for the rest of his life however he pleases. Alexander should be well on his way to Media. Antyllus has taken sanctuary in the Mouseion, and Kleopatra assumes that Octavian will take the boy back to Rome to live with Antony's relatives. These are her assumptions, patched together with the small bits of information that slip into her room with her meals, none of which she can eat. She has not taken food since she heard that Hephaestion, offered his life in exchange for serving Octavian, replied that the suggestion was beneath his dignity and was put to death. She herself is teetering between choosing to live or to die, and Charmion knows this. She tears tiny bits of food with her fingers and tries to put them in Kleopatra's mouth as she did when the queen was a child. And, as if that stubborn child has returned to take over the queen's body, the food is met by clenched lips.

Kleopatra cannot decide if the fate of her children will be a happier one if she lives or if she dies. She receives no answer to her requests to know if they will be allowed to inherit the throne, to know if they will even be allowed to remain in the country. She has made the ultimate offer in a letter sent two days ago—my life in exchange for the children inheriting the throne. To this, she has had no reply.

And here is Cornelius Dolabella, the son of the man whom Caesar had admired and Antony had not. Dolabella the father was a charming profligate, perhaps too much like Antony himself, whom the latter had accused of committing adultery with his wife, Antonia. Caesar, always one to gossip, had told Kleopatra that Antony made up the charges because he despised Dolabella, and because he wanted to get rid of Antonia so he could finally marry his longtime lover, Fulvia, while she was widowed.

Dolabella the son looks to be the handsome scoundrel his father was, a man who loved Caesar, deserted him in death, and then found his way back to Caesar's cause, falling on his sword rather than being captured by Caesar's assassins. Young Dolabella had fought with Antony against Octavian, so the only way he is standing here, head still connected to body, is if he is as adept as his father had been in changing loyalties. He must have declared fully and unequivocally for Octavian, so that whatever he says will be a message. Undoubtedly, he has been carefully selected for this mission.

She intends to meet his deceptions with her own dissembling, but Kleopatra can barely meet the son's eyes without crying. He is perhaps thirty years of age, and until a few days ago, she would have passed for his contemporary. Now she cannot look into a mirror. Her face is flushed with fever scattering a web of tiny red veins over her smooth cheeks; her eyes, swollen slits, looking terribly like her father's after he had taken ill. She has lost weight, and her long, queenly neck is scrawny and chickenlike. Her hands, only weeks before the same as in her youth, are lined with waterways of thick blue blood vessels, the skin cracked from fever's dehydration.

"Your Majesty." The young man is on one knee, pressing one of those shriveled hands to his cheek. She hears the pity in his voice, the almost ironic use of her title, and she withdraws her hand.

"How is it that you got permission to see me, Cornelius, when your general thinks me either too dangerous or too lowly to set eyes upon me?"

"The general is all too familiar with the stories of your charms, madam. He heard them directly from his uncle. He is a man like any other and does not wish to make himself vulnerable to your famous enchantment."

Kleopatra finds that she is long past parrying with charming rogues. Despite her intention to use charm, she feels impatience insisting its way into her words. "Please! There is no need to invoke the ghost of Caesar, nor to taunt an ill woman with outrageous flattery. The general has my money and my country. There is nothing more I can offer him. And that is his conundrum, is it not?"

"I'm not sure what you mean, madam," Cornelius says as if genuinely puzzled. He takes a seat opposite the queen. "The general sent me to check on your condition. He heard of your illness and wishes to know if you are improved."

"Why is he so concerned over my health? Does it really matter to him whether I live or die? Tell me, Cornelius. You have his ear, or you would not be sitting here. In which condition does he prefer me? Dead or living? Which would serve his purpose?"

Though they are alone, Cornelius gets up from his seat and kneels next to Kleopatra so that he might whisper in her ear. "That is what I have come to tell you. In the name of Julius Caesar, for whose memory my father died, I did not want to be the bearer of this news."

Oh, these Romans, so deficient in the theatrical arts, are such natural performers. She feels her anger rise—a sign of improving health. "Then let us not prolong your agony."

"Madam." The eyes are as wide as a cow's and threaten to spill conjured little tears. The brows are knitted in false anxiety. "The general asks me to inform you that he is preparing to leave Alexandria for Rome. You are to prepare to leave as well. In three days' time, you and your two children will travel to Rome."

"Prisoners?"

"Yes. And marched as such in his triumphal parade in the capital."

She takes her time responding. His words send chills through her body. She is not sure if it is the fevers returning or the fear that what he says is true.

"I see. The general is to march the mother of Caesar's only son in chains through Rome, along with two of the children of the Imperator? Do I understand that correctly?"

"That is correct, Your Majesty."

"Thank you, Cornelius. You may leave now."

He looks amazed at his hasty dismissal. Clearly he had anticipated some greater scene, some wonderful histrionic episode that he might relate to his commander. "Is that all you have to say on the matter?" His voice is shaky. Caesar will be so disappointed at the abrupt conclusion to the meeting.

She smiles. "That is all I have to say."

Charmion returns to the room as Dolabella leaves. "Is your fever worsening? Is that why you sent him away?" Charmion's serene hand is on Kleopatra's forehead. "I'll send for cool compresses."

Kleopatra stops her. She stands and begins pacing. "No, wait. As a matter of fact, this visit has remarkably improved my condition."

"Kleopatra, please get back in bed. You are no better than when you were eleven years old. You are not well."

"I did not think Octavian would take me for a fool. I don't know what he has planned, but it is certainly not what he sent young Dolabella here to say."

"And what is that?"

"That he will send me and the younger children to Rome and march us in his victory parade."

"Don't be naive, Kleopatra. Do you think that is not within the scope of his evil?"

"No, but I don't think he is so stupid or so short-sighted. He plots and schemes with the skill of a Sophoclean dramatist. He is not a man of the moment; the tentacles of his schemes reach far into the future. No matter how desperate he is for my humiliation, he knows that even the barbarous citizens of Rome will not take kindly to a queen marched in chains like a common animal, much less the children of Antony."

Charmion is skeptical. "He has maligned you much in that city. Are you so sure the barbarians are not calling for the degradation?"

"Charmion, do you not remember that all Rome was outraged when my sister Arsinoe was marched in chains in Caesar's parade? The women of the city rallied behind her though she was a declared enemy. Remember, Arsinoe declared herself Caesar's enemy. Octavian declared *me* an enemy of Rome. There are too many in the city who know better. He wouldn't risk it. Not with Antony's death fresh in everyone's mind, particularly his soldiers. Their loyalty to Octavian is new and tenuous at best. The sight of Antony's little ones—oh, and do they not look just like their father?—might be just the catalyst to turn at least a few of them on their new commander. I don't know what he means by sending me this news, but I am sure it would be a mistake to take it literally."

"But what are you going to do? What if in three days' time his men come and put you in chains and take you and the children away? Will you take the risk?"

"Yes. Because I believe I know why he sent the message. He is hoping that the news will either worsen my illness and kill me, or that my pride will outweigh my will to live and I will kill myself."

"And is he right on either charge?"

"He thinks he's the cat and I'm the mouse, Charmion, but I will surprise him yet."

"But what will you do?"

"Watch me." Kleopatra takes a seat at a small table. She picks up a pen and begins to write, but the sleeves of her dressing gown drag across the page. She stands, throws off the gown, and takes up the pen again over Charmion's protests that she is killing herself by not keeping warm.

She mouths the words of her letter to Charmion as she writes:

To: General Gaius Octavian
From: Kleopatra VII, Queen of the Two Lands of Egypt
I have received my old friend Cornelius Dolabella and heard the news from him that I and my children are to be taken to Rome as your prisoners. I ask that you allow my women access to my full wardrobe so that I shall not disappoint the Roman populace with my appearance. In addition, my health is so improving that I wish for full meals, prepared by my staff in the manner that they know I like, to be sent to me three times a day. I do not wish to relapse on the long voyage and die ignobly en route in a strange land or at sea. By the way, it would be extremely generous of you to allow me to make one final visit to the tomb of Marcus Antonius, as Fate in her wisdom has now decided that those who vowed to always be together shall be separated for all time.
Thank you for your attention to these small matters.

She signs the letter with a grand flourish, laughing so hard that her chest rattles and she begins to cough.

"Despite your intentions, Kleopatra, you *are* going to kill yourself if you do not stop this nonsense."

Kleopatra brushes off Charmion's worries. She opens the door and hands the letter to the guard. "See that the general gets this immediately." She hopes her smile and the levity that has returned to her voice does not raise his suspicions.

Swift, brutal action is the most expedient way to success. Julius Caesar had taught him that, and he wonders now what his uncle would have thought of him turning his own cruel philosophy on Caesar's alleged son. Ah well. Perhaps Caesar would have been so incensed at how far Kleopatra was willing to carry the ruse of the boy's paternity that he, from his Olympian vista, is smiling down upon Octavian for putting an end to it once and for all.

He had been left with no choice, he reflects as he surveys the riches confiscated when Little Caesar's party was intercepted in the desert. When the solution is simple and obvious, why debate the ethics or the means? He has silenced the solicitous Arius, who cannot stop talking about what was done, as if he believes that each detail he furnishes will put another gem or coin in his pocket. Octavian does not wish to burden himself with an itemized account of the assassination; suffice it to say that the insignia ring and the money and the eyewitness chronicle of Rhodon, who under Arius's supervision would know better than to lie, is proof enough that only one Caesar remains upon this planet. The account of the death of the other boy, Antyllus, whom he knows personally, causes a tear to fall, just as he had shed one for Antyllus's father in a moment of uncharacteristic sentimentality. It is not remorse or sadness or grief or even guilt that make the tears well up at these times. It is the realization that all life, even his own, is temporal. The strange notion that a life can be taken so easily, and that this power is available to anyone who is willing to seize it. Why more do not exercise this ability is beyond him. Why these philosophers, Arius and Rhodon, do not right now strike him down and make off with all this gold before them is a mystery to him. Perhaps, as Caesar used to say, some men eschew leadership. Some men, most men, are simply happier to follow a man who will make those unhappy decisions and take responsibility for them.

But a man must also exercise caution. The case might be made that Caesarion and Antyllus were of a dangerous age—an age when Alexander was already at war on behalf of his father's kingdom, subduing tribes that the king had yet to conquer. He saw the boy Antyllus when he came with Antony's offer; saw how the boy already carried Antony's square jaw and puffed-up chest and long straight nose—and arrogant attitude. Octavia would have to forgive him that one.

Everyone henceforth would have to get used to forgiving his actions because, well, they will have to. At any rate, surely such boys—scions of Caesar and Antony; sons of the celebrated lover of those men—would have united against him and caused another episode in Rome's continuing civil wars, the wars Octavian now claimed to have ended forever. Surely the assassinations will be interpreted as necessary politics-as-usual. He has found that if one simply acts and offers no explanations and no remorse, those who surround one will quickly come up with reasons in one's own defense. See how Arius and Rhodon are doing this right now, words tumbling together as they offer how Octavian has acted wisely, and listing all the reasons why. He is tempted to put to them the question of the little ones, but that is against his philosophy. He will decide their Fates and then act without seeking outside advice. But he does not think he will be able to satisfactorily explain the deaths of small children, even to himself. Well, those he would take back to Rome with him where he might keep an eye on them. What could be the harm? The twins were not yet nine years old.

Octavian dismisses the two philosophers because he is weary of them waiting around for additional rewards for betraying their charges. He has given them money and their lives. Can they not see that despite the fact that he demanded the betrayal, he also has disgust for the betrayers? He slips a few more coins into each flat and eager palm and sends them off.

Left alone with these magnificent additions to his personal trove, he tries the insignia ring on his index finger. It is tinged with something that he thinks might be blood, but it is easily wiped away with a stroke of his cloak. The ring is too small. Little Caesar must have inherited his father's thinness; or, if he correctly gauges Kleopatra's cunning, inherited the thinness of the person with whom Kleopatra copulated, selected for his keen resemblance to Caesar. She would have thought the entire scheme through, he is sure. The ring does fit nicely on the little finger, and that is where he will wear it for a while. It is heavy gold and engraved with the eagle of the Ptolemies, that beast who hangs over almost every room in the palace. It is so like the eagle that flies on the Roman standards, and he wonders if this is just a coincidence. At any rate, it is a convenience, a symbolic bridge from Greek to Roman rule. A sign from the gods that Egypt has always been destined for his command.

He plucks the prize from the lush landscape of glittering treasure, gingerly at first, holding it between the thumb and index fingers of both hands. It is lighter than he anticipated, and he laughs at how hard he was prepared to try to lift it. In the end, it is effortless. He turns it so that his eyes meet the emerald eyes of the cobra—inscrutable, defiant. He pets the inflated chest of this asp, this symbol of pharaonic power, making slow friends with it, running his finger over the diamond-shaped scales, tapping its pointy tongue. He places the diadem on his head. How well it fits. It seems the sons of Caesar are the same circumference at the head. Poor Julius! Stabbed so viciously by his countrymen for wishing to wear this very crown. Ahead of his time. Sometimes, it is left to the younger generation to fulfill the ambitions of the elder. Sometimes, it simply took a different sort of man to accomplish the deed.

⌐⛺𓅃𓅃𓊖⌐𓁹⌐⌐

She is in the middle of the first meal of the day when she hears the news. She has awakened refreshed and without fever for the first time in many days. The sun is already bright, which means that she has slept long and hard, dreaming of her father and the ritualistic dances to Dionysus that he used to perform for family and friends. In the dream, her father wears a transparent sheath so that his audience watches his ample flesh as it dances with him. The audience is Kleopatra and a roomful of Roman soldiers—some whom she recognizes as the dead from the battles in Greece. She does not wish to see them, for even though she is a child, all that has happened in her life has already passed. She tries to concentrate on her father's agile movements as he sways his large body in time with the pipes, but the Romans keep distracting her. *No one dances unless he is drunk,* they mock. Her father does not hear them and continues dancing as if in a trance, the false curls of his hairpiece shimmying down his back as if he were a young maiden. But she, a little girl of ten, is all too aware of the ridicule. She looks for Antony, the only Roman who might make them understand that her father is not drunk but reverent; not mocking the god but honoring him. But Antony is not there.

She shakes off the dream quickly, more quickly, she knows, than if Antony had appeared. She has already dreamed that he still lived, and upon awakening, her sadness was so great that she took medication and went straight back to sleep hoping to find him again. But this morning, her face is cool and her feet and hands are warm, sure signs that she has mended. Her chest is ugly and bruised but not swollen. She calls for her breakfast and it is delivered not by Charmion but by some silent servant whose name she does not know. She dismisses the girl and has taken the first bite of an orange when Charmion enters the chamber and asks her to stop eating.

Still chewing the pulp, she is told that Charmion has been visited by the old philosopher, Philostratus, once a great lecturer at the Mouseion, and now a bent-over fellow with a long white beard and a mind half gone. He has spent the morning with Arius, who let it slip that the son of Julius Caesar and the elder son of Marcus Antonius have both been mysteriously murdered. By whom, the philosopher could not say. But he had been told by Arius to deliver these two items to the queen: a moonstone worn about the neck by Antyllus, and the medallion of Horus the falcon-god, which Caesarion wore always, even to sleep. Charmion slips the items into Kleopatra's hand, very cold against her skin as if they had long been removed from the warm flesh against which they had once rested.

Kleopatra puts her hands to her mouth and vomits the small bits of her food. The remaining contents of her stomach quickly follow. She is grateful to be ill again, to have the acid burn in her throat take away the pain in her heart. Charmion cleans the mess from the queen's hands and tray and tells her that she must collect herself. There is more. The old philosopher said that Arius, a former tutor of mathematics, asked him to convey one equation to the queen's lady: five minus two equals three.

"I asked him to repeat it, for he is half mad these days. And he did, three times, angry with me as if I were one of his students who had not studied his tables."

Kleopatra pushes the quilts away from her legs. "We have very little time," she says.

For once, Charmion does not question Kleopatra, does not spout the usual precautions over health. Health is no longer an issue. She gives the queen her hand, helping her out of bed. Kleopatra is dizzy as she stands, and pauses a moment to shake off the blackness that tries to take her over. "Get Iras right away."

"Will you dress for mourning?"

"There is no time for that. I will have plenty of time to mourn when I am dead. But we must accomplish one final masquerade before that happens."

Charmion leaves without asking why she is being sent—a first in some thirty years. Alone, Kleopatra can review her choices: She might keep herself alive to see the rest of her children die. She might continue to wait out Octavian on the chance that he is not demonic enough to slaughter little children, nor stupid enough to parade a woman in chains before his fickle populace. She might end her life and save her youngest three—perhaps. She realizes that she no longer has any guarantees for her actions. What animal is as unpredictable as he? There is none; even the earth's fiercest creatures act savagely only to save themselves.

So many have disappeared now, and she wonders if they are waiting for her to join them; if Antony, missing her, has petitioned the gods to hurry their reunion. She cannot watch as more who are her life go to their deaths. With each death dies hope. How many times has she said that hope is an expensive commodity, borrowing from the historian Thucydides? Until today, she has not realized its cost.

The robes of Isis are heavier now that she has lost so much weight and strength, and she is relieved to be lying down in the litter. The dress is of many colors—blood red like the sun in late afternoon, yellow as on a clear summer day, and white as a winter moon—and its pleats fold out from her like the rays in the crown of the sun-god Helios who lies fallen on the beach at Rhodes. The mantle alone must weigh several pounds. Black, fringed, it hangs on her chest like a shield, embroidered at the hems with glittering moons and stars that catch the flashes of light intruding into the dark carriage through heavy brocaded curtains. Everywhere on the dress are fruits and flowers, the earth's beautiful bounty made manifest by the grace of the goddess, the mother of the earth, the queen of the moon, the daughter of the sky, the giver of life itself. When she stands, she must walk carefully to balance the big bronze orb of the crown that sits on her head, hugged on either side by snakes wrapped round golden ears of corn. But this is the final performance, and she will not falter at the end.

She has announced that she is making a last visit to the tomb of her husband before she is taken to Rome. The physician Olympus reported to Octavian that the queen was too ill to walk and had to be carried to her final communion with Antony, lest her weakened condition prevent future travel. Her small procession includes Charmion and Iras, and servants carrying decorations for his grave—garlands, a goblet of his favorite wine to pour as a last libation, and baskets full of flowers and grapes to lay on top of his gold sarcophagus. They follow her litter on foot, along with the ubiquitous Roman guard. She has heard that Octavian laughs at her constant surveillance, saying that the queen must be quite satisfied now; that she always wanted a Roman army at her side.

Her only regret is that she cannot take one last look at her city, and perhaps that is best. She is as weak—or as strong—as Antony, who did not want to leave this life, despite that he had lost almost everything. Though she has been ill, she feels her body on the mend, and she is incensed at the irony. She has lived only to die. Isn't that the human condition? What has been the point of it all? she asks herself in these last moments she will have to think. What is the point of so much suffering? So much activity? So much effort that has resulted in the opposite of her intentions?

She remembers the voice of long-dead Demetrius—was he in her dream as her father danced for the Romans?—the philosopher who tutored her for years at the Mouseion. It is not the outcome but the effort, he would say, reminding her that there was no quantifiable sum of a human life, no way to measure Virtue, that elusive quality that

Socrates said could never be taught but was remembered by the soul. Has she lived the virtuous life? Demetrius used to tell her that a life of action and not philosophy was her destiny. How right he had been. But was it possible to reconcile a virtuous life with a life of action? That was a question she had neglected to ask. War, politics, rivalry, lust, love. She has spent her life in these arenas. Wars, Socrates said, were undertaken for money, and for the concerns of the body. We are slaves of the body, and we must acquire wealth to please it. The body keeps us enchained all through life and we must look forward to death so that we might be finally free of the body's demands. But Kleopatra cannot agree with the philosopher's assessment. She did not go to war to build wealth but to preserve what was left of the world's beauty after it had been trampled and bled by Rome. Her kingdom she tried to defend to honor her ancestors and to secure the power of her children. And if she might choose right now whether to be relieved of the body's concerns or to resurrect Antony and relive the body's pleasures, she would choose resurrection. She would choose to wrap her arms around her children rather than free herself from the responsibility of protecting them. Perhaps death will be the great liberator the philosopher promised, but at this moment, Kleopatra is angry that she must make an abrupt end to this body that might have gone on enjoying the sun on her face or the air through her hair as she rides her horse in the mornings on the Nile's marshy banks.

But if there is any hope—that damnable word again—that the three little ones will not have the same bloody fate as Caesarion and Antyllus, she will happily trade the pleasures she has known for the mysteries of death.

She hears her name sounded outside in cries and whispers by the people. She is grateful that she cannot see the faces. They have come to catch a final glimpse of their queen, for word of her long journey has spread to every quarter of the city. Little do they know that it will be entirely different than the one they believe she will be making.

At the mausoleum, she insists that she be carried inside before she gets out of the litter. She does not want her dress to give away her plans to the guard. She listens to the guard inspect the baskets of decorations and libations and offerings for weapons, for instruments of death, and she holds her breath. Someone makes a joke about the plumpness of the figs, and Iras invites him to try one, but he says that no, he only wishes to split one open and lick its insides, which he does, lasciviously, because she hears his fellow soldiers snicker. Satisfied, they admit only her and Charmion and Iras. The litter is put down by the bearers, and the baskets are placed on the ground, and the servants and guards leave, closing the great doors behind them. Iras helps her out of the carriage, and she is dizzy and disoriented as she stands in the room where she held the body of her bleeding, dying husband. The treasures have been removed and little remains but for the statues she brought in to honor Antony in death, and the golden couch upon which he died.

In Antony's death chamber, she smells the sweet, dying roses laid on his sarcophagus days before. She sweeps them aside so that she might look at his visage molded in bronze. His arms are folded across his chest and cannot reach out to her. She takes the bottle of wine she has brought for the occasion and pours it over the coffin. "Are you ready for me, my love? I am coming to you, and I do not wish to catch you in a dalliance with Persephone or any of the Nereids or Muses who have caught your eye in the next world. Like Hera, I am a jealous mistress." She runs her fingers over his full lips, teasing them with wine as she had done so many times, expecting the cold cast to turn into his warm receptive mouth and take her finger inside. She wonders who will be waiting for her, and if, in the underworld, she will have to choose between Caesar and Antony. She wonders if all of life's trials are continued, or if the philosophers are correct and she will be free from worldly anxiety. *Ataraxia.*

"We must hurry," Charmion says. "You will see your husband soon enough."

Yes, time is essential. It seems that every moment she breathes, the lives of Selene and Alexander and Philip are threatened.

Kleopatra is depending upon the skills boasted by Iras that he can handle a poisonous snake. She is dubious about this, yet she has little choice but to believe that his fascination with Egyptian snake charmers led to this strange ability. She has taken no chances and has a vial of fast-acting poison wound in the knot of hair at the nape of her neck. But even the physician Olympus, consulted at the last minute, admitted that no death was as swift or as seemingly painless as the venom of a cobra. "The Egyptian executioners used to administer the bite to the condemned," he said, "but found it too merciful a death for a criminal." Olympus had treated the Royal Family since the birth of Caesarion, and she did not doubt his loyalty. Even if he had agreed to join the roster of Octavian's payroll, it would take some time for his heart to follow his pockets. He promised her, with tears in his eyes, that she would feel "a sharp sting, at first unbearable, but quickly it turns into numbness. I have seen victims laughing as if drunk, so there must be a pleasantness to the venom. Soon, your eyes will close, and you will begin to dream, quickly slipping into the eternal dream of death."

Iras tells her that whoever is bitten by the cobra goes directly to the gods, for the snake carries an immortal elixir. The cobra, the reptile whose face rises above the Egyptian crown, has protected Pharaoh for thousands of years. When the Egyptian people hear of the means by which the queen has gone to the gods, they will know that she has not died, but taken her place among the immortals.

Kleopatra warily eyes the baskets that contain the asps. "You do not have to join me," she says. "This is my voyage, my Fate."

Charmion merely shakes her head. Iras says, "Do you think I will let my queen meet the gods with unkempt hair and a rumpled gown? I am going to the gods with you as your divine dresser."

Charmion takes her hand. "We are many years past words, Kleopatra. You have been my life here on earth, and I am yours in death. It is a promise I made to the king."

"My father?" she asks.

"I made the vow to two kings, your father, and the Imperator," Charmion replies. "It was his final request to me. 'Keep her safe until we meet again.' I am to deliver you to him or be haunted by his angry ghost."

"I never believed I would have heard you call the Imperator a king."

"He was because he was deemed so by a great queen."

Kleopatra cannot believe that this gentle eunuch who runs brushes through her hair so softly, who winds beautiful jewels and golden pins into her locks with such precision and love, will pick up a long and deadly snake and hold it to their arms. But he opens the baskets eagerly, carefully removing the garlands that guard their secret.

"How is it that they have not stirred?" Kleopatra asks.

"Fear and cunning keep them dormant until they have a sure strike at their victim." Iras's eyes are vibrant, like shiny peanuts soaked in oil to soften them. He has made up his face impeccably for the occasion, eyes ringed with sleek black lines, cheeks reddened to a virgin's blush. Kleopatra believes he is a little drunk. In recent months, he has worn a coal black hairpiece to cover the bald spot at the back of his head. Charmion wears the same Greek chiton she has worn since Kleopatra has known her. She has not had to alter her dress nor her hair nor her cosmetics to suit her age because she has always had the air of a dignified old woman.

The mausoleum is cool though it is the tenth day of August, a notoriously hot month in Egypt, even by the sea. The morning light intrudes through the high windows, making a white haze above their heads. Kleopatra lies on the golden couch where Antony breathed his last. She is tired of words. Every minute she lives might rob one of her children of their lives. "I will say no more," she tells Charmion and Iras. "Come and kiss me."

Iras kneels next to her and puts his head into her bosom as if he were a child. He is trying not to cry, and she tells him that he is the one who must be brave. He cannot fail her. The stakes are too high. "I love the little ones, too, Your Majesty," he weeps into her chest. He pulls his face away and she sees that the black around his eyes has streaked. He intuitively knows this and wipes his eyes clean with wet thumbs.

Charmion kisses Kleopatra's cheek. "I shall see you shortly. It is no more than if I left to fetch you a blanket."

"You have been mother to a motherless child," Kleopatra whispers to her, suddenly aware that she has never before realized this, much less thanked Charmion for taking a mother's role. But Charmion puts her finger on the queen's lips. "It is enough to have been near you," she says. For the first time, Kleopatra feels the full force of Charmion's love; she has been its only recipient, a fact and condition she has taken for granted all these years. Kleopatra thinks of all the love that she has given to men and to children and to the people of Egypt. Charmion has hoarded that watershed of love for Kleopatra alone.

She is floating in this love and crying. She urges Iras to hurry, but

he no longer seems aware of her. He has locked his attention to the
creature in the basket. He is utterly still. It seems that nothing is happening at all, until she sees a hook of an almond-colored head rise out
of the basket as if waking up to its morning. Iras kneels, locking eyes
with the creature. Kleopatra wants to close her eyes. She does not want
to see what Iras will do, or if he will be hurt trying to do it, but it is
too fascinating a sight, this man and this asp riveted to one another.
Charmion kneels by her side, stiff and still. Iras moves backward, and
the snake follows him, rising higher and higher out of the basket.
Kleopatra thinks her heart has already stopped. Charmion takes the
queen's arms and spreads them wide, just as they had discussed, expos-
ing the vulnerable white flesh. Kleopatra does not want the creature
near her face, so they have decided to let its venom enter her left
arm—near the heart so that death will not have far to travel. She
knows that if she screams, if she protests, if she utters a word, she can
alter the text of this drama, but she remains silent, waiting. At some
moment of his choosing, Iras reaches forward and takes the snake by
its body. It does not lunge at him but allows itself to be grasped. If it
escapes, it will not matter because there are two more snakes in the
baskets, each waiting to take another life.

   Iras has the thing securely in his hands now, holding it away from
his body and walking toward the queen as if offering some unholy gift.
She tries to take in the features of the snake—the diamond cuts of its
skin, the pale gold eyes, the flaring hood of its neck, the forked
tongue. Precisely the likeness she has worn upon her own head for so
many years. She tries not to move though her heart has returned to her
body and is beating wildly in her chest. She closes her eyes so that she
does not leap off the couch in some natural instinct to protect her life.
She hears Iras's labored breathing approach. "Yes," he says. And she
feels a sting in her arm that reminds her of the worst pain she has felt,
that of childbirth. There is a searing in her arm so bad she wishes she
might call for a surgeon to cut it off. But she remembers that the last
time she felt this agony she was bringing life into the world. This time,
the pain is keeping those she loves in this world and alive. The sting is
unbearable, but she tries to smile just a little. She realizes that her
muscles are going numb. She must see the world one more time. She
opens her eyes and meets Charmion's stare. There are no tears in her

eyes. She is like a butcher, or a priest at the sacrifice, performing his grim task without emotion. Once Kleopatra is dead, Charmion will be the asp's next victim, and then Iras will turn the snake on himself, and the three will go to the gods together. Iras has urged Kleopatra to wait for him so that he can adjust her hair before she meets with any divinities.

"Is this a fitting death for your queen?" Kleopatra asks them.

"Yes," replies Charmion. "Fitting for a queen who is descended of so many kings."

She is very tired even though she hurts so badly. She feels Charmion put a silk pillow beneath her neck, straightening her crown. Fingers place the tendrils of her hair about her face. She is aware of her breathing, and then, no longer aware of anything at all. She is drifting back to sleep, back to the dream with her father. She sees his face, heavy with concentration and reverence as he picks up his flute. He puckers his lips, but seeing her, smiles.

Kleopatra. The glory to her father. The glory of Egypt. It is about time that you have come to see me again.

He gives her a look of mock chastisement, and then he puts his big bear lips on his pipe and plays the reedy melody that is her favorite.

They are in the Royal Reception Room, just the two of them, as they have been so many times waiting for visitors, and his music fills the room. She sinks deep into her throne, grateful for this stolen time alone with her father, propping her head on her hand, and letting his glorious melody wash over her, cleansing away all the anxieties of the world and bathing her in heavenly delight. She is drifting again, so peacefully that she feels as if she is entering a new dream. Suddenly, a fruity, fine wine is on her lips, waking all her senses, and she hears Antony's deep laugh, the one that rings out in pleasure and abandon, and the tinkling of goblets meeting one another in a toast of victory.

Author's Coda

After Kleopatra's death (30 B.C.E.), Octavian surrendered his power to the Roman senate, and they honored him with the name Augustus (January 27, 29 B.C.E.) which means "the Revered." He took the new position of First Citizen, and with the skill of a magician, created the illusion of restoring the old values and forms of the Roman Republic, while garnering sovereign power and making himself Rome's first emperor. He ruled in peace until his death in 14 C.E., using Egypt's confiscated wealth to rebuild Rome's infrastructure. He understood Rome's yearning for their mythical Republican past as well as the impossibility of its actuality in the face of its enormous empire. If I have been unkind to him herewith, it is only to balance the historical record, which has been extremely harsh to Kleopatra and to Antony for two thousand years.

Ultimately, history was written, or rewritten, by the winners. As early as 36 B.C.E., Octavian had begun his revision of historical events and conflicts. The works of Cassius Severus, Titus Labienus, and Timagenes of Alexandria—Octavian's critics—were destroyed, along with an estimated two thousand books. We can only guess at their contents, but it is safe to assume that any writings favorable to either Kleopatra or Antony were eliminated. During Octavian's reign, court historians such as Nicolaus of Damascus wrote histories and biographies that lavished praise upon Rome's new emperor. In fact, Octavian wrote his own autobiography, fragments of which are preserved. Consequently, Kleopatra's legacy comes down to us from the pens of the most grievous enemies of Antony and herself.

I find it fascinating that historians inevitably overlook Octavian's extraordinary acts of cruelty and eagerly proclaim him a great and benevolent ruler. He did, in fact, force a pregnant Livia to divorce her husband and marry him. Comments are rarely made on the depravity of this event. He did, in fact, sacrifice hundreds of his fellow Romans after the siege of Perugia. He reneged on his commitments to Antony. He had Caesarion and Antyllus murdered in cold blood. And later in his life, he banished his only child, Julia, to exile on a deserted island for committing adultery. She eventually died there of starvation. It is most interesting that in light of his deeds, Kleopatra is the one who has been marked by history as depraved, coldly ambitious, and amoral. I believe a psychologist would label this "projection."

Octavian was not always cruel. After Kleopatra's death, he took her three younger children back to Rome, where they were raised by Octavia. Octavian treated them very well, marrying Kleopatra Selene to King Juba, a learned Numidian monarch and ally of Rome, sending her brothers to live at her court. Selene gave birth to at least one son, but there history loses record of Kleopatra's line. Antony's Roman children continued the family tradition of political prominence, and he was ancestor to several Roman emperors.

Some historians have made the case that Kleopatra was the true successor and heir to both Alexander the Great and Julius Caesar; that she and Antony had a more humane and intelligent policy than Octavian and his imperial successors. Her vision of a Graeco-Roman empire was eventually achieved in the Byzantine empire three hundred years after her death. In any case, Octavian must have seen the wisdom of their vision, because he kept all of Antony's policies and appointments in place after Antony's death, even while disgracing his memory in Rome. Kleopatra, a great ruler and politician, may have come down to us in history and myth as a seducer and the downfall of two great Romans, but she was beloved by her own people, and for many hundreds of years, her reign was considered great. As a famous historian once said, in all its history, Rome deigned to fear two people; one was Hannibal, the other was a woman.

Acknowledgments

The knowledge, experience, and intelligence of many people are on the pages of *Kleopatra* and *Pharaoh*. The books arose out of an ongoing conversation with Mikal Gilmore about the ways in which history has portrayed women. He was there when the idea struck, and his encouragement and support lo these many years have been invaluable. Bruce Feiler took up the dialogue in Nashville and spent more time talking about Kleopatra, form, structure, and ideas than any man ought to have been made to do. I am blessed to have his friendship and intellectual camaraderie.

The late Nancy A. Walker of Vanderbilt University guided my research and daily kept me from feeling overwhelmed by its enormity. She was a prolific scholar, a generous mentor, and a dear friend. Marina Budhos taught me more about the art and the craft of writing fiction than I knew I had to learn, and in the process, raised the standard and caliber of my writing to a new level. My daughter, Olivia Fox, provided a perfect role model for an adolescent princess and helped me breathe authenticity into the young Kleopatra. Professor Susan Ford Wiltshire inspires me always, and she and Dr. Kaye Warren made sure the books passed historical muster. And I have said before, but herewith reiterate, without my mother's generosity, *Kleopatra* might never have been completed.

Friends patiently read drafts and gave crucial feedback and other needed encouragement: Will Akers, Patsy Bruce, Gilbert Buras, Cynn Chadwick, Gian DiDonna, Mary Bess Dunn, Keith Fox, Michael Katz, Beverly Keel, Lee Lowrimore, Clarence Machado, Allison Parker, Cathie Pelletier, Camille Renshaw and Pifmagazine.com, Dorothy Rankin, Richard Schexnayder, Molly Secours, Tom Viorikic, Jane Wohl, and Andrea Woods. I would also like to thank the faculty and students of the Goddard College M.F.A. in Writing program.

Ben Sherwood made the impossible possible. Warren Zide and Jennie Frankel saw the cinematic potential of the books and acted accordingly. Harley J. Williams, Dawn Weekes Glenn, and Zeke Lopez bring grace and class to entertainment law. Jonathan Hahn is a publicist who works with heart and soul. I also wish to thank Miriam Parker, Ana Crespo, and Chris Dao at Warner Books, and especially Jackie Meyers for two gorgeous covers. And, I am very grateful to have Bryan Hickel and Adam Schroeder in my corner.

These books are in print because of the intelligence and energy of three women. Susanna Einstein acquired the book with great enthusiasm, and Jackie Joiner has since been its loyal and ebullient supporter. Amy Williams—agent, travel companion, pal—has the energy of a hurricane, the heart of a lion, and a soul that is dead center in Apollo's triangle.

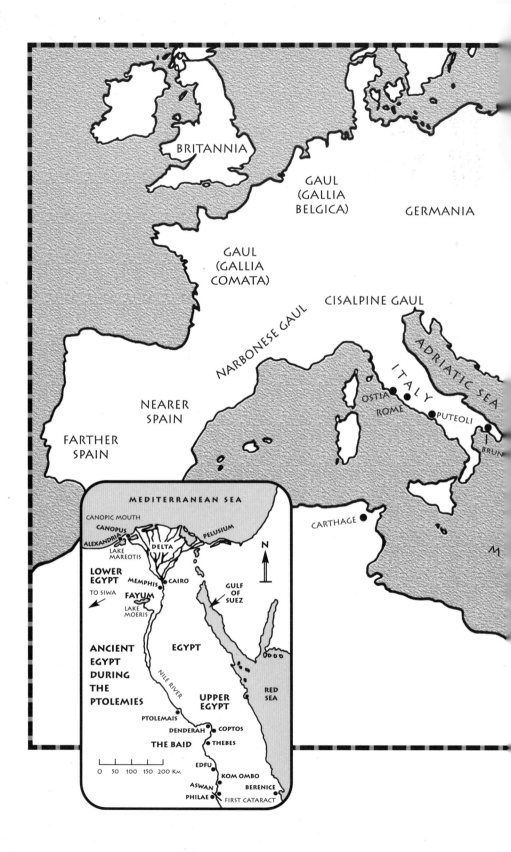

BRITANNIA

GAUL
(GALLIA
BELGICA)

GERMANIA

GAUL
(GALLIA
COMATA)

CISALPINE GAUL

NARBONESE GAUL

ADRIATIC SEA

ITALY

NEARER
SPAIN

OSTIA
ROME
PUTEOLI

FARTHER
SPAIN

BRUN

CARTHAGE

MEDITERRANEAN SEA

CANOPIC MOUTH

CANOPUS
ALEXANDRIA
PELUSIUM
LAKE
MAREOTIS
DELTA

N

LOWER
EGYPT

MEMPHIS CAIRO

GULF
OF
SUEZ

TO SIWA
FAYUM
LAKE
MOERIS

ANCIENT
EGYPT
DURING
THE
PTOLEMIES

EGYPT

RED
SEA

NILE RIVER

UPPER
EGYPT

PTOLEMAIS

DENDERAH COPTOS
THE BAID
THEBES

EDFU

KOM OMBO

ASWAN BERENICE
PHILAE FIRST CATARACT

0 50 100 150 200 Km